Doom Spore San Diego

A DarkSF Novel
(Science Horror)

by
John Argo

Clocktower Books
San Diego, California

Doom Spore San Diego

Clocktower Books (clocktowerbooks.com)

P.O. 600-973, Grantville Station

San Diego, California 92160-0973

e-mail: editorial@clocktowerbooks.com

Author's 2017 Preface

After some marketing adventures, I have returned to an earlier title (Doom Spore San Diego) to emphasize that this is a San Diego novel—not only because the author wrote it there, but because most of the action is based in San Diego. Motto: *Today San Diego—Tomorrow the World.* The text has remained substantially the same throughout.

In the FZ Edition (January 2015), I underscored a real-life zombie theme that arose, surprisingly, from the subject matter itself. My original intention was, and remains, to align the book thematically with the classic 1956 DarkSF or Science Horror film *Invasion of the Body Snatchers*, which was based on an equally classic Jack Finney horror novel (1955, *The Body Snatchers*).

The zombie sidestep is not frivolous. A young friend (the talented artist Ryan Osga) pointed out to me something I had not realized—that in nature there actually are real zombie life forms. At least one of them is a kind of fungus (zombie fungus), identified in tropical rainforests in 1859. It takes possession of insects and directs their actions in a manner that is beneficial to the fungus rather than the insect. I'm not joking. You can look this up: *Ophiocordyceps unilateralis*, an entomopathogenic fungus that acts as a parasite of insects and kills or seriously disables them. As often happens, truth is far stranger than even DarkSF or Science Horror.

Speaking of which: what is DarkSF or Science Horror? Science Fiction, as opposed to Fantasy, is a genre based on the plausible and possible (definition by famous SFFH anthologist Judith Merril in the 1960s). Fantasy, she said, is a literature of the implausible and impossible, like fairies and elves.

As an aside, I have identified a subspecies of speculative fiction that I call SciFae, or Tychnik, based on the nostrum that often, today's magic is tomorrow's science. Lighting a flashlight a few centuries ago in the Eurocentric world, if you happened to be a time traveler, could have gotten you burned alive at the stake as a witch or sorcerer. Today, flashlights are technology (applied science). In that spirit (no pun intended) today's vampire might well turn out to be a scientifically engineered android in 2222 CE or whenever. In the same way, my spores have turned out to be not only DarkSF (and Science Horror) but plausible.

A novel (and movie) like Jack Finney's *The Body Snatchers* is not fantasy, because the insidious pods floated in from space (no magic involved). The term actually originated in 19th Century Britain as a way of describing the theft of corpses (typically for medical experiments, which were not legal at the time). Robert Louis Stevenson wrote a famous short novel titled *The Body Snatchers* on that theme. His 1884 story was already historical fiction, as it reflected on the old-hat activities of corpse thieves like Burke and Hare (operating, again no pun intended) around 1828. In that year, Edgar Allan Poe was yet a teenager, and RLS hadn't been born.

Now we know: the zombie behavior of the spore people in my novel *Doom Spore San Diego* is entirely plausible, at least in affecting ants. As humans, you could argue we stretch the point by having them affect aunts, which presumes that they therefore must also affect uncles, and in fact any members of the species *homo bipedalis*, sometimes optimistically referred to as *homo sapiens*. The latter assumption blithely ignores such dark (and true) phenomena as world wars in which countless millions die for no reason, or the rise of demagogues and tyrants to cause those wars, and so forth. But that's fodder for some future novel of fingernail-biting and hair tearing importance.

Meanwhile, happy reading. Keep the lights on at night, and perhaps a little hatchet or something under your pillow just in case these stealthy, beautiful, deadly spore people start stepping out of your nightmares. They and their ilk have been known to silently step out of shadowy bedroom corners or from curtains that blow in a breeze even if the window is shut.

Despite yet another mutation in title, you may continue (more than ever now) to think of these spore people as zombies. My own sense of the etymology of zombie is not merely as the name of an African deity brought to Haiti by enslaved humans, but a mangled form of the French for *sans vie*, meaning without life. That is outside the scope of this novel, which I wrote many years ago (before I had ever heard of fungal zombies) because I love San Diego as well as Jack Finney's work, and wanted to write my own poddish sort of spine-tingler. Here is is, in the flesh.

Somewhere in my half-conscious mind, like a gloomy attic filled with half-galvanized plots and ideas, is the germ of a sequel. I may yet write it, and bring back Linsey Simon and the other characters.

Chapter 1. San Diego Today

Jimmy Mendez lived in a little house on a side street in the Grantville neighborhood of San Diego with his mom, who was a housewife, and his dad, who was often away at sea.

Jimmy was nine years old and would be starting fourth grade in the fall. That seemed like a long way off to him. At the moment he was still in Third Grade, but that would be over in a few weeks. That too seemed like a long way off. More importantly, Jimmy had just gotten brand-new tires on his Christmas bicycle, and as soon as he delivered the horror mask to his mom, he ran out to the back patio to see how the bike rode.

"Thanks, Jimmy," his mom called fondly from the kitchen. A heavy, dark-haired woman with pleasantly dimpled cheeks and loving eyes, she raised the mask over her face and said "Boo!" It was a face Jimmy had cut out from a pattern. It was on a kind of round piece of gray construction paper, and glued to a Popsicle stick with white office glue. "What is it?" mom called out as she looked through eye-holes cut into a puffy gray shape.

"A mushroom," Jimmy said as he lifted the bike.

"Were you studying mushrooms today?"

"Oh, yeah. Funguses." Remembering a school assignment, he dug in his back pocket and extracted a crumpled sheet of paper. He unfolded it carefully on the table. "See these lines here?" He pointed to a beautifully symmetrical pattern of fine spokes radiating from a central blank spot. "Those are mushroom spores. We cut the head off one and put it on a white paper under a glass jar. In a couple of hours it made these lines." He added proudly. "A mushroom puts out two million spores a minute."

"That's very interesting." Mom cleaned a few last dishes.

Jimmy forgot about kindergarten and gripped his bicycle. He hefted it by the handlebars. The tires felt nice and fat and hard. "Yeah, this is going to be great. It'll probably be a lot easier to pedal. Thanks, mom!" He rode out on the sidewalk, raced up and down the dips of driveways.

"Jimmy!" his mother called from their driveway a few minutes later, when he had reached the far street corner, and was thinking of crossing even though he knew he wasn't supposed to.

"What?" he shouted back. He turned and rode toward her with the big old Schwinn wheels twirling. Their spokes reflected sunlight. Patches of shade and light alternated on Jimmy's upper torso as he sped along.

"Watch the driveways! Car could come out any second."

"I am!"

"I'll call you the minute daddy calls to say he's home."

Lima Voyager, a nondescript cargo ship under Peruvian flag, approached San Diego harbor one cloudless, sunny morning. The ship came crawling over the sea and slunk toward land like a dark, furtive animal that hoped not to be noticed. The few who noticed her, particularly members of law enforcement agencies on duty around the clock to protect American shorelines, got the creepy feeling that something was wrong about her—something indefinable and deeply troubling.

She was a boxy looking antique—27,000 tons, small, strangely high in the water as if her cargo holds were empty, and a smell of decay about her like the fungus rot of the jungle. A cluster of strangely reticent crewmen stared down from the rails above her flaking black hull. They regarded the U.S. shore with hollow eyes and open mouths, as if speechless at some impending and unstoppable doom that, so far, only they knew about. In the lolling seas outside the harbor mouth between Point Cabrillo and North Island, Lima Voyager was challenged for a routine U.S. Coast Guard inspection.

The boxy freighter hove to with foul orange-colored water spouting from her bilges. She rocked on the splashing sea, showing rust streaming down from dirty black upper hull down to her flaking red Plimsoll line. A Coast Guard cutter sent a team of inspectors on board. A Coast Guard chopper circled above to provide cover. U.S. Navy SEALs and other crack police and military units were within a few minutes' call—after all, eight nuclear submarines were berthed just within the dark, brooding arms of Point Cabrillo with its centuries-old fortifications and Ft. Rosecrans cemetery. A harbor master's pilot approached Lima Voyager on a launch and boarded at about the same time. Lima Voyager's last port of call had been Peru, which was one of the Treasury Department's red flags for drug searches. The T-Men of the Coast Guard took a drug-sniffing dog on board. Unlike the military services like the Navy, the Coast Guard are a U.S. law enforcement agency with powers of search, seizure, and arrest like any other police jurisdiction, and naval patrols in offshore waters are usually accompanied by a Coast Guard officer to lead arrests.

Lt. Linsey Simon, of the uniformed Harbor Police Division, watched the proceedings from a small police patrol boat within her jurisdiction inside San Diego Bay. As she kept binoculars before her eyes, she steadied her elbows on the control panel on the canvas-topped bridge as the small patrol boat heaved lightly in calm channel currents. Linsey Simon was a trim, 30ish woman wearing a dark blue uniform and baseball cap of her police service. She looked swallowed up by a red life vest and belt full of equipment, including a 9 mm Gluck and extra clips. The swallowed-up look was deceptive, and her small, wiry body was like a steel spring curled up in all that gear. She was one of the fastest runners and strongest swimmers on the force. With a black belt in Judo, she was known for good instincts and making good critical decisions under fire. Her husband, Jack Simon, locally well-known and tough-talking journalist, had ample respect for Linsey's determination and capabilities and enjoyed her attractive feminine side. Her associates respected her, and at the moment her partner Cleveland "Cleve" Bartlett and two other uniformed officers looked relaxed as they waited on the main deck below for her leadership. The three men—wearing the same dark uniforms, orange vests, and armaments as Linsey—comfortably eyeballed their leader and the decisions she was making about the strange ship clanking slowly toward the harbor mouth. Cleve wasn't actually Linsey's partner anymore, not since she'd made rank, but he was the colleague she always took with her when she went in the field and needed a backup person in the car or boat, wherever her duties took her. Recently, she'd been doing plain clothes liaison work uptown with a Federal task force, and that was taking her ever more away from being grounded in her chosen profession. But it was all interesting.

As she watched Lima Voyager chugging in on the tide, Linsey thought there was something painfully strange about the ugly ship that was about to enter the harbor and tie up at a private pier within the 32nd Street Naval Yard. Maybe it was the ship's tawdry appearance versus the clean Coast Guard and Harbor Pilot vessels surrounding her. In Linsey's business, you looked hard—real hard—for the hidden drug deal, the approaching terrorist, the bomber, the smuggler. It was something every peace officer took deadly seriously, because the nation was under constant threat of attack from those who fanatically hated her, and the slightest slip or oversight could mean the death of thousands. So what was it about this clattering tub? Some corporation was paying top dollar for this piece of scrap to float into an expensive berth. What was that all about? Lt. Linsey Simon had a funny idea she wasn't seeing the last of this cargo tramp. Drugs? That was the likely profile, but something about this vessel didn't quite jibe.

As Coast Guard and harbor pilot boarded, Lima Voyager's captain and first officer stood on the bridge with their hands on the railing. With hooded, inscrutable eyes, like zombies, they watched as the Americans fanned out and checked the usual spots in such a ship. The inspection took an hour and resulted in a broadband burst of routine web form reports. Finding nothing obviously amiss, the inspectors and their dog rejoined the cutter. Several would later remark on the chill feelings they'd gotten on board. Nobody could put their finger on what might be amiss, but they all had a bad feeling—starting with the odd, unpleasant smell of earth with something dead in it. And yet—the small cargo of machine parts, lumber, wine, and gourmet mushrooms seemed properly tagged and invoiced, and neatly stacked in the holds in wooden crates secured with chains. The Coast Guard vessel roared off north toward Torrey Pines State Beach to join a surf rescue, and Lima Voyager chugged at one quarter speed through the channel entrance into San Diego Harbor.

To hear the dog handler tell it weeks later, the dog had not picked up any drug or blood scents—but it had begun acting skittish. The dog had sidled against its handler's dark blue uniform leg as if spooked, even frightened. This was a courageous dog, which on previous occasions had attacked on command, even under gunfire, to bring down violent suspects. The same big-hearted dog had refused to go near any of the dark-eyed crew or officers of Lima Voyager—and, to hear talk in a dockside tavern around 32nd Street—oddly, not a single crew member or officer had so much as offered to pet the animal. They had stared at the German shepherd, which had its hackles up and a low growl never leaving its throat, with an unfathomable discomfort—as if it were a species of animal with whom their kind had never before bonded.

Chapter 2. San Diego Today

In the Grantville neighborhood, Jimmy Mendez was pedaling happily along the sidewalk when he heard his mom's excited voice over the hedges: "Your dad is home!"

"Oh, yay! Let's go pick him up."

"Put your bike away, quick, Jimmy." Already, Mom stood with her purse in one hand and the keys to the old green Dodge in the other. Jimmy sailed around the corner, up the driveway, and into the garage. He had a way of dismounting by swinging his right leg over the seat so that he stood on the left pedal with the right leg wrapped around the back of the left leg, and this way he coasted into the garage and let the bike fly so that it drove in by itself, standing up, and came gently to rest still upright between two piles of plastic bags containing wood chips for the yard. Dad had bought the chips two years ago and never quite finished the back yard project. He'd promised to build Jimmy a swing, but then he'd been called out to sea on his Merchant Marine contract. By now, Jimmy had given up on ever having a swing set in the yard.

"That's odd," Mom said to herself as she headed down Waring Road to Interstate 8 and headed west toward the sea.

"What's odd?" Jimmy asked. With his softball glove on one hand, he casually tossed his ball into the glove over and over.

"I'm supposed to pick him up in National City."

"In Mexico?" he asked hopefully. It was where some of Jimmy's ancestors came from on his dad's side. On his mother's side they were Anglos who'd come from Oklahoma during the Great Depression. His mom had told him these things, and he'd also learned them in school.

"No, in National City, halfway down there."

"Dang." He'd hoped for a trip into Mexico for fun and to pick Dad up. "So what's odd?"

"Well, son, he usually has me pick him up at the dock where the ship pulls in. I'm sure there is some explanation; like someone owed him money or he owed some money and had to pay it. I hope he wasn't playing poker and losing his shirt."

Jimmy tossed his softball gently and watched absently as Mom took the high freeway ramps out of Mission Valley to head south on Interstate 15. Traffic was heavy but moving fast. Palm trees breezed by on either side of the road in hazy sunshine.

In about ten minutes they entered National City and took an exit ramp. High up, a passenger jet worked its way across the Palm Avenue freeway ramp for a landing at Lindbergh Field. The jet's twin tail engines left a white vapor contrail glistening in the blue sky. Lots of moisture in the air today.

They pulled up at a house surrounded by blue jacaranda trees in full bloom. Mom blared the horn, and a door opened. Out came a man who looked like dad.

Mom seemed excited and waved. "Hi honey!" she called out in a high, singsong voice. "Welcome home!"

The man noticed her. He looked in her direction as he came toward the car with his sea bag, but he didn't wave or smile. His eyes seemed to somehow not really recognize her.

Jimmy sat up and stopped tossing the ball. That man wasn't dad at all. He looked like dad, but something was wrong. A lot of things were wrong. The shape of his head, the way his eyes didn't focus on the same things dad's would have, the way he walked, the way he carried his heavy sea bag over the wrong shoulder. Worst of all, if it were dad, dad would be smiling and waving and calling Jimmy's name. This man just came toward them at a slow walk, looking more worried or something; busy; like he had someplace to go.

"Honey, move to the back seat," Mom said.

"Why?" Jimmy said. He was going to say "That ain't dad," but Mom seemed too excited to let him talk.

The man who looked like dad didn't seem to care. He got into the back seat as if he were climbing into a taxi in some big city and didn't care to learn the driver's name.

"Aren't you going to kiss me?" Mom said.

"I'll kiss you later," he said. Jimmy thought he smelled something dry and earthy. "Let's go home. I'm tired."

"Okay, honey," Mom said. She pulled away from the curb, hiding her obvious disappointment. "So you're tired, huh? Probably hungry too, huh?"

"I ate on the ship."

"Really." Mom looked in the rear view mirror and saw Jimmy staring at her. Her fake smile disappeared, and her eyes looked worried now, just like Jimmy felt inside.

That smell—it reminded Jimmy of the garden shed. It had taken him a few seconds to place it. It was the smell of earth, whether in the basement or the garden shed. "Daddy, have you been digging in a garden someplace?"

The man looked at him, and Jimmy realized this man did not recognize him at all. It broke his heart, though he hoped there was some mistake. Kids have instincts adults do not have. Jimmy knew deep down there was no mistake. Something indescribably horrible had happened. Was going on. Was just the beginning. Jimmy was too scared to even cry. What he saw in those lifeless eyes—a kind of reptile hate—made his knees knock together and he nearly wet his pants.

Chapter 3. 1945 Operation Jitensha (Bicycle)

Except for a speck on the horizon, and a cloud above that speck, the South Pacific Ocean tended into infinity in all directions.

World War II raged around the globe, but this moment on a late April day seemed silent and primordial, as if mankind did not yet exist. The only killing was by a pelican snatching a sardine, with a muted splash, and flying off.

That distant speck was the mountainous coast of Peru.

Tropical sky sweltered ominously in a gray-blue haze. Wind brought alternating whiffs of distant, rotting jungle and chalk-dry highlands. The ocean surface heaved and sank in ever-shifting crests and troughs laced with yellowed foam. Sunlight stabbed into resistant water. Shifting hills of heavy water looked translucent near their thundering, collapsing tops with kelp and splinters of wood tumbling over.

A periscope suddenly sliced through the water's surface in the direction of Peru. The looking-glass left a knife-cut wake of swirling foam. Ten minutes of cautious scanning, plus coded messages from several spy ships disguised as fishing vessels, eased for the moment any fear of Allied patrol planes in the area. A steel conning tower broke through and heaved up above the water. Gliding at a smart 10 knots, a vast torpedo shape breached amid rips and tears of flying jade sea water. Acres of dark steel plating glistened as sheets of sea water clung momentarily by their own tension, and then crashed down like broken glass.

Japan's largest submarine, one of the mammoth I-400 class, rode on the surface like a building lying on its side—399 feet long and four stories tall. She carried a crew of 145 sailors and thirty officers, scientists, engineers, and technicians. As soon as she breached, a hatch atop the conning tower opened. Several petty officers with binoculars rushed out. They threw themselves chest-first against the rails to begin scanning for enemy activity.

Operation Jitensha (Bicycle) was on. It was late in the war, Japan was losing, the situation was desperate, and dangerous action must be taken.

Diesel generators roared to life. Thick bluish gray smoke smelling of burned oil drifted away over the waves. A large hydraulically powered deck hatch swung open toward the tower. A rectangular opening now gaped. From the opening's shadows rose a steel elevator platform. On the lift stood a ring of sailors and in the center, tied down by its floats, was a sea plane.

High up on the sail, the boat's captain and several intent Army scientists watched the proceedings avidly. They would momentarily begin reporting back directly to the High Command in Tokyo about the operation's progress.

The platform rose until it completed the final twenty-foot stretch of a 115-foot flight deck along the top of the boat's spine. The several I-Class subs of the Imperial Japanese Navy were, in effect, underwater aircraft carriers designed for long-range operations against the U.S.A. On this mission, two of the ships had sailed to Peruvian ocean waters on a top secret germ warfare mission. Both subs had steamed rapidly near the surface. They had false superstructures to disguise them as tramp steamers, although a flyover by an Allied patrol plane, at just the right angle of light, might have spotted the enormous bulk under the surface. Now this sub's companion boat had refueled her and then turned north for a suicidal mission (the Panama Canal, but she would be sunk before getting near enough to send her own planes aloft to bomb the locks).

Aboard the remaining I-Class, technicians unfolded the unmarked Comet float plane's wings. The pilots tested the plane's new 1,560 hp Mitsubishi Kinsei-62 14-cylinder, two-row radial nose-mounted engine—revving it in test bursts. When all was ready, sailors unyoked the wheels from the deck plates.

Pilot and navigator nodded to each other under their long, glass-paneled canopy. The pilot waved and grinned at the deck crew. Sailors lined up and saluted. The pilots returned the salute. Moments later, a 85-foot-long pneumatic catapult sent the plane careening into the air. Yawing and pitching uncertainly for a moment, the Comet straightened out. Pulled by its powerful engine, the plane climbed at 2,000 feet per minute.

High over the Pacific Ocean, the Comet, having climbed to just under 35,000 feet (seven miles), leveled off, and raced toward the interior of South America.

The pilots maintained radio silence to avoid being picked up by Peruvian defense forces. The government of Manuel Prado had recently severed ties with the Axis Powers and seemed ready to declare war on Germany and Japan, in return for U.S. support in Peru's war with neighboring Ecuador. Far below, grayish water gleamed in the morning sun. The sun shone in a clear blue sky marked only with thin, distant clouds. The thin coastal strip, or Costa, loomed ahead one moment, with the steep slopes of the Andes Mountains a few miles back. The land ahead was one of the most arid on earth, despite its proximity to the Pacific Ocean.

The Comet flew at full cruising speed, 300 mph given the pontoons, on a bearing of east by northeast. The aircraft seemed to gobble miles as it shot toward the hulking mass of the Andes, which loomed ahead, swathed in a thin cloud layer. They crossed the coastline near Puerto Caballas and immediately flew over the Nazca Valley with its enigmatic line drawings scratched for miles into the sandy soil. Shooting straight ahead, the propeller plane roared into the heart of ancient Inca territory, toward the lost empire's most deeply guarded and dangerous secret.

The unmarked, enigmatic plane flew past the ancient capital of Cuzco, to the south a bit, and then almost over the high sanctuary at Macchu Pichu. Soon, the Andean highlands lay behind, and now came the slope down into the jungles that would eventually lead to the Amazon Basin where half the rivers of South America drained into the Amazon River and out into the South Atlantic. But this was still Peru, which contained the westernmost expanses of dense jungle whose eastern extents lay in Brazil.

Tokyo, on that spring day in 1943, displayed timeless beauty in the form of cherry blossoms falling like light snow over temple roofs. But the war was turning against Japan, and her true situation was better represented in a dark, smoky conference room at the Naval Operations Offices in Tokyo Bay. A dozen tense men in Army and Navy uniforms stood smoking and listening in a pillared hall while a young Navy officer waving a pointer stood before a slide projection screen. On the screen was a map of northwestern South America, including Peru. The Army officers present were from a chemical and biological warfare unit. The Navy officers represented the functional reality that Operation Jitensha (Bicycle) was largely a naval operation.

Outside the Naval Operations conference room, around the Tsukiji Fish Market area near Tokyo Bay, pinkish-white blossoms tumbled through the sunny air. By contrast, the air inside was heavy with the smoke from military issue cigarettes as well as hard to get in wartime Tengu and Peacock brands.

The young Navy officer in dark uniform pointed to the next slide: a map of the Pacific Ocean off the coast of Peru. "Our I-400 Class submarine will surface to discharge a modified seaplane—Yokosuka D4Y Suisei (Comet)—two-seat carrier dive bomber, with range 1575 kilometers (945 miles). Flying empty, dragged somewhat by pontoon landing gear, the aircraft will fly at 500 km/hr (300 mph) and reach its destination in one hour."

Pausing to look at stony faces around him in the smoky conference room, the officer continued: "The mission will be accomplished within several hours as the two officers go on shore to collect specimens that they have been trained to recognize. The return journey will be in one hour."

Maj. Gen. Shunji Sato interrupted the young officer. Sato was head of Unit 731's Canton branch, and had been flown in from China especially for this briefing. He would report back to the commander of Unit 731, Lt. Gen. Ishii Shiro, the microbiologist doing human experiments on countless Chinese and other Allied prisoners. "Lieutenant, you realize that the war is at a crossroads and we must not fail in this Peruvian mission. How do we know the intelligence behind this effort is solid?"

The officer clicked his heels and bowed deeply. "Sir, our source is one of the many thousands of Japanese ex-patriates living in Peru. While these people, scattered through much of South America, are of course regarded with justified suspicion among loyal Japanese, many of them are poorly treated in their new homelands. Many of them resent their Caucasian rulers and would like to see those regimes weakened. As a result, our source, who bears a Japanese surname and is the son of first-generation immigrants to Lima, is one of those overseas Japanese who has developed a considerable loyalty to our Emperor. Although Peru has become officially hostile to open Axis activities, we still enjoy considerable support from Chilean and Argentine Axis supporters."

"Hah! Spies, you mean, which is not the same as saying openly loyal allies or devoted soldiers." Sato puffed hungrily on his strong cigarette during this explanation, and now exhaled yellow-white tendrils of smoke from his mouth and nostrils while turning to the man beside him. That was Major Tomio Karasawa of the Headquarters unit. He leaned close and said softly: "Major, let's make sure that this new weapon does not leak out into enemy hands. The results would be disastrous not only for Japan, but for the entire world."

Karasawa nodded sharply and unscrewed a silvered fountain pen to make notes on a pad of finest quality sube rice paper. "I will begin a file on it, Sir, and coordinate with Intelligence."

Sato added for emphasis as he smoked his Peacock cigarette to his fingertips: "Japan cannot afford for this information to leak to enemy newspapers and anti-Japanese propaganda radio."

The officers continued to hear testimony from several colonels. One, a biochemist, proclaimed: "Our source in Peru has introduced us to a treasure trove of priceless biological warfare agents that will make Japan number one not only in Asia, but across the entire earth." Cigarette smoke veiled the listeners' worried eyes, glittering spectacles, and gritted, exposed teeth as they considered the ramifications of unleashing such a powerful nightmare upon the world.

Already, things seemed to be silently going wrong. Thousands of miles away in the South Pacific, the I-400 class submarine waited dangerously past her deadline as the two aviators did not return. Every passing hour exposed the giant submarine to further danger from patrolling enemy aircraft.

Nearly 11,000 miles away from Tokyo, on the eastern slopes of the Andes Mountains in Peru, looking toward the Amazon Basin rather than the Pacific Ocean, a different smoky scenario played out its timeless beauties and terrors. As the Andes sloped downward and eastward from high, dry, freezing cold above a mile high toward the jungles of the continent's center, an ancient fold lay open in the cliffs hundreds of feet above the tree line. This thin fissure that dropped straight down was dark inside with jungle growth, widening in a steep drop to a yawning volcanic caldera in the high jungle. The volcano had been extinct for eons, and the blasted remains of its crater were thickly overgrown with lush growth. The crater contained a lake a quarter mile across, which glittered dark blue in the filtered light coming down through the fissure. In the middle of the lake lay an island the size of several aircraft carriers, formed by cooled lava left from the volcano's last eruption. This plug, rising several hundred feet above the steaming lake surface, was covered with green forest growth that should harbor a great variety of living organisms, but looked strangely quiet, motionless, and devoid of bird life.

The Comet followed the minutely detailed maps held by her navigator. They located the natural fissure in the Cordillera Orientale slope near the beginning of the vast Manu River rain forest area. Spiraling down to half a mile altitude, the float plane entered the magical-seeming environment of the fissure. Below, as the two men looked out speechlessly, was a circular lake, colored dark blue. In its middle rose a 300 foot high island covered in green tree crowns that masked what looked like rocks and buildings. As they descended, a mile-high granite rock face with two curving, sheltering arms was on their west, while on their east the endless jungle opened up. On the east, there was endless blue sky in a swollen humid haze over the topmost canopy. The plane kept circling lower. They saw a few wheeling gulls and hawks, and even two condors circling high up, but lower down there was a noticeable void of bird life. As they circled lower and lower, they gaped at what looked like an abandoned city on the island in the middle of the caldera. The architecture was oddly sinuous, superimposed upon the more massive, squat stonework typical of most South and Central American civilizations. The two men caught only glimpses of the buildings buried in leafy tree crowns. Soon, the aircraft set down on the glassy, opaque surface near the island's shore. The water had a stony quality, like green jade. Bits of fog drifted over the surface amid a brooding stillness. The two men slid back the plane's canopy and threw out a large package—their life craft, which hit the water and inflated in staged popping noises. The two men clambered out, coughing in the noxious air. They carried backpacks containing hatchets, flashlights, and anything else they might need during a stay of several hours. They knew that their I-400 class submarine was by now submerged and hiding from U.S. and other Allied planes, for the boat was a juicy target, and its mission was too important for it to be lost to some random accident. The two pilots in the caldera about 500 miles away were well aware of the sub's vulnerability, and worked with a sense of urgency to get their mission over with.

The air was thick and sulfuric, almost unbreathable. Coughing and wheezing, they rowed the raft toward a slimy little shore under a dark overhang of thick forest leaves. They climbed out and made their way through thickets of thorns toward the beckoning cities that had been abandoned centuries earlier. Not even the Inca had ventured into this place, though most likely they had known of it. The city had the characteristic pyramids and monolithic statues of the region. It also had great, multi-colored growths that hung like sconces and pediments on the buildings. Here and there, a huge round sphere opened its mouth and exhaled a black trail of swirling spores. Too late, the men realized they had stepped into a place whose treasures would not easily be given up. The inhaled the earthy, metallic, odd scent of the place. Their lungs filled with a dull mushroomy taint that slowed their stop and made their hearts labor in their chests. They staggered about the streets of the lost city in awe, forgetting their mission, as a different set of realities took over. Here was a city sculpted in fungi. Its creators had long disappeared, having died in a lost war with an insidious enemy. Now it was the turn of these two Japanese pilots to succumb to the powers of this place. The two men sank to their knees, then slowly collapsed face-down. Even then, green and white molds began to cover them as if they were slowly drowning in decay.

After a long silence, the two pilots returned to their rubber raft. Each, visible only as a dark silhouette in the deep shade under so much jungle growth, carried two large, round objects—one under each arm. As they emerged from the shade, they looked perfectly normal and calm as if nothing had happened. Placing their burdens in the dinghy, they pushed off and started paddling to their quietly waiting sea plane.

Suddenly, from the outer shores of the caldera, where vines and leafy tree branches hung over the edges of the volcanic crater, arrows hissed over the water. Arrows cut through the drifting fog and crossed over waters bubbling with subterranean gases that killed birds dead if they even flew near the water's surface. The two Japanese pilots, even in bulky flight suits, were pierced by multiple arrows and slid into the water. Their bodies sank below the surface. The rubber raft drifted toward the float plane but gradually deflated and sank bubbling under the surface.

Copper-skinned Guardians stippled with white and red dots stood watching as their handiwork found its proper result.

Frantic radio exchanges between I-400 and her network flew back and forth with Tokyo. Lingering through the night, as Allied sub hunter planes flew out on routine patrols, the disappointed monster finally sank beneath the waves and cruised back toward the homeland.

The float plane in the jungle remained sitting on the waters for many years, until finally its pontoons rusted through in the extreme warmth and moisture. The plane tipped nose forward into the water and disappeared beneath the surface. A trail of oily, rusty bubbles boiled up through the alkaline waters, and then all returned to normal. By then, men had walked on the Moon and other great events had come and gone. The new Millennium came amid a welter of violence in New York City and elsewhere. New fanatics appeared and human history rolled on.

Wars came and went, their reasons forgotten as soon as the last body bags rolled off the evac planes. But there was one more chapter to be written on Unit 731—to be added to Major Tomio Karasawa's memoirs—carried thousands of miles through Burma and China, and eventually to show up in San Diego, California.

Chapter 4. Several Years Ago

Lee Collwood VI was 35 years old and sweating about his inherited corporation in the desert of Southern California.

Lee sat in his corner office overlooking the unchanging desert as he awaited the arrival of his unlikely new business partner. Anaconda Chemical, founded and successfully nurtured by generations of his forebears, had missed a few vital turns on Lee's watch and was tens of millions of dollars in debt, with the spiral deepening month by month. In plain English, not enough money was coming in, and tons of money was leaking out from myriad holes. Loosening the collar around his prickling neck, he thought: Today is the day I will stop the slide and get the ship back on an even keel.

He was a tall, lean man with very dark glossy hair and a naturally pink cheeks. He generally wore dark suits that he had especially tailored in ultra-conservative Santa Barbara County, where he had a 7,000 square foot mansion with horseshoe driveway and white-pillared porch, on five acres near a country club he partially owned, not far from the former Reagan Ranch. For three or four days each week, he spent the day at work in the family's main industrial plant. He owned a Lear Jet that took off from Santa Barbara Airport and landed on Anaconda's company airstrip. This airstrip was built and maintained by the U.S. Air Force for contractual reasons involving the Department of Defense, because Anaconda Chemical not only made substances that went boom, but in recent decades had become heavily involved in pharmaceuticals and silicon-based computer parts. The Air Force had recently sent notice of intent to pull the plug. It was like that on all fronts.

Lee awaited a special box of papers, being driven from San Diego to his plant by a young man and his father. They were the Robertsons, and right now they seemed about the only saving grace in Anaconda's dismal looking future.

Neither James Robertson, 50, nor his father James, 80, smiled much on this trip. Etta Robertson, the elder James' wife and the younger James' beloved mother, had recently died after a long illness. Etta's cancer had left a pile of debts, and her two surviving men were doing what they must to at least save the house in Point Loma. The father had retired from the FBI toward the turn of the century, and had spent some more years in Civil Service. The younger man was balding and heavy, with thin frizzy white hair around a sun-burned, salmon-colored pate. The father was lean, with folded-putty skin that suggested he didn't go outdoors much anymore. His teeth were large and yellow, what he had left of them. He had wisps of thin white hair. Both men dressed alike: business shirt open at the neck; no tie or jacket; good suit pants; comfortable loafers that looked scuffed and about two years past their usable prime.

The younger man had a degree in Liberal Arts, and did peripheral engineering work—technical writing, web design—when he could find a temporary gig at one of San Diego's midsize firms. James Jr. drove, while James Sr. fussed with a map that kept fluttering in the hot wind entering the car. The air conditioning didn't work too well, and there hadn't been time or money to get it repaired—a fact the two regretted now as they crossed the desert. The old man, who was now also dying of cancer, and wanted to leave something to his son, got a distant look in his eyes and reminisced about his days in China and Burma, where his had been one of the O.S.S. units cleaning up after the Japanese withdrawal.

James Jr. was a quiet man, and he listened patiently. It was the Japanese documents that Collwood wanted so badly, and was willing to pay good money for.

"There she be," James Sr. said, waving a bony hand at the distant, bluish shadows of Anaconda Chemical buildings on the horizon. "Almost there now. Wonder how much he'll offer."

"Depends on how excited he gets about what you have."

"You know," James Sr. said, making a strained face with haunted eyes, "I've been losing sleep over doing this. You know what's in those papers, and I can promise you whatever this man wants them for so badly, he is up to no good."

The plant and offices of Anaconda Chemicals sprawl across the Southern California desert between Brawley and the Salton Sea. This is a region known as the Imperial Valley, which borders on Mexico to the south, San Diego County to the west, and Arizona to the east. The region contains some of the hottest, most arid terrain on earth.

North lies the Salton Sea, former salt flat into which Colorado River water accidentally flowed in 1905 to create a lake that has been choking on salt and chemicals ever since—despite its better years as a fishing spot and tourist attraction. Its fathoms are said to contain more than one bomber or fighter plane from nearby military installations over the generations.

A few dozen miles east, in San Diego County, lies the Anza-Borrego Desert, another place where you can fry an egg on the sidewalks of Borrego Springs at five o'clock on a July afternoon. You could probably bake a loaf of bread in your car trunk, though nobody is known to have tried it. And the desert is littered with the bleached bones of men and animals.

In this atmosphere, the patriarch of the Collwoods and founder of Anaconda, Lee Collwood, thought it would be good to join or sunder massive amounts of earthly chemicals for great profit, in privacy far from civilization. It wasn't until the later 20th Century that Uncle Sam actually built any major freeways in Anaconda's neighborhood.

The plant is of World War II vintage, with a sawtooth roof of many symmetrically angled skylights. Because of the various products made here, some of them used in war, the plant has always had a top U.S. Government security rating. It is surrounded by high, electric fencing. Its perimeter is patrolled by armed guards with dogs, riding air conditioned Hummvees. The plant has dozens of buildings large and small, spread over hundreds of acres of varied terrain, so that horseback and aircraft patrols are also necessary. The buildings are of a consistently mayonnaise yellow painted over stucco or wood, as distinct from the sandy, gravelly terrain with its mix of vegetation.

It is the kind of landscape in which tumbleweed rolls over wind-carved dunes, and the air has a kind of tense, overheated hum that overlays a graveyard silence. In spots where there is water close to the surface, perhaps in a dip, some stunted Manzanita oak might ply its twisting branches and sparse leaves, enough to offer cover to small birds warbling with joy. This is a place where you might see a sidewinder cruise by at high speed, sampling the air with its forked tongue while its body undulates like a coil in perpetual motion. You might see a roadrunner or a fox or even a Mexican wolf. You might see the U.S. Border Patrol (La Migra) drive by in their cream color and green SUVs with thick-knuckled thread tires, and moments later see a group of illegals (men, women, children) breaking for cover to cross a road and disappear among the sage and cactus, perhaps never to be seen again until their decaying remains are found a year or a century later. Except for the whine of La Migra vehicle's transmission, or the distant hum of a spotter plane, or the warbling of that bird, or the caw of a larger bird of prey or a flock of vultures, it all happens under a blanket of silence. This is where the Collwoods have cooked up their business schemes the way the chemists in their laboratories try new assays in boundlessly many combinations.

Lee Collwood VI had already taken calls this from two ex-wives demanding money, and threatening he'd be denied visitation with his two sons and two daughters. He could only stall them while he got his lawyers to file renegotiation papers for the alimony. Lee's hands were tied. He was low on cash and he had to be extremely careful about liquidating assets, for fear of tipping off the investors. The people whom he had talked into sinking money into this company were expecting big results, but the two big cancer drugs had both come up very short in in-house tests, and Lee was stalling about giving the Food and Drug Administration samples. He knew the clock would be ticking all the louder, and once he handed the FDA his best samples, there was no way left to cook the books. His goose would be cooked in thirty to ninety days. He could appeal and claim they'd botched the tests, but it was a fool's game. Lee Collwood knew he didn't have the talent of his forefathers who had built this empire, but he had their shrewd maneuver capability, and a burning desire to win at all costs.

He had the Robertsons figured. He knew the two men sitting before him were desperate for money, and he wasn't too concerned about the amount they needed. He wasn't interested in dickering—just in getting what he knew would be the key to his future. "What did you bring me?" he asked brusquely, while ordering a silver tea service and ginger snap cookies.

Secretly, he pressed a button that caused a digital recording system to make audio and video files of the transaction, just in case things ever wound up in court. Lee had let his own father's lawyers train him well. One could never be too careful, when playing with dynamite like this.

The spacious, luxurious office with its plate glass windows overlooking desert vistas began to fill with faint aromas of sugar, vanilla, and almond. "I have the papers I told you about," the father said. The old man reached into his inner pocket and took out an envelope that looked as if he'd held it a lot, maybe sweated into its wrinkled paper. Lee sensed that the old man and his son had misgivings about how the explosive information they were handing over might be used. Lee was used to this feeling in people. They sensed, somehow, that he wasn't being sincere with them. Screw them—these two were a pair of cheap, trashy opportunists without a pot to piss in. He was from America's equivalent of royal stock. Let them sweat, and hand over their secrets, and walk out with a few thousand bucks to mend their tattered and tawdry little lives. Lee caught himself before he might radiate contempt at the two.

"Excellent," Lee said. He stirred his tea and said: "So you flew with Chennault's Flying Tigers before the war, and later on the U.S. Army Air Force Himalayan airlift into China, and after the war you came into possession of Major Karasawa's notes...?"

"You studied my report well," the old man said, trembling as he clutched the manila envelope to his chest with both arms as if protecting it. Lee watched in surprise—almost afraid that the old man might change his mind as he sat there with wide eyes behind lenses glittering in the harsh desert sunlight that filtered laser-like through the blinds and into the air conditioned office. But the old man's mouth opened in a yammering wail and he rocked violently with the baby-like envelope in his arms: "Please, Mr. Collwood, promise me. Swear to me, your oath as a gentleman, that you will keep this information, you and the Government, never to make an offensive weapon, but to study it and to make sure no other country can ever duplicate what Karasawa's people found in the jungle."

This was easy. "Sure," Lee said, smiling. The old man slumped in relief and passed the envelope across the desk to Lee, while the younger man looked mistrustful and unhappy. Lee swept a gold pen into his hands and signed a check for tens of thousands of dollars with a flourish. "You have my promise as a gentleman, and this should make things easier for you."

As the father and son walked slowly to the door, Lee said cheerfully with all the faithly nectar he could summon: "You've done the right thing, Mr. Robertson, for yourself, for your family, for the United States of America." He thought about rising and adding: "God bless these United States," but decided not to. It would be over the top.

He sat back and breathed a huge sigh after the door closed and the two men disappeared from his life, leaving him this thing on his desk, this envelope that he leaned over and was almost afraid to open, so radioactive did it seem, so vastly dangerous and crazy like that atomic bomb project back in the 1940s. It was a Pandora's Box, he knew, and he hesitated with both hands held over the envelope in the chill twilight of his empty office. Then he remembered he had no choice. He must save his company and his own integrity and cash flow, not to mention his reputation. Zestfully, he tore open the crinkled Manila paper to expose the aging and brittle papers inside.

Chapter 5. San Diego, Two Years Ago

One evening, a few days later, when James Jr. had finished helping his father to bed, and was in the middle of doing the last few dishes before going to bed, he heard a noise at the back door. He froze, standing in the brightly lit kitchen with a towel in one hand and a dripping wet plate in the other hand. There. He heard it again—a scratching, almost a knocking, but not quite either. Putting the plate aside, he flicked off the lights to minimize his silhouette. For a moment he deliberated about going upstairs to get his dad's old service .45, but he was tired and he didn't want to wake the old man, and this was probably nothing. There, again. Drying his hands with the towel, he walked softly to the rear of the house. He stood on tiptoe and looked through the small leaded-glass window at the top of the door. He was startled to see two figures standing out there—an old man and a young woman. Looked like illegals from south of the border. They knocked again softly, and he was torn between calling the police and helping them. Illegals rarely ever bothered anyone, but were in a hurry to go north away from the border area. If they were stopping here, it meant there was some emergency. He opened the door a foot and stuck his face out. "Yes? What's the matter?" There was a metal-framed screen door between him and them.

They stared at him, and a shiver went up and down his spine. The old man looked downright spooky—a leathery face, clearly Amerind features on reddish-copper skin, and short white hair. His clothing was dark, baggy, nondescript, and dusty. The dented brown hat's round crown and short brim suggested the Andean region, maybe Peru or Bolivia. James had a degree in International Relations, and had taken one or two courses on the history and sociology of South and Central America. The young woman was even more unsettling—her eyes especially. She was as tall as the old man—both were short, almost tiny people—and dressed like an American in a cheap kelly-green suit with awkward black flat-heeled loafers and a busy, foofy blouse. She too looked Hispanic, with lots of Native American in her genes, and she the sclera of her big, dark eyes showed white all around.

"Is someone hurt?" James whispered. "Is there a problem?"

The old man radiated hypnotic strength as he stood there like a little fireplug, with tension and focus written into his weather-beaten frame. He said something, probably in a dialect of Quechua, the language common to many Andean areas. Whatever he said, it was a command, curt and muffled, not to James but to the young woman. She in turn said in lightly accented English: "You are Mr. Robertson. He knows it."

"Yes, I am. How do you know me?" A chill went through James' guts. He fumbled with the lock on the screen door to make sure it was locked.

"My father once met your father. Not in Peru, but in China."

The old man spoke again, and she translated. "He wants to speak with your father. It is a matter of the utmost urgency."

"My father is very ill," James said. "He is dying." He started to close the door. The old Indian man's eyes opened wider and he looked up, as if he had seen something above James' head. James and the old man's daughter exchanged surprised looks, and before James could react further, he heard James Senior's gruff voice behind him on the stairwell. He whirled to face his father, who stood there trembling in pajamas and trailing a bed sheet. James Senior held the railing with both hands, trembling, but said in a firm voice. "Let them in . I'm afraid Collwood is a bad man, and I made a huge mistake letting him have the papers. I only hope it's not too late."

The old Indian nodded with terrible intensity. "Offensor!" he said cryptically—a term James Jr. had not heard before.

Chapter 6. San Diego, Current Time

On a typical clear, sunny day with a playful breeze ruffling the water, Lima Voyager passed her Coast Guard inspection. With a harbor master's pilot on board to guide her, she clanked slowly past Point Cabrillo, past the nuclear submarine pens and other Federal installations on the north side of the harbor entrance, and North Island Naval Air Station and the aircraft carrier berths on the south lip. Lima Voyager was one of a constant stream of ships making the journey in or out of one of the best salt water ports on the West Coast, and, aside from a few Harbor Police, nobody took much notice. And why should they? Looking on the bright side, her paint was reasonably fresh, if a little rusty around the seams, and her engines throbbed with quiet strength, and thin streams of water spouted from two or three bilge ports to signal that all was working well in her guts. She to be simply heading to port for a refurbishing.

Two other persons watched her arrival with considerable interest. Standing stock still on the docks on Harbor Drive that had once been home to the greatest tuna fishing fleet on the North Pacific, a man and a woman stood like statues. He was an elderly, white-haired man with a dented round hat and baggy, dark clothing, while she was a slender, still youthful woman wearing jeans and a dark T-shirt along with a simple red baseball cap. Both had strongly delineated, pure Indian features. They stared at the passing freighter, which clanked like the forges of hell, and in their eyes was written bleak prophecy of a great evil entombed within those rusting black steel plates. Rusty bilge water spewed out as if gargoyles were taunting the two on the dock. But the two had disappeared— melted away into the heights of the city above India Street toward Cortez Hill and the vast urban groves of Balboa Park.

Lima Voyager bypassed the Coast Guard station and former tuna fleet docks, on one side, the aircraft carrier berths at North Island Naval Air Station on the other side. She clanked past the tourist attractions around the B Street Pier—like the Star of India iron-hulled sailing ship dating to 1863— and under the Coronado Bay Bridge. Slowly, she angled left, portside, and disappeared into the mass of mostly gray Navy vessels laid up around the 32nd Street Naval Yards. Somewhere in there, at a small civilian cargo dock surrounded by high wire fences topped with barbed wire, she had a civilian harbor tug nudge her to rest. Engines off, she coasted silently as crew members readied for tying up.

After the harbor master's pilot went ashore, nobody else left the ship. Mariachi and song could be heard echoing across the steel decks from someone's large radio—a Tijuana station—and several sailors could be seen cleaning and securing the decks after their ocean voyage from deep in the Amazon. For Lima Voyager had not just steamed north from Peru. She had also been halfway up the Amazon River on the other side of the South American continent—a river that at times seemed like an ocean in itself, in that one could sit on its currents in an ocean-going steamship and not see land in any direction. She had left the Amazon Basin by its great estuary near Belem, had crossed through the Panama Canal, and briefly journeyed south to Lima before turning north toward the U.S.

That night—as related to Lt. Linsey Simon and other investigators by a U.S. Navy Shore Patrol petty officer who happened by on routine duties—the heavily fortified wire gate opened briefly. Almost furtively, the captain and his two dozen complement left in civilian clothing, carrying sea bags, and locking the facility behind them. They left the ship totally unmanned, with lights on and radios playing as if men were living on board. Only one other figure saw them do this, and he would never testify.

Chapter 7.

Hearing a gate creak in the nocturnal fog, the old security guard froze in his tracks.

The old man lived on a very meager Navy pension plus his Social Security. In a way, he had little to bitch about, he figured. He had three meals and a roof over his head at a cheap hotel downtown. He got his cigarettes, coffee, and liquor at the Navy Exchange at rock bottom prices, and he made a little on the side black-marketing cheap goods to local guys at a slight markup. He had cable TV, including several raunchy channels, and he drank himself to sleep every day with the cheap plastic curtains blowing in and out of the Victorian-era windows in the Gaslamp district. Plus, he made his drinking money and some to spare with his security guard job. Not that he needed the money so much, but he needed something steady and regular to do.

He didn't mind the noise of the young men and women partying two stories below—kind of made him feel not lonely. His schedule, though, was topsy-turvy. He would leave the room at 10:00 p.m. five evenings a week, walk over to the trolley exchange, and take the Orange Line down to the 32nd & Commercial trolley stop. There he'd walk through the Navy gate, showing his I.D., and then down the narrow little paths of dusty asphalt amid high wire fences, until he arrived at the concrete black building where his guard company had their headquarters. The guard company had people all over the city, all three shifts, 7/24, but the old man had this shift in this place sewed up and he liked it. He liked walking the quiet docks at night. About the worst he had to do was carry a heavy round time clock in a black leather case, on a black leather strap over one shoulder, and go from one key to another, turning it in the time clock to prove he'd been there—each key was numbered, and left an impression marking just that moment on a paper disk inside the time clock. He liked being near ships. He was an old Navy man, after all. He was just glad not to have to do all that work anymore, or supervise anyone, or put up with any more crap from poker-faced senior NCOs or wet behind the ears officers. He liked the solitude and the silence. He liked to stand sometimes and watch the nigh lights twinkle in dark, rippling water, or hear waves splashing softly under wooden piers, or hear the flap of a seagull's wings at night as it moved from one roost to another.

So what was different about this night? He froze in his tracks in mid-round, with the heavy time clock slung over his shoulder. About 150 feet away, seen through two or three wire fences, a group of men were leaving their ship. That much was obvious, from the lights and music aboard the small cargo freighter. They looked like Central or South Americans, he thought, wearing pea coats and watch caps, and carrying sea bags on their shoulders. Something odd about that scene made him stop and be very still, hoping he wasn't spotted. He had a little phone to call the dispatcher if there was any trouble, but he'd never had to use it so far in his three years with this company. What was it about those people? Their silence? Their lack of laughter or conversation? A certain deadness in their eyes? Must be 30 of them, and not one said anything to the man next to him. Usually men told jokes, laughed, lit cigarettes, nudged each other in a friendly way. Not these jokers. They moved in a way that suggested they didn't want to be seen. That aroused the old man's suspicions. Stealth. Could they be terrorists? Probably not 30 of them all at once, carrying sea bags unless those were filled with explosives. But there were easier ways to cause mayhem. What were they up to?

The old man realized too late that they'd seen him.

Clever outflanking maneuver.

He was watching the body of them walk away toward the main 32nd Street entrance, when he suddenly realized that three of them had detached themselves and had made a detour so that they came up behind him.

He turned, just in time to see a burly man in a pea coat draw near. "Hey," the old man said, "can I help you?" but it was too late. With one of them on either side, grasping his elbows, the burly one put his sea bag down and wrapped big powerful arms around the old man. The old man tried to cry out, but the other man opened his mouth and exhaled something that made the old man relax. As darkness closed in, he noticed the smell of the man embracing him— like a forest mushroom. The old man noticed that the man seemed to be made of old mushy plastic foam. He looked like a man, all right, but beneath the skin he was something else. Something moist, alien, dangerous. As he was dragged out of sight across a wooden dock, under the dock, to where the black silky night water lapped up on wet rocks, the old man relaxed and let himself go. He could just picture that cheap, torn plastic curtain billowing in the sweet night air as the thing that got him under the dock put its head close to his neck. The thing bit a hole open, inserted a shiny black tube that snaked into the old man, and started sucking life out of him.

Sometime much later that night, many hours later, a shape detached itself from under the dock. The shape that crawled up from the darkness and stood upright on the wharf was that of an elderly security guard with a severe case of missing personality. He wore the security guard uniform, looked just like the security guard, and flashed the right I.D. at the Navy gate, but he did not head for the trolley station. Instead, he began walking in the opposite direction—south, toward National City. He left behind him a long shape under the dock, in the darkest shadows where the gravel rose up to meet the rotting wood underbelly. There, a long wavy wood-like shape with many thin layers, and with powdery edges, now occupied a formerly empty space.

In fact the late night fog, a feature of the marine layer common in San Diego at this time of year, was filled with the figures of men silently walking away from the harbor. Each carried a sea bag over one shoulder. Each walked steadily, at a deliberate pace, toward some destination. Passing police cars did not stop to question them, because they looked like ordinary seamen.

The city, with nearly two million people, beckoned to the silently walking zombie spores.

Chapter 8.

The owners of a private patrol company notified the police that one of their elderly security guards, a retired U.S. Navy petty officer, had disappeared from his duty station. The relief, a young college student, had arrived at 7:45 a.m. and found the gate unlocked, lights on despite the misty daylight, radios playing, and no sign of the old man. The college student did find the old man's watch clock lying, dew-covered, on a gravel walk.

A company patrol officer, arriving soon after, opened the clock and determined that the old man had been making his rounds. San Diego Police turned the investigation over to the Harbor Police.

Two Harbor Police officers, a man and a woman, arrived in a patrol car. For a time, they waited by the padlocked gate, making cell phone calls, and looking out over the waters. After a while, two more vehicles arrived. One was a San Diego Police Department car with a dog, called in for backup and search. The other was a utility truck, whose operator cut the lock with a heavy-duty clipper before leaving. The police went in with the dog, and searched high and low. The absence of a living soul, and the eerie lights on in the ship and the Mexican music cheerfully playing on the ship, somehow did not hang together.

The supervisor, Lieutenant Linsey Simon, arrived to take over the investigation. She was greeted at the dock by the initial officer on the scene, Patrolman Cleve Bartlett, a dark-skinned young man with a slight Southern accent. They'd worked many hours together, and were comfortable in each other's company, with never a jealous moment by Linsey's husband Jack.

Linsey rumpled her nose. "What's that smell?" There was a vague odor, like mushroom soup starting to rot.

Cleve shook his head and grinned, with the macabre humor that emergency personnel regularly summon to mask their feelings about a disquieting situation. "We checked the galley first thing. Nothing but some rotten food."

"So what's with the missing guard? Sleeping off a hangover somewhere?"

Cleve shook his head. "Guy has never been drunk on duty. Very regular old Navy man, set in his ways. Been with the company several years, never missed a day of work, steady as a rock. That's why they are alarmed."

She nodded. "Got all the bases covered?"

"Sure. Normally, we wouldn't be concerned until he's been missing at least 24 hours, but this is in a sensitive Federal area, and there is the proximity of water which could suggest an accidental drowning. We walked the dock and down along the little gravel beach further down, but nothing turned up."

"You found his time clock."

"Yeah, their supervisor did. Lying on the gravel. The old man wouldn't have just dumped it there and left. If we can't find him here, dead or a live, there is some possibility someone might have snatched him for some reason—ransom, who knows—and might be in Mexico with him by now."

"Is he Mexican or Mexican-American?"

Cleve shook his head. "Regular old white Lutheran from the Midwest, settled here after retiring, 30 years in the Navy. His wife died some years ago, and she was WASP also."

"Then I don't think Mexico is a good bet. Guy had no money, no family to speak of, or we'd know it by now." She frowned. "Why is this ship sitting here with radios and lights on, and nobody home?"

"That's what everyone's wondering."

"What is the history?"

"Ship docked yesterday afternoon. We have a Coast Guard report that they checked it out at sea. Nothing suspicious, just the dog handler says their dog went nuts. Couldn't figure out why."

"Like that?" She pointed to the SDPD dog team. The young African-American handler looked expert, and the dog looked sharp, but he was having a hard time reining the whining, salivating animal in.

"Yeah," Cleve said. "I imagine so."

"Probably the smell," she said. "Maybe some illegal chemical. I'm going to check that out." Her gaze lingered on the poor animal. Amid the strangely disquieting smell that seemed neither natural nor manmade, but had a discomforting sharpness—an odd tang—the dog whined and growled and licked its lips nervously. The dog kept its ears pricked, tail between its legs, keeping a low, spread-legged stance very close to its handler.

"Hey," she told the handler, "can you run her through the ship, one good pass, and then take her home? She's not happy."

"She's very unhappy," the strapping young man said. He wore yellow leather gloves and a dark blue jump suit. He spoke comfortingly to the animal, but she barely calmed down. "Man," he said, "something is wrong here, Linsey."

"Yeah, I'm starting to think so more and more." Linsey had gotten to her present rank not so much because of any political savvy—she just knew how to look good, keep her mouth shut, and not seem like a threat to any of the more aggressive movers-up in the department—but because she had a nose for trouble, and once she sank her teeth into a case, nothing could make her let go. This was starting to look like one of those.

Right now, she had to make some field decisions. She told the utility guy: "Thanks for popping the gate. I'll let you go." She told Cleve, "Let's get on deck and back up the dog team."

They strode up the metal gangway and emerged on the freighter's eerily quiet deck. "Man," Cleve said, "I sort of get the creeps here, or is it just me?"

"It's creepy all right," she said. Mexican mariachi tunes blared happily, and the lights blazed. She had no intention of changing anything for the moment. "I guess," she told Cleve, "we need to treat this as a crime scene until or unless the old man shows up. But there's more. Something about this ship isn't right. Where is she from?"

Cleve checked his PDA, which uplinked to a database downtown. "Been to Brazil and Peru, then made straight for San Diego. The cargo is listed as machine parts, going from a Fuentes Ltd in Lima to an Anaconda Chemicals in San Diego with headquarters near Brawley, California."

"Has the cargo been touched at all? Still secure?"

She heard the dog barking loudly inside the ship—savage, scared hacking barks that echoed amid all those dark steel corridors.

"I have way of knowing if anything has gone out the Navy gates at 32nd Street."

"No way?"

"This is a private, civilian ship at a private, civilian dock."

"Why do they own a dock in the middle of all this Navy acreage?"

"Because Anaconda Chemicals has been a defense contractor since World War II. They are grandfathered in here. "

The dog and her handler appeared at the top of a stairwell. "I've never seen her like this," the handler said. The handler looked sweaty and flustered. The dog's hackled were spread, and she had foam dripping from her muzzle. She looked at Linsey and barked loudly. Linsey understood: the dog was telling her this was a bad gig, and wanted to get let the hell out of here. The dog seemed to be saying *You humans are nuts for hanging around this place.* Linsey had been around working dogs for many years, and this was a message she rarely received. She nodded to the dog and raised a palm in acknowledgement. "See anything unusual?"

"Ship's empty. Nothing in the cargo holds," said the handler.

"Nothing?" It immediately made her wonder if there had been a drug shipment that got ditched somehow when the Coast Guard drew near. "Why would Anaconda Chemicals pay to have a freighter come from Peru and dock here—*empty*?"

"You got me," the handler said, barely able to restrain the dog, who eagerly pulled toward the gangway to leave the ship. "Not our job."

"Do me a favor and take a good look around the grounds before you stop to write your report. That will be the benchmark for whatever investigation goes forward. Remember, our immediate concern is a missing persons case."

"Right," the handler said as he let his dog tow him off the ship on her lead.

She called after the handler: "We're going down for a look. Come back and make sure we're okay." He waved, and she said: "Come on, Cleve, let's take a look around below."

She and Cleve descended into the darkness below. It was spooky, walking among the corridors, whose lights were off. The air conditioning was off, too, leaving that dank smell that penetrated everything. She said: "Let's make a preliminary run through and then get out. If the old man turns up somehow, we'll cancel the investigation and I'll write a report that someone higher up can take up with Anaconda Chemicals."

The only thing that struck her notice were some unusual looking growths along the baseboards in some especially dark cargo holds. She knelt beside one and ran her flashlight beam over it. "That's a huge mushroom," she told Cleve, who hung back with a dubious face. "No, I'm serious, Cleve, this ship came up from the tropics and seems to have brought with it some fungus thing."

"That thing looks gross," Cleve said at last, looking pained.

"It's a mushroom," she said. "A fungus. This is a bracket fungus, the kind I used to see along the bottoms of downed redwood trees up in the Olympic Peninsula rain forest when I was a college student in Seattle." She ran her fingers over the long, multi-tiered growth. Its surface felt cool and tough, but spongy and springy. "This is where the smell is coming from. They got a bad case of the fungus-among-us."

"That why they abandoned ship?"

She frowned. "Good point, Cleve. I'm going to wash my hands real well after touching this specimen. Lord, it's six feet long and a foot tall. Just big enough to hide a human body."

When they arrived on deck, she took a quick look through the bridge and the officers' quarters. She found nothing unusual—just not a soul anywhere, and that music and those lights. She tugged Cleve's arm, and they started down the gangway. The dog handler appeared on the dock below. "Hey, Linsey, we found another of those long mushroom things."

"Where?"

"Under a little wooden walkway near here. The only reason I noticed it was because the dog started going nuts again. I climbed down underneath and got some samples." He held up several plastic baggies in a gloved hand. "Looks like the same sort of mushroom things on the ship."

"Good, get those to the lab," she said.

She walked across the dock, down a path, and clambered under the wooden walkway. Sure enough, there it was—a bracket fungus just like those on board. The dog team had taken samples, so she didn't feel the need to. She ran her fingertip along the powdery edge of its several shelves. If these things were on board, she could explain them. It was a reach—the jungles were filled with weird life forms, and a ship coming out of the tropics might pick up something weird like this. But why would this appear less than a day later under a dock nearby on land?

"You okay?" she heard Cleve said somewhere behind her.

"I'm deep in thought," she snapped, and immediately regretted it. "I'm sorry, Cleve. That came out wrong."

"That's okay," he said. "I'm still getting used to your style after all these years. I see that you're onto one of your bulldog capers and this won't end until we either find the old man or the UFO that ate his lunch."

Chapter 9.

Lee Collwood, shaken and enraged at the news about his ship, had his private jet make a 15 minute hop from the Salton Sea to Lindbergh Field in San Diego. A long black limousine met him on the tarmac. The driver, a Filipino man in a black suit, got out to open the rear door so he could enter the private luxury of a backseat office with wet bar and satellite uplink for the communications center. In minutes they were speeding south toward National City. En route, his operator back near Brawley finally was able to patch him through to Henry Morton.

Collwood shouted into his phone. "What the hell do you mean, the ship docked and now it's sitting there empty?"

"That's right," said his patient manager of San Diego operations, a six figure a year CEO with 5,000 people working for him. "Don't shoot me. I'm just the messenger."

"Aw for God's sake…" Collwood flipped the phone shut and thrust it into his inside suit pocket. Raising his sunglasses so they rested against his forehead, he frowned at the passing city streets, the buildings, the pedestrians, palm trees framed in sunlight and clear blue skies. The limousine crawled through the shady streets downtown—Broadway, Ninth Avenue, Island Avenue, lined with jacaranda and queen palms—until they arrived in the industrial district around 32nd Street. The limo had stickers to get past Navy and Marine Corps gate guards, and briefly crawled along Government shipyard property before taking a number of narrow dirt alleys among small parcels of heavily fenced private property, and arriving before the northern fringes of NASSCO shipbuilding yards. There sat the Lima Voyager, a 35,000 ton freighter that looked like a toy in a bath tub. She was 250 feet long and broad in the beam, towering four stories above the cracked and mossy pre-World War II dock.

Accompanied by assistants and body guards who kept out of sound range, Lee Collwood strode across the dock and shook Henry Morton's hand. Both men were tall and lean, with the look of those accustomed to giving orders and getting things successfully done. "I'll show you what we have," Morton said as he pushed open the tall, narrow gate of a shiny new inner fence that enclosed the aluminum ramp leading to the ship's main deck. "The Harbor Police were here yesterday, as I mentioned."

"Did they find anything?" Collwood asked. Morton did not know the exact nature of the cargo that was now evidently missing along with the crew and captain. Morton only knew it was a sensitive pharmacological source cargo from somewhere in the South American jungle, and that seemed to be enough for him to understand a successful new line of drugs could rejuvenate Anaconda.

"Their notes are still being reviewed," Morton said as he followed Collwood up the ladder. "I should have a preliminary on my desk by tomorrow, and of course you'll get a copy."

"What about our friend?"

"Miss Hazleton," Morton said with a slight chuckle. He was having an affair with an executive assistant, 24 year old Dolly Hazleton, at the Unified Port District Authority. "She already looked at the notes made by a Linsey Simon, who was the principal investigator."

"And?"

"Basically, nada." Morton shrugged. "Dolly tells me Simon is a shrewd investigator and may be having some second thoughts about this situation."

"Can we move the ship to another port? Sink it?"

"Not right away. It's tied up in red tape here at the dock and has to stay here. In case you didn't notice, we are surrounded by military facilities, and probably a thousand Federal police of various kinds."

Collwood swore as he stepped onto the dusty steel deck. He clapped his hands and looked around as Morton joined him. "Looks deserted."

Morton nodded as he too clapped his hands. "Eerie, isn't it?"

Standing in silence, the two men listened to the creak of a loose door, the slap of stagnant water in bilges, the whistle of wind across an open window.

"I turned off the lights and the mariachi music," Morton said.

"What?"

"They left it looking like the crew's on board."

"Drugs," Collwood fumed. "It's the only explanation. They must have been a bad bunch, from the captain on down. Probably smuggled in a ton of cocaine and had a few samples."

Morton said: "Good scheme, now that you mention it. But the Coast Guard went over the ship with a fine toothed comb."

"And?"

"Our spy there says the dogs were skittish, but they didn't find a trace of illegal drugs in the air. That would tend to run against your theory."

"Unless they were towing it underwater. All that stuff happens. Come on, let's look around below."

Together the men searched the bridge and the First Mate's quarters for flashlights. Then, armed with crowbars and strong lamps, they toured the ship. The galley had a stale, greasy smell. The refrigerator smelled of rotting meat—a large package of hamburger meat had thawed, and blackened blood had leaked over the steel shelves and dripped down to the lowest white enamel surface. Cockroaches scuttled in a swirling mass like brown liquid as Morton quickly slammed the door shut. A tour of the crew quarters revealed open doors, unmade beds, missing suitcases, a forgotten shoe here and an open book there. Nada.

"Catch that smell?" Morton said. "We opened the windows topside to air the place out."

"What is it?" Collwood sniffed. His heart pounded as he recognized the faint, earthy smell of strong fungus. He knew what it was. He had seen pictures of the Peruvian caldera island and its mysterious city. Morton had no idea. Nobody did—only the captain and first mate of this blasted tramp.

So where the hell is my fungus? he fumed inwardly. Grimly, he thought: This is a mess, and I'm going to have to fix it myself. When I track down those bums...

"Someone said it smelled like mushrooms," Morton said, laughing at such a silly idea.

"Like with a huge steak," Collwood joked to cover his own anxiety. If the infestation had escaped, then he knew a disaster was about to happen that would make his troubles at Anaconda look like child's play. He also understood the Feds were smart enough to trace the epicenter to this ship. Suicide was not an option—he knew he'd be too scared to put his 9mm automatic in his mouth and pull the trigger. But he could take the weapon, in whose use he had trained himself well, and find the scurvy crew of the Lima Voyager and fix their wagons. At the same time, it might be a good idea, just in case, to secretly start planning for his escape to some faraway country, maybe in the tropics, without an extradition treaty with the U.S.

He must get a manifest of the ship's crew and their addresses. He'd start with the captain. But first, he must humor Morton—the man's blindsided investigation might lead him to the captain. They climbed down a narrow passage below decks. The mushroom smell was stronger here, but mixed with a dozen other odors—machine oil, cleaning fluids, a man's cheap cologne. Hearing a buzzing sound, they stopped. "What's that?" Morton said. They took a few steps further. They stopped again. The buzzing was louder. Twin flashlight beams played back and forth on the dusty, cobwebbed steel ceilings and down to the gray deck. "There," Collwood said. "Something spilled."

"Smells like maple syrup."

"Probably is." Their beams focused together and revealed thousands of skittering insects and a large rat. The rat lay dead on its side, and a stream of roaches issued from a hole eaten into its fur. Its black eyes still gleamed, although looking filmy, as light shone on them. It was a miniature La Brea Tar Pits, caused by a five gallon jug of pancake syrup having been tossed from its shelf. The plastic had cracked, causing this inch-deep lake. It indicated the ship had a faint list to one side.

"Look here," Morton said. He pushed open a small door and stepped over a high threshold into a small office. "The Harbor Police investigator mentioned this in her report." He played his beam along a strange object stuck to the baseboard. It was about six feet long, composed of wavy little shelves. It was dark in color, with faint powdery-white edges.

"I'll be darned," Collwood said, looking at a huge bracket mushroom of the kind found in rainforests. They grew along the bottom surfaces of fallen logs near the damp, spongy forest floor.

"What is it?"

Collwood guessed the fungus was a relative of what he had surreptitiously had his men smuggle out of the Peruvian cordillera. "These boys really did sail through some tropical wonderlands," he mused out loud, not caring what Morton thought. It was too late for that now. The Offensor fungus had morphed somehow, and was taking on a life of its own that nobody could have guessed at. After all, it had been kept in check for eons. Now, for the first time, it was free to take on the world. Funny, Lee thought, that's what I'm doing, and now perhaps I have a worthy opponent—some damned mushroom that's a serial killer.

Chapter 10.

Lieutenant Linsey Simon of the San Diego Harbor Police had begun splitting her time between old, white-washed headquarters on Harbor Drive and a fancy glass skyscraper several blocks away downtown. She'd just been given her new orders. She would be working half time as a uniformed patrol supervisor, and the other half of her work week as a plain clothes detective liaison with the Feds.

She would be her agency's representative to the San Diego Unified County Investigation Agency (SDUCIA or 'Stoosha'). She was 32, a solidly, athletically built blonde with a freshly attractive face and clear blue eyes. Those eyes switched easily between friendly, sunny disposition and crisp, businesslike coolness. She now reported for work two or three days a week in a large, anonymous skyscraper near the foot of Broadway not far from the B Street Pier complex.

Here on the tenth floor of an air conditioned tower—so new that it still smelled faintly of construction chemicals—she joined representatives from SDPD and over two dozen other area police organizations that were part of a yet larger network ultimately reporting to the Federal Government's anti-terrorism activities.

Linsey enjoyed her small but modern looking office. Surrounded by multiple layers of curving, smoky glass that afforded a semblance of privacy, she also shared a small slice of clear plate glass overlooking the harbor. Her husband, Jack, 35, was a reporter at The San Diego Times. Often, he would drive over from his Mission Valley office to meet her for lunch when he wasn't busy with one of his City Hall stories. They owned a two-bedroom condo at Fenton Parkway, centrally located about five miles from the ocean at the far end of Mission Valley. They also owned a getaway cottage on an acre of oak forest on the far side of the Laguna Mountains, on the down slope leading into high desert. They had no children as yet, but hoped for a boy and girl some day soon.

This morning, the phone at Stoosha rang, and Linsey picked up to hear a strange story from her patrol partner, Cleve, about a battered old cargo ship that had just arrived from Peru. With nobody on board. Lights on, salsa music playing loudly, and not a soul in sight.

A bit later, Jack Simon called from the newspaper office. Linsey was in her little glass office, enjoying a cup of apricot yogurt and a view of San Diego Bay while talking with her husband on the telephone. He had meetings and was begging off on their dinner date. She said: "Yes, honey, I'll let you off the hook. But you have to promise me a movie."

His voice sounded close to her neck, and she closed her eyes and imagined him kissing her there. "I'm going to promise you a movie, and something else besides. You know what it is. It begins with S, ends in X, and spells L-O-V-E."

She laughed. "Okay. I can meet you at our house now if you'd like."

"I'd like, but I have several meetings with people who have faces like old mules and wouldn't understand."

"Ah, the Mule People," she said, licking her spoon and doing a half-spin on her chair to put her feet up. The water outside looked gunmetal blue, filtered through the thick window, and rippled with myriad wavy twinkles as the sun and wind ruffled it. "Hey, let's skip that movie and make a date to go sailing. We can rent a boat this weekend."

"If you're up for it, so am I. We'll leave the Mule People in their barn."

"Deal," she said. A courier slipped an interoffice memo envelope across her desk. She waved to the young woman, and opened the manila envelope, with its many holes perforated for viewing, and pulled out a printout labeled LAB RESULTS, PRELIMINARY. Jack was still talking, but suddenly she didn't hear him. She read: ...Upon UCSD Medical Center Toxicology and Mycology Consult, preliminary results indicate a lichen-like structure containing not only algae typical of that genus, but also a complex viral and bacterial symbiosis not seen here before. More remarkably, there are strong traces of human DNA, and a substance resembling pulverized human bone and marrow...

Linsey sat bolt upright, and her spoon clattered away over the desk. She interrupted some clever joke Jack was lovingly murmuring into her ear, said "Honey, I'll call you back later, okay? Bye-bye sweetie, I love you."

She stood up and felt fingers of horror crawling up her face to make the hair on her head feel as if it were standing out straight. This is it, she thought, staggering from her office on legs that felt like stumps, this is it—the terrorist biological bomb we've been dreading. How long would it be before the entire city succumbed to this monstrous attack? She hurried to her boss' office with the papers fluttering in her hands.

Chapter 11.

Lee Collwood flew back to Brawley to collect a few things, most notably his 9mm automatic. It was an older weapon that had floated around in the family for over twenty years, and there was no way anyone could trace it to him. He had an old fart in Jamul, a retired sheriff's deputy, who hand-made rounds for him with some extra grains of gunpowder in a partially hollowed tip, and he always paid Rosa cash because that was what the old coot demanded. Paranoid old fellow—thought the Federal Government was after him. Another UFO story. Speaking of UFO stories, Lee called his lawyer in Los Angeles, Syd Applebaum, and had Syd text him a list of the names and addresses of the Lima Voyager crew on his cell phone.

Armed and ready to rock and roll, Lee Collwood stepped from his private plane on a back lot at Lindbergh Field. His Porsche was waiting for him with the key in the ignition and the tank topped off, courtesy the faceless legions paid to service wealthy patrons like Lee Collwood with no questions asked.

Lee wore his usual dark suit and white shirt, with a maroon tie on loose at the neck. He wore black sunglasses that glittered in the hazy sunlight, and an expensive gray cotton baseball cap with a slightly longer bill than usual—custom tailored for him by a London designer.

Armed with Syd's list, Lee drove into traffic and headed for the first of the thirty or more addresses he'd been given. Some of the men on that list were probably shady characters with multiple passports, he realized, and might not pan out. But at the top of the list was one Ramon Murphy, First Class Master's License, captain of the ship. That would be a good place to start.

Ramon Murphy lived at the far end of El Cajon on the eastern outskirts of Greater San Diego. As Lee drove east on I-8 and exited onto Mollison Avenue, he checked the safety on his gun. He drove several blocks until he came to an upbeat neighborhood of a generally downbeat suburb with a reputation as a redneck fringe. He parked under a jacaranda tree that was shedding mauve blossoms. He checked to make sure the gun was ready, tucked the gun into his belt under the jacket, and stepped from the car. He walked up to the house and rang the bell. Hearing the dingdong deep inside, as if underwater, he raised the sunglasses to his forehead and peered over a wooden fence. He saw a swimming pool and several middle-aged men and women having a barbecue. Soft elevator music played, in just about as bad taste as the women with wigs smoking cigarettes and swilling beer, and the pot-bellied men laughing at dumb jokes from some abysmal Fox television program. The door opened a crack, and Lee tightened his grip around the gun. Under his jacket, where nobody could see, he pointed the muzzle at the gray-haired, fleshy woman in the doorway. "Yeah?" she said, and he said "I'm looking for Ramon Murphy."

"Oh yeah? Well, he's at sea. He was due home yesterday, but hasn't showed up or called. Who are you?"

"Fred. I owe him money." One squeeze of his finger, and she would be blown away backward into the house, dead, amid that dreadful cigarette smell that lay like a sewer odor in the air conditioning. He took his finger off the trigger. He was learning something here.

She brightened. "Well, he'll be glad to see you. Fred is it?

"Fred, yes. Where is he? Any idea?"

She shook her head. "I'm his wife, and I'm getting tired of his baloney. He's probably lying in some tavern down near 32nd Street, wasting all his money. He can guide a ship 10,000 miles without an accident, and then fall over his own feet after having two beers. That's the difference between sober and drinking when it comes to my husband. I tell you—"

"Thank you," Lee said, backing away. "I'll call tomorrow."

"You can come in and have a hot dog and a beer."

"Thank you," Lee said and walked away. He stopped, turned, and asked: "What is the name of that tavern?"

"The one he goes to?"

"Yeah," Lee said in imitation of her slovenly English.

"The Dew Drop Inn."

Oh how original, Lee thought. How dreadful. "Thank you."

"Don't mention it," she shrilled.

Lee had the list of names, including the first mate, but he thought it worth dropping in at the Dew Drop Inn. A 20-minute drive west on I-8 took him to downtown San Diego, and ten minutes south lay the shipyards. He spotted the rotting sign ('Dew Drop Inn') over a decaying block of buildings that were an afterthought of the neighborhood's glory years after the wars. America had produced two thirds of the world's gross national product during a period bracketed by World War II, the Korean police action, and the Vietnam non-war. After that, things had gone to heck, as the pious say, and this neighborhood was no exception. Lee made sure the gun was between his belt and his skin as he walked into the dim recesses of this air conditioned purgatory. The music that met him was a mishmash of noise and punk, belonging to no era in particular and all eras in general. He walked up to the bar, and figured the safest thing was to order a beer. Around him were the drunks who showed up at six a.m. to start drinking, took occasional naps with their foreheads soaked in spilled beer, and only went home at 2 a.m. when the law forced the bar to close. Their only exposure to daylight was going out every 30 minutes to smoke a cigarette. In this alien environment, Lee asked the beefy woman tapping his beer from the keg: "Captain Ramon Murphy, seen him around?"

"Ramon?" Calculations flitted behind her dull blue eyes. "He ain't been here recently. Why, does he owe you money?"

"No, my name is Fred and I owe him money."

"Jeez, you must be a deeply religious man.

Chapter 12.

"Mom, that guy isn't dad." Jimmy Mendez was in the kitchen, arguing with his mother. "Jimmy, what has gotten into you?" his mom said. She knelt by his side, washing his face and hands with a warm washcloth. Behind her, the kitchen curtains blew in a pleasant spring breeze, belying the fear Jimmy felt. Everything wanted to seem so normal, from the apples smelling nice in a bowl like mom's love itself, to her dish soap drying under the rinse rack—but it wasn't. Nothing could be normal again, not while Dad was missing and this stranger was pretending to be Dad. "I'm telling you, mom, I've known Dad all my life. That guy looks like him on the outside, but he ain't dad on the inside."

"Hold still! How could you see inside of him?" mom said with gentle reproach, pushing a washcloth finger in one ear, then the other, while Jimmy squirmed. It felt like worms eating his brain when she did that, and he hated it when she twisted that luke-warm cloth inside his head. "Jimmy, I said hold still!"

"Mom, he looks at me like we're strangers. He hasn't kissed you or hugged me. Can't you tell?"

That got her. Mom paused, with a strange frown. "Well, that's true but I assume he's tired from his long trip. Maybe he isn't feeling well. It's not easy being a sailor."

"You go to the bedroom and smell him." Jimmy pointed down the long dark hallway to the master bedroom, "He even smells weird."

Mom rose, sighing, and rinsed the muddy washcloth out in warm water. "Why don't you run along and play on your bike? I have to go to work soon, and daddy will take you to MacDonald's so you can get a toy when he wakes up?"

"Do you have to go to work?" Jimmy said, feeling a bit sick. He knew that if he got sick enough, she would take time off from work. Maybe he could will himself to get sick. The flu!

"Jimmy, what are you doing making that face?"

He expelled air and opened his eyes, sadly recognizing it wouldn't work. "Nothing."

"Practicing holding your breath?"

"Not really." Couldn't she get it?

"So you can be on the swim team?"

"I'm going to be a deep sea diver when I grow up."

"Oh, okay. Want something to eat before I go?"

She made him a bowl of chocolate ice cream with whipped cream and nuts. While he ate, sitting in the sunny little kitchen with its greenish décor, mom disappeared down the hallway.

"Well?" Jimmy said, licking his spoon as the brown ice cream melted and worked its way over his hand.

She came back from the bedroom, wrinkling her nose. She had changed into her loose, greenish nursing scrubs. "He does need a bath. Smells like stale fish or something. He's sleeping like a log, the poor guy." She threw her coat across her arm for later, picked up her purse and big jangling mess of keys, and kissed Jimmy on the forehead. "You let daddy sleep, and bring him some hot cocoa when he wakes up, okay?" She wet the washcloth and wiped his hand. "Try to stay clean for a little while, okay?" She kissed him again and darted out the door.

Jimmy sat in the silent kitchen as he heard the car start up. He frowned, hearing a sound coming from the bedroom at the end of the hallway. As mom backed her car out of the driveway, Jimmy ran to the front window to wave goodbye. He was always asleep by the time she got home from her evening shift at UCSD Medical Center. He sighed as he returned to his ice cream. Everything seemed to sunny and normal, and

Chapter 13.

Three airplanes cruised slowly back and forth in the sky above San Diego, the connection unnoticed by all but three young men doing a roofing job.

As the three young men stood atop a two-story house in Serra Mesa, overlooking the great expanse of Mission Valley, they shielded their eyes from the midmorning sun and enjoyed the spectacular view. The morning marine layer fog had not burned off, so that the larger buildings were shrouded in a cottony mist right out of a science fiction movie.

The American college dropout, Hugh Milton, was new at the roofing trade. His colleagues, Fritz Juergen and Max Waldmeister, were sympathetic enough. Fritz and Max, friends since childhood, had failed as bakers in their native city of Speyer, Germany, and had immigrated to the U.S. to try their hands at a new trade. They were a pair of pale, burly cousins with curly blond hair and a watery look in their blue eyes that bespoke their fondness for beer. They needed an extra hand now and then on an extra big roof, and Hugh was their man. They lived in the same apartment complex at Parkway Plaza in La Mesa, overlooking I-8, and their alliance stemmed from a few casual parking lot greetings.

They were starting a lucrative new job. The hardest part was over—they'd spent two or three days stripping and scraping the old roof, ripping out old bent roofing nails and filling a dumpster below with curled black paper and torn grayish-blue tar shingles. Then they'd spent a day carrying heavy rectangular packages of new tiles and rolls of fresh undercoating paper, which now lay arrayed along the crest of the pitch all along the roof.

"The fog that ate San Diego." Fritz chirped the fake movie title in a German accent. They all laughed.

"But do we have enough beer?" Max asked. They all looked at the cooler which had a twelve-pack, sandwiches in water-tight baggies, and a mass of ice cubes tightly sealed and sitting in the shade behind the brick chimney.

"Yah," Hugh said in an imitation German accent, "Yah, ve heff ze Bier, unt zo ve are gutt to go." They all laughed. "Eat oll ze buildings you vant, fog monster!"

"Ja!" They all said and started working. Together, they laid strips of black undercoating. They worked their way up from the lowest edges, overlapping the long, four-foot-wide sheets so that water couldn't get under them as it ran down in a rainstorm.

As they worked, the sunlight grew more intense and the marine layer fog started rapidly to thin. They took a break, sitting on the roof with beers and sandwiches. Each had tied a red or blue bandanna around their heads, and they had plenty of colorful zinc for their noses and ears. They had spray bottles of sun block with which they often misted each other down to guard against skin cancer.

As they sat eating, they gazed out over Mission Valley, noticing several airplanes that slowly buzzed back and forth. At first, there didn't seem to be any connection between the three planes. From their high perch, the three young roofers looked southward across the mile-wide valley to the opposite rim, which averaged about 300 feet high.

Mission Valley formed through eons of erosion. During the age of dinosaurs, the region had been under shallow seawater, and the boulder-encrusted low mountains around the coastal edge of the county had been islands and sandbars on which huge saltwater lizards had basked while enormous crocodiles circled below the surface to jump on the lizards or some passing herd of dinosaurs. As the sea level had fallen (largely because millions of years of gradual cooling had built up ice packs on mountains and at the poles, thereby releasing less rain runoff back into the seas) a huge river had pushed through San Diego County. The river had been one of several draining the seas covering much of the Southwest. Today, the San Diego River was a tame meander at the low point of Mission Valley—barely a shadow of the raging giant that had gouged the mile-wide, 300 foot deep valley. It was easy to picture the scene millions of years ago, with the mile-wide river slowly subsiding, and tributary waterfalls dumping acre-feet of churning sandy water and foamy spray into the river. By the time the last sabertooth tiger had roamed through the mud flats, and the last herd of woolly mammoths had meandered past in search of forage, humans had established themselves up and down the coast. That was at the beginning of the Holocene, the present period in Earth history—the age of mankind.

Max, Hugh, and Fritz sat on the rooftop watching the planes as they zigzagged back and forth. "Man," Max said, "those look like they are crop dusting."

"Nothing is coming out the rear though," Hugh said.

"I don't see any nozzles," said Fritz dubiously.

They slowly finished their meals. To the east, where Mission Valley narrowed into Mission Gorge and then disappeared into the first of several mountain ranges—the 1000 or so foot tall Fortunas—sunlight already shone brightly as dry, warm desert air pushed the fog back out to sea. Directly below the three men, the big shapes of the football stadium, the I-15 and I-805 overpass exchanges with I-8, and numerous high rise office buildings were still partially shrouded in fog. To the west, where Mission Valley broadened into a flood plain as the river dumped into the Pacific Ocean seven miles away, a wall of fog still shrouded the Mission Valley and Fashion Valley shopping centers.

During Superbowl days, the men had seen as many as seven or eight large blimps circling like prehistoric whales around the packed stadium, and the skies had been filled with press and spectator planes. Today, there was only mild local or regional air traffic from Montgomery Field a few miles north in Kearny Mesa, and Gillespie Field a few miles east in El Cajon. Choppers from a nearby flight school rose and fell. Traffic, police, and rescue choppers periodically cut a quick line across the valley. Military craft from North Island Naval Air Station as well as the Marine Corps Air Station at Miramar were among several military fields yielding up their own air traffic. Trumping it all, of course, where the huge Boeings and Air Buses lumbering in and out of Lindbergh International at the water's edge downtown, and Rodriguez International just across the border twenty miles south. With all of that going on, it was easy to dismiss three small planes zigzagging in a systematic pattern all morning.

After an hour, one of the planes made a direct pass about 300 feet overhead. Its shadow briefly rippled across the hot roof.

Fritz exclaimed "Hey!" and stood up straight, rubbing his neck. He spotted broad black letters N followed by some numbers and a red ball with a diagonal line through it. The other planes had similar markings.

"What's the matter?" Hugh and Max said, stopping work and waiting at a crouch with hammer and roofing nails in hand.

"Something stung the back of my neck." Fritz looked at his palm, which had a light coating of something sticky and nasty. "This crap is light green or yellow, and has little black dots, thousands of them."

Max shielded his eyes and looked after the plane, which made a sharp banking turn and headed south-southwest into Mission Valley toward the huge bridge of the I-805 overpass.

Hugh wiped sweat away and reached for a water bottle. "You don't suppose they are dropping some kind of bug spray or something, do you?" As he brought the clear, sparkling plastic bottle to his mouth he froze. "Hey, this bottle is coated with something." There was a fine fuzz like faint yellowish flower spores over the whole bottle.

"It's all over the roof here," said Max, grabbing his white shirt with both hands and shaking it. "Sticky stuff!"

"Stuff doesn't want to come off," Fritz said through gritted teeth as he rubbed his elbow against his shirt and squirmed.

Hugh was too hot and tired to care much. He pulled the plastic spout on the bottle open with his teeth and drank deeply. As the water gurgled down his parched throat, he thought it had an odd, flat taste like something that has gone stale in someone's freezer ice cube tray.

After a while, Max looked up and noticed the three planes flying away in a sort of arrowhead formation, eastward over the Fortuna Mountains near Golfcrest Avenue and Mast Boulevard. The three tiny black dots disappeared over the mountain range in the direction of Santee or El Cajon, the three men tiredly thought in a brief discussion.

As quickly as the onset of the yellow ick, it seemed to blow away. Within an hour or two, the smell and stickiness no longer bothered the three men as they finished laying the under-paper and started laying rows of brand-new brick-colored shingled speckled with white gravel to deflect sunlight.

By midafternoon, when the San Diego Police and Fire Departments had processed several calls about sticky material dropping on roofs and streets, large red HazMat trucks roared out to several locations to collect samples, but the annoyance had passed. It was mentioned briefly on a late afternoon news broadcast, and one or two news choppers did low fly-bys to look at rooftops, but the issue had disappeared from local news by the five p.m. evening broadcasts.

Chapter 14.

Based on the lab result and Linsey's excitement, her boss gave the printout a quick scan and called a meeting of the Ready Team. At any time, there were at least three to five representatives in the office from among the several dozen on the task force.

The boss was Louise Trost, Chief Special Agent on site and Federal regional anti-terrorism coordinator for the San Diego part of Southern California. She and Leslie got along fine. Louise was a heavyset Afro-American woman with a singer's thick, mellifluous voice. Looking older than her years, she seemed to Linsey almost grandmotherly. Louise had a patient chuckle and a way of slowing things down so they could be looked at from all points of view. She could also be biting with those who crossed her, or disagreed with her without having the facts to back up their argument. Linsey found her a good person to work for—smart, nurturing, get stuff done.

"Linsey dear, I do have one little reservation. Why would enemies of the United States use mushroom bombs? Don't get me wrong, there is something dreadfully anomalous here, but I would think they'd attack us with some sort of gas, or pour something in our water supply."

"I know," Linsey said, starting to sweat under the collar. "Maybe I reacted a bit too quickly."

"No, you did just fine," Louise purred. "We do need to find out why there is human DNA in a mushroom found under a dock where a guard disappeared. Be cool, child, we'll sort this out."

Mrs. Louise Trost, MBA Harvard School of Business, was 38, the daughter of an Afro-American Air Force General and a Caucasian German woman of Turkish and German descent.

The former Louise Berry spoke several languages fluently, and by age 14, when her father retired to Spokane, Washington, she had lived in six different countries and visited at least two dozen. When Louise began high school as a socially shy but precocious learner, the adjustment to U.S. life was the hardest she had ever made. Because of her features—light skin, blue eyes, tightly curly black Afro hair, full nose and lips—she was the subject of a fair amount of prejudicial heckling from her mostly White school mates. That she was chubby made things all the more difficult. She had been trained to believe in herself, and never lost faith in her wider goals. She sang in choir at the Resurrection Episcopal Church, and took first place in Debate Society. Always a bit heavy, and with a history of childhood asthma, she shied away from sports. She ended her high school days as Class Valedictorian, and her proud parents sent her packing for a successful four years as a Business major at Yale University, followed by graduate school at Harvard. After years in private industry, she'd switched to police and forensic work, and raced up the management track at Homeland Security.

Louise Berry had been married 18 years to Frederick Trost, a Black airline pilot stationed in San Diego with Pacific Airlines and its successors. The couple had met while Louise, as a 20 year old business school summer interne with a large corporation in Virginia, had met the young Naval aviator who had just finished Annapolis and was stationed at Norfolk Naval Air Station. They'd married three years later, in her first year of grad school. the couple had two boys and a girl, all in high school now, and lived on the slopes of Mount Soledad with splendid views of the Pacific Ocean from high up. The kids had attended Muirlands Middle School and now La Jolla High School, and all were honor students.

In recent years, Louise had begun taking an interest in Yoga and Tai Ch'i, and had lost twenty pounds from a still generous frame. Because of her lifelong shyness, which sometimes manifested itself in an appearance of seeming closed or unfriendly, when she really felt vulnerable and defensive, she had also joined Toastmasters and was just learning how to tell jokes. Public speaking was a real terror for her, and she still felt like crying even as she stammered out a good clean joke.

Two detectives filed into the room—a tall, skinny man with slick black hair representing SDPD, and a petite blonde with a boyish figure and pink face—as well as an FBI agent.

Louise put the issue on the table, adding "There is no question something is wrong. We need to figure out if this is our problem or someone else's."

"Someone else like who?" the FBI agent asked. He was a macho Japanese-American with a blue-black buzz cut and highly toned karate build. His off the shelf beige suit sort of floated on his sinewy body. He peeled an orange as he sat in on the meeting with one leg pulled under him and the other casually stretched over a pile of books under the table.

The smell of orange peel oil filled the room, making Linsey thirsty. Funny how that worked. She was beginning to wonder if she'd jumped the gun.

"Well, if the guard was murdered, it's the Harbor Police. If terrorists murdered him, it's us. You read the memo. Now if the DNA in the mushroom turns out to be his, then maybe it's a case for some Federal Agency we haven't heard of yet."

"X-Files," the blonde cop snickered.

"Twilight Zone," the tall, skinny detective said. Linsey expected he'd start mimicking the TZ theme, but he didn't.

Louise said: "I've taken the liberty of contacting a mycology expert at UCSD. Mycology is the study of fungi. The University of California's San Diego campus has many wonderful little departments and subdepartments, and that's one of them. They actually have someone on staff or on call at UCSD Medical Center in Hillcrest, and I'm expecting a call back any moment."

"We have to try really hard," the blonde said, "not to take on the police work of other departments. This sounds like a case the Harbor Police should work first."

"Maybe," Louise said, "and that's where we got Linsey Simon from. She's working the case and has alerted us there may be a biological bomb angle here. Please understand, I don't believe in the notion of letting a hot case bounce around among various entities and departments until someone somewhere decides to take possession. You know, unless there is a chance of political glory somehow, they are all going to say no. Meanwhile, some crime scene languishes or some perp gets away. The policy here is to be proactive rather than push-away. It may get us in to trouble now and then, but hopefully we'll be first out of the box on that one real case that involves blowing up half of San Diego, or poisoning a lot of people."

"Better safe than sorry." The FBI guy sucked an orange slice.

"Hello?" said the conference call speaker on the desk.

"We hear you," said Louise.

"This is Professor Sean Nolan. I'm a senior scientist at UCSD Biology specializing in Mycology, and a consultant to UCSD Medical Center. How can I help you?"

Louise introduced herself and the others at the table and told him the problem: "We have a situation that looks to our laymanly eyes like a great anomaly. A man has disappeared, and a huge man-size mushroom not native to this area has been found. It turns out from the preliminary lab report that this is an unknown species and, I repeat and, it has human DNA inside. Our principal investigator, Lieutenant Linsey Simon of the Harbor Police, seems to feel it's worth looking at a terrorist connection. My question is: does the DNA match that of the missing guard? Can you help us?"

"Ummm...well, if I had a sample of the missing guard's DNA—a pristine swab from the in his cheek, or some blood—I could start our lab working on that. What does that buy you?"

Louise said: "Well, if the DNA is that of the missing guard, then this huge mushroom must have eaten him."

Amid silence, Linsey heard shocked breaths.

Louise continued calmly: "I'm of the inductive school of reasoning. We investigate just the facts. Do I need to spell it out? We have a huge growth, it has human DNA, we're missing a guy, is the DNA his? If it is, we have a major hubbub. If it's just some random chatter, some fragments that look like human DNA but aren't, then we write it off as an anomaly. We need you to look at the DNA in the mushroom."

"In a mushroom?" the professor echoed incredulously. "Okay, well, send us the mushroom and the DNA, and we'll check it out. Get us missing man's DNA—a stool sample, blood, whatever you can manage."

Louise said drily: "We'll see what we can do. Since he's missing, we can't ask him for a cheek swab." She muted the speaker phone and pointed to the SDPD detective. She mouthed: "Get to the guard's hotel room with a forensic team, stat." She put Professor Nolan back on for thanks and goodbyes.

Linsey had a picture of some cheap hotel downtown where the missing guard had lived. "Hey, do guard companies routinely get DNA samples? They do have the guards fingerprinted."

Louise snapped her fingers. "Thanks, Linsey. We'll hit that asap also." After the others had filed out of the meeting room, Louise and Linsey were alone. "Linsey, you jumped the gun."

"I know." Linsey felt mortified. *What a fool!*

Louise spoke, unruffled. "Child, we are swimming in a pool of sharks. Think about what you say and do."

Linsey felt mauve and purple and burgundy shades of mortification cross her cheeks.

Louise said: "Don't feel bad. We've all inked that square."

Chapter 15.

Jack Simon was in his large window office at the San Diego Times making a pot of coffee when the department secretary, Jovia, walked in with an armload of supplies. "Oh, Jack!" she said as she dropped a paper bag of paper clips and other goodies in his In Box. She appeared to be surprised to see him.

"What's up, Jovia?" he asked. She was a tall, attractive young black woman who wore power suits and dreamed of a corporate exec job after evening classes at National University. With three kids and a husband in medical school, that was proving a tall order, and Jack always offered sympathies. She appreciated the understanding and liked him.

"There was something..." She bit her lip, frowning. "I can't quite remember—oh, yes, a Mr. Robertson. He called."

Jack had two different stories going in his mind, one about City Hall and the other about a brewing City Council crisis, and he was just glad to be able to move around a bit as he went through the motions around his coffee pot. "Don't know him."

"He left his name and number." She dug a scrap of note paper from a vest pocket and put it on his ink blotter. "He said he wanted to talk to you about that big flap going on with the airplanes spraying in Mission Valley."

Jack was interested. "Did he say he knows what's behind it?"

"He was very secretive, and noticeably nervous."

Jack stopped. "Nervous? Hmm. If he knows anything you'd think he would go to the police."

"Unless he's in some real trouble."

Jack poured a cup of steaming black coffee and sat down at the desk. He forgot the coffee as he looked out over Mission Valley. "Most people who come to me, when they are in trouble, try to smear someone else to cover their own tracks."

"And the other few?"

He shrugged. "Nuts of one kind or another."

"I'll let you deal with it," she said as she started to walk from the room. He watched her shapely figure—something a man couldn't resist, no matter how much he loved his wife—and she turned. "Jack, I almost forgot, Dylan Matthews' wife called. She said he wants you to call him. It's kind of urgent."

"Thanks. I'll give him a buzz."

After she had left, Jack finished fixing his coffee—light cream, one sugar—and then called Dylan Matthews' number from his rolling card catalog. Dylan had been a fellow journalist, down the hall, until his alcoholism had gotten him "unhired," as he liked to put it in his perpetual blend of bitterness and humor. He'd been asked to resign in lieu of being fired after a lot of absences, missed assignment, and a few faux-pas like misquoting the mayor on a critical budget issue and almost creating a political firestorm. Dylan's wife Maggie answered. "He's out for a walk, Jack. How are you? How is lovely Linsey?"

"We're doing fine, Maggie. You?"

"Oh well, you know—" She left a lot unsaid. The grief and worry in her voice suggested Dylan was still slipping downhill.

"Do you know what he wanted to tell me?'

"I'm not sure, Jack. He's, you know, incoherent half the time."

"I'm so sorry, Maggie."

She started to sniffle a bit. He waited until she composed herself. "I'll have him call you when he gets back from his walk."

"Thanks. Take care of yourself."

Jack sipped half his coffee and tried dialing the other number, that of Mr. Robertson. The phone on the other end rang and rang, but nobody answered. Soon, Jack was on his second cup of coffee and typing away at his computer. His head was full of City Hall information, and he forgot all else.

Chapter 16.

Jimmy Mendez had been to the store two blocks away with some older kids, but now he was scared he'd be in trouble. It was starting to be late afternoon.

He could tell, as he raced home on his bicycle, because he could smell hamburger cooking in houses as he went by. The ice cream truck came by with its jingling music rolling over the rooftops, and Jimmy could have kicked himself for the bad timing—had he been home five minutes earlier, he might have copped an ice cream.

Turning into the driveway, he swung his right leg behind his left, and stood on the left pedal as he cruised into the open garage door. Stepping off, he let the bike gently sail to rest standing up between piles of bags. He stopped and listened for signs of trouble, like mom and dad arguing about why they weren't stricter, or mom calling his name in that quavering, scared voice when he wasn't immediately nearby.

Hearing nothing out of the ordinary, he pushed open the inside door from the garage into the hallway near the kitchen. He stood still and listened. The TV was on, with a bowling game. That meant lots of laughing people, bouncy commercials, commentary from some old guy with weird hair.

Jimmy tiptoed into the house and pulled the door shut. He was about to sneak down the hall to his bedroom, at the other end of the house from mom and dad's, when he heard a noise. He froze again. It sounded like a groan or a sigh. It wasn't words—Jimmy could tell that much. It seemed to be coming from the living room at the back of the house, so he tiptoed to the doorway between the kitchen and the dining room and looked diagonally across toward the living room. Mom and dad stood there, locked in an embrace. Her back was toward Jimmy. She wore this wrinkled white blouse and dark skirt that came down to the backs of her knees. Her nylons and shoes were gone. Dad was taller than she, and her head was back while he leaned over her. Jimmy couldn't see dad's face, but he hoped it was back to normal—not the cold, distant stranger who had come ashore. Mom's arms seemed limp, as if he were really planting a long-lost-love kind of French nuke on her. Maybe things were okay after all. Grinning faintly, Jimmy turned and headed for his bedroom. His stomach was beginning to sound early, faint hunger pangs. He grabbed his softball and glove on the way.

Sometime later, the hunger pangs began. Jimmy looked up from his computer, where he'd been playing a game of chasing monsters through a castle, and shooting them with ray guns. It was noticeably darker outside. The clock on the wall, with the big easy to read numbers, said it was 5:00. Mom should be preparing dinner about now, but Jimmy couldn't smell anything. He left his bedroom and walked down the long, dark, carpeted hallway to the middle of the house. The TV was still on, but now it was billiards instead of bowling. The kitchen was as it had been when he walked through earlier. Weird. They wouldn't have gone out for pizza without him, and he would have to be babysat. That was the law. He walked around the kitchen table, noting that no dishes were on it, and the stovetop was cold. No hamburger, no potatoes, no pudding, nothing.

Jimmy headed down the long hallway to his parents' bedroom. It took forever to get there, and he lightly tossed his ball and caught it with the gloved hand, over and over.

The door was slightly ajar, and he paused. He didn't hear any noise from inside. He knew that adult moms and dads sometimes lay on the couch together and necked, or got into bed without clothes on to look at each other or something. Sometimes they made weird wailing noises, or growled at each other. It was scary, like watching people attack each other. You'd think one was going to kill the other, or eat the other. Kids at school said it was *Sex*. Jimmy was too embarrassed to ask what it meant.

When he pushed the door open and stood staring, he saw them lying in bed together. He smelled this icky smell, like dirt, but it had something garbagy in it. *Nasty*. They had their clothes on, but rumpled. They must have fallen asleep together. A fan was on. Distant TV talk about billiards made it hard to hear if they were breathing. He didn't want to look closer.

He went back to the kitchen to fix some ice cream and cookies. Maybe drink a glass of chocolate milk. He found ice cream, and potato chips, and cola, and peanut butter. He climbed up and got some cookies from the jar on top of the refrigerator. Almost fell down and broke his neck in the process. Finally, when he was ready to eat, the ice cream was starting to melt, so he said "Oops!" and quickly took the carton back to the freezer. Should have thought of that. A puddle of chocolate was on the table. *Now I'm in for it.* Hearing a sound from the dining room, he paused and listened with his heart racing. If mom saw the mess, she would yell, and that would make dad take down the ping pong paddle.

No further sounds. Jimmy got a sponge, filled it with warm water, and started to mop up the mess. All the water from the sponge leaked out and made twice as much of a mess. Finally, he used a whole roll of paper towels to sop it up. He took the whole armload of wet towels outside to the trash can. Then he realized his shirt was now covered with chocolate, so he took it off. The neighborhood girl, who was eight, made a nasty sound and stuck her tongue out, imitating his physique. He stuck his tongue out at her and hurried into the house. Were mom and dad still sleeping? It was so quiet in here.

He walked down the long hallway again. "Mom?" His voice sounded thin and quavering in his ears. It sounded like someone else's voice. He wasn't ready to call out "Dad?" yet. Something made him shy away from that. He wasn't sure yet if that man was really his dad. "Mommy?" he said in a frightened little voice.

The smell in the bedroom was stronger now. It reminded Jimmy of mushroom soup, but stale somehow, almost rotten. He started to gag. He just glimpsed both of them, still in their embrace, only they weren't on the bed anymore. Mom lay pressed against the baseboard, and dad had his arms around her and his face over hers. He had his back to Jimmy, and Jimmy couldn't see either of their faces, but he knew something was terrifyingly wrong here. They didn't seem to be moving, and he didn't see dad's shirt moving up and down with breathing. A glossy black hose ran from Dad's mouth out into Mom's neck, and Dad's cheeks were slightly puffed out as if he were blowing something into her—something, industrial, sharp, mushroomy.

Jimmy didn't have the time or the courage to go in and find out more, because barf came up and ran between his fingers as he cupped his hands over his mouth. In the gloom, he could make out that it was mushroom-colored barf, sort of clay colored. He ran down the hall, crying and barfing at the same time, with that awful mushroom smell rising up into his sinuses and choking him. He just made it to the bathroom and stood on his box under the sink, when the whole ice cream, cookies, everything he'd eaten, plus the orange juice and chocolate milk, jumped up out of his throat and splashed the sink. Just seeing it made him barf all the more, and he started crying inbetween barfing, crying for mommy to come help him, but she didn't, and he was afraid to go down that hallway again.

Chapter 17.

Patrolman Cleve Bartlett of the Harbor Police stopped before the highrise, and Linsey sprinted out the main door and into the squad car. She wore civilian clothing, including white silk blouse, dark brown skirt, and beige purse, and had her badge and gun on her belt under a brown blazer. "Hey Cleve, thanks for picking me up."

"Always a pleasure," Bartlett said. He was a big, dark-haired, dark-skinned man with an easy-going nature but a sense that he was coiled like a spring ready to go off. She'd seen him run four blocks in full gear, including utility belt with ammo and gun plus Kevlar vest, and catch a 17 year old high school sprinter wanted for purse snatchings by the Star of India on Harbor Drive. "Where to? Back to our Mysterious Mushroom?"

As he pulled with lazy carefulness into traffic, she buckled up. "Yep. The Fungus Among Us. You realize, Cleveland, that this is probably the strangest case we'll ever work in our lives."

Cleve nodded. "When you call me by my full name, I know you are speaking profoundly."

"Indeed."

Cleve drove south on Pacific Coast Highway and down into the 32nd Street Naval Yard, under brooding skies that made the forests of masts, antennas, and tall cranes all the more gray for their military paint. Cleve wheeled the car down the narrow driveway to Anaconda Chemical's dock, where the black-hulled freighter with her dirty white decks and bridge loomed like a foreboding question mark.

Minutes later, a sleek gray Mercedes convertible sports car pulled in. A tall, graying man with a closely shaven salt and pepper beard got out. He was well-dressed—a lady's man, Linsey thought—with a well-tailored light gray suit, no tie, light lemon shirt open two buttons to expose a tanned chest and a crop of white hair. He was all business now, though, as he strode over extending a tanned hand. "I'm Dr. Nolan, the mycologist from UCSD. You are?"

"Lieutenant Linsey Simon," she said, shaking his strong, dry hand. It was a nice enough hand, sort of taut and bony in an intelligent way, if that made any sense. "We spoke over the phone."

"Yes, I was impressed by your comments." He and Cleve shook hands and exchanged names and pleasantries. "Show me to this find of yours. I'm intrigued."

"If you're a mushroom man, this'll make your day."

"Actually, I'm a fungus man. Mushrooms is the nonscientific name for certain edible fungi with caps. Some people call the poisonous ones as toadstools—also not scientific lingo."

"Can you educate us a little?" Linsey asked as they strolled down the gravel walk to the dock. A light breeze ruffled their hair and rattled the tackle on a nearby flag pole.

Nolon said: "There are generally considered to be three major domains of life on earth. These have superseded the older classification into five or six kingdoms. The exact categories keep being refined over time, but it will help to think of it this way. There are three main types of living things, and the distinctions are based on the nature of the fundamental building block of life, the cell.

"The cells in our human bodies, for example, contain an outer membrane, then a largely liquid part inside containing all the functioning stuff to process nutrients for energy to keep the ship going, and finally at the center is a nucleus containing genetic information. There is a lot that goes on in the nucleus—it's almost a cell within a cell. Each of the domains of living things have many examples."

"First, there are very simple life forms that do not have cell nuclei, especially most types of simpler bacteria.

"Then there are more complicated life forms made up of one or a few cells with nuclei, usually made up of a single cell type whether it's one cell or several. These include more complex bacteria, and some of the organisms living around black smokers in the ocean bottoms.

"Finally there are the advanced life forms that have very complex arrangements of often very specific types of cells. In other words, we have skin cells, eye cells, fingernail cells—different cells for every function of the body. These advanced life forms include plants, animals, fungi, and some other odds and ends like the algae. I am a biologist specializing in fungi, so I am a mycologist." He added, smiling: "I am a bit sentimental, calling my subject the Fifth Kingdom."

They came to the boat dock. "It's under there," Cleve said, pointing to the shadowy underside of the dock.

"Fascinating," Nolan said. He took his jacket off and laid it carefully aside. As Linsey and Cleve watched with wide eyes, he proceeded to undress. "Nothing to be alarmed about. I generally wear my swimming trunks for moments like this." Linsey almost laughed out loud as the handsome, tanned gentleman stood there wearing nothing but a pair of red trunks that came almost to his knees, and a banana-yellow tank top. The trunks had an array of grabby logos from some computer game involving a space station. From ladies' man to nerd, she thought. "Excuse me." He produced a small flashlight and a sample kit, and crawled into the slime under the dock.

Exchanging horrified looks with Cleve, Linsey took off her blazer and crawled in after him as far as she dared—avoiding the green slime that bobbed around river rocks in the water's edge. filtered light reflected in wildly undulating patterns and blobs over head on the bottom sides of the dock planks. The smell wasn't so bad here. Saltwater, decomposing algae, and seaweed almost masked the odor of the six foot long thing anchored along the rocks. Each end touched one of the thick, round pylons that were smeared black with pitch and preservatives.

Nolan probed with a hand wearing a latex glove. "Ah," he said. "Interesting. Quite wild, really. This is not precisely a fungus. Looks a bit more like a lichen."

"Can you enlighten me?" Linsey said, squirming as the round rocks hurt her knees.

"This thing looks truly unusual. I'm glad to have a look *in situ*. A lichen is a symbiotic—that means, living together, helping each other—relationship between a fungus and a bunch of algae. They do different jobs, and they complement each other. Usually they are very small life forms you'll see attached to rocks from the tropics to the polar regions. They are not the same as moss, which is a primitive plant. This thing is huge, if it is a lichen. This is definitely far more complicated." He held the flashlight in his mouth and, with a scalpel, took scrapings and cuttings, which he placed in little baggies.

He slipped a latex glove over the other hand, so it made a snapping noise. "So you sent samples to the lab already," he murmured, running a fingertip over the cuts already there. "I'm wondering what the reproductive cycle of this thing is like. This exemplar looks dry and spent, but I would bet my last buck that it has some way of coming back to life. Usually, fungi produce a vast number of spores, like two million a minute for your household button mushroom. I don't see any evidence here of spores—there would be piles of fine black dust here."

Linsey said: "Unless the tide washed it away."

He frowned. "You may have something there. Are you suggesting a reproductive relationship involving sea water?"

She laughed. "What do I know? I'm a cop. I'm not suggesting anything, just thinking out loud with my poor sponge of a brain. This thing is stuck to the bottom of a dock by the sea."

He nodded. "Very good. You are trained in inductive logic. You start with the facts at hand, and try not to introduce any theories based on facts not present."

"It's called evidence," she said, and couldn't help the little tone of sarcasm in her voice. Despite his efforts to keep things simple, he seemed to want to say simple things in complicated ways. *What a nerd*, she thought. *Likeable, but a nerd.*

"Right." He ignored her and continued his inspection. He crawled around the thing, murmuring "It does look like a polypores bracket fungus, maybe a sort of ganoderma, and probably a tropical genus. That would make it more advanced than a common gilled mushroom in the way it out-spores. I'm not sure we've encountered this precise specimen before." He peered at it from below and above. She squirmed as he put his face close and smelled its surfaces.

At last, he crawled out and placed his specimen kit on the dock. As he dressed, he said: "I don't know what we have here. For a bracket or shelf fungus, I would expect more of rounded or seashell shape rather than these long ribbon shelves that seem layered like..." He frowned with inspiration as he pulled his trousers on. "...almost as if it were mimicking dryrotted wood. Now that's an interesting hypothesis. Maybe this thing hitched a ride on a ship, maybe this one here. You say this freighter came from the tropics?"

"Yeah, South America," Cleve said. Linsey put her blazer back on. Nolan packed his specimens in his fine jacket pockets and clambered on the dock. "My initial guess is that it's a new bracket fungus that grows on fallen logs in a rainforest. It often helps kill the tree, and then feeds on it for months as the tree lies on its side. Mosses and other opportunistic vegetation help provide cover and keep the wood damp."

"Ick," Linsey couldn't help saying. "By the way, there are some others in the ship. The reason we took you to this one first is because we thought all along there was some connection to the guard, whose time clock was found on the gravel here."

Nolan eagerly followed them to the freighter. Cleve waited outside while Linsey gave him the tour of the ship. As they climbed on board, she said: "That smell is stronger here."

"Could be spores," Nolan said, "or it might just be the natural decay of the thallus. Most fungi have their visible portion—the part you call a mushroom—made of very fine fibers. Huge numbers of these form a sort of network that forms the cap. More technically, the fibers are hyphae, and they form structures called mycelia which include stems, caps, gills under the caps for producing spores, and so on.

They gingerly felt their way around below decks by the light of his little flashlight and her larger police light. He took a few more samples, but murmured "More of the same." She couldn't tell if that meant exciting or boring.

"I can assure you of one thing."

"What's that?" They climbed back to welcome daylight.

"An organism has a certain specific nature. It evolves in a niche that includes other life forms. No matter where it goes, it tries to behave in the manner that it evolved to behave in. So whatever is going on here, these fungi are imitating the conditions in their place of origin."

Chapter 18.

Hugh Milton bade good evening to his two German friends, Max Juergen and Fritz Waldmeister in the parking lot of their apartment building on Parkway Plaza, La Mesa. Hugh had driven home from the Serra Mesa job in his pickup truck, they in their beat up old VW Golf. All three men were tired and in need of a bath, a nap, a meal, and a cold beer. The beers they'd consumed on the roof during the day had long since worn off, except for a muzzy feeling that made Hugh feel extra tired.

Hugh trudged up the stairs, hoping Annie was home. Annie was his 22 year old live-in girlfriend. She was a small, cute young woman with gray eyes and short brown hair and, as Hugh thought of it, a tight little body. She had just finished her degree in English at San Diego State University, and was about to start a summer program to get her teaching certificate for city schools. Until then, she'd be working part time as a hairdresser. Things were tight, but they knew they could make it. She was trying to urge him to resume his studies in Engineering at the University of California, San Diego. They'd been talking seriously about becoming engaged, and he thought of her as his fiancée. Sure enough, when he rattled the key in the door of their one-bedroom on the third floor, Annie pulled the door open and smothered him in a happy embrace. What a great way to come home, he thought, as he hugged her and nuzzled his nose in her neck.

"You go take a hot shower," she said enthusiastically, "and I'll make us a nice dinner." She wrinkled her nose. "You smell of beer and sweat."

"I've been working hard, baby."

"Bringing home the bacon?" She made a money-money gesture with thumb and index finger.

"Yeah, actually—" He reached in his overalls pocket and fumbled out fifty bucks. "—They advanced me some cash because I told them we need grocery money and gas."

"How nice!" Annie said. "I'll get you a nice cold beer."

"Thanks." Truth was, he reflected as he shed his dirty clothing on the way into the bathroom, he was beered out for the day. Fritz and Max could inhale it down like oxygen, but at 25, Hugh thought he must be slowing down with old age already. His skin was red and hot from exposure to the sun, but the two Germans were good about using sun block. Hugh took a hot shower amid loud rock music. He whistled happily as he soaped up in the steamy air. He heard a knock on the door—"Honey, dinner is ready!"—and replied "I'll be right out!"

They sat together on the tiny balcony looking east over a huge willow tree sitting on a slope. They felt lucky to have this place, because the eastern exposure meant they could enjoy early morning sunshine, but weren't baked all day and evening as the sun turned along the southern horizon and beat into west-facing apartments late into summer evenings. It was shady here, and they got a nice breeze. They toasted each other with cans of beer, and ate sloppy joes on buns. She always made salads, and this evening was no exception. He loved the tangy raspberry-lime dressing amid chopped lettuce and other goodies. After dinner, Annie went to clean up, while Hugh got himself a large glass of cold water and lay down on the couch. He wasn't feeling so well.

Annie came out wringing her hands in a dish towel. "You okay?" He managed to groan in reply, holding his stomach while lying stretched out on his back. She pressed: "What's the matter?"

"Not sure. Are you okay?"

"Yes," she said. "I feel fine. It couldn't be my dinner."

"I didn't mean that. My stomach is all up in knots."

"Maybe you're coming down with something."

"Maybe."

"I'm sorry, Honey." She knelt by his side and hugged him, kissing his chin and neck. "Maybe later we can have a little fun and you'll feel better."

"I'd like that," he said sincerely, hugging her to him. A long moan escaped him. "Sorry," he said.

"Maybe you should take a magazine and go sit in the bathroom," she said with a laugh.

"Yeah, I'll try that." With effort, he hove himself erect and staggered off to the bathroom. He wasn't in there a minute before he had a severe bout of diarrhea. When it seemed he was empty, he discharged water. Then he threw up—a lot of lettuce and little bits of this and that. He flushed the toilet each time, until it seemed he had nothing left but empty cramps.

At one point, Annie knocked on the door—quick nervous knocks. "Are you okay in there?"

"Yeah." His own voice rang hollow in his ears in the confines of the small bathroom. He managed to make it to bed, where he lay curled up in a fetal position. "Honey!"

She poked her head in. "What is it?"

"Can you call Fritz and Max and ask them if they have this?"

"Sure." She reported back ten minutes later: "They say they feel fine. If you can't make it tomorrow, no sweat. They'll pay you the full nut, because you worked so hard on the hard part."

"Wonderful." Cramped up, he fell asleep.

He awoke at the first light of dawn, feeling pretty good. He felt thirsty, a little dizzy, a little weak, but otherwise fine. He downed a quart of orange juice, hoping it wouldn't give him the runs again. He made himself bacon and eggs with toast and jam while Annie slept peacefully. There was a gentle knock on the door—Fritz—"Are you coming along?"

"Yeah, man, just give me five minutes, okay?"

He kissed Annie goodbye as she slept, gathered his work clothes and water bottle, and marched out the door for work as if nothing had happened. He felt a little odd, and thought it must be all the beer he'd consumed the day before. No more beer, he resolved. Only water and sodas. Clean living! Then maybe this odd feeling would go away.

Chapter 19.

When Jimmy Mendez awoke, his mouth tasted terrible. He was thirsty, and had a headache. He didn't know where he was, but that wasn't the worst of it. He just couldn't quite remember what the worst of it was.

As he sat up, squinting in foggy dawn light, he remembered this much: scared to death, he'd gotten his blanket, his bear, and a box of cookies, and locked himself in mom's car. In the middle of the night he'd woken up, afraid to go into the house, and crawled along the little sidewalk to the garden faucet. There he'd let water drip quietly into his cupped palms, and he'd drunk from that. The water had tasted flat, but cold and fresh.

Now he just wanted to be with mom. He sprinted from the car, down the gravel walk, and up the concrete side stairs. The door was unlocked, and he pushed into the house. It wasn't like he'd expected. Usually in the mornings, mom had the radio on, and the house smelled of toast and coffee while she hustled about cleaning and humming to herself. Now there was this gloomy silence. It was as if nobody were alive in the house.

Could they still be sleeping? Of course. It was early. He sprinted down the carpeted hallway, falling over some slippers in the dark, but quickly getting up unhurt. He burst into the bedroom and just then he remembered—

But the bed was empty. There was a long dark-brown thing by the baseboard, about as long as a small adult. It looked like a long wooden plank all rotten and full of holes, and frazzled at the ends. Its sides weren't smooth, but wavy, with some powder on them. Actually, it was like a board made out of layers, like thin sheets in one of those crumbly layer pies that mom sometimes made. Looking closer, he thought he could see a long curve in this thing. That was it. It the faintest curve to it, as if it was somehow female. He stared closer, wide-eyed. It smelled like mushrooms, and when he touched it with one tentative fingertip, it was dry but kind of springy or squishy like soggy newspaper...

"Jimmy?"

He whirled.

"We have things to do today."

Mom stood in the doorway. Or rather, the person standing there looked exactly like mom, except her eyes were totally lacking in love. He could sense the cold about her, like at the bottom of the sea where no sunlight ever penetrates. If he let her, she would suck the life out of him. He somehow sensed it; he knew this deep down. And dad? Maybe—he looked at the fungus thing, then at mom, and at the dusty stain on the carpet beside the fungus thing—somehow, the thing that had taken dad's soul away now had taken mom away too.

The person who wasn't mom stepped into the room and said in a perfectly normal voice, but one that had no love in it—it didn't even seem to recognize him as her son—"Jimmy, what would you like to eat?"

He waited until it cleared the doorway. Pretending to approach it, he broke suddenly and ran out the door, down the hall, and out into the street bawling, blinded by tears.

Chapter 20.

The being that had been Maria Mendez stood behind the curtains and watched as the little boy ran out in to the street screaming hysterically.

When a police car arrived, the fungus zombie *was-Maria Mendez* prepared to leave hastily by the back exit. When the police did not come knocking, but left with the boy, was-Maria Mendez picked up a telephone and dialed. The voice at the other end was that of the being that had been the Captain. "Yes?"

"It is I." It closed its eyes and hoped the was-Captain understood who was breaking contact silence by calling.

"Mendez," was-Captain said, speaking as if to the human it had known on board ship. "What is the purpose of this contact?"

"To alert you that Mendez' child is in police custody. Our operation will start becoming visible."

"Our operation will become visible soon enough, but we do not want to hasten that moment," was-Captain said. "Stay there and wait for them to come. I will consult with our advisors and tell you what to say."

After the phone call, was-Maria Mendez waited fifteen minutes standing stock-still behind the curtains. It stood in the shadows while motes of dust danced in the still beam of sunlight stabbing in through a slit in the otherwise thick drapes. It thought.

Chapter 21.

Neighbors hearing a small child screaming hysterically in the street called police, and a black and white unit came cruising down the street within three minutes.

Officers found a small boy lying on a grassy sidewalk shoulder, sobbing and incoherent. As officers approached, the child tried to run away in panic. With the assistance of another marked unit, offers were able to apprehend the child several houses down, where he was hiding among bushes.

The child was taken to UCSD Medical Center, where he underwent an emergency examination to determine his general health, possible rape or molestation, trauma of any kind, exposure to HIV, and possible involvement in crimes by adults including parents, relatives, neighbors, or other parties. The child was determined to be in reasonably good health with no signs of abuse, drug or alcohol involvement, HIV, or other compromising factors. The child was taken to Children's Hospital for psychiatric evaluation, which took the rest of the day, and resulted in an ambiguous finding. The child was found to respond normally to standard tests, indicating an absence of standard psychiatric markers for physiological or psychological compromise. However, the child was found to be frightened and hysterical, claiming his parents had been abducted or eaten by large imaginary shapes.

The child's name was determined to be James Mendez, Jr., only child of [BLANK] and [BLANK], residing at [BLANK]. Father is a licensed merchant seaman while mother is a licensed practical nurse. A social worker from Child Protective Services evaluating the case visited the home, accompanied by uniformed police officer, and found it to be in good order. A woman identifying herself as the mother of Jimmy Mendez answered the door and took the social worker inside for an inspection of the house. Seeing no cause for further worry, the social worker dismissed the police officer and proceeded to do a detailed workup, talking with the kid's mom in the living room.

When asked where the father is, the mother replied that he is away at sea. When asked why the child claimed his father had been present, the mother said she did not know. The mother said the father was due home any time from a cruise on board a cargo freighter, and she did not know the name of the ship or any other details about it. When asked to show bank statements and pay stubs verifying income and expenditures, the mother produced all the required documents showing incomes considerably above the median for Greater San Diego, and bank statements as well as credit card statements consistent with high incomes and considerable but responsible debt payments—no apparent expenditures for illegal street drugs.

Upon a second examination of the house, social worker found no evidence of violence in terms of broken and repaired furniture, windows, or other property. Bathrooms and other living areas showed no evidence of drug paraphernalia.

Social worker adds this note: "I did not go further in asking about the child's claims about hallucinatory visions. I did, while in the parents bedroom, detect a faint foreign odor that could be described as musty, but the premises were clean and showed evidence of a considerable cleaning as one would expect. The mother mentioned she had the day off, and thus might reasonably be expected to do household chores like cleaning. I did notice that there was a faint, elongated mark on the baseboard near the bed, exactly where the child had said there was a growth of unknown type. I asked the mother about the stain, and she said she had spilled a cup of coffee while getting out of bed, and had used a Teflon scouring pad and dish soap to clean it up. Such a stain could be consistent with a small child's frightened vision of something ordinary made to look like a monster." Social worker concludes: "I asked the mother if she was concerned where her son had been all day, and she said that he was out riding his bicycle and playing with neighbor children. She said he had been in and out all day. When confronted about this lie, she displayed some emotion, including tears, and stated that she was having marital difficulties and was having a hard time focusing on her child care duties, but that she had learned a lesson and would take good care of her son from now on." Recommendation: "Return child to [MOTHER ONLY] immediately."

Chapter 22.

"Bingo," Louise said, poking her head into Linsey's office. "The police had some DNA on file for our missing guard. They've had a courier run it to UCSD Medical Center for lab processing."

"Great!" Linsey had been working at her computer and listening to music. She set her earphones before her as she rose. "Hey, Louise, I may have another little lead."

"You're just cooking today!"

"Remember that the Coast Guard report mentioned there was a pilot who went on board?"

Louise snapped her fingers again. "Yes."

"I called SDPD and nobody has interviewed him yet."

Louise frowned. "Now why would that be?"

"Because he hasn't answered his phone."

Louise said: "If you're going looking for him, take someone from SDPD along—if he lives in San Diego. Got to avoid any inter-agency wrangling."

"Actually," Linsey said, "he lives in Coronado, so I'm not worried about jurisdictions. They are pretty good over there."

"Be careful."

"I will." She strapped on her weapon. "News from our mushroom man, Dr. Nolan?"

Louise shook her head. "Mycologist. I'm going to let you handle the yakkety yak with him. I just keep checking my email to see if he's hollering about lab results yet."

"Okay, Louise. I'm going to meet my husband for lunch and then I'll swing over to North Island to look for our elusive harbor pilot. That definitely sounds like my jurisdiction."

"It does indeed. Well, I'm sure you can talk your way out of just about any sticky situation."

Linsey noticed something odd as she drove out of the parking garage in her private car, a dark green Lexus with cream colored leather interior. Either the entire world had become dotted with tiny yellow dots, or maybe some tree or bush was flowering madly, or else her eyesight must be failing—was she seeing little dots everywhere?

As she drove up Broadway, she was held up at a stop light by Horton Plaza, the fancifully architectured shopping mall that dominated the center of town. Looking down, she saw a tiny yellow mushroom growing from a crack in the street. Any moment, a car would run over it, but it had sprouted on the dashed white line separating lanes.

She saw more and more of them—tiny, frail dots no bigger than a dot at the end of a sentence, atop hair-thin wavy stems.

She took scenic California 163 with its rows of palm trees south to I-5, and then cut across California 75 atop the soaring Coronado Bay Bridge. Descending as if from a helicopter ride, she breezed into the City of Coronado. Along with Naval Air Station North Island, this was an elongated thumb of land that stuck up north-south from Imperial Beach and San Ysidro by the Mexican border, and enclosed one of the best natural harbors on the West Coast. A century or more ago, before the Silver Strand road had been built up, North Island had actually been an island. If one considered the naval air station as the tip of a thumb, then the fingers meeting that thumb ended at Cabrillo Point, which stuck out into the sea and formed the northern boundary of the harbor. A narrow but deep channel a few hundred feet across allowed sea traffic in and out. That included nuclear submarines berthed at Point Loma along with other Government ships, and the touristy Harbor Drive area where the Star of India sailing ship, and the retired aircraft carrier U.S.S. Midway were docked, among numerous seafaring attractions that included a decommissioned Soviet B-39 Class diesel attack submarine.

She met Jack in the Babcock & Story Bar at the Hotel del Coronado—the Del, as San Diegans generally called it. Parking by the seawall, she walked two blocks along the sandy sidewalk. To her right, she heard the surf booming as a Pacific storm sent rows of good surfing swells. It was windy here, and she was glad to have a jacket on because there was a slight, coldly humid bite in the air. Still, it was bright enough to warrant sunglasses. She called Jack on her cell phone. "Hi, honey, where are you?" There were at least six major restaurants and bars in the complex.

"The main bar topside. Come up through the beach side and I'll wave to you."

"Done deal. Order me a margarita."

The Hotel Del was a famous 1888 Victorian ramble of white wooden buildings distinguished by its brick-red roofs. In particular, it had a large round structure on the seaward side with a huge red cone-shaped roof, and other, smaller cone shapes. The big cone sported a U.S. flag. Linsey entered the stately, dark-wood lobby with its high-beamed ceilings. *Very posh.* She descended to the shopping arcade on the beach level and followed the curving corridor among pricy shops with indoor display windows, and out onto the rear terraces overlooking the blue Pacific. There, Jack waved to her. He had been working steadily at his laptop while sipping a Bacardi and cola. They kissed as she slipped into a comfortable wooden chair with leather padding beside him. "What are you working on?"

"City Hall. The usual."

"Have you noticed these little yellow mushrooms growing everywhere?"

"Yeah, what's that all about?" Jack was a muscular, balding, powerhouse kind of man. Though mild-mannered, he liked to excel at most things, from work to jogging and boating. He tolerated her addiction to Saturday morning softball league, and she enjoyed sailing with him on Sundays—they had a 24 foot single mast boat, but sometimes he could borrow a larger boat from some of his many golfing buddies, some of them multi-millionaires. Jack's hair was still dark, but it had receded from a high, narrow forehead. It was still thick over the ears. He had a rugged face with beard shadow, a small hawk nose, and a little rosy mouth she loved. He was nearsighted, and wore glasses with heavy dark horn rims. When he wasn't tense and working, he grinned a lot and said silly things. He wore a white linen shirt today, with the sleeves rolled up to reveal hairy arms. He had square, pink fingertips, and hunted and pecked at the keyboard. "I am a hunter-pecker," he once told a paleontologist he was interviewing for a story on local hunter-gatherers of eons past.

"I'm working on a mushroom case," she said as her margarita arrived, ferried by a busy waitress amid the noon rush. She told him a little bit about the case of the missing guard and the human DNA found in a six foot long mushroom under the dock. Their hamburgers arrived, cradled amid lettuce leaves, pickles, and tomato slices, with hot broasted potato wedges reddened with paprika. They shared a side of cole slaw.

Jack frowned. "You said mushroom?" He nibbled at a potato. She told him a little more, about the abandoned ship. He waved his potato wedge. "There was some kind of flap the other day about a plane spraying some yellow stuff over Mission Valley. The HazMat people analyzed it and said it seemed to be fungus spores or something."

She gripped his arm. "Jack. I remember hearing it on the news, and it sort of went away. What if these little mushrooms are from that spraying?"

He shrugged. "Why would someone spray mushrooms?"

"I'm on the Terrorism Task Force, remember?" She whipped out her cell phone and pressed the predial for Louise.

"This is Louise," the familiar voice said.

Linsey poured out her story to Louise.

"Whoa, honey, we've rushed into one situation already. Now you think terrorists are spraying mushroom spores?"

"Has anyone analyzed those little yellow critters yet?"

"I don't know, child, but I can sure find out. I'll make a few calls and get back to you. Thanks for the heads-up."

Linsey picked up her burger in both hands, so that Russian dressing dribbled out on the lettuce. "I got burned once already, yelling fire before the match was struck. She's going to check it out for me. I'm meeting the harbor pilot this afternoon."

He grappled with his burger. "Want me to go with you?'"

She brightened. "Could you?"

"Absolutely. I'm just waiting for a call back from the Mayor's office about the city pension plan problems. I feel better when I see old Cleve by your side."

"Give me some credit. I have a black belt in martial arts, and I can shoot off Washington's wig on a dollar bill at 25 yards."

"You are mighty indeed. Still, if you run into some goon, I'd rather think of Cleve behaving like a Sherman tank." He suddenly remembered. "Oh, on a sadder note, I spoke with Maggie Matthews the other day. Dylan's been hitting the sauce again."

"Oh no, I'm so sorry to hear that."

"Yeah, she sounded pretty grievous." He paused eating until his moment of sadness went away and the marinated tomatoes could taste great again.

"Why were you talking with Maggie?" She dabbed at Russian dressing around her lips.

"Oh, er, what was it? Someone called. Jovia said someone called about the spraying thing, and then Dylan called but didn't say why. Probably looped and looking for someone to tell one of his war stories to." He made a mental note to try those phone numbers again once he got back to his office.

Chapter 23.

Hugh Milton completed a full day's work with Max and Fritz. Hugh felt a little fatigued at times, but he dutifully stayed away from the cooler of beer. He had a slight lunch of cottage cheese and toast, followed by an apple and a banana. They had maybe another day to go before the roof was done and the big payoff came along. Annie would be very happy, Hugh thought as he drove home in his pickup.

They had a light supper, and he made love to her after dark to candle light and soft rock music. They were both passionate and went a long way. They fell asleep in each other's arms.

After midnight, Hugh woke up and realized immediately that something was terribly wrong. He looked at his hands and arms, which seemed yellow. Staggering to the bathroom, he looked into a flushed face with huge bags around haunted eyes. What could this possibly be? He didn't want to alarm Annie, so he wrapped himself in a blanket, took a quart of fresh spring water, and sat alone outside on the balcony. He was shivering and uneasy, almost to the point of panicking. Did he have a fever? Was this some weird flu?

Dozing on and off, he felt as if the world were spinning. His body felt as though it were undulating, and it was beginning to hurt. His joints hurt—classic flu, he thought—and his bones seemed sore. His back in particular was sore, and it hurt no matter which way he squirmed. He found a bottle of aspirin in the medicine cabinet, and took a handful. All the while, he remembered feeling sick the other night, and then miraculously better the next day. Maybe, with luck, he'd wake up from this nightmare and feel fine in the morning.

It didn't turn out that way. At dawn, Hugh was writhing in agony. Both sides of his middle back felt as if they were on fire. His thinking was clouded, and his body felt as if it were reacting to some poison. It was a weird, painful, scary complex of feelings he had never had before. Max and Fritz stopped by, asked Annie if he were coming today, and wished their best condolences when she said he couldn't.

Annie decided to skip her class at State that morning, and called in sick for her hairdressing job. Around noon, she helped Hugh stagger down the stairs to her car, and she took him to the Emergency Room at UCSD Medical Center in Hillcrest. There, he sat in a wheelchair for hours, while all sorts of other patients swirled about. Some were mental patients. Others were prisoners heavily chained, escorted by Sheriff's Deputies from the County Jail. Others were heroin addicts shivering and sweating as they writhed in their chairs waiting for intake. There were alcoholics, druggies, all kinds of sick people, and Hugh did not receive top priority at first. Then a doctor came and looked at Hugh in a closed area. The doctor took his temp and other indicators, seemed to panic, and had Hugh put in quarantine. The medical staff had absolutely no idea what was going on with their patient. Hugh was becoming delirious by now. Distantly he heard Annie's voice—he still recognized her—as she argued and pleaded with important people. An ambulance came and removed Hugh to a place somewhere with lots of clean white bed sheets where he could be observed closely without compromising anyone else if he were infectious.

Hugh overheard, dimly, a conversation: "His organs are starting to fail. We have comprehensive results back from Lab, and they show his kidneys and liver are failing at a rapid rate. An increasing rate, in fact. This man is desperately ill and failing fast. So what's going on? Why is this happening?"

"Mushrooms," said a wise voice. "He must have eaten some mushrooms. He has all the classic symptoms of mycotoxicosis." It was a man, Hugh could detect through the walls of delirium in which he now hovered. It was a man, a doctor man, a man perhaps talking to Annie or to some other doctor. What have we, doctor? A white rabbit, a hookah pipe, a tunnel to another world.

"Renal failure," said another man somewhere nearby in the darkness. "His liver is also sliding into failure, and his heart can't be too far behind."

Hugh loved Annie and was sure she would do well in teaching school. That meant they would have a marble sanctuary together on a green hill in sunshine. It meant that they would be married soon, and that would make her happy. He only hoped he would not forget to attend the wedding. He had an urgent situation going on with this tunnel that was trying to pull him down its long pleasant slope toward a light.

Chapter 24.

After lunch, Linsey and Jack decided to take a brief walk along the beach before looking for the harbor pilot who had guided Lima Voyager into her dock.

Jack had his car parked several streets over, so he locked his laptop in the trunk of Linsey's Lexus. Walking hand in hand, they strolled by the booming breakers. Usually, the sea was much more still. Today, there were hardly any people sitting on towels soaking up the hazy sunlight. The beach today seemed to belong to surfers in full-body wetsuits, and large sea gulls brazenly inspecting passers-by to see if perhaps they had any fish to offer. Bird logic. The fresh air drove away the slight buzz Linsey still felt from the margarita.

"So where does this harbor pilot live?" Jack asked as they returned to her car.

She showed him the man's name, phone number, and address. Lester Sapolsky, First Class Harbor Pilot, lived off Orange Avenue. Linsey read Jack some of the qualifications Sapolsky held a Federal Masters License and a Federal First Class Pilot's License of Unlimited Tonnage issued by the United States Coast Guard.

"Wow," Jack said. "Sounds like a top notch guy in his field."

"Yeah, he's no fly by night."

They pulled onto Coronado's main drag, a mile or so long. Orange Avenue could have been the downtown of any New England village or small town in the USA. Two lanes each way, with a spacious green median divider with trees, it stretched from the southern end of town, where the Silver Strand passed the Hotel Del Coronado, to the northern end overlooking the harbor. The City of Coronado was a municipality situated on the former North Island, now joined to the mainland by the Silver Strand parkway which ran down to Imperial Beach. Coronado was joined at the hip with the U.S. Navy community at North Island Air Station. This was the same air base seen the hoary old 1930s flick Devil Dogs of the Air starring James Cagney. The two massive Quonset-like hangars made of poured concrete, seen in that movie in aged black and white Cagney flybys were still in use, housing modern aircraft. The northwestern part of Coronado was famous for being a retirement community of old admirals and generals of various services, and there was a military golf course on the beach, under the approach lanes for carrier-based aircraft landing at NAS North Island. On the Silver Strand, home base of the Navy SEALs, trainees could be seen working out under grueling conditions in sweat shirts, baseball caps, shorts, and combat boots.

Jack and Linsey located Lester Sapolsky's house on a quiet side street shaded by old willow trees. The houses were generally two-story add-ons, reflecting the upscale nature of the community. What had started as a one-story Victorian gingerbread house might by now be merely the ornamental entrance to a six-unit condo, or to a millionaire's ten bedroom, ten bath mansion with pool, and view of Glorietta Bay. Sapolsky's house was a modest two-story, New England-style salt box. The simple but elegant house sat in a shady lot overgrown by huge Brazilian pepper trees on either side. The house had been added onto around the edges in eclectic styles.

"Try calling him on your phone again," Jack suggested.

Linsey did, as they sat parked in the shade, and got a recording. "This is Les. I can't come to the phone right now..." She snapped the clamshell phone shut. "I guess I'll go knock on the door. Eyeball me, will you?"

"Want me to come along?"

"Nah." She got out, smoothing her jacket. "But thanks." She almost regretted having him come along, and thought of suggesting he drive around the block out of harm's way if there were any harm. "I'll be back in a few minutes." She strode up the concrete walkway that was littered with mauve jacaranda droppings—that time of year. There was also a very fine reddish powder, almost like nutmeg or cinnamon, but earthy smelling. Linsey surreptitiously touched her gun with her fingertips, checking it out, while looking around. From a second story window across a canyon, a toothless elderly woman glanced out at her and then slammed a window shut. Otherwise, nobody was in sight. The concrete walkway was strewn with ankle deep pepper tree detritus—poor maintenance. Was that because the owner traveled a lot, just didn't care, or something else? She came to a recessed doorway set in an archway of stones. A lantern glimmered under the doorway's ogive peak. A pile of yellowed newspapers lay rolled up amid ankle deep leaves. A bench beside the thick oak door looked as if nobody had sat on it in a while. Linsey rang the door bell. Not hearing chimes inside, she rapped on the little leaded window pane in the door. "Hello? Mr. Sapolsky?" *No answer.*

She clambered through bushes, making a circuit around the house. This involved leg-over climbing onto the rear redwood deck with its predictable flotsam and jetsam—enameled plates standing on edge, candle in wrought iron and glass cage, thick table covered in loose pepper tree leaves and twigs, and so forth. She clambered over the far rail after briefly noting a view of hedges with a peep at the bay, and ended up back at the front door. She saw more of the reddish powder dusted very finely and evenly in a fan as if it had emanated from inside the house.

She tried the handle and found that the front door was not locked. Glancing about for neighbors to talk with, and not seeing any, she drew her weapon. Wrapping her hands around the grip and keeping her finger on the trigger, she pushed the door open with her foot. "Police," she said, "is there an emergency?" Without a warrant, she knew she was stepping on thin ice.

There was no answer. She smelled a strong odor like wet, decaying leaves and soil. There was dark red powder everywhere. "Hello?"

Her own voice sounded thin and lost itself in the dark shadows that seemed to permeate the house. All the curtains inside were drawn. A chair lay on its side in the kitchen. She should call for backup, she knew. She should do a lot of things, but there was something far more frightening at stake here.

For the first time in her career, Linsey Simon deliberately violated a number of department policies, and that in another jurisdiction yet. Her own coolness amazed her, but she was viewing herself almost as a stranger. She didn't understand the situation that was enveloping her at every stage in this investigation, and she didn't know exactly what she was doing, so it was like watching someone else in action and wondering what they were doing.

"Hello? Anyone here?" She knew better than to bother. She followed the smell as it grew stronger. She followed her nose into a bedroom, where she flicked on the overhead light.

A mass of bed sheets and blankets lay off to one side, as if someone had struggled in bed and then rolled off. She followed the avalanche of twisted sheets and blankets with the sight of her gun, until the gun pointed to a six-foot-long fungus resembling a rotting dark brown board. It was attached to the baseboard along the wall.

A noise.

She whirled this way and that, pointing the gun.

"Honey?" said a man's voice.

Jack. She stayed crouched, desperately trying to figure out the situation. "Jack, is that you?"

Her husband stepped slowly into the room behind her.

She whirled and pointed the gun at him.

He loomed in the doorway with his powerful frame, bull head, and beard shadow. The eyeglasses twinkled in the wan electric light. He held a pump-action shotgun in his hands—hers, from the trunk of her car.

She lowered her automatic. "Jack, are you insane?"

"Are you okay?"

"Crack that shotgun."

He opened the breach and laid it over his forearm so the barrel pointed downward. "You were taking a long time, so I came in to make sure you were okay."

"You scared the living daylights out of me."

"Sorry. You had me pretty worried too."

She holstered her gun. "We're getting out of here."

"Aren't you going to call—?"

She grabbed his shirt and towed him out, down the hallway. She pulled a paper towel off a rack as they went through the kitchen. "Don't touch anything. Did you touch anything in here?"

"No, I just—"

"You were holding my shotgun with both hands?"

"Yes."

"Didn't leave any finger prints then. Good. Get out the door." She used the paper towel to wipe the door handle she had touched earlier, then wadded the towel and stuffed it in her pocket. "Just get in the car and let's book."

They stashed her shotgun in the trunk where it belonged, and got into the front seat as fast as they could without seeming in a hurry. She pulled out from the curb and drove away.

"What was that all about?" he asked.

She told him: "Every instinct in my being was screaming for me to call for the Coronado PD. Every fiber of training said I should call for backup, whatever. But I felt some higher instinct that said it would be the wrong thing to tip Them off."

"Them?"

"Whoever is doing this mushroom thing. There are some seriously whacked out people at work here. I don't know what the game is, but they are out to hurt someone. I don't know whom they want to hurt, but I suspect it's a lot of innocent people. Right now, I feel I walked in on a crime scene, though I can't prove it, and I messed it up just by being there. I erased fingerprints, and failed to notify the local PD, and who knows what else. Like basically, Jack, I just put my career on the line. Or it's a slippery slope. If I haven't put it on the line, I'm not acting like a good cop now. Yet, I'm following my instinct."

Jack was silent, the way he got when he didn't know what to say, but wanted to be darkly and silently supportive. The glint of worry in his eyes had a sheen of fear. How well she understood. She reached over and gave his knee a reassuring squeeze.

Chapter 25.

After dropping Jack off at his car, and kissing him goodbye, Linsey took the Coronado Bay Bridge back into San Diego. One minute the downtown cityscape lay just across the harbor, less than a mile away, almost capable of being touched while sails glided over still waters. The next minute she was hundreds of feet in the air, looking down on the 32nd Street Naval Station shipyard below on her right, including the dark lozenge that was Lima Voyager, and on her left North Island and downtown, with a hazy Cabrillo Point in the distance. Inland, the Laguna Mountains loomed like dark gray shadows in distant sunshine.

Linsey drove down onto I-5 going north and exited at 6th Avenue, from where she drove down into the center of the city. On Broadway, she entered the parking garage of her agency's building. Within minutes, she was in Louise Trost's office, spilling her guts.

Louise took it all in stride. "Child, I'm not exactly happy to hear you violated some rules, but I'm far more disturbed by this bracket fungus thing. No sign of the harbor pilot?"

"AWOL," Linsey said. "I called his department earlier, and they had not heard from him. Something has happened to him."

"You think the City of Coronado should open a criminal investigation?'"

Linsey bit her lip and couldn't say. "I'm not sure. The only possible sign of struggle was a chair on its side, but that's hardly reason to declare a crime scene. No body, no motive, nothing—there is no case. He hasn't been declared missing." She shook her head. "I backed out of there, knowing it was a dumb idea to go in in the first place. I do highly recommend surveillance."

"For what?"

"Oh come on, Louise, I found another one of those fungus things. What more do you need to hear? Until we know better, we should keep the possibility of a terrorism link open. Whatever is causing this, it's connected to the Lima Voyager somehow, and her whole missing crew."

"Nobody has yet filed missing persons charges on a single missing crew member," Louise said.

"Right." Linsey pondered. "Okay, I want to know more about the ship. Who owns it. Who paid for the last cargo. What was the last cargo?"

"Okay," Louise said, "Good instincts. I'll talk to the police chief in Coronado. Meanwhile, I have something else for you. Look at this." She slid a handful of papers across her desk.

Linsey glanced through what appeared to be County Medical Examiner reports and Fire Department reports. "Let me make sure I get this," Linsey said. "There is now an investigation by the San Diego Fire Department because of the reports a couple of days ago of planes crop dusting in Mission Valley."

"Yes," Louise said. "It's a possible terrorism issue, and I have Feds coming in from Fort Detrick and the National Centers for Disease Control. So far, I've kept it out of the news, but who knows how long before the Fourth Estate picks up on this."

"They had the story and dropped it," Linsey said. "The story of the yellow toxin and the crop dusting planes got on TVbut vanished from public notice."

"The media are hopeless," Louise said. "They are the thin membrane of information that separates us from absolute tyranny, but they've done a lousy job in recent years of conveying the truth to the average person. Sensationalism is what they feed on, and I'm afraid there will be a feeding frenzy once this whole thing breaks open."

"So where are we?"

Louise said: "Three fellows doing some roofing in Serra Mesa the other day got bombed with that yellow rain stuff. One of them got some in his digestive tract, and died a few hours ago. The M.E. report concludes that it's the same strain of fungus that the HazMat people collected the afternoon three planes were seen crop-dusting Mission Valley."

"I think I know what I need to do next," Linsey said. "I need your blessing as Federal umbrella lady, so that I can cross jurisdictions. I want to start tracking down those three planes. Who flew them, where did they take off from, where did they land, and above all—why? Why any of this?"

"Good idea," Louise said. "I'm making you the principal investigator. Next bit of information: We've checked every airport in the region, and not a single one has a record of the three planes in question. They came from nowhere, did their thing, and vanished into thin air."

Linsey scratched her head. "Did you say there were roofers? Maybe I can start by interviewing them."

"That, and track down the information on the Lima Voyager. You're suddenly a very busy woman. Want an assistant?"

"How about my old friend and partner Cleve Bartlett?"

"I'll see if the Harbor Police can free him up." Louise winked. "You could deputize your husband."

"Jack? He'd be after a story the whole time, showing up with an arsenal at the worst moment. I'll keep my love life out of harm's way."

Both women laughed.

Chapter 26.

Jimmy Mendez sat on the edge of his hospital bed, looking out the window. He sat in his cotton pajamas, holding an orange between his knees but too numb to peel it.

Someone walked suddenly into the room. Hearing the door open, and seeing the shadow stabbing over the bed and over the floor, Jimmy let out a yell and dove under the bed.'

"Jimmy?" said a lady in squeaky white shoes and baggy clothing—green scrub pants, flowery top. She was Filipino and had a nice smile. "Jimmy, I won't hurt you. Come out so I can take your temp. I'll give you some ice cream if you help me out."

Jimmy rose. "I thought you were—"

She stood calmly, holding a little box in one hand, and in the other something to stick in him. "I was who?"

"I thought you were—" Jimmy lowered his voice, "—mom."

The nurse stepped forward. "Let me put this in your mouth. It won't hurt." He let her. The thermometer tasted vaguely like strawberries. "It has a fruit pop flavor kids like. So why did you jump under the bed? You thought I was your mom?"

"Not my mom," Jimmy said heatedly as a little beep sounded. She took the thermometer out of his mouth and looked at it. "Not my mom, but the thing that looks like her."

"Temp is normal, Jimmy. Very good. Your mom is not your mom?"

He shook his head.

"Okay, Jimmy, thank you."

He could tell she thought he was crazy. She didn't meet his eyes, but he could see alarm in her eyes. She wasn't mean. She seemed worried for him.

A while later another lady came in. She was also nice. They sat side by side on the bed. She was a tall young black lady with dark red lipstick and glossy, curly hair. She smelled nice, and she had a beautiful smile. "I'm Annette Lewis from the Polinsky Children's Center. Jimmy, tell me what you want most."

"I want my mom. My real mom."

"What if I told you your mom was on the phone with a social worker this morning, and she'd like to see you back home." She reached out to touch him with silver wrist bangles and long brown fingers with rings.

Jimmy pushed her hand away and jumped down to stand on the floor. "I'm not going home until my mom comes here to pick me up. My real mom."

"So you don't want me to take you home?"

"No!" He felt angry and also scared. He felt like crying.

"Okay, nobody is going to make you do anything you don't want to do. I promise."

"The thing I saw at my house was not my mom. My mom loves me. That thing is—empty inside. Hollow. Like a rotten apple." He stammered, looking for words, but the image overwhelmed him: the way a freshly cut apple quickly turns brown; the way you bite into an apple and it makes a hollow sound, because there is a tunnel with brown stuff, and when you look at it, a green caterpillar is looking at you from inside the apple, wiggling its antennas. Gross.

Miss Lewis must have read his mind. She put her hands together pensively and said: "Okay, sweetie, tell you what. I'll call your mom and ask her to come here. Does she drive?"

"My real mom is a nurse. She can do anything."

"Good. Why don't we call her now?" She took out a cell phone. "What's your phone number?"

"I don't want to talk to the other thing."

"Do you remember your phone number?"

Jimmy told her. "You talk to her first, okay?" He held Miss Lewis's brown pants leg with both hands, feeling some sense of protection with her long thigh between him and the phone.

"Hello, Mrs. Mendez?" Miss Lewis paused. Jimmy tried to read the look on her face. She made all sorts of little changes with her large brown eyes and beautiful white around the brown part, but Jimmy couldn't read her thoughts. "This is Annette Lewis from the Polinsky Center. I have Jimmy here with me." Pause. "Yes, he is fine." She glanced at Jimmy while listening. "Yes, of course. Want to talk with him?"

Jimmy felt his heart pounding as she handed him the phone. He shook his head and gestured that she must hold it, so she held it and he gingerly stretched his neck, leaning over her firm, warm, safe thigh. He gripped her pants with his fists as he put his ear against the phone. He said in a tiny quaver: "Mom?"

"Jimmy," said the thing. "Come home now."

Jimmy shoved the phone away, whacked Annette's hand, and ducked under the bed. "That's not my mom. That's the thing that killed my parents!" he yelled. He found an old black plastic knife someone had dropped long ago, and held it up like a stabbing knife to protect himself. He held the knife in both hands over one shoulder, beside his face, and pulled his feet up close so that he was almost in a ball sitting against the wall, as far from Annette as he could get.

"Shall I call you back later?" Annette said while kneeling beside the bed. She made to effort to come under and retrieve Jimmy. "Really?" she asked. "Really?" From under the bed, Jimmy tried to read her eyes. He got a confusing set of messages. Annette alternately rolled her eyes in shock or surprise, then nodded in agreement, and then shook her head in disagreement. "They will have to come to the Polinsky Center then. There is no way I can drop him off at someone else's house. And you'll have to sign over custody to his aunt and uncle. What's that?"

She waggled a finger for Jimmy to come to her. He laid his knife aside and cautiously crawled out from under the bed. He trusted this Annette Lewis with the nice smile and warm eyes. He walked over and put his arms around her while she still knelt on the floor. He laid his head on her shoulder and wept softly. He heard the phone snap shut and disappear with a little zip noise into her pocket. She put her arms around him, lifted him onto the bed, and sat beside him. "Jimmy, your mom—"

"That wasn't my mom."

"The woman on the phone claims to be your mother."

"She's not."

"Let's pretend for a moment. She says she is unable to take you home at the moment, and she has asked your aunt Nellie and Uncle Sim to care for you. Would you like to go with them?"

"I want my mom back." He felt as though his heart were breaking, he missed her so. His dad too, but the mom-pain was so big that the dad-pain was sort of hidden behind it. He sobbed, and Annette soothed him. She held him close and stroked his hair. "You have a cousin Maribel, don't you?"

"Yes." Maribel was pretty nice.

"Your m—the woman I spoke with says that if I drive by, she'll sign the papers. It's a temporary remand of custody to the Walesky family. That means you can live with them. Of course they have to agree to it, but the woman I just spoke with says that they'd love to have you."

"Okay." He thought about times he'd played with Maribel, and it was pretty good. She was a year older, and could be a little mean when she was in a bad mood, but generally it was like having a sister. Since they were both only children, it seemed okay. At least he'd be with family.

"So is that okay with you?" Annette said.

"Yeah, I think so. At least they are family to me, and then I can wait for my mom to come for me when she gets back."

"Do you have any idea where your mom might have gone?" Annette asked with a very confused and troubled look.

Jimmy shook his head. He had no idea. None at all.

Chapter 27.

Not long after, Jimmy sat in Annette Lewis's cool car. It was a dark blue one shaped like a dagger. It had sand-colored leather inside, and a bunch of red, green, and orange lights, real small ones, for the radio and the other stuff in the dashboard. Cool, Jimmy thought. Soon, they were driving down Jimmy's street. He sat gaping behind the passenger window, while reflections of familiar houses and trees and street signs flowed through the prism of the glass, flowing like water over the reflective surfaces. It was his familiar street, where he went bike riding every day, and yet now it was like an alien world. House windows that had once seemed friendly now looked dark and hostile. "Hey," he said, "can I get my bike?"

"Is it at the house?" Annette asked.

He nodded. "Can you get it for me?"

"You don't want to come to the door and say hello to her?"

"No!"

"Okay, we won't go there, sweetie. You're doing fine. Just relax and I'll do the talking."

Annette pulled over at the curb. Jimmy ducked down low and looked over the edge of the door at eye level. The house looked black inside, as if nobody was there. It looked as if the inside was 1000 feet deep down in the ocean, where it was pitch black and cold. Annette got a pen and clipboard from the back seat. "I like to be ready," she said in her warm, musical voice. "Just grab, sign, and go. You learn to not spend time in front of people's doors. Hang in there, Jimmy, I'll be right back."

He said: "Don't let her ask to see me."

Annette gave him a shocked look and froze for a second. "I won't, Jimmy. You really feel that strong about it, huh?"

He didn't answer, and she got out. He watched her go up the driveway. She was a tall lady. Her hips rocked from side to side as she walked. He locked all the doors. He put his arm on the window ledge, rested his chin on his forearm, and watched.

Annette knocked on the door. She waited. She did a little dance to the left, looking in a draped window, and a little dance to the right, looking in there. Then she rapped with her fist. Jimmy could see the little black window panes dancing. To his amazement, the door opened. A slit of blackness appeared, as if hell had opened a crack. He couldn't see the thing that looked like his mom, but Annette was talking to someone. It didn't take long. Annette held up the clipboard. A hand appeared—lefty, like mom—and signed. Annette nodded and said thanks as the door slipped shut. Annette came down the walkway looking troubled.

Jimmy unlocked the driver's side door. Annette got in, and he expected she'd chew his butt for locking the door. Instead, she seemed to have difficulty speaking. "She didn't ask to see you," she said. "She didn't ask how you are." It was all she said, as she turned on the car and drove away.

Jimmy looked back at the silent house, shivered, and buckled up his seat belt. "Did you smell anything funny?"

Annette rumpled her nose. "Yeah. I did. It smelled kind of like earth or something. Loam. Soil."

"Mushrooms," Jimmy said, folding his arms together. He nodded. That's what they are, he thought. Mushroom people.

"So you like the Waleskys," Annette said by way of opening a conversation.

"Oh yes," Jimmy said, thinking of times he'd stayed over. "Aunt Nellie makes great French toast. Uncle Sim tells stories. Maribel is a girl but she has lots of gun toys and the best computer games. Hey, we forgot my bike!"

"Oh dear, we did, didn't we? Shall we go back?"

He shook his head. "No." He felt glum. "Maybe Aunt Nellie will drive over later and get it for me."

"How old is Maribel?"

"She's in fourth grade."

"And what does Aunt Nellie do? A nurse like your mom?"

"No, she is a housewife. She does sewing for people."

"And Uncle Sim?"

"He's a merchant marine sailor, like my dad."

"I see. Do they ever go sailing together?"

"Yeah, like now. They were at sea together." Jimmy held his head with his hands and frowned. He felt like he had a headache.

"What's the matter, Jimmy?"

"I can't figure it out. I think they were both supposed to be out on the same ship, but some guy came back looking just like my dad. He disappears, and my mom turns into a mushroom or something. So if they went on the same ship together, and this guy who looks like dad came back, then will Uncle Sim be a regular guy?"

Chapter 28.

Later that morning, was-Maria Mendez walked across the lawn. It looked like an attractive young dark-haired woman in a slightly disarrayed red blouse and a skirt that came to just above the knees. It had shapely calves and flat black leather shoes. It knocked on the neighbors' door and waited.

The Muellers opened. He was a thin, white-haired man of about 70 with age spots and a tremble in his hands. She was a roundish, white-haired woman with watery blue eyes and age spots on her hands that held a wool shawl around her shoulders.

"Hello," said was-Maria. "I am Maria from next door. I am looking for Jimmy."

"Who?" he asked harshly—he seemed hard of hearing.

"My little boy. He is nine years old. Have you seen him?"

"No," Mrs. Mueller said. "The little boy with the bike?"

"Yes," was-Maria said. "Can I come in? I need your phone."

The old couple looked at each other in surprise. Mueller said: "If you need help finding your boy, of course."

Mrs. Mueller added graciously. " Is it a local call?"

"It is local," was-Maria said. It followed them into the house and closed the door.

Chapter 29.

The Muellers brought was-Maria into their home. "We're old and slow," he said jovially, "but we still get the job done." He spoke in an old man's high-pitched, wheezing voice.

"You have to put up with our slow pace," Mrs. Mueller said in an old woman's tremulous voice. They shake like autumn leaves, these two old humans, was-Maria thought. It was not a sentimental thought but a tactical assessment.

While the Muellers fussed over her in the parlor, was-Maria picked up the telephone and dialed. Soon, was-Richard answered. Richard Bloomstrom had been a sailor aboard *Lima Voyager*. The voice at the other end was not quite his. "Yes?"

"This is was-Mendez. Are you prepared?"

"Do you have a host?"

"Yes."

"Where is it?"

She told him, and he hung up.

Mueller hovered before it. "My wife has gone to lie down for a while. That's all we do all day, lie down and take naps, then dodder around. Can I offer you a drink of something?"

"I am not thirsty. A friend of mine is coming to pick me up."

"Okay. I hope you find your little boy."

The thing that had been Maria stepped up close to him.

His features changed, grew confused. His eyes widened, seeing the form of her body, and hungering for its shape. His lips grew dry and he licked them. "Is this friend of yours coming soon?" he asked and for the first time there was a hint of alarm or even fear in his voice as he saw the flat, black naked animus of her eyes. "Wait a minute!" he cried in his thin, whistling voice full of old man's chalk and phlegm and bad-smelling breath. His eyes grew wide in alarm.

The being that had been Maria formed its lips into a circle and blew out a cloud of slightly dark air.

Mueller ceased being afraid and relaxed as the natural poisons entered his lungs and started the process of shutting them down. Was-Maria took him by the hand and led him past the bedroom where his wife lay on her side, stirring fitfully in half-sleep. They walked down a hallway and came to a bedroom that seemed to function more as a storage place than anything else. There were pictures of a young man in blue graduation gown. They were old pictures, indicating their child had left home years ago. There was still a bed in the room, and on this was-Maria made Mueller lie down. He was old and slow, and it had to lift his legs for him. He was half-oblivious from the drug it had blown into his lungs, so he moved all the slower. But he ended up on his back the way it wanted him to be, and it crawled up onto the bed and lay with one arm and one leg over him. It found the spot in his neck where it was best to bite, and then it snaked a tube into him. It lowered its face so that its forehead rested against his cheek, and its mouth was round with the slimy black hose that came out and entered his neck. This was a process its kind had learned from spiders in the jungle—numbing the victim by subtle but powerful poisons, so the extraction of DNA and the exchange of cellular instructions went painlessly.

Bess Mueller was in pain with her arthritis and other ailments, but she still had a sharp mind. As she lay on her side on the bed, trying to nap, she saw that woman lead her husband by the bedroom, and instantly her feminine wiles snapped into focus. Something was terribly wrong here.

Slowly she fumbled for the walker by the bedside. When she grew agitated, it was harder for her to walk properly and she needed this dreadful gadget to get around. Still, it was better than being bed-bound. She swung slowly erect, and eased behind the walker. Step for step, like a snail, she made her way from the bedroom into the hall way. She wished these damn things weren't so long. What did elderly people need with long hallways? She went down to Chris' old bedroom—he was a successful 30-something real estate developer in Chicago these days, and didn't keep half as much in touch as he should. Bess got down the hall, took one look into Chris' room, and saw all she needed to see. It was all she could do to keep from shrieking.

That woman had her husband in bed with her. All she saw was that woman's sweet young behind, and her bare legs, wrapped around her husband's old stiff gams. The old fool looked like he was her prisoner, the way she was wrapped around him and her head was bent down over his neck.

Bess turned slowly and inched down the hall with her walker. She reached the living room and started for the phone. Now she grew confused. Had she called the police already?

Someone was knocking at the door. Was the phone ringing? She listened carefully, but it seemed not to be making any noise. Someone was ringing the doorbell and banging on the door. Bess turned in that direction and made her way toward the door. "Hang on, officer, I'm coming!"

She opened the door, and there stood a stranger in a combination of jeans and leather. He had a head of curly hair and black eyes. "Yes?" she said.

"I am Richard Bloomstrom."

"Who?" she cried out in a high, quavering voice full of fear and suspicion. She felt the onset of panic.

Mr. Bloomstrom formed his mouth into an 'o' shape and blew something at her. *Air. A stream of dark air.* She felt herself relax. Now this wasn't bad at all, was it?

The being who had been Richard Bloomstrom got the old woman on the couch and had his extractor tube in her neck before she had any idea what had happened. Soon, was-Richard lifted her and put her against the baseboard. Then it pressed against her, pinning her against the wall low down, and started the extraction process. In the exchange, was-Richard would become was-woman—but not the old feeble crone. The new Gestalt would be of a fresh, vibrant young spore containing the aggregate DNA of all the persons was-Richard had already killed. The old woman's body would morph into a bracket fungus, still containing much of her remains. It would in a few weeks begin generating billions of new bracket spores.

In the bedroom, was-Maria was changing into was-Mueller. As it extracted Mueller's DNA, the genetic instructions flowing across from him to it changed the being's cellular makeup, and it began resembling Mueller. At the same time, Mueller began resembling a Peruvian bracket fungus as was-Mueller began to be set up as a spore generator for a whole new generation of Offensor fungi. The war of the mushroom people against the humans was off to an auspicious start.

Chapter 30.

When Jimmy Mendez, 9, got out of Annette Lewis' car, and saw his cousin Maribel Walesky, 10, waving to him from the porch of the Waleskys' house in Linda Vista, Jimmy did something he had never done before. He ran up to the house, seeing Maribel waving and dancing with happiness to see him. He ran up the stairs onto the wooden porch, and embraced her. It wasn't a rough embrace, but a tender, needy one. Maribel seemed astonished at first, then a little embarrassed. Maribel looked at the strange black woman in the fine business suit walking up to the house. The woman nodded. Maribel knew then it was okay, even necessary, to hug her cousin. Maribel comforted him for a minute or two, tousling his hair and rocking him back and forth while he clung to her, eyes closed, cheek on her shoulder. The woman climbed the stairs. "Hi, I'm Annette Lewis."

Maribel extended a hand. "I'm Maribel." She was a tall, slender girl with long dark hair and big dark eyes. She had a pink mouth and lean face still soft with the last echoes of baby fat.

"Is your momma home, Maribel?"

"Yes." Maribel put her arm around Jimmy's back and guided him toward the door. "Come on, Jimmy, let's get you some chocolate milk or something."

Jimmy felt drained and let her guide him. She'd grown a few inches and towered above him since last time he'd seen her, when they were the same height. The feel of her warm skin, and the smell of her, were familiar and good. The Waleskys' house smelled as it always did, a cross between Polish sausage and Mexican frijoles and a half dozen ethnic dishes.

Aunt Nellie came out of her kitchen, wearing an apron over good clothes. "Jimmy! For Heaven's sake, child, what is going on with your family? Come on in, Miss—"

"Annette Lewis," Jimmy heard the nice lady say. "I have temporary power of attorney papers here for Jimmy's custodianship. Are you Mrs. Walesky, his aunt?"

"I sure am," Aunt Nellie said with that way people have of talking when they are missing a few teeth. Sure becomes Fure, sort of. Aunt Nellie had a heart of gold and could be relied on for a safe, secure place to be—a second home with mom's older sister, the next best thing to mom herself.

"I have a few questions for you," Jimmy heard Annette say.

"Sure," Aunt Nellie said. Fure.

Jimmy, realizing he had not slept well in days, walked or crawled toward the living room couch. He remembered times when he was being babysat, and was not feeling well, and Aunt Nellie had made a nest for him with blankets on this couch, and he'd recovered there from the flu while watching cartoons and eating dry, sweet cereal. Now he sought that same refuge.

He heard Maribel say: "Jimmy, what's the matter with you? Want a blanket?"

He nodded, and curled up in a ball on the couch which smelled of dust and stale chips and Uncle Ernie's farts and all kinds of other reminders of several thousand evenings of family TV watching. He felt Maribel's soft hands tossing a blanket over him, and sighed as the blanket descended in a sheltering cover over his trembling body. He felt the warmth of Maribel's bony but soft body as she sat beside him and stroked his hair. They had fought some angry battles in the past, a lot of it due to his temper, but he resolved never to be mean to her again, and to be understanding when she was being selfish or snooty.

As he drifted off into feverish sleep, he heard Annette say: "So tell me a little bit about your husband, Mrs. Walesky."

"Fure. Well, he's a good man, basically, when he ain't drinking. He's a sailor, you know, and he has a way, when he gets into port and gets paid, of stopping here and there and eventually arriving here in a taxi half-broke and half-beat up. He still brings home a good wage, and he's a good man when he's sober, so I ain't kickin'."

"Where is Mr. Walesky now?"

"Darned if I know. He was due in on the same ship as Jimmy's dad. I've tried calling Jimmy's folks a bunch of times, and can't get through to my sister."

"Mrs. Walesky, the boy has been suffering from some traumatic nightmares. He believes his mom and dad have been somehow—I can't quite explain because it's a child's nightmare and it's not quite coherent—somehow been eaten by giant mushrooms or something."

"Oh, is that so? Ain't that weird," Jimmy heard Aunt Nellie say. He could understand why nobody would believe his story. He had trouble believing it himself, except when he thought about it, he always arrived at the same point: I saw what I saw.

"Children who have these ideations have often been through some severe trauma that makes them substitute a fantasy for something real that is too hard for them to process. I'm going to recommend strongly that Jimmy comes back to Children's Hospital for regular counseling visits so he can get medical and psychological assessments. Understand what I am saying?"

" You think someone's been—doing something to him?"

"I'm not saying anything, Mrs. Walesky. All we know is that Jimmy is having a very hard time, and his mother has turned him over to you because obviously she is unable to cope. Do you know if his parents have been having difficulties?'"

"No, can't honestly say I do. His dad, Jimmy Sr., never drank, unlike my dear old how-do-you-do Ernie. Maria went through college, unlike dumb old me, and works as a nurse. I have never had any idea that anything was wrong, but then you never know, do you?"

"You're right, Mrs. Walesky, and that is the major point. One never knows what is going on in a family until its most vulnerable members say Ouch."

Jimmy heard Aunt Nellie say: "I almost wish it was mushroom monsters. That would be so much simpler, wouldn't it?" She sighed. "Well, I should be used to it. Ernie is a licensed airplane pilot also, you know? Sometimes, he puts the buck ahead of all else. Maybe someone hired him to do a flying job, and he's just forgotten to call me. Ernie would forgot like that. He's a good man though. He'll come home with a wad of dough. Seven sheets to the wind, but he always takes care of his family. We just got to wait and see."

Chapter 31.

The beings who had been the Muellers waited patiently in the house. In addition, the two bracket fungi were growing nicely, one in the living room behind the couch, the other in the bedroom out of sight from the door.

Then opportunity struck in the form of two bright-eyed, earnest young men who knocked at the door. The two beings in the shadowy living room looked at each other. When the knock came again, was-woman opened the door.

There stood two young men in their early 20s, holding religious scripture books, and dressed in dark suits. "Hello, we're here to tell you the great news about our religion," one of them said, in words to that effect.

"We have a great religion that will change your life and make you happy. Can we come in to tell you more?" the other said, in words to that effect.

"Why sure," said was-woman. "Come in." It stepped aside to let them in.

"Have a seat on the couch while I make you some lemonade," was-man said from the parlor.

"Thank you," the two young men said in unison. They rushed to sit on the couch and open their books to certain pages so they could start reading verses to their hoped-for converts.

"Did you know that—" one of the young men began, and told about the amazing powers and remarkable kindness of his deity if one believed all sorts of arbitrary things made up long ago. If you didn't believe these things exactly so, their deity would do horrible things to you in quite inventive ways.

The other man told them from personal experience how uplifting it was to worship this deity, and how deleterious not to."

"Is that so?" commented was-woman, pushing a hassock close to the first young man's feet as she knelt innocuously on the living room carpet.

Was-man came from the kitchen holding two glasses of cold water in which floated lemon slices and ice cubes. Sugar granules danced around and around in the liquid where it had stirred and it was still circling. "Is that so?" was-man said to the second young man. It made an 'o' of his lips and blew a little cone of dark air into the young man's face.

Taking its cue, the former woman said to the first young man: "We are anxious to hear more." It blew dark air in his face.

The two young men relaxed completely.

The two was-people crawled onto their victims and did the arm and leg wraps and then the neck bite. As the glistening, wet black tube slid from the beings' mouths into the humans' neck, the beings lifted their victims and carried them into a spare bedroom with space available along the baseboards. This house would become a good breeding ground for the bracket fungi that would launch countless tiny spores into the atmosphere. Those spores, in turn, would be sacrificed in their trillions so that, for each human they killed, a single mature carrier spore of the Offensor species would walk the streets of human cities to kill more humans and create more bracket fungi.

Chapter 32.

With a lot of hot soup from Aunt Nellie, Jimmy Mendez began to regain his strength. He felt a sad sometimes, when it occurred to him maybe suddenly in the middle of running or playing that he had not seen his mom and dad for a while. Maribel always cheered him on and got the other kids to help him forget for the moment, and Jimmy was a pretty strong kid.

Still, if he smelled certain smells or thought of that woman who had taken his mother's place—those flat, black eyes—he felt paralyzed. At moments like that he couldn't move. He'd feel waves of sheer terror rolling up and down his back.

Aunt Nelli was very smart. She went over to the house and got his bicycle for him. She had to explain to a couple of undercover cops sitting in a car on the street that she was Jimmy's aunt. There was no yellow police tape on the house, and they reluctantly let her go because she happened to have the papers from Annette Lewis in her car, and she had a spare key to get into the Mendez house. Like a panzer tank of wrath, Aunt Nellie came out of that house loaded with bike and ball and bat and a few other important kid things, and had an expression that dared anyone to stop her. Nobody did.

The strategy, and Aunt Nellie told Jimmy this, was to get him totally tired out during the day so that he could sleep at night without waking up screaming several times. Even so, Jimmy sometimes had nightmares, and woke up next morning curled up either in Maribel's bed or Aunt Nellie's.

Aunt Nellie came into the kitchen beaming as Jimmy and Maribel sat having hot chocolate and French toast. "He called!"

"Who called?" Jimmy said.

Aunt Nellie put her arm around Maribel, who perked up. "Your daddy called. He's in town, coming home today or tomorrow. Seemed tired or something, but sober, and pleasant."

"Great," Maribel said without total conviction. She glanced at Jimmy, who looked as if he were choking on his French toast (an impossibility, so it must be terror). Jimmy's eyes were bulging as he turned shades of pink and red.

"What's the matter?" Aunt Nellie asked.

"Nothing," Jimmy said, grabbing his remaining French toast in a muddy hand and running out of the room.

"What's the matter with him?" Aunt Nellie asked. She wiped her hands in her apron and looked happy about the phone call.

"I know what he is thinking," Maribel said.

"What?"

Maribel had a way of not answering. She sipped her hot chocolate deliberately and did not meet her mother's gaze. Inwardly, she trembled and hoped Jimmy was wrong. Jimmy had told her about his dad, and then his mom, after his dad had come home from the sea.

"What?" her mom asked in a harsher tone.

Maribel didn't answer or look at her mom, but reached out with one hand and took her mother's hand, and squeezed. Her mother stood with her mouth open.

Chapter 33.

A serious discussion occurred over coffee and cereal at the Simon household the next morning. Linsey and Jack sat on the patio overlooking Point Loma rooftops and the broad, gunmetal blue Pacific with its rolling breakers and glinting sunshine seen through a heavy marine layer. It was her turn to cook breakfast, and she made a classic American breakfast of eggs, sunny side up, on toast, with bacon and sausage. Instead of ketchup, they put slices of tomato over everything, British style. It was a habit Jack had picked up during his years as a U.S. Navy liaison officer in London, and later as a traveling journalist in various countries.

"Jack, I know you smell a story here," Linsey said as she poured them each a hot, fragrant cup of coffee.

"I smell coffee," he said with a coy expression, rolling his eyes. "Smells good."

She sat down. He was teasing her and being extra thick, and she wasn't biting. "I am not going to let you annoy me. You know what? If you become impossible, I'll have you arrested."

"Oh really. I've heard that before."

They started eating.

"Jack, this is a very serious case. I'll tell you that much. If you behave yourself, I'll give you an exclusive."

"Okay, start giving me an exclusive. Is the Federal government involved?"

"Yes, dodo. I'm working on a task force that includes the FBI. If you leak even a word of this, I'll never speak with you again. We'll make love in private. From separate rooms."

He laughed. "Okay, okay, I'm underwhelmed. What do you want me to do?" He raised his cup to sip.

"I want you to keep quiet about this investigation until we get a break. Then I'll make sure you have a scoop."

"I'll tell you what," he said, setting the cup down with a definitive clink. "I'll follow my nose, and I'll decide when and how to release what I find. But I promise you that I won't jump the gun with anything I learn from you."

"I have to watch you every minute, don't I?"

He laughed. "Oh, come on, Linsey. I'm not going to forget that you're my wife and the love of my life. I'm just not going to forget that I also have a job to do."

She glowered at him.

"Linsey, in the end you'll thank me."

"If I don't spank you first."

Jack was hoping to have lunch with colleagues at a Chinese restaurant in Mission Valley, but a story intervened. By the time he wrapped it up, it was two in the afternoon. Jovia came and brought him a half a sandwich and a cold perspiring can of cola, for which he profusely thanked her. She said: "That Chinese food was great. Have you ever eaten there?"

He said absently "Long ago" while unwrapping the plastic wrap to discover a tuna salad on rye with pickle and pepper. "Oh God, this looks good."

Jovia hovered in the doorway. "Did you ever get hold of Maggie Matthews?"

"Oh yeah. Dylan's still hitting the sauce. She sounds sad."

"That is really sad. What about that other guy?"

"Oh, what's his name." Mouth full, Jack dug around among the papers on his desk until he found her tattered note from days ago. "Oh yes, Robertson. Here it is."

Jovia said something pleasant and wandered away, while Jack devoured his sandwich and dialed the phone number. A man answered. "Yes?"

"Mr. Robertson?"

"Yes."

"This is Jack Simon at the San Diego Times. You called here a few days ago about those planes spraying Mission Valley."

"Oh yes. I have some information that may help."

"Are you involved in the spraying, Mr. Robertson?"

"No."

"I'm a newspaper reporter. Why me? Why not the police?"

"Because there are broader issues involved and I don't want to end up in extremely bad shape."

"What do you mean?"

"Dead."

"Oh come on." Jack nearly hung up.

"Please, Mr. Simon. You are an investigative reporter. You are well known in the region and quite famous for your exposés."

"I'll give you thirty seconds."

"Does the name Collwood mean anything to you?"

"Collwood, Collwood." Jack tapped his foot impatiently. Then he stopped. "You mean the guy who owns Anaconda."

"That's him. My father and I met him a few years ago. My father has passed away since, but Mr. Collwood has some information about Peruvian fungi that we both felt was going to the wrong hands. My father was desperate and had to trust him."

"Are you bullshitting me, Mr. Robertson?"

"What could I possibly gain if this weren't true?'

"Okay, you have my interest. Can we meet?"

"Yes. Want me to come to your office?"

They made a date, for tomorrow afternoon, to have James Robertson Jr. drive from the East County into the City of San Diego and meet Jack at the newspaper's Mission Valley offices. Jack was reluctant about it, because he'd had such meetings that usually fizzled when it turned out he was dealing with some opportunist wanting to capitalize on an ongoing disaster of some kind. Nevertheless, it paid to leave no stone unturned, particularly when the guy was willing to come to him.

Chapter 34.

Professor Shaun Nolan, Ph.D., mycologist at UCSD Medical Center, was on his way to meet with Louise Trost downtown. She had invited him to join her for a light lunch at the ornate Victorian fountain at Horton Plaza.

He was beginning to notice a large species of what looked like a fine, light green Dictydium sporangia. More likely, he felt it was a new type of mycena. He was at a red light, and got out of the car to harvest a handful of these fungi by hand. The light turned green, and people behind him started honking, but he ignored them as he got back into the car. He sniffed his catch, but did not find the characteristic iodine smell of many mycena. The sporangium was a form of slime mold, and these were too large to be of that species. Cars roared around him. Angry shouts floated in the air. When he looked up, the light was red again.

Dr. Sean Nolan, 48, was a senior scientist at the University of California, San Diego. A jogger and basically a youthful, happy man, Sean felt privileged to work in a series of small wooden structures on a 200-foot-high sandy bluff with a spectacular view overlooking the Pacific Ocean. Sean was a botanist, on the faculty of the Biology Department. His specialty was mycology, the study of fungi.

Sean, who had a solid, dry sense of humor, liked to call himself an ambassador to the Fifth Kingdom. Over the past century, scientists had classified life on earth into kingdoms at the highest level. They'd started with three such kingdoms in the 1890s —Protista, Plants, and Animals—and, as their understanding grew more sophisticated, five and later six kingdoms (subdividing the 'all else' Protista into four subdivisions including Fungi). More recently, many scientists preferred a more simplified scheme of three domains (Bacteria, Archaea, and Eucaryotes or 'those with cells'). Somehow, Sean preferred the simple romance of the Fifth Kingdom. After all, the fungi were a powerful and creative bunch of life forms, with over 60,000 variations of stunning diversity.

Pete's wife Eileen, 42,a vivacious dark-haired woman, shared his enthusiasm for the daily ten mile jogs that they referred to as 'cleansing' or 'flushing the pipes.' She had been a champion bicycle racer a U.C. Santa Barbara, where she earned her M.D. degree, as well as a softball enthusiast. Rosario was in Family Practice with the old Hillcrest-based hospital of the U.C. San Diego Medical Center near downtown San Diego. They lived in a 4,000 square foot town home in a gated community in Del Mar (very upscale) but also owned a 1,200 square foot condo in the Gaslamp district in downtown San Diego, where they could spend the night if they'd had a beer too many at a Petco Park baseball game, or took in a late movie downtown during their sparse hours together. They had no children, and it was starting to look unlikely that they ever would. It had always seemed that their busy lives pushed childbearing yet another year or two out into the future.

Arriving downtown, he entered the parking structure behind the wildly colored and imaginatively shaped Horton Plaza mall. Parking in the shady garage, he bought a pretzel and a hot tea on the 5th floor food court, and got his parking ticket validated. Taking the complicated mid-air tangle of stairs and elevators down to ground level, he found Louise. She sat on a bench under the shade of a queen palm in the small rectangular park. Traffic and pedestrians were thick downtown, for it was the noon hour. The courts had let out, and jurors and court officials were rushing to Horton or the Gaslamp for a bite. The air smelled delightfully of mingled cuisines—Japanese, Mandarin, Italian, Greek, Persian, anything one could desire. Shaun found Louise, meanwhile, calmly munching a peanut butter and grape jelly sandwich on plain white bread, and sipping a can of cola. He joined her with his pretzel and tea. They nodded by way of greeting, as if they were old friends, though they had only known each other vaguely from years of floating through the court system on various cases.

"What's that sticking from your pocket?" Louise asked.

"Oh this." He'd almost forgotten. "Not sure." He reached down and pulled a handful out of the gravel at their feet. "It's some sort of fungus, probably not a gilled mushroom but something close. It may actually be a more primitive thing called a sporangium, but I won't know until I get it on slides and under a microscope, plus do various tests."

"Is it poisonous?" Louise asked.

"It's sure to be toxic to some extent. The County M.E. autopsied a roofer who died of classic mushroom poisoning symptoms, and he had some of the genetic structure of this in his blood and lungs."

"He died from inhaling it? Why aren't we all panicking?"

Shaun considered this for a moment. "There are over 300 species of poisonous plants in San Diego County. The oleander, for example, has been used in murders. We're not in an alarm over the common philodendron or the deadly nightshade, both of which, while not native, abound here. I do think if a few more people die from this, we'll have a public health uproar."

"And you're going to wait until that happens," Louise goaded in her soft, grandmotherly voice loaded with poisons of her own.

He felt the back of his neck crawl hot pink. "Louise, I'm sitting here having lunch with you. Ease off, you stinkhorn."

She chuckled. "Shaun, I'm just rattling your cage. In my own slow, quiet way, that is what I do. It works very well. You will have a report for me by the end of the day, won't you?"

"Yes. I want you to put in an official request through channels just to back me up."

"I can do that." She flicked out her cell phone and spoke with her executive assistant. She put the phone away two or three minutes later. "She'll have it typed up and waiting for my signature after lunch, and it will be on your desk by 3 p.m."

"Great."

"So what is going on, Shaun? Terrorists?"

"Well, I can't rule it out. There are at least nine types of mycotoxins, or fungus poisons, that have been weaponized by various countries, from aflatoxins to zearalenones. There have been historical precedents of fungal warfare. For example, from the late 1970s through the early 1980s, Soviet client militias in Laos and Cambodia may have used what the peasants called Yellow Rain (trichothecene mycotoxins)."

"Is there an antidote, just in case this turns out to be mushroom warfare?"

"None. However, there are counter-measures. For example, soap and water washes it away. If you feel strongly—in other words, if you think it is warranted from a law enforcement perspective—I would start calling people like the U.S. Army's Chemical Corps, which knows about mycotoxins. And the National Centers for Health."

"A little precaution is always warranted. I'm going to make some calls, if you'll give me phone numbers for the best people. I want to keep it quiet for now so we don't start a big panic."

"I suggest we do more," Shaun said. "Let's go through the media and advise people with compromised respiratory systems to stay indoors for a few days if possible. I'm almost certain that the roofer died from an over-ingestion of live spores."

"I can see that, no matter what we do, we're going to get beat up later for not doing more sooner."

"If only we knew what to do."

"I'll tell you what," Louise said, "I'm going to call Washington, and have them contact the Governor of California to get the state and city apparatus rolling. No harm in being prepared. Meanwhile, you go back to your lab and find out what we are dealing with."

They sat for a few moments in pained silence, finishing their lunches which had lost all flavor. Then, with a quiet handshake, they parted company for the moment.

Chapter 35.

Lee Collwood IV, CEO of Anaconda Chemicals, sat in his car on lower Broadway in downtown San Diego. In the passenger seat was his subordinate and local San Diego CEO, Henry Morton. They sat in the shade of the Koll Center, a spacious 20-story marble and glass office building two blocks east of the sparkling harbor water.

Collwood was on the phone, for the 15th time hearing a dumb voice message on the answering service of Lima Voyager's Captain Gus Tidjeman.

"Any luck?" Morton asked.

"No." Collwood slipped the phone into his inside jacket pocket near the side-holster of his 9mm Glock. "No, I think he may have skipped town." Collwood had considered taking Morton into full confidence. Telling Morton everything opened up new risks, but Morton was in fairly dire straits financially. He had a gambling habit he thought Collwood didn't know about. Collwood's detectives, hired through Syd Appelbaum the lawyer in Los Angeles, knew most of his corporate officers' terrible secrets. The time didn't seem quite ripe yet, but in another sense, time was running out. It wouldn't be long before this disaster spread, and the fingerprints of Anaconda Chemicals were all over Lima Voyager. The other option was to talk to the Coast Guard or the Harbor Police and come clean. After all, the fungal samples he'd had his agents smuggle out of Peru included the one responsible for the disaster that was about to unfold.

Suddenly, Collwood had a bright idea. Perhaps all his troubles might be over soon anyway. What if he developed a counter-toxin to the nightmare that was already spreading throughout San Diego? Somehow, he would figure out how to sidestep the bad publicity if more people died. That was what Syd Applebaum's legal team and the publicity team in Los Angeles got paid for. Ultimately, though, it was up to the man at the helm—himself—to figure out the broad strategic course. It would not be a defensive course. The best defense was offense, and already Lee Collwood was about to orchestrate a new campaign to rescue himself from the failing Offensor campaign.

"Tell you what," he told Morton, "let's drive by Captain Tidjeman's house one more time. I'll drop you off at your office."

"Oh God yes, I am days behind in my work."

They talked a little bit about work on the way to University City, where Tidjeman owned a sprawling two-story house with a pool overlooking a leafy canyon. Morton's San Diego branch of Anaconda Chemicals had been feeling the pinch of the home company's cash shortage for two years now. Sales were stagnating, and there had been two layoffs terminating 20% of the work force. Investors had downgraded Anaconda's stock and bond offerings twice already, with the result that a riskier kind of investor was gobbling up larger chunks of common stock in an ominous takeover mood. Morton was eager to get the new mycology research and development project that Collwood had promised him in glowing lengths, and now it must be starting to be clear to Morton that something was morbidly wrong with Anaconda. Keeping him and six other CEOs around the country at a subsidiary level allowed Collwood to cook the books creatively and hide it from his CEOs. It was just a question of how long, unless Collwood became even more creative. One thing Collwood's intelligence operatives had informed him of: Morton had his resume making the rounds on the East Coast under a John Smith cover name. Of course CEOs did that a lot, but it tipped Collwood off to be careful to trust Morton.

They drove I-5 north, east on State 52, and north on I-805, then exited at Governor Drive. Near Genesee, they drove down into a middle-class neighborhood, then into a cul-de-sac overlooking a canyon of eucalyptus trees and palms. It was the third time that day, and at least the tenth time in the last several days, that Collwood had made this drive—with or without Henry Morton at his side. He didn't want Morton tor realize how desperate he really was.

"My God," Morton said. "Look. There is a light on at the front porch. And the door is slightly ajar."

"There is his car," Collwood said. "He must have just rolled in from wherever he's been." He reached under his jacket to take the safety off the Glock. At the same time, he braked to a rocking stop directly behind Tidjeman's car, blocking it.

"I can't believe I'm doing this," Morton said as they got out. "This is like Hawaii Five-Oh."

Instinctively, Collwood looked around so see if they were being watched, but they were surrounded by dense, tall ficus and willow trees blocking the view of nosy neighbors. The house, sporting two large pillars on a three-stepped portico, faced the sprawling canyon from the left. The only neighbors were one house behind, on the left, and one across the street beyond an ancient, giant ficus whose yard-thick trunk had broken up the sidewalk all around.

They walked up to the door. Morton knocked and stood waiting. Collwood stood just behind him and to his right. Collwood sensed that Morton was hungry to get his pharmaceuticals R&D going, and was even more eager than Collwood to confront Tidjeman.

"What is it?" said a booming voice with a slightly flat affect.

Collwood sensed movement behind the slightly open door. Maybe it was a shadow moving on the wall, or the wind blowing a leaf somewhere.

"Captain Tidjeman, I'm Henry Morton, CEO of Anaconda Chemicals. Mr. Collwood and I wish to speak with you about our missing shipment."

"Oh yes," said Tidjeman. He was a tall Dutchman with pale blue eyes (now looking strangely like smoky glass) and very white skin. He must have been blond in his younger years, but now his bulbous head featured a ring of closely shorn gray stubble around a waxy bald spot. He wore nice summer clothing, and smelled somewhat like loam as he opened the door with a pasty-skinned hand. "I'll let you in," he said.

In that moment, seeing the man's oddly dilated black pupils, Collwood had a sense that he was up to no good. As Collwood reached into his jacket for the gun, Tidjeman formed his mouth into an 'o' and blew some dark air in Morton's face.

At that, the Glock was in motion.

Morton dropped like a sack, and Tidjeman caught him with both hands to prevent Morton's head from smashing on the concrete. Tidjeman was in a forward-bending, slightly squatting posture looking up into the muzzle of Collwood's Glock.

"The shipment," Collwood said.

Tidjeman blinked thoughtfully.

"Don't think about shooting that crap at me or I'll empty this gun into you before you can blow."

Tidjeman, still with that thoughtful look on his face, took Morton in a head-hanging, under the shoulders grip and dragged the limp man into the dark hallway.

Collwood took a step closer and blocked the door with a foot against its bottom edge. "Don't get cute with me, Tidjeman. I don't care how much dope you smuggled or whatever atomic bombs you brought in to blow the whole country up. I don't give a shit. All I want is my fungus."

"I am the fungus," Tidjeman said in that flat voice.

"What?"

"Maybe we can do business," Tidjeman said. "You need raw pharmacopia, and I need hydroponics space in you laboratories out in Brawley so I can develop my own little project."

"I've already done my business and paid cash," Collwood said. "That's why I carry insurance." He waggled the gun. "I'm used to dealing with people who try to take my money and run. Don't screw around with me. I warn you."

"You need me," Tidjeman said, laying Morton's body against the wall for later action. He straightened up and dusted his hands. Collwood noticed that fine clouds of skin cells fell of his hands as he slapped them against each other. "You won't hurt me. You'd be crazy to."

For a second, Collwood felt himself wavering. What to do? If anything happened to Tidjeman, who else could he turn to?

In the next second, Tidjeman started forward while making that 'o' mouth to blow spores in Collwood's face.

Collwood was faster. The gun barked one, two, three times.

A mix of dry gray stuffing and wet black slime hit the wall behind Tidjeman. What was left of Tidjeman dropped to the floor with the sound of a department store dummy dropping. He even bounced, stiffly a few times. His head rolled like a big ball of papier mache down the hallway and came to rest against a sliding glass door overlooking a concrete patio with red steel railings overlooking a canyon.

As Collwood stood thinking about what to do next, the headless body stirred. It rolled over onto one elbow. The other hand went flat on the floor. Pulling up one knee, then the other, and pushing with both hands, the headless body rose into tottering standing position. Collwood recoiled, stepping back. He glimpsed the inside of the creature's neck—a mass of gray pulp, with vestigial streaks of human bone and nerve endings amid rusty-red streaks of blood and other human body fluids. Several tough but resilient black tubes hung inches out of the severed neck. Each of the tubes was about the thickness of a pencil, round, and shiny gray-black like wet eel hide. The tubes seemed to probe about for their missing ends.

With the head gone, and therefore the stabilizing mechanisms of the inner ear, the body lurched toward Collwood. Its arms stiffly rose as if to embrace him. He stepped back, glancing to his right at the distant head. Its eyes were open and its mouth was round. Maybe it was sending messages to its body, so Collwood thought, for small gouts of black air came out of the flattened bronchial openings in the bare neck. Collwood unloaded two more rounds into the head. He aimed dead at the 'o' shaped mouth. The bullets trashed the lower face so that shattered teeth pebbled the jelly mass now exposed and slowly dripping. The rounds left huge spider web cracks spreading in the plate glass behind the head.

Collwood kicked the torso away from him, so that it sprawled over Morton's inert form. He unloaded the rest of this rounds into the torso. He went into the high-tech kitchen and pulled drawers out, leaving cascades of silverware to sail and dance in rows and curves on the dark blue concrete floor. He found the inevitable junk drawer and took out a roll of sturdy twine. He pulled a ceramic knife from a fancy Japanese cutlery block. With knife and twine in hand, he went back through the living room to the front hall.

The torso had risen again, and stood groping its way erect along the wall. Collwood judo-swept it by the feet. It smacked down on its side. Collwood cut a length of twine to tie its ankles together. It tried to lean forward and unleash a feeble gout of black air at him. He rose and kicked it in the chest so it stretched out with the neck pointing away from him. He tied its hands together behind its back, and threw a little rug over the neck so it would stop shooting spores at him. He tied the rug down, looping twine under the armpits and up around the back. He went into the kitchen, and found a fancy black and white plastic shopping bag from some upscale fashion shop in University Towne Center Mall. He went through the back area and kicked the head into the shopping bag with one foot. Returning to the front door, he dragged the still feebly struggling body outside.

Making sure as best he could that nobody was watching, he threw the shopping bag and body into the trunk of his car. The body and head weren't as heavy as a fully functioning human's, there being less liquid than in a human body.

What to do with Morton? Leaving him here would make one more loose end enabling the authorities to track their mystery to Collwood's doorstep all the sooner. He dragged the unconscious Collwood by the ankles, and effortlessly lifted him into the trunk. He slammed the lid down.

He stopped to get gas, and stocked up on cold sodas and sandwiches. It would be at least a four hour drive to Brawley. At least now he had some material to work with.

Chapter 36.

Lee Collwood reloaded his Glock as he drove the long miles toward the Salton Sea. At one point he had a scare, because he encountered a State roadblock. Agricultural agents in dark green uniforms were looking for illegal shipments of fruits possibly containing some insect that was ruining crops in both Arizona and California. Seeing his destination—in the desert not far from Brawley—they didn't bother checking his trunk.

He also encountered a similar stop by the Migra, or Border Patrol. They, however, were checking cars coming north from Mexico, and he was heading southeast. He could well imagine the looks on their faces if they did open his trunk. Then again, the first tell tale sign that a man had illegals in the car was the extent to which the car rode low on the road. Five or ten people could lower the chassis—a sign the Feds would spot.

He sailed through this roadblock and prayed to make it okay to his plant. At six p.m., the desert was still hot while shadows grew long, and the light frying the walls of buildings turned from incandescent down to an increasingly honeyed, soft glow. It was almost sad and poetic in a way. Melancholy, if you swung that way. But Lee Collwood was all action, lights, music, no time for sentimentality. He had no time for fear or self-doubt.

Long ago, when his mother lived, she had taken him to see a bearded doctor with a Vienna accent and African statues on his bookcase. This doctor had diagnosed the pubescent Lee as having touches of sociopathy and megalomania, embedded in a mild bipolar condition that made him at times hyper, at other times lethargic. Another doctor some years later—after he had pushed a girl from a horse at a riding stable during classes, and the parents sued because she had become paraplegic—had said Lee was narcissistic. It meant he loved only himself, if one could call that love, and he didn't care whom he hurt. He had no feelings for other people. He didn't know where he ended and other people began. His mother had cried for weeks, and regarded him with large, tragic eyes while holding a hand up to stifle sobs. He kept getting thrown out of schools, usually for doing things to other boys that went beyond the normal pranks and black eyes. Lee mellowed with time, converting his brute physical energy and raging carelessness into more subtle maneuverings—manipulation, lying, cheating. While he was physically violent earlier, he'd always been outmaneuvered by those who resorted to cleverness rather than physical cruelty. When Lee learned that it was more effective to be psychologically cruel, and easier to cover one's tracks—especially coming from a billionaire family that could always clean up the mess, fix the problem, buy the next pony, pretend Lee was getting better—then Lee switched gears from brute to just plain creep. Of course, that wasn't how he saw himself. That was from the lengthy, hateful depositions made in divorce court by his three ex-wives. He saw himself as being a victim of the 'lonely at the top' syndrome of those who are better than their peers. His burden in life was to inherit a billion dollar fortune that others had let slide to the brink of ruination. It was his duty, a patriotic duty to his country as well as to his family, to restore Anaconda Chemicals to its former glory. That end justified any means. And since he paid generous amounts of child support and alimony, always on time, he figured he was a far better fellow than these awful women made him out to be. After all, he'd never struck any of them, or their children. One could easily tally up the plusses and minuses, the debits and credits, as Lee tended to do, and come up with a wholly different accounting.

Lee Collwood drove up to his personal entrance at the south end of the plant. At a press of a button in the car, the three-wide steel garage door rolled up for him as he drove into the cool gloom. Sensors noted the entrance of his car and closed the door behind him. He pulled to a stop in the 18 car garage and motor pool that contained his prized Lamborghini and classic Porsche, among other treasures.

First, there was the matter of the bodies. He opened the trunk and stood back, gasping. Even for his strong stomach, the sight he saw was revolting. The entire trunk was gauzed over with a light mesh of very fine threads. Through the threads, Collwood saw that the headless torso of the mushroom man had managed to wrap its arms and legs around Morton, apparently killing him. The mix of human decay and mushroom bloom was overpowering. Morton must have been rotting for at least three hours in the hot trunk going through the desert. Strangest of all, the head had somehow gotten out of the bag and loosely reattached itself, by just those glossy black eel-belly tubes. The head was now also firmly attached to Morton's neck by such a tube coming out of the head's mouth and entering Morton's left jugular artery. Morton's eyes were slightly open with an odd sheen, and his mouth was open in what looked like a deflated, final scream. Collwood was tired and disgusted. He yelled out an obscenity and slammed the trunk lid shut.

He climbed into a golf cart and drove across the garage, up the ramp, and back into sunlight. He entered the inner courtyard of his personal estate, which contained a large swimming pool, jacuzzi seating up to 18 people, and amenities to throw a rolling party for hundreds who had arrived by jet at his private runway on the desert floor outside. In recent years, the celebrities who used to come to his grandfather's and father's parties didn't come anymore. Lee didn't make friends very easily. He managed to attract women who liked his money, were okay with his reasonably good athletic looks, and tolerated his roller-coaster personality and personal disconnection.

At the moment, he lived alone in the sprawling estate. Locals from the entire county still showed up for work at the adjoining plant. Parts of the plant had shut down over the years, and entire buildings stood empty like a ghost town. Anaconda Chemicals today employed more workers at its San Diego facility (5,000) than at the home plant near Brawley. Since his last wife had moved out a year ago, taking their last child with her, he'd been alone here with his guns, his cars, his planes, and his dreams. He had plenty of time to fly in experts in various fields to deliver one and two day briefings on mycology, lichenology, and other tributaries of the great river of biology, the study of life.

When old Robertson had brought him the translated journals and notes of Major Tomio Karasawa, Lee Collwood had quickly grasped the implications. Karasawa had been on the headquarters staff of the Imperial Japanese Army's infamous Unit 731 stationed in China. Lt. General Ishii Shiro, a microbiologist and commander of that unit, had performed horrific human experiments on hundreds of thousands of Chinese men, women, and children, in addition to thousands of Allied prisoners of war. The unit's very existence had been covered up by MacArthur's Japanese occupation government after the war, for various political reasons. In a manner reminiscent of the treatment of certain Nazi war criminals—who were valuable assets for the ensuing Cold War with the Soviets in Europe—the U.S. and her allies seized the information about Unit 731 and buried it in deeply secret classifications to avoid having it fall into Soviet or Red Chinese hands. Robertson had been a minor U.S. official involved with Chiang Kai Shek's Nationalist government before Mao Tse Tung's Communists drove the Nationalists from the mainland to form the Republic of China (Taiwan). Robertson later, by his own account, received the Karasawa documents from an alcoholic and debt-ridden U.S. officer in San Diego. Robertson, who understood both Japanese and Chinese, translated the documents and planned to release them to the press after his death by means of his will. His wife's illness, and his own illness, and his looming bankruptcy as a result, forced him to seek a buyer. Because of the nature of its business and proximity to San Diego, Anaconda Chemicals had been first on his list of candidate buyers, and he'd hit the bull's eye on his first shot. He had been cagey in his discussions with Lee Collwood, but Collwood was desperate and Robertson didn't need much at all by Collwood's standards—half a million dollars.

Collwood mixed himself a drink and walked out to the pool. The evening was cool, and the interior of the pool twinkled slowly as waves on the surface mixed light sources in and above the water in hypnotic dancing patterns. Collwood dropped his clothes on a deck chair, pulled a swim suit out of a metal dresser full of them, and dove into the pool. He swam several laps, letting the cool water flow over his body and wash away the dirt of the outside world. Purified, he wrapped himself in a large towel, turned on a gas heater, and lay on the deck chair. He was a bit hungry, and resolved to make himself a sandwich later. He had no staff anymore, having let them all go for lack of cash.

He was awaiting a phone call, and it came shortly. His phone warbled and he popped open the clam shell. "Yes?"

"This is Thomas Blake. Who am I speaking with?"

"Lee Collwood. Where are you?"

"Driving to your place with six of my associates."

"Great. Call me when you're outside and I'll open the gate."

It took several hours for the van full of men to arrive from Phoenix, where they had been especially recruited by some of Syd Appelbaum's friends in L.A. Meanwhile, Collwood dozed off. The warbling of his cell phone awakened him from a deep, tired sleep. Blake and his men were outside. "I'll let you in. Give me 15 minutes, okay?" He dove into the pool to wake up. He clambered out, dried off, popped several uppers to get himself going, and drove his golf cart out to the garage. He raised the steel door remotely, and a dark green van glided quietly into the garage even as the door unrolled itself back to the shut position.

The passenger door opened, and a strapping man of 30 got out. He was blond, with a sort of page boy hairdo that turned frizzy at the ears and ended at the collar. He had a strong jaw, small broken nose, and features Collwood had seen on body builders and extreme martial arts guys. He wasn't bulked up, but had solid muscle in a lean frame. "Nice to meet you."

"Same here," Collwood said. "I have a severe problem, and I need you guys to fix it for me."

Blake grinned, showing small white teeth. "That's what we're here for." He sounded vaguely Commonwealth, now that Collwood began to notice, and he recalled that Blake was South African. Syd's people had recommended this guy as tops in the field. He'd been a mercenary in several wars, including those fought by the U.S. in the Middle East. The guy was said to be intel material—trustworthy, dedicated, tied by an umbilical to his employer's wallet and therefore loyal to a fault.

"Let's meet your men."

Blake bellowed over his shoulder: "Okay, gents, show the man your face. Don't scare him to death."

Six men climbed out—two white, two Asian, two black. "That's the whole six pack," Blake joked. "These boys will cut their finger off for you, honest."

"I believe it. Do they scare easily?"

Blake guffawed, and the others followed suit. They were all cut from the same jib—youngish, hard, lean, ready to scrap. At the look on Collwood's face, their laughs lost some of their heartiness. Collwood gave them a brief rundown, warning of the blowing of dark air full of spores, and of the ruthless inhumanity of their opponent. He assured them a total license to kill them.

"Let me give you an example of their kind," Collwood said. He had them gather around the trunk of his car and unlocked it. As the trunk groaned open on its spring-loaded hinges, Collwood gasped more than the others.

The bodies in the trunk were gone—head and all. The gauzy mess had been torn so that only a few shreds remained to blow in the wind. Against the far wall of the trunk stretched a dull brown mass—a bracket fungus. Henry Morton's shoes and clothing lay wadded in a corner, covered with slime. The being who had been Tidjeman had apparently chewed or cut his way—oh yes, the ceramic knife!—through the firewall behind the back seat. It would have been easy to reach up and pull the lever that made the back seat fold forward.

Collwood whirled to confront several snickering faces. "You think I'm nuts, eh?" He reached into the trunk and pulled Morton's clothing out. He shook the klutzy brown shoes. "You see these? The thing's a mimic. Your first assignment is to get out there right now and hunt down this killer, this mimic, this fungal freak. Here is your challenge. You think it's a joke, you get careless, and this thing spots you before you see it—you get a blast of black air in the face, and you're done for."

Blake betrayed one instant's uncertainty. "Mr. Collwood, you're quite sure now—?"

Collwood got in his face. "I'm paying you guys top dollar per diem and you do what I pay you for. Hunt this thing down and get the practice you'll need when you go hunting in the city!"

Chapter 37.

Linsey Simon returned to the office, and saw Louise Trost waving through the smoky glass of her office. Louise had a serious, animated look about her. Linsey, holding a cup of coffee, walked in and sat down. Louise finished a phone and sat forward, steepling her fingers. "Linsey, the fudge is going to start hitting the fan."

"Oh?"

"I had a meeting with Dr. Nolan at lunch time. We've decided to raise the alarm level a few shades of color. We've had one guy die, and it looks like the whole city is coated with this unknown yellow fungus." She pointed to a plastic cup full of mushrooms, sealed under a sandwich baggie tied down with several rubber bands. "What if this starts an epidemic? What if it's some terrorist launching what could become a plague?"

Linsey shook her head and winced as she sipped hot coffee. "Keeps us employed, but is a real nuisance."

"No time for flippancy, young lady; what's the action plan?"

"I'm planning to take Cleve out to interview the two surviving roofers. Seems the dead guy, Hugh Milton, may have inhaled fresh yellow spores and/or drunk a lot of water with the freshly fallen spores in it. I want to try and get a lead on those crop dusting planes."

"Every police and military agency in Southern California is on that case. Good luck."

"And I want to track down whatever there is to be tracked down about the Lima Voyager."

"I like that better. Good luck again. Sounds like you have your hands full. Say, Linsey, have you had a talk with that muck-racking husband of yours?"

Linsey grinned. "You mean Yellow Press Jack? I threatened his life if he coughs up as much as a single syllable about what I may mutter in my sleep."

Louise picked up a pair of long-bladed, scary looking scissors—usually used for cutting cloth or newspapers. "You tell old Jack I'm going to personally emasculate him if he does that." She cackled with laughter. Then she added: "Seriously, keep this as hushed as you can until we come out with a joint statement."

"You think it's that far?"

"My gut tells me it's a sleeper, honey. I've been in law enforcement all my life, and I still have a vivid imagination. This story is going to cause a sensation."

That afternoon, as Jack Simon sat in his office typing a story about City Council kickbacks scandal, the phone rang. "Simon," he answered curtly while squinching the phone under one cheek and continuing to whale away on the keyboard with both hands.

"This is Jim Robertson, Mr. Simon. Just wanted to confirm that we are meeting this afternoon in an house."

Jack's stomach lurched. "Mr. Robertson, I hate to tell you but I am on a deadline right now with a front-page story..."

"It's extremely urgent."

"I have to postpone, Jim. I'm really sorry."

"I have a friend here, from Peru, who can explain—"

A red, angry looking face under a wave of white hair poked in. *The Publisher.* "Is it done?"

"Almost," Jack said to the Publisher. To the man on the phone he said: "Jim, God just stuck head in and asked for my rear end on a platter if I'm not done with this front page story in time for a review meeting at five. I'm trying to be a nice guy and not hang up on you, but this is costing me seconds I don't have."

"I will come with this man and we will sit outside your door until you have a free moment. It's urgent."

"Okay, you do that. I can't guarantee I'll have a free moment, but maybe after five?"

"We will be there shortly. Thanks so much, Mr. Simon."

Jim Robertson, a balding, graying man of 50 with the soft, paunchy physique of a man who has spent his entire life at a desk without ever kicking a ball or swimming a lap, walked down his front drive. It was hot in the East County, with clear blue skies and a sun whose fierce light reflected hotly on chrome and glass all around. Accompanying Jim were Paco Tlocl and his daughter, who had Americanized her distant, jungle Quechua name to Marie Passos.

"Did you bring a sample?" Jim asked as they got into his car at the curb. Marie sat in the back and explained: "He is not allowed to carry even a grain with him, for fear it would cause calamity." The old man rode shotgun and remained stony, projecting his usual focused, intense, thoughtful air.

Jim shook his head. "I think it would have been good to drop a few spores on his desk and convince him by demonstration." He pulled away from the curb and started driving down East Main Street in El Cajon. He planned to take Interstate 5 westward into San Diego—a drive of less than half an hour. It was mid-afternoon, and the rush hour had not yet begun. Besides, the afternoon rush came eastward as city workers returned to their homes in the suburbs.

As Jim drove through the quiet streets of his working class neighborhood, Marie and Paco conversed in their obscure, sibilant dialect. Jim's mind was on a variety of matters, from a late electric bill to a rattle in his engine and a missed phone call from an attractive divorcee he'd been courting in Rolando. Jim paid minimal attention to the simple actions of driving, and paid no attention to the softly murmuring Indians.

As he turned onto Johnson Avenue, he sensed that something wasn't right. Something around him, in the traffic, something bothered him suddenly. Already, Marie had noticed and he heard her gasp. As they waited under a red traffic light, he heard the roar of an approaching automobile. He had just time enough to turn to his left. He heard Paco remark in an even, unexcitable voice, and heard a drawn out wail from Marie.

At the same time, he glimpsed the older model, heavy 1960s American car making straight for him. The car cut across lanes of traffic like a torpedo seeking its target in some naval vessel. None of the dozens of drivers all around on the broad avenue had time to register what was going on, much less blow their horns in protest. Like in a staged motion picture, the car made directly for Jim's car. Jim could see the dark-skinned man behind the wheel. He heard the engine accelerating. A second later, the impact slammed Jim's car sideways across six lanes devoid of traffic. As the right wheels hit the curb, they buckled. Jim had the breath knocked out of him and was losing consciousness, but he had time to note that the T-boning car kept pressing them and that he was heading across a lawn into the side of a furniture store. As his consciousness faded, he heard glass from the showroom window raining down on concrete. He felt a terrific pressure in his left side.

"On purpose," someone was saying. Jim heard voices as he tried to put his thoughts together. "Like one of those terrorists," said someone else. "A suicide bomber with a car for a bomb."

Sirens wailed, and Jim looked through a veiled haze at the wreckage of his car. He was in the wreckage, but alive. He couldn't move, but he deduced that the long, hard torpedo of steel had sliced through the rear of the car. Somehow the middle steel post between doors had deflected the left front fender of the attacking car, so that it completely crushed the rear half of Jim's car. He couldn't even move a hand to help, but he could turn his head to the right. As his vision came into a focus a little bit, he saw that Marie was buried in a mass of metal and glass. Only her face was visible, and the shattered window behind her revealed her blood splattered all over the gray-painted furniture store wall. Her facial features looked flaccid, but there were a few seconds of life left in her large, dark eyes.

Paco seemed unhurt, but for the first time, Jim saw him emote personal feelings. He'd known the man on and off for several years now, ever since that night when dad had still been alive and these two had come scratching furtively at the back door. Paco knelt on the seat, moaning softly in grief and shock. He fumbled with small brown hands and tiny fingers to undo that mass of metal, chips of safety glass, and viciously cutting seat springs that had torn and impaled his daughter in addition to the slamming between car and wall. In that tangle of materials, Jim saw, was the mangled and ripped, bloody body of the attacker, and much of the blood on the wall was his rather than Marie's. Must have come right through the windshield on impact and landed in Marie's midsection like a rocket.

Paco managed to find one of his daughter's hands and held it while she turned her eyes to look up at him. He brokenly cried desperate words of endearment as her eyes sank slowly shut and she died. Sirens sounded and rescuers came running—those things Jim heard, but was focused on what happened next. The dead assailant's body began to sprout fine yellowish tendrils, and Paco raised both arms as if in some religious ceremony, and spat on the man's body. While he repeatedly spat on it, he produced a small knife and, with two swift gestures, cut a tiny pouch open. Reddish powder filled the air, and the green tendrils wilted and turned into tiny dead brown grains that blew away. Paco continued his prayerful pose, grasping Marie's battered head in both palms, until Jim saw Paco literally will himself to die out of grief.

That afternoon, Dylan came around. Jack rose from his keyboard to meet the older man. "Dylan, good to see you."

"And I'm halfway sober for a change." They shook hands. Dylan looked awful—red-skinned, pot-bellied, with stick limbs under his thick sweater and suit. "Have you had lunch?"

Jack glanced at the clock. "No, I was waiting for a guy to show up. Big deadline, but I got the story in early."

"If your date never showed up, why don't you let me buy you coffee and a sandwich."

"Yeah, I'm starving. It wasn't a date, just some crank." Jack rose and slipped his jacket on while he found Jovia's crumpled note again and read from it: "James Robertson Jr."

Dylan looked stunned. "That's who I came to tell you about."

"Oh?" They walked out of the office together, and down the carpeted halls to the elevator.

"This man came to see me about a year ago. Had an Indian with him, from Peru. I was too drunk to be coherent, but you know how it is. I put on a show of listening while twenty or more ounces of expensive Scotch swirled in my blood stream. I only heard half of it, and thought it was pretty uproarious, but just crazy enough that there might be some truth to it."

The elevator came and they rode down in its carpeted, steely ambience. Jack said: "That's how I look at it too. Usually it's cranks and limelighters, but once in a while if you can't figure out what they might gain, it is just possibly for real."

They stepped out into the balmy sunshine and crossed the parking lot to Jack's car. "Someplace close, like in Hotel Circle?"

"Yeah, yeah, fine," Dylan said. They got in and Jack wondered if the frail looking other fellow had much of a stomach left to be eating lunch. Dylan said as Jack drove: "I couldn't figure this guy's game out, but it was something wild. Seems his father had been in the Flying Tigers back in China before the Second World War. Joined the Army Air Forces during the war, and afterwards spent some time in China. That's where he met this fellow Paco's old man, who had been brought by the Japanese from Peru. Now I only have a garble of it, but if you can connect with Robertson you can probably get the full story. If it's got anything to do with this mushroom story, you're sitting on a gold mine."

"I gather it involves Anaconda and Lee Collwood."

"That worthless on of a bitch," Dylan spat. "Ran someone over once, drunk of course, up in Santa Barbara. Daddy's money got him off the hook as always. They get these expensive lawyers that can lie their way through an iceberg, and you can get anyone off the hook. The Collwoods had plenty of money, but I think this is the last one. I think they're going belly up."

"Is that the angle?" Jack asked. What was Robertson's game?

"Nah," Dylan said. "I think Robertson is a believer. Believes his story. Is eager to pitch it to you, but very selective about whom he approaches. Like he's afraid for his life, or worse."

"Or worse?" Jack said with bite in his voice.

"The country, the world, what do I know?" As they parked outside a diner, Dylan launched a fragmentary story that Jack found baffling and interesting—he wasn't sure about plausible.

Chapter 38.

"Yessir," Blake said in response to Lee Collwood's instruction to hunt down the being that had been Henry Morton—or so Collwood claimed—the men were still skeptical but kept their doubts to themselves. "Okay, you guys, mount up. You heard the man. Flashlights and side arms. Let's move out."

The door rolled up. Bristling with weapons, the van roared out of the garage. Collwood left the door standing open so that starlight could be seen twinkling over the moonless desert dunes. He quickly lost ear contact with the quiet, powerful van. He hoped they had four wheel drive, for they'd need it.

The question on everyone's lips was: *How nuts is this guy?*

Blake had the driver stop. "Listen, you guys. We're professionals, here to do a professional job. Our employer believes there is a thing out here that looks like his late business partner who gnawed his way out of the trunk of his car. We go find that partner and bring him back. If he tries to eat your hand off, kill him. It's that simple. Got that?"

"Right," they all said. Each was an independent agent hand-picked for this job. They thought highly of Blake, and he thought highly of them or they wouldn't be here.

"So if you were a walking fungus mimicking a man, where would you be right now?" Blake asked.

"This guy have dogs?" a man asked. "He got dogs, we let them loose, and we just follow as they hunt down Mr. Button."

"No dogs," Blake said. "But listen."

They heard a distant sound like laughter—silly, yippity, spilling giggly laughter.

"Coyotes."

"Yeah."

"We let them do the hunting for us."

"Yeah."

"We ditch the van. Blake, can you stay here and play base?"

Blake shook his head. "I want to be in on this." He pointed to a man he thought might make a good second. It was a Chinese named Lo. "You stay here to guard the truck. Watch your back."

"Yeah, boss." Lo was a small but solid guy, wearing a watch cap jammed low. He carried an assault rifle slung over his right arm. He wore a dark wool sweater and black jeans, the kind cut baggy enough at the legs to fit over boots, which he wore also, black engineer boots.

Blake liked the scent of the desert at night, and the promise of the hunt. He'd enjoyed this in Saudi Arabia at an oasis with some royal princes many years ago, hunting lion at night. Never mind the lion were largely extinct, and game wardens released them for the princes' pleasure. It was still a taste of ancient Arabia. Blake said: "Let's go, guys. Good luck!"

The six men melded into the darkness. There was no moon, but the desert still glowed with reflected ambient light, mostly starlight. They knew their eyes would get used to it. There was precious little to stumble over but some creosote bushes and the like. Sparse, tough vegetation.

Blake wished they were on horseback. Still, it was refreshing, invigorating, and exciting to be tracking at night like this. He liked the smell of the Southern California desert at night, when the day's heat was done, and a cool wind played over the scrub and coaxed wildlife out of their lairs.

"Wish we had dogs," said one man; "this could take a week."

"And horses," another said.

"We'll give it an hour or two," Blake said wisely, "and if nothing turns up, we'll go back and tell Mr. Money we need a chopper and some sniper rifles. That's how I'd do it."

"Yeah," they all said in unison, thinking it a bully idea.

Back at the van, Lo paced slowly on a low ridge above the parked vehicle. From this vantage point, he had a good view of the tops of the dunes for a mile around. Gradually it dawned on him that the brighter night light higher up was impairing his vision of the darker shadows among the dunes flowing around his feet like waves of the sea. The van looked solid and boxy, and he decided to stick with his high vantage point.

Unseen by Lo, the being that had been Henry Morton stepped out of the shadows near the van. It had its hands in its pockets, and seemed to be wearing the clothing Morton had worn in the trunk. It wore a dark suit, a slouchy dark hat, and a white shirt with a dark vest over it. It had on the most absurdly large brown shoes, and it was intently hunting for what it needed. It heard the breathing of the man atop the dune, and stood in the shadows of the van to watch him pace back and forth in the dim light.

Lo paced up and down, hoping the others would come back soon. He had spent a little time in the Libyan desert at one point in his checkered mercenary career, but he considered himself a Taiwan city boy. He'd been selected for urban duty in San Diego, and this desert nomad stuff was like something out of a movie. He didn't like it.

The creature stalking the man on the dune moved slowly and deliberately forward. Suddenly it heard a man speaking.

"Lo, this is Blake. Are you okay?"

"Blake, this is Lo. Bored stiff, but happy. You find our allegedly weird mushroom man?"

"Not a medium rare chance. We'll call it off in another hour."

"Very good."

Was-Morton heard all this and made a great effort to adjust its vocal chords. "Blah," it croaked softly trying to say Blake.

Lo whirled. "Is someone there?" He listened.

"Blah," someone said.

"Blake?"

"Lo, this is Blake."

"Yeah? Where are you?"

"I'm down here by the van."

"I thought you said another hour."

"It is baloney. I'm coming in early. The others will follow."

"Gotcha. Hey, got a cigarette?"

"Yes, right here."

"Be right down. Hold your fire."

"I am holding it."

When Lo clambered down the sandy slope to the van, his eyesight took time to adjust. He still saw dark muddy blobs as he groped his way along the side of the van. "Blake, you there?"

"Here."

Lo rounded the front of the van. "Oh, hey, there you are!"

One second he saw the man's dark figure looking the other way. The next second the figure turned and it wasn't Blake but that scruffy guy they were hunting. He had his mouth shaped in an 'o' and before Lo could bring the assault rifle around, blew a stream of dark air over Lo's face. Lo saw no reason to keep the gun, and dropped it. Smiling, he waited for the dark figure to act.

Was-Morton had the collective DNA, but also the collective memories quite separately obtained from brain material, of Morton, and before that Tidjeman, and before that a Peruvian merchant sailor, and before that an Andean Indian. Was-Morton had a compendium of experience stored up, and knew better than to lie here sucking out this man's genetic material, when his fellows might arrive at any time. So it threw the anaesthetized Lo into the back of the van, started the engine, and drove off.

Forty minutes later, Blake and the first stragglers arrived.

"Wasn't the van here?" a man asked.

"Yeah, look, there's the tracks."

"I'm afraid we've been had," Blake said. "Either our employer has played a trick on us, or this business is far more serious than we ever gave it credit to be."

When they arrived on foot near dawn, banging on Lee Collwood's steel rollup door, he almost didn't want to answer.

Collwood waited until they were all seated sheepishly around his pool. A catering service brought in Mexican fast food—it was the only thing available at this hour—while Collwood harangued them. "You've lost one of your men, and you lost your vehicle. Big deal. I can send a chopper up and have them find the van. I guarantee what we'll find. Dammit, now do you believe me? We're up against something diabolical."

"I'm sorry, Mr. Collwood," said Blake, "we really didn't take it seriously enough, and here I am, minus a good man. I feel bad about that. Makes me want to find this mushroom crap and flush it down the toilet. Only I know it's not going to be that easy."

"Right," Collwood said. "You've had your first encounter with Homo Mycotus, and he killed your guy and stole your van. Hopefully by now you have enough common sense to understand you are up against one of the most successful biological adaptations in history."

Somewhere out in the desert stood an abandoned van. In it, a bracket fungus stretched along the back wall. It contained the DNA of Lo and Henry Morton and Captain Tidjeman and many other souls, and was preparing to become a spore launcher—not in the secondary reproductive cycle of mimicked humans, but the species' real, native way of reproducing, in which each bracket community released an endless series of billions of spores.

As a red sun swimming in yellow clouds rose, and the cold night air began to warm up, a figure walked along a rural highway. Eventually, a bus came by and slowed to a stop with a pop of air brakes. The bus opened its doors with a pneumatic hiss. The former mercenary Lo climbed on board, heading toward San Diego.

Chapter 39.

Linsey Simon drove the unmarked car, a loaner from the SDPD Detective Bureau, with Cleve Bartlett riding shotgun. Cleve had chucked the uniform for a handsome tan twill suit with blue shirt and dark blue tie. She wore her preferred blouse and dress trousers that covered her Doc Martens boots.

She and Cleve pulled up on a quiet, sunny street in Serra Mesa and got out. "Hi there!" she called out toward sky so blue it almost looked dark blue, matching Cleve's tie, but that was an illusion of pupil-overload.

A shadowy figure on a rooftop waved back.

Moments later, Max Juergen and Fritz Waldmeister clambered down the ladder and joined Linsey and Cleve on the sidewalk. Linsey had arranged the meeting by cell phone.

"Oh yes," Max said, "what a shame. He was such a nice young man." He and Fritz looked 30ish, blond, in good shape. They had that dark-red look of fair-skinned people with chronic sunburn, despite wearing broad-brimmed straw hats, long-sleeved shirts, and long pants.

"Did you know Hugh Milton long?"

Fritz said: "He worked with us for a few months and he was doing well. College dropout—looking for himself, as they say— had a nice girlfriend."

"Annie," Max said. "We saw her at the funeral. Very sad."

"Was he ever sick? Miss a day now and then? Drug problems? Did he drink too much?"

"No, nothing," they both said. "Few hangovers now and then, but we probably caused most of those with our beer drinking. We are German, you know. Beer is our second bread."

"The report from SDPD, or actually from the Fire Department, a hazardous materials incident report, says you saw planes that appeared to crop dust."

"Half of San Diego saw them," Max said.

"At least, half of the people around Mission Valley."

"Did you see any markings on the planes? Numbers, symbols, anything meaningful?"

The two men looked at each other. Fritz said: "I think they had large black letter N or NT followed by a hyphen and some numbers and a red ball with a diagonal line through it."

"Can you remember the numbers?"

He did, and he told her. It was all the information they had. Various police agencies had made reports on the planes, but these were the first two witnesses who could offer details. It hadn't occurred to them to come forth with the information—they'd assumed the police already had the information.

As many witnesses explained it, the planes appeared to be systematically flying back and forth over Mission Valley in a grid pattern. San Diego Police and County Sheriffs had compiled a kind of map, of which she had a copy, showing similar activity on that day—that day only—in several canyon areas stretching from the coast inland about five miles, and from Del Mar in the North to Otay Mesa almost on the Mexican border.

"If we knew where those planes landed," Cleve said after they bade the two men goodbye and drove away. "Where they refueled, where they came from."

"This information might help," she said. "Can you call the local FAA office and scare someone up to investigate this?"

Cleve spent a half hour on the cell phone and used the car computer to FTP information. Meanwhile, Linsey drove to a shady place under a large tree in the Harbor district. She had another line of inquiry going—background on the Lima Voyager. Cell phone squeezed under one ear, she brought coffee and one donut each back from a bakery. Cleve groaned guiltily but grabbed his sugar donut. With the two of them talking simultaneously, the car was like a small office. The computer screen flickered with changing images, and the car printer chirred out little printouts on cash register style paper.

In the end, Cleve related: "There were probably as many of five nearly identical one-engine Cessnas in the air. The registration number clue is frustrating. None of the airports in the region has any planes with that prefix registration. In fact, the FAA guy I spoke with at Lindbergh Field guessed that we were dealing with a temporary registration that could have been issued anywhere in the region. The block of numbers used is probably fake. We don't know the fuel capacity, load condition, or any other information about those planes. All we do know is that they did not originate or land at any of the airfields like Brown, Montgomery, Lindbergh, or any of the military air stations. But they couldn't have flown too long without refueling."

Linsey related: "I found out *Lima Voyager* is under Liberian flag, and she's in limbo. She's in the middle of a bankruptcy case involving her owner and several creditors. The owner is a XenoX Shipping out of Seattle, and nobody there has answered a phone in months, so the creditors' lawyers tell me. It's a mess." As she spoke, she looked at the pile of printouts on the console tray between them. The car had a sort of miniature desk with a lamp over it, and the computer in a steel framed case that could swivel to face driver or passenger. As she ran through the litany of woes about the ship, her subconscious mind was on an divergent thought track. "I did manage to get a list of the captain and crew, with addresses and phone numbers, courtesy Louise Trost and the FBI. So we can start running through those one by one in hopes of finding the guys that were on the ship. There is no record of the cargo other than Cargo: Industrial, Cleared (meaning the Coast Guard has checked and found no bombs, drugs, parrots, or other no-nos), General. Cleve, what's that?"

"Huh?" His eyes roved to a pile of papers where she pointed.

They reached for a printout with a round dot in the logo. Cleve said: "Wow, Linsey, the logo. you're on to something."

She snatched it from him. "It's an attachment from one of the creditors up in Seattle, and it's an invoice by which XenoX is obligated to pay the sum of $1.3 million on demand in return for the cargo of Lima Voyager, again unspecified but mentioned in broad terms as Chemical, Cleared, Class [something or other, long numerical identifier]. Look at the logo. It's a circle with two Xs in it and the letters ENO through the middle. ENO is the smallest, the second X is larger, and the largest is the first X, whose northwest/southeast legs poke slightly through the circle." She grabbed a clipboard and drew the logo on a piece of scrap paper. "Maybe the planes had that XenoX logo on them in black, like it is here, and someone painted over it. Why wouldn't they just use the same dull white as the planes?"

Cleve shrugged: "Maybe fresh white paint would have stood out too much? Maybe red was all they had?"

"Good enough for me." She whipped out her phone and called Louise. "This is Lieutenant Linsey Simon of the Harbor Police in San Diego. I'm on an important investigation. Is there a XenoX company or corporation in San Diego County, or maybe in Riverside, Orange, or Imperial Counties?" Two minutes later, she had the information.

"Cleve, XenoX is a chemical company here in San Diego County. They are a subsidiary of Anaconda Chemicals, which also has plants here in San Diego and over in Brawley. Brawley is the home office."

After bouncing around through the bureaucracy of the huge corporation, Linsey finally got through to the Public Relations Officer in San Diego, a youngish man named Ricardo Chavez. "How can I help you, Lieutenant?" asked the ebullient Chavez.

"Mr. Chavez, I wonder if you can tell me—does your company own any aircraft?"

"Aircraft? Sure, lots of them."

"Lots?" Her heart nearly skipped a beat.

"You mean corporate jets, experimental craft, what?"

"Crop dusters?"

"No, none at all. We don't even make agricultural products here in SoCal. We do have a Chicago subsidiary that makes fertilizer boosters. I don't know how that's delivered, though. I think farmers use a tow spreader on the back of their tractor."

"You have any planes at all in the county?"

"Let me look through my fact book. Here. We have two corporate Lear Jets, one at Lindbergh and the other at LaGuardia in New York City. We lease those out to other companies because we're on sort of a tight budget. We have a rain making division outside Borrego—east of the Volcan Mountains."

"You do? Rain making?" Linsey gaped.

"Oh yes, it was one of Mr. Collwood's pet projects. He is quite an innovator. Actually, I think it's been shut down for some time because of tight funding."

"Mr. Collwood?"

"The CEO of Anaconda Chemicals. He's the big boss. Our CEO, Henry Morton, is under him. We are a wholly owned subsidiary. Say, Miss-?"

"Lieutenant Simon."

"Lieutenant, would you like to come tour our San Diego plant? It's right up here in lovely Mira Mesa."

"I may take you up on that soon. Thanks."

"What was that all about?" Cleve asked.

"Ready for a little overtime?"

He shrugged. "My wife has tuna casserole tonight. One of my favorites, but it gets better each time it's reheated."

"Good," she said. "Gimme your trash." She took the empty coffee containers and donut bags out to the trash can. "We are taking a drive out to Borrego, my friend. I'll explain as we go."

Chapter 40.

Jack came home just as Linsey was grabbing a quick shower. She dried herself behind the steamed up shower door while he came in to briefly whiz. "Had a late lunch with Dylan Matthews."

"Oh? How is he?"

"Terrible. Looks awful. But he ate a sandwich and sipped black coffee. I don't know if he slipped any schnapps in there."

"Cleve and I have to go out on an investigation."

"Oh? Anything good?"

"The fungus thing. Every cop in SoCal is working on the case."

"Dylan had a very interesting story to tell me about that."

She snapped the door open. Steam came out—he wasn't sure if it was hers or just vapor. "You are not working on a scoop, Jack." She saw the serious look on his face, and felt startled.

He shrugged. "Honey, time to put the cards on the table. It's as crazy a story as I've ever heard." He looked her over. "I wish we had time to reminisce a bit. You look ravishing when you are hot and pink and wet."

She stepped out on bare feet, stood on tiptoe to kiss him so he smelled her damp, fruity hair. "Sorry, darling, Cleve calls."

"Good old Cleve. Glad I am not a jealous type."

"Cleve is not my type, sweetheart. You know that. I like him as a partner, but that's where it ends." She embraced him for emphasis. Jack, who had never worried about Cleve, took the opportunity to French kiss with her for a few minutes and enjoy the firm but yielding curves of her athletic and loving body. When he found himself reaching deeper than time permitted, she laughed and tore away. "God, Jack, where do you get the goat hormones?" Laughing, wearing only a towel, she ran down the hall, and locked herself in the bedroom. "I better stay away from you, or my investigation and my career go down the drain."

He stood outside the door, leaning on one arm with his face close to the wood, and started telling her the story that Dylan had told him. After a few minutes, she unlocked the door quietly and let him in. She had changed into a kind of dark commando-style uniform that made her look like a female comic book hero, or so he had once told her. She sat on the bed and blew a wisp of blond hair from her face while putting on black combat boots. Jack told her the Robertson story and she listened intently.

Chapter 41.

The drive to Borrego was a pleasant one, and ran through a cross-section of San Diego County's varied landscape. Both Cleve and Linsey were long-time County residents with back-East roots. No matter how long she lived here, she thought, she'd never cease to marvel at the place with its various micro-climates—most areas containing high, arid mesas and sharply dropping, winding canyons filled with brush, palms, and trees—oak, eucalyptus, Manzanita, and many more species. Linsey told Cleve as much about the Anaconda matter as possible. She held back a bit, because rightfully she should first discuss it as a top secret matter with Louise. No matter what Jack wrote or to whom he blabbed, she must cover her behind. So she let herself enjoy the ride quietly. Both she and Cleve were tired after a long day's work, and he wasn't too talkative at the moment.

Horizontally, there are five major climate areas (and too many small ones to know them all). There is the arid coastal strip, about five to eight miles wide, with the mild, sunny weather for which the city is best known. Second are the inland valleys, like La Mesa and El Cajon, which are generally hotter and drier in the summer. The transition from coastal to inland, in the Mission Valley area, occurs around the 1,000 foot high Fortuna Mountains as Friars Road runs east from Mission Gorge and climbs to Golfcrest, followed by a sharp drop in to the slightly more extreme climate in Santee. Third is the mountain area, starting about an hour's drive from the coast. The mountain ranges generally run north-south. Fourth are the high deserts on the eastward slopes of the mountains, whose stony formations have that bluish tinge full of crazy shadows and twists. Further out are the low deserts, like Anza Borrego, sun-baked expanses of mostly flat, grainy sand like broken glass studded with well-spaced, hardy survivor plants. The whole region millions of years ago was the bottom of a shallow sea filled with ocean and lagoon-dwelling beasts from the dinosaur age. One of the richest areas for such fossils is right in the heart of Chula Vista, a coastal city between San Diego proper and the Mexican border.

    Vertically, there are also several climate zones. One begins with the valley floors and canyons, which tend to be overgrown and sometimes even lush. The

San Diego River runs the length of it, meandering west from the mountains around Julian near Borrego and Volcan Mountain to a smallish coastal delta emptying out of Mission Valley. Downtown San Diego lies on the coast, south of the coastal plains and marshes.

A second vertical tier might be the half-mile zone, like at Julian. This is a former mining town, now a touristic community about 2400 feet above sea level, whose major export are delicious home-grown and baked apple pies. Julian has four seasons, including colorful leaf changes in autumn and some snow in winter. Weather forecasts in San Diego in the winter inevitably mention 'snow levels,' and 2400 feet means snow in Julian. There is considerably more rain at this altitude than near sea level. The third and final tier is in the mountains up to just over a mile high. That includes Mount Palomar, Mount Laguna, and Mount Volcan. The climate at the one mile range is more like that of the Pacific Northwest rainforests—at least ten times that of the lowlands along the coast in a wet year.

Linsey drove a little over two hours to reach the desert area around Borrego Springs. She passed through Mission Gorge, past the rolling green hills of Mission Trails Park; crossed over the dark Fortunas with their covering of enormous caramel boulders, through the lowlands of Santee and Lakeside. She drove north on Japatul Road (Route 79), gradually climbing, and winding through tree-shaded mountain roads toward Julian. Beyond Julian, the landscape continued to be more forested, but tapering gradually into the bluish twisted fantasies of the high desert. In the next half hour or so, the twisting road took her down toward the low desert around Borrego with their sandy flatlands. Instead of going into Borrego Springs, however, she followed a complex map that Cleve managed to locate and download from the Web onto their computer display. She wished these cars had Global Positioning, but that was beyond the City's current broken budget. They followed a narrow private road about five miles through some mountain passes with oak forest on one side and steeply dropping granite and sandstone cliffs on the other. Thus, they came to a rise in the road overlooking a small valley. A gate-fence blocked the road. Signs warned No Trespassing, and Private Property, and XenoX RainMaker R&D, a subsidiary of Anaconda Chemicals, and finally: For Sale. In keeping with the For Sale theme, the buildings below looked deserted. Loose papers blew along the rusting metal fence posts. The place had a general air of abandonment and disrepair.

"So," Cleve said as they sat unable to drive further. The rusty chain and padlock on the gate looked terminal.

"Yup," she said. "There's the airstrip." They looked out over a square mile of green grass and grayish-brown scrub in a roughly square valley. At the far end were a number of sand-colored buildings with black numbers painted on white squares. The way the buildings were numbered, they had that flavor of huge corporation. Running north-south, perpendicular to the road, was a modest macadam strip. To their right, toward the southern rim of the valley, was a hangar. The hangar had a roof but no sides, and two one-engine Cessnas filled its interior. Parked outside, with their wheels chocked and their wings tied to ground anchors, three more Cessnas. All bore the round XenoX logo with protruding legs like Saturn's rings.

She walked up to the fence and put her chin against it, between hands gripping the wire." There are the planes."

Cleve looked through binoculars. "That's got to be them. Do you know—the logos are a nice dark green, and they are back on the planes, as are the real registration numbers. Take a look."

She accepted the binoculars and looked. She saw the green logos and the real registration numbers. "If those are the planes...yes, I think I see streaks that could be where they've been repainted on the tail wings and fuselage. That's a smoking gun. Now we have the problem that, if we've been spotted, whoever is down there can be destroying evidence."

"We should boogie on out of here," Cleve said.

"I agree. We'll come back with warrants and a search team."

"Did we say spotted?" Cleve said.

"Huh?"

"Look." Cleve pointed to a white SUV laboring along the inner perimeter along the fence line. "Security."

The vehicle looked dusty, and its windows seemed opaque in this light. There was a thick layer of dried mud all around the bottom. It labored to a halt in the middle of the road.

"Let me do the talking," Linsey said. "Stand your ground."

Two security guards in khaki got out. They carried side arms and spray, along with handcuffs and night sticks. Brown baseball caps and jet-black sunglasses completed the uniform. Their badges were stainless steel squares with Anaconda Plant Police engraved in curving letters top and bottom. In the middle was a logo, a green circle with Xx in the middle. "Can we help you?" the driver said in a curiously accented and flat tone. Both men seemed to be from some foreign country. They had dark gray skin, and moved somehow just a hint stiffly. There was a curious, very faint mothball smell about them.

"Can we help you?" the driver repeated as the two neared the fence. They didn't come too close, however.

"We're sort of lost," Linsey said cheerfully. "Cool place you have here."

"What are you looking for?" the passenger guard said.

"We are," she said thinking fast, "from Animal Control. We are monitoring endangered species. Today we are counting green condors. Have you seen many around?"

The two private cops looked at each other, then at Cleve and Linsey. "We do not recognize that species," the driver said.

"That's just it," Cleve injected. "They have become so rare that you don't see them around anymore. It's a tragedy."

"Are you taking photographs?" the passenger guard said.

"Heavens, no," Linsey said. "The flash would scare them. We just try to sneak up on them, where they may be nesting..."

The driver grew louder. "There are none here. You should leave the area before there is trouble."

"Absolutely," Cleve said. "They get nervous when there are more than one or two humans around. We're just on our way back to town, and we won't bother you again."

Linsey added, waving, as they backed away to their car. "Bye now. Sorry to have bothered you."

They glared for a minute, then returned to their SUV.

Cleve took the wheel, and Linsey quickly buckled up as he wheeled the car around. She took one more sweeping look before they left. Through the binoculars, she could see exhaust vents behind the wings and along the fuselage. Probably for dropping cloud-seeding chemicals, she thought as she lowered the binocs. On a small, rusting metal sign tucked out of sight among weeds near the gate, she noticed also the address of the parent company outside of Brawley. That might be a good place to visit sometime soon.

"Hey look," Cleve said as he slowly drove away from the gate. He pointed to a row of cars. "I wonder what those are."

"Privately owned cars," Linsey said. "Pull over a minute. Let's get the license plates."

"Yeah," Cleve said, "what I find unusual is that they are all covered with dust. Around San Diego, that happens to any car that sits for a day or two, because it's basically an arid climate and there is a lot of dust in the air. You can see those cars have sat for a few days, because there are dew streaks in the dust."

"Good observation," she said, writing models, makes, and registration numbers down. For good measure, she got out and copied down the Vehicle Identification Numbers or VINs on a metal strip under the right corner of each windshield on the driver side. "If nobody works here, and these look like expensive cars, they could only belong to the guards. But the guards would park inside the plant." There were easily a dozen dirty cars in a row. "They'd take their cars home each night. These cars have a lot of dirt on them as if they'd sat here a good while. "

"How many planes are there down on that strip?"

"I think I counted five. Maybe six." Cleve slapped his forehead. "The pilots! But why haven't they come back to get their cars? Why not drive home when the job was done?"

"Maybe they're dead," Linsey guessed wildly, almost petulantly. "What do I know? There is some huge mystery here, and we need to clear it up fast. Tipping our unknown opponent off by raiding this place isn't the best policy right now."

Louise Trost would have the best answer to that question once they got back to the office.

Chapter 42.

Collwood spoke briefly with Thomas Blake as the five surviving mercenaries assembled on Anaconda's private air strip at the plant complex near Brawley.

A white twin-engine turbofan jet sat on the runway with its engines whistling loudly during preflight tests by the pilot and co-pilot. On short hops like this from San Diego, a technician also flew along for checkout purposes. That left room for seven passengers and up a ton and a half of cargo, which in this case consisted primarily of weapons and ammunition as well as a hastily developed Swedish model military gas mask with NBC anti-fungal filters. Blake's men were about to start boarding the plane, which had a wingspan of just under 40 feet. Its two engines were pod-mounted tight against the fuselage just above the trailing edge of the wings. It was just under 50 feet long and had a maximum range of 2300 miles, traveling at up to 530 mph (Mach 0.81, 461 knots at 41,000 feet (12,496.8 meters).

Hot desert air whipped their short hair about and rattled their clothing. The early morning light was reddish, but turning lighter to reach its incandescent brilliance at noon. "You see now what you're up against," Collwood said, feeling a trace of frustration, yet also a certain satisfaction.

Blake, like his men, had lost any touch of skepticism or doubt. "Sir, I apologize for our shaky start. The good thing is, now my men and I are motivated like never before. We understand there is a deadly enemy out there, and we'll find him and neutralize him—including the thing that was my man Lo."

"Excellent. A lot is riding on this, and I'll pay you all double if the mission is a success."

Blake brightened. "That's ' another excellent motivator, Sir."

Collwood watched as they tromped off toward the waiting plane, a converted C-21 medical evac jet Anaconda used to ferry small cargoes among its plants, as well as brass. It was his West Coast jet, and he had another in New York City. There was no time now to have these men drive to San Diego—they must be flown in. A regular plant courier could drive their van into town. The van would be parked at Tidjeman's property for now.

Collwood watched the plane taxi down the runway and angle up for ascent. It lifted with a thunderous noise that rolled back and forth on the desert floor and among the reddish outcroppings on the horizon. Glinting in the sunlight atop a stream of exhaust, the jet banked to one side and streaked off to San Diego. Within a minute or two, its thunder grew distant and faded into silence.

Wind whipping in his ears, Collwood got into his golf cart and picked up the phone. He called the San Diego plant and ordered Martin Delavalle, the operations manager, to take charge as Acting CEO in Henry Morton's place. The first order from Collwood to his new Acting CEO was to announce that Henry Morton had to attend to a sudden death in his family and left for an unspecified city far away. That would stall off curiosity for quite a time, Collwood thought. He also ordered Delavalle to come to Brawley immediately to confer.

Within two hours, as Collwood sat lunching alone by his pool, he heard the return thunder of the jet. The C-21 had dropped off Blake and his men at a private hangar near Pacific Coast Highway in San Diego, and picked up Martin Delavalle. After a quick checkout and refueling, the plane returned to Anaconda Brawley Airport. Collwood, in his golf cart, met the plane on the runway. As always, Collwood shook hands with the pilots and technician. Delavalle had come alone, carrying a suitcase and wearing a light gray business suit. He was a balding man with a fringe of curly red air over his ears and around the back of his head. At 45, he had the rugged, lined features of the outdoorsman that he was, and sharply competitive—almost predatory—blue eyes. He had a strong grip. "How do you do, Mr. Collwood? Thanks very much for the honor."

"You're welcome," Collwood said heartily. Delavalle was his man in the San Diego organization. Morton had recruited him from an East Coast manufacturing firm, as he had all his staff, but this was the man Collwood had most courted over the past few years to obtain intelligence on Morton's operation. It never hurt to have eyes and ears on everyone's inside. Delavalle had another excellent use: he was Morton's liaison with the Mayor and the City Council. Collwood felt good about having this fellow in charge. "Come join me by the pool for a drink."

"Thanks."

They got into the golf cart, and Collwood drove it fast over the bumpy walkways among palm trees and flowering bushes. "As you know, things are tight these days, and I've let much of my staff here go. I hope you will help me turn it around."

"I think we can manage that," Delavalle said confidently.

"I'm glad to hear it. If you'd said 'I'll do my best, Sir' I would have packed you back on that plane and fired you."

Delavalle grinned with that hard, unfazed look. "I wouldn't have it any other way."

Collwood prepared drinks for them both, along with a tray of hors d'oeuvres from the outside refrigerator. "You're a tough man, Mr. Delavalle, and that's what I need now. Someone who doesn't flinch, no matter how ugly things get, and someone who gets the job done, no matter what, recognizing that the greater good is at stake. There are over 20,000 Anaconda Chemicals employees worldwide, and this is a company I need to turn around so they can all stay employed—which means 100,000 family members are affected by what you and I do here."

Collwood set a tray of luncheon meats, pumpernickel squares, crackers, dip, carrots, and the like between them on an umbrella-shaded glass table. The two men sat on either side of the table on dock chairs, sipping gin and tonics while the hot, dry desert wind gently raked their faces.

Carefully, revealing only as much as needed, but it was an awful lot, Collwood told Delavalle the story. "I took a huge gamble, sending a team of special operatives down into the Peruvian jungle. They retrieved for me about a hundred samples of various fungi from a location deep in the jungle, where I knew from an old World War II source these were located. Circumventing a bunch of useless red tape, bribes, and bureaucratic meddling, I had the samples brought into the country by cargo ship. Unfortunately, events took a bad turn. Something in that shipment took on a life of its own and has been killing people, including the ship's captain. I have people on the ground in San Diego as we speak, finding the samples and tracking down whoever stole them. I can also tell you that I've sent back my original insertion team to get more samples—and to handle them with far greater care."

Delavalle looked astonished. "How will you handle the samples once you get them?"

Collwood pointed to the large, weather-beaten buildings beyond his private enclosure. "I have state of the art assay facilities in there. We can rapidly micro-test for thousands of chemical combinations with our automated facility." He explained that he had thousands of assay or test trays ready for any desired test. The trays contained thousands of different combinations of organic (carbon-based) and inorganic (every other element) molecules. Each unique combo or sample had a minute amount in an inert jelly base sitting at the bottom of a tiny hole in the tray. If one wanted to test substance X, one ground up substance X into a fine powder, mixed it with purified and totally neutral water—in fact, Collwood's laboratory created its own water by bringing vapor forms of oxygen and hydrogen together under very controlled conditions to prevent explosion. One added a substance called reactin that would respond if any chemical combination turned out positive. The substance X/reactin/water solution then got injected into the thousands of test holes in the trays by a row of injection needles poised over the tray as the tray rolled through an injection chamber. It remained then to run the trays through a series of ultraviolet chambers. If a particular combination had any sort of interesting response, the ultraviolet would show a glow where the reactin was interacting with the substance. In this way, Anaconda Chemicals could do thousands of tests in a day that would previously have taken months.

Delavalle nodded with composure. "Biochem hasn't been my strong suit over the years, but I understand what you're saying."

Collwood said: "I have plenty of people who understand biochem. I need a man who can lead this company during a time of crisis without falling apart. I think you're that man."

"I believe that I am."

"I can promise you one thing," Collwood said. "Stick by me through thick and thin, and you'll come out of this a very wealthy man. Aside from company stock, you'll be cash rich—a multimillionaire. The sky's the limit."

"I am with you through thick and thin. Who do we kill first?"

"I have a team on the ground for that, Delavalle. I don't want you getting your hands dirty. I need you to understand what is going on so you don't get rattled."

Delavalle left within the hour on the jet.

Collwood called Syd Appelbaum in L.A., using an encrypted line. "Uncle Syd, I need you to turn around that insertion team and get them back into the jungle. We've got to do the exercise all over again, but this time we'll fly the material out."

"No problem," said Appelbaum, a spry man of 70 who had run a successful law firm to the stars and wealthy for decades and then retired to do, as he put it, 'more exciting things.' "I can arrange for a legitimate shipment of antibiotics and such to an orphanage near Cuzco, and they'll bring out test samples. You know, sick children, blood work, needs to be tested in the U.S.A. It makes Customs inspectors and other uniformed filters go mooshy in the soul, just thinking of all that patriotic singsong. We'll get your mushrooms in without a problem."

"Thanks, Uncle Syd, you are a gem."

"No problem, kid. The old man wouldn't want me to do anything other." Syd and Lee Collwood's father had been friends in the Army in their youth—two young captains assigned to desk jobs, processing JAG paperwork for a large stateside command—and Syd had been the old man's chief legal beagle for decades. They were like family.

No sooner had he rung off with Syd, than another call came in on the crypto line—from Martin Delavalle, who had just landed in San Diego and hadn't even left the airport. "In fact," Delavalle said, "I'm in the jet again, calling via scrambler. You have a problem downtown, pal."

"What is it?"

"There is a Federal task force that's starting to look at you. Check this out, for starters."

As Collwood waited impatiently and with growing consternation, he looked at the computer screen at his side. There was a black and white, somewhat grainy snapshot of two persons looking through a fence. "What is this?"

"Those are two cops from San Diego, being challenged by guards at the XenoX plant yesterday."

"So? That plant's been out of commission almost a year."

"That's what you think. Look at this." The image changed, showing a patrol vehicle and two men standing outside of it.

"Yes? What's the problem?"

"We changed private security firms months ago because we couldn't afford to put Anaconda guards at union pay out there."

"I don't believe it."

"I checked it out just now. Someone canceled the contract Morton's people had set up with a private firm for cheaper rent-a-cops. They have fake Anaconda people driving the trucks."

"Who is doing this, dammit?"

"The name on record is a Captain Tidjeman, supposedly acting on behalf of Henry Morton. Morton has left town, I hear."

"What's going on at my Volcan plant?"

"I assumed you knew, because I sure don't."

"So who are these cops?"

"Lieutenant Linsey Simon and Agent Cleveland Bartlett, both of the Harbor Police, but they've been attached temporarily to a Federal anti-terror task force run by a Louise Trost."

"Harbor Police!" Collwood said. "It's starting to make a little sense now. The Lima Voyager is in their jurisdiction, even though the civilian dock is in the middle of Navy property. So she must have gotten suspicious and has been investigating—and there is no telling how close she is getting to me, or to you, now that you're taking Morton's place."

"What aren't you telling me, Collwood?"

"I'll be in San Diego tomorrow," Collwood ad libed. "We can talk then. In the meantime, get on this. See if you can stop her investigation, and go check out the Volcan plant and let me know what is going on there."

"I'm not going in there alone."

"I'll send some heat," Collwood said. He considered having Delavalle take some plant security people from the Mira Mesa plant, but thought better of it. Blake would me more discreet. "Hang on." He rang off, got Thomas Blake on the phone, and arranged to have three of Blake's team meet Delavalle at the Volcan plant gate where the two cops had been photographed by a surveillance camera yesterday.

Delavalle hung up the phone and sat back in the cool dark of his office in Mira Mesa. The venetian blinds were shuttered, but if he opened them, he'd be looking over the roofs of Anaconda Chemicals' San Diego operation. Around the office, he had photographs of Henry Morton's wife and family smiling at him from all sides. Fortunately, they were in Kansas somewhere, and it would be a while before the separated wife would start inquiring after her husband. As long as the monthly support checks kept flowing eastward from Morton's bank account, that would be in order—Delavalle had seen to that.

Now he had the larger problem. He didn't trust Collwood for an instant. The man had been playing him for years. Even Morton had advised Delavalle to be careful, given Collwood's reputation. The question now was—how to maximize the opportunity to milk Collwood and leave with a bundle, before the situation started to stink so badly that the Feds came in. He knew also that Collwood would take any opportunity to hang him out to dry if it meant saving his own neck. It was tempting to just walk out of here and not look back. But the lure of millions Collwood had promised was too strong.

Collwood phoned his old Republican Party buddy. "Danny? It's Lee Collwood."

"Oh, hi, Lee, how are you doing?" They made friendly chitchat for a few minutes, catching up on the past few months since they'd golfed together. After promises to renew their game, Collwood explained: "Got a situation here in San Diego. It's about the Anaconda Chemicals plant at Volcan Mountain. You know, we've been good to you over in your district—"

"Oh I know you have, Lee, I know you have."

"—I need you to delay a loose cannon down in San Diego from snooping on that government contract we set up for the biological warfare deterrent R&D."

"Oh really? What's going on?"

"Seems that a couple of Harbor Police cops have stuck their noses in something they shouldn't. I don't know how we breached our security. We were bringing in a shipment of fungus from South America. Looks like the stuff vanished off the dock."

"No!"

"Yeah, but I have it all under control. I have a private team tracking it down, to keep everything quiet and under wraps."

"Is there any danger?"

"Nah. None whatsoever. I think what happened is that the captain and a few of the crew were smuggling illegal drugs, and they took my mushroom samples along with their dope. The mushrooms are harmless until we genetically engineer them."

"Glad to hear it." Metrick was swallowing the story—hook, line, and sinker. Metrick said: "What do you need me to do?"

Last time he'd asked Metrick for a favor, he'd sent him a gift of $100,000 through a third party by way of a campaign donation. "Danny, it's important, and I will double the support," Collwood signaled—carefully, in case they were being wiretapped. One never knew, even though Collwood paid top dollar to keep his electronic and digital net swept clean by the remote network managers in Mira Mesa.

"I understand, Lee, and your understanding is always so very deeply appreciated."

"I'm always profoundly touched and moved when I am able to support your cause."

"What can I do for you, Lee?"

"I'd appreciate if you can step in and slow down this Louise Trost who is the task force supervisor of this female harbor cop. They are about to start investigating my Volcan Mountain plant, which has been out of operation for almost a year, and we cannot afford to have a messy, stupid investigation going on that hits the papers and exposes resources and ultimately hampers or cripples our national security effort."

"I buy you a little time, Lee. That's the best I can do."

"That will help greatly. Hey, golf soon?"

"You got it. God bless now."

"God bless you and your good works," Collwood said.

Chapter 43.

Linsey and Cleve sat with Louise Trost in her office downtown at ten p.m. that night. All three were tired. Linsey shared Jack's Robertson story, and Louise said: "Write it up. Get all the details and pass them along to me. I think Mr. Collwood is getting deeper into kimchee as the hours pass."

Cleve yawned, and the two women laughed. "Time to go home and get some sleep?" Linsey said to Cleve, as much a suggestion as a question. Cleve nodded. "I don't think we can get much more done today. It's been a full day and a half."

"Well done!" Louise said told Linsey, while shaking Cleve's hand. We're onto Collwood but it's too early to tip our hand. We don't know who the real enemy is, if there is an enemy, and what we need now is intelligence." She picked up the phone. "Patch me through to" [she mumbled something and hung up]. She folded her hands on the desk and said: "I've been on the phone with the Governor's office and also the Director of National Intelligence or DNI, among other people. That's my job—pulling resources together seamlessly to meet any eventuality in the area of counter-terrorism, and secondarily to direct resources to other agencies for non-counter-terrorism related situations. This is, as far as I am concerned, still a counter-terrorism situation. However, based on some of the characteristics—cargo ship from South America, empty cargo holds, disappeared captain and crew, etc—it could also be drug related. Thus, I'm going to call upon our friends in the Border Patrol and the Drug Enforcement Agency to call upon their resources, and there will be a plane in the air within the hour to start infrared and microwave echo reconnaissance. We'll want a closer look at all of Anaconda's facilities, particularly the ones at Volcan Mountain and in Brawley. I'm talking warrants, searches, the whole nine yards."

"How long before we know anything?"

"Noon tomorrow."

Linsey and Cleve looked startled. "How is that possible?"

Louise smiled. "I have a sneaking suspicion there's going to be so much pressure up the pipe that we'll have U.S. Air Force spy planes in the air within the hour. They'll map the place inch by inch in the dark and also in the morning light.

Signal goes back to an analysis station, probably at Langley, Virginia, or NSA headquarters, and I'll have printouts of maps, photos, and analysis text from experts—noon tomorrow."

"That's effin'-A," Cleve said.

"You got that effin' right," Louise told Cleve in her grandmotherly fashion. "Well, you each have a spouse waiting up. What's on the agenda for tomorrow, Linsey?"

"I'd like to get Cleve assigned to work with me for at least a week, if that's possible."

"I'm sure it is. I can pull any resources I need, and if you say you need him, you've got him."

"And," Linsey said, "I have a list of the crew, so we should put teams together to find the men and interview them. I'd say two people for each crew, so about sixty people should do it."

Louise nodded. "I'll see what I can scrape together. I guess I don't go home tonight, but then so don't a lot of other people."

Linsey said: "Someone will need to talk with the top brass at Anaconda. I understand there is a Mr. Collwood who owns the company, and a Mr. Morton who runs the San Diego show."

"I'm a little leery of that. Let's see what the reconnaissance tells us. If his planes have been crop dusting San Diego with yellow seeds or pods or whatever, and at least one person has died, then I'd say we had better be careful what we say to whom. Chances are, if they are his planes, Mr. Collwood knows something about it—or can point us to the person who might."

"One other thing," Linsey said as she shuffled through the handful of quickly yellowing printouts from that afternoon. "We can be reasonably certain that there is a connection between the Lima Voyager and Mr. Collwood's company. What that connection is, I don't know yet."

As they got up to leave, Louise handed Linsey a printout. "That's a report I requested from the Department of Motor Vehicles while we were talking. They ran it on an emergency basis through the night duty sergeant at the County Marshal's Office. Names, addresses, and phone numbers of the owners of those vehicles you saw parked near Volcan Mountain."

"Thanks," Linsey said. One of the names immediately caught her eye. It was that of Ernie Walesky, a man whose brother Joe worked for the Harbor Police. Sometimes San Diego was still such a small town, even though it was America's sixth or seventh major city. Ernie Walesky might be a good guy of whom to start asking questions tomorrow.

That night, as they lay in bed reading, Jack remarked: "I haven't seen you this tense in quite a while. We need a vacation together, you and I."

"I'm sorry, honey. My head is whirling like a blender."

"You sure you haven't inhaled some of those spores?"

"What do you know about spores, Jack?" She turned and leaned on one pajama-clad elbow, facing him. He seemed to use his fat anthology of Jack Finney novels like a rampart to hide behind. "Well, honey, the entire county is covered by those little yellow fungi. I have two rivals at our newspaper alone, not to mention every television and radio news desk in town, trying to put together a story. We have a dead roofer, a lot of yellow fungi, and the nagging question of those supposed crop dusting planes. Frankly, it stinks."

She had a horrible thought. "You're going to be really mad at me if you get scooped, aren't you?"

He laid his book down on his washboard and folded his arms. "I'm going to go nuclear, yes."

She thought about it. "The last thing I'd want to do is curtail your curiosity and ambition."

"Well said. Or my innate intelligence, considerable analytical skills, and drive to serve truth, justice, and the American way of life."

"Or your ability to shovel manure with the best of them."

"I rest my case. I am a misunderstood genius."

She whacked him with her pillow. "All right, Jack. Let's make a deal."

He dropped his show and sat in eager anticipation. "Yes?"

"Historic events require a reporter with the inside scoop."

"An embedded journalist, as it were."

"Right, like in the recent war. The exception is that, if you report anything, your butt will sit in a Federal prison."

"I'll keep mouth shut, nose clean, but you'll feed me truffles."

"Something like that. I'll take you along on some of my investigations. You and Cleve can protect me."

"Deal." He hugged her and slid close. He was breathing hard and emitting fever-like body heat over her side of the bed. It was catching—she responded with similar symptoms.

Chapter 44.

Linsey kissed Jack hurriedly goodbye in the morning as he sat having his morning coffee and reading his e-mail. "I'll call you if anything exciting seems to be breaking."

"I need a total rundown to start a journal," he called after her.

"Okay—tonight!"

Cleve waited at the curb in the unmarked car. He wore jeans, combat boots, a rugged-weave black sweater over a white shirt. "No suit today?" she asked while buckling in as he pulled into traffic.

"Nope. I see dirty work ahead. I won't ruin my good suit."

"Smart man."

"Where to?"

"Let's start with the Lima Voyager today. I want to check the visitor logs for the past week. I'm sure it's been covered, but I want to see if Mr. Collwood and Mr. Morton have been down to see their cargo."

They stopped at the main U.S. Navy gate, and with a phone call to Louise's office and an admiral's office, Linsey got to check both the manual, paper logs and the digitized, on-network lists of people who had shown I.D. It was a side effect of the age of terror—everyone's comings and goings seemed to be increasingly under scrutiny.

"Here it is," Cleve said. He loomed over a service counter with loose-leaf binders stacked all around him. "Three days ago, Collwood and Morton came through here with several assistants. They stayed a little over two hours and then left."

Linsey checked the verifying initials. The young Navy petty officer who had checked them in and out remembered them. She was an attractive blonde woman with blue eyes and a slight Heartland drawl, wearing her white pants uniform and green web gear including a holstered automatic, a whistle, and various belt kits. On her left upper arm was a large black leather sleeve with an American flag and the words Security Police. "I remember those guys," she said. "They were all excited, almost rude, the way they rushed in and rushed out. I noticed it because they seemed so upset. Especially the tall, handsome one with the cold fish eyes. I think that's Collwood."

"Did you overhear any of their conversation?" Cleve asked.

The petty officer shook her head.

"Thanks. You've been a great help," Linsey said. Leaving the young woman looking pleased, they returned to the car.

"We're slowly tying the threads together," Cleve said, "and we still have no idea what the big picture is."

"Right," Linsey said. "I'll drive. Let's go see Ernie Walesky. He crewed on this last trip, and I know his brother Joe."

As she drove to the Linda Vista section of town, Linsey called Harbor Police dispatch and had herself patched through to Joe Walesky, who happened to be working the boat channel off the old Naval Training Center that morning. "Joe?"

"Linsey? What on earth—I haven't spoken with you in over a year. How are you?"

"Good, Joe. How are you? Hey listen, I'm working something, and your brother Ernie's name has come up. Nothing big, just a friend of a friend. I'm wondering if you've seen Ernie."

"Not the past few days. I understand he's been missing a bit."

"Missing?"

" Ernie is fond of the bottle. Meek as a lamb, even when drunk, but hard to take. He and Nellie have had it out many times. Usually, when he comes back from a long sea voyage, he goes off on a bender for a few days, gets it out of his system, goes home to Nellie, takes a week to recover. Is he in a jam?"

"I don't know. His car is sitting abandoned near Volcan Mountain. I'm going to interview his wife—Nellie?"

"My sister in law. Holy Jeez, Linsey, maybe I should take the day off and see what's what."

"Why don't you wait until I talk with Nellie?"

"You got me worried now. That's my brother."

"I understand. I didn't call to get you alarmed, Joe. I'm sorry. Does he by any chance fly planes too?"

"Oh yeah. Ever since we were kids. Me, I get air sick. Ernie can handle planes the way a country boy handles horses."

"Does he ever do jobs for people as a pilot?"

"Sometimes. Don't tell me he's flying drugs or something."

"No. That's not even up for discussion. Hey, while I have you, do you know anything about Anaconda Chemicals?"

"Who?"

"Never heard of them?"

"Nope."

"Never mind. I'll call you after I see Nellie."

As she had expected, by the time Linsey got to Nellie, Joe had already called. It worked that way in large, close-knit families. It didn't bother her. She found the small house on a side street in a quiet neighborhood. Linda Vista had some rough spots, but this one was good. Nellie was a rough-hewn but salt of the earth gray-haired grandma, long-ago probably a blonde surfer or beach bunny from the seams in her face. Shame what the sun did to its worshipers.

Nellie was a housewife, an old fashioned stay at home mom. She had a daughter, Maribel, 10, and a slightly younger male cousin named Jimmy Mendez on the premises. Nellie had Linsey and Cleve sit out on the back patio, in the breezy sunshine but under an outdoor café style umbrella. Moments later, she appeared with a tray of iced tea for three. All the while, her hands seemed to shake, and she looked terribly nervous.

After pleasantries, Linsey honed in on the visit's purpose. "Have you heard from your husband yet, Mrs. Walesky."

"Why yes, Ernie called and said he'd be home any time now. That was two days ago—the time seems to be stretching."

"Interesting." Linsey told her about the abandoned car at Volcan, without mentioning the rest of the story. "I'd say the car has been there a number of days, judging from the amount of dirt on it. So why would your husband call you when he's not close to his car. We're Americans, after all. The car is to us what the buffalo was to the Indians."

"You don't know Ernie. He could be holed up somewhere three or four days at a poker game, as long as he's got whiskey and beer going down."

"Must be very frustrating."

"You get used to it. He's a good provider. Been kind to Maribel. She loves him dearly. It would tear her up if anything happened to him."

"Mrs. Walesky, how long was Ernie at sea this last time?"

The haggard woman thought about it for a minute. "I'd say three weeks, maybe, he's been gone from here. Not a long time by merchant sailor standard—much worse back in Navy days."

"Joe, from the Harbor Police, says Ernie is a pilot."

"Oh yes, he loves planes. Makes extra money flying things for people, or just flying people."

"Do you have any idea where he might be right now?" Linsey began to feel a frustrated sense of going in circles. The woman seemed sincere and probably wasn't covering up for any illegal drug activities. It seemed like a very safe, pleasant middle class home. Something was troubling Nellie, however. Linsey sensed it, and was determined to work at the edges of it until Nellie spilled the beans. Cleve sat quietly by, sipping his tea.

The woman shook her head, and they sat in silence for a moment. "You ain't asked about the other thing, have you? Maybe you don't know."

"Know what?"

Nellie rolled her eyes toward the children playing quietly in a far corner of the yard. "The boy, Jimmy, he's staying with us. His dad was on the same ship with Ernie."

"Really?" Blood rushed in Linsey's ears. Alarm bells rang.

The woman's eyes had a tragic cast. "Poor little fellow. He was always such a strong, regular kid. All of a sudden he got hysterical, saying his mom and dad took off on him."

"Oh? We seem to have a lot of missing persons here."

"I'm not sure he means they are missing."

"What does he mean?"

"He has some fantastic story that landed him in the psychiatric ward at Children's Hospital before they farmed him out to me. Claims his dad returned but wasn't his dad, and then his mom stopped being his mom."

"Can I talk with the boy?"

She shrugged. "Sure," she said, slurring her Ss because she was missing a couple of crucial teeth. "Jimmy!" she called.

The boy came running. "Yes?"

"This police detective lady wants to talk with you."

Jimmy stood panting. "Yes?"

He seemed like a very sharp little guy, Linsey thought. "Jimmy, what's been going on in your life?"

"If I tell you, you won't believe me. Nobody does."

"Jimmy, I'm not here to judge. I'm here to ask questions."

He told her his story. The girl, Maribel, who was slightly taller, stood behind him and wrapped her arms around him.

Linsey let him tell his story, and was aghast at the implication that—she had to fight herself to even formulate the thought—some nonhuman life form had taken over Jimmy's parents—if one took the boy's story literally. Of course there were bound to be psychological explanations—transference, sublimation, whatever—but one thing he mentioned made Linsey's blood run cold. Very innocently and truthfully, the child described a strong fungal odor or mushroom smell. She remembered the odor around the harbor pilot's house. The ship Lima Voyager seemed to be at the heart of a dark mystery whose tentacles kept spreading.

"So what do you think?" Jimmy asked challengingly.

"I am starting to think there is a lot of truth in your story."

Instantly, the boy became a pleading child. "Can you help me find my mommy and daddy?"

"I'll do what I can," Linsey said. She didn't feel very positive about the prospects. "Let's keep in touch, okay?" She rose. Nellie extended her hand. They all shook hands and Linsey left each of them—Nellie, Maribel, and Jimmy—a copy of her business card.

As they spoke, there was a knock at the door. Maribel ran to answer. A tall, attractive young woman in high heels and red business outfit stood twirling her sunglasses in one hand and holding a thick leather portfolio under her other arm. A long, thin black leather purse was tucked under the portfolio arm. "May I come in?"

"It's Annette!" Maribel yelled.

Jimmy's face went through a range of contortions, from pleasure to fear.

"Don't worry, Jimmy, I didn't come to take you back to Children's Hospital. I just came to say hello—see how you are."

"I'm fine," Jimmy said, ready to fight or flee. But he stayed sitting on the couch. He picked up a rubber softball and squeezed it so that Linsey thought it must break.

Linsey rose and shook hands with the elegant woman. "I'm Annette Lewis, Jimmy's social worker."

"Linsey Simon. I'm a police lieutenant."

"Investigating the situation that brought Jimmy here?"

"Pretty much, yes. Just following up, mostly, because I don't have very much to work on yet."

"I drive by Jimmy's house every day, and there is nobody home. I assume there is a missing persons case in progress?"

"We're doing the best we can." Linsey noticed Cleve looked a bit put off, and frowned at him to keep his cool.

"Of course you are. I apologize for interrupting. May I ask Jimmy a few questions?"

"Go ahead. We were just finishing up. I'd be interested to hear what he tells you."

Annette turned her attention to Jimmy. "So, big guy. How's the chow here? Getting your three hots and a cot?"

Jimmy grinned. "You're weird, Annette."

"Ex-Army officer. Sorry." Annette grinned and sat next to him. She flipped open her portfolio and started writing with a gold pen. She had perfectly shaped, ornately decorated fingernails that made Linsey wish she could afford to dress like that. Not in police work, unless maybe undercover. "Jimmy, are you still having nightmares?"

A tear ran down his cheek. "Yes."

"Miss your mom, don'tcha?"

He nodded.

Linsey felt a bit choked up, and Cleve looked as if he'd swallowed a golf ball—his eyes were bulging.

"Tell me about the nightmares."

"It's dark" (sniff) "and I'm walking down this tunnel" (wiping eyes with sleeve) "and" (quaver) "I hear my mom's voice but" (sniff) "when I get to the room at the end of the hall, there is something else in the bed."

Maribel handed him a box of tissues, and sat with her arm around him. Jimmy's shoulders slumped as he dabbed his nose. "My mom is gone, and there is some kind of fake in the bed. Dad is there, but he is fake too."

"What are they doing?" Annette said.

"They are lying here. Spooning."

"Are they dressed?"

"Yes."

"What else?"

"He has his head turned down like he's kissing her from behind, under the ear, here—" He put his finger on his neck.

"The neck," Annette said.

The jugular vein, Linsey thought.

Jimmy said: "There is a shiny black tube sticking out of his mouth and it goes into her neck. He's not my dad but some imitation and he's sucking the life out of her, but she's not my mom, she's some phony imitation."

He broke down sobbing, and couldn't speak anymore. Linsey and Cleve rose. Linsey said: "I'd like to give you a call, Annette, if you don't mind."

"Sure," Annette said, extending a business card with two immaculately groomed fingers. "I'll stay with him a while and see that he feels more comfortable."

Linsey and Cleve were both glad to leave. Linsey drove.

Cleve said: "The kid could be stark raving nuts."

"I don't think so."

"I don't think so either," Cleve admitted. "Up to the black tube part, anyway."

Linsey said: "The child could be imagining things to cover up something really horrible that may have happened."

"Like someone broke in and murdered his parents?"

"Yes, that kind of thing. Something like that." Rape, or some other form of violation.

"That's the social worker's job, to help him figure out what's wrong, or get him to a shrink for therapy."

Linsey's mind went back to mushrooms: "I think it's time we start assuming the worst."

"Which is?"

"Some kind of virus, some kind of disease, maybe even a form of mass hysteria is at work. Maybe the zillions of tiny yellow mushrooms don't mean a thing, or maybe it's a terrorist plot, or even the end of the world. Who the hell knows."

As they drove back through the suburbs to their downtown office with Louise Trost, they noticed suddenly that the yellow mushrooms had begun to disappear. Where they had formed a carpet in some places, they were now hard to locate.

However, what they began to notice was that there seemed to be large mushrooms everywhere. They first noticed it when they were stopped at the red light at Genesee and Balboa. On two of the corners, where cultivated plants grew, erect cap mushrooms reared up inches tall.

"I've never seen them this large," Cleve whispered.

"And they look strong," Linsey said, "healthy."

The phenomenon was not going unnoticed on the radio. Every news station had some mycology expert on. The fungus gurus cited global warming, climate change, exceptional marine layers and moisture, for the robust mushroom crop.

Cap mushrooms reared up in bunches. On lawns, flat mushrooms grew in colonies of a dozen or more. Trees began to show shelf or bracket mushrooms at their bases. It was a subtle thing at first, but now it was becoming noticeable.

According to the news, twenty persons had now died from the yellow mushroom dust in the air, but the yellow mushrooms had begun to disappear. In their place, thousands and millions of mushrooms were cropping up in rich yields all over town.

Chapter 45.

Joe Walesky was standing at a hot dog stand near the Convention Center. His Harbor Police cruiser sat parked at headquarters nearby. He was in uniform, armed, and taking a much deserved lunch break. He'd written 30 tickets, made three arrests, written six reports, and issued 20 warnings including several heated verbal exchanges with inebriated tourists who couldn't hear a kindly reproach but had to make a scene. He still had ten reports to write, during lunch break.

Joe was waiting behind a few tourists in the hot sun to order a ballpark frank and a huge-gulp root beer. He was having a fairly slow day, and felt relaxed. In his mind was a whirl of thoughts including family matters. His brother Ernie was still missing, although he'd phoned Nellie and told her he had some kind of flying job to bring in a little extra money. Ernie usually went on a bender for a few days after each cruise on a merchant ship, so this actually seemed more positive than usual—taking a small aircraft piloting job rather than winding up drunk in some barrio tavern and getting rolled. Joe had picked him up more than once and taken him home, snoring and with a black eye. This time, something was different, and Joe had a twinge of worry. Something was different, but that didn't mean things were necessarily okay. He wondered if Ernie had gambled all this money away and was trying to make it up by running drugs in from Mexico, or some other dumb scheme.

Joe had been with the force for nearly 15 years and had seen San Diego's downtown area blossom. When Joe and Ernie were kids in National City, San Diego had been in its last long, slumbering decades as a Navy town. One could still, in the late 1900s, drive north along Pacific Highway. Passing the Navy yard at 32nd Street, one would come through the city's civilian rail yards, freight yards, factories, and warehouses before entering the modest and quiet downtown area around lower Broadway. Today, the freight areas were mostly gone—a few old brick walls with fading signs kept for historical purposes, absorbed into new structures like Petco Park. The Convention Center dwarfed the dockside west of the Gaslamp Quarter. A small, futuristic city of high-rise condos, hotels, and office buildings had sprung up. In any nook where they could be fitted were small parks with fountains and shady walks. The red trolley had two rail lines going through here, with stations every few blocks. The huge hotels tied in with the Convention Center had vast, fanciful lobbies. A new building style had emerged—Joe liked to call it Comic Book Gothic. Others might call it neo-Victorian Fantasy, playing off the Victorian era flavor of the Gaslamp Quarter. The lobby reception desk dwarfed its uniformed concierge and clerks. Above them towered an odd mix of neo-pastoral wall murals showing rural scenes from Louis XIV's France (maybe). On either end of the desk were enormous bracket-shaped lanterns taller than a man and curving from desk to ceiling like the rear ends of large sailing ships. These lanterns consisted of a wrought iron grid with panes of soft yellowish glass like soapstone inset. The building style was no longer functional, like that of the 1900s, but fanciful. A tall building might have one corner rise straight vertically, and another sloping downward like the edge of a pyramid, or upward and outward in defiance of gravity. Some buildings rose straight up, but had high levels sticking out like hat brims, suggesting futuristic landing pads or bridges to other buildings. To Joe—who liked to read old comic books and moldering SF books, which he'd collected all his life for considerable side money—it was the future foreseen in the 1930s, 40s, 50s, finally arriving after the ugly decades of the Cold War and culminating in the disasters around the turn of the century.

Joe got his ballpark wiener and his tall root beer, sauntered over to a free spot at a little concrete table and bench, and started eating in the deep shade of an oak tree. He enjoyed the cool breeze that smelled of the sea and of jasmine. His phone chirped, and he answered. "Yeah?"

"Joe, it's Ernie."

"Ernie, how are you, man. Are you sober?"

"I'm sober. I need to see you."

"Sure. I'm having lunch. Where are you?"

"Lima Voyager."

"The ship?"

"Yes."

"I'll eat my hot dog and come over. You sure you're okay?"

"I will wait."

Joe sighed. He was glad to hear from his brother, although Ernie sounded kind of funny, as if he had a very dry throat or something. Joe hurried through his lunch. He rose, tossed his trash in a container, wiped his hands and tossed the paper napkin after the rest, and headed over to his car. The reports would have to wait, which meant he'd probably be doing overtime unless he could check in early if things stayed slow.

It was a short drive, about two miles, through the familiar gate manned by sailors and Marines at 32nd Street. Joe drove slowly down the gravel street that stretched between high fences. With his customary policeman's eye, he observed all around him. It was an instinctive scanning to look for people or things out of whack. It might be a civilian who looked rumpled and out of place, a sailor wavering along drunk, a workman who looked like he'd stolen something and had that tight, furtive walk. It could be a lot of things and you didn't know what they were until they floated into your field of vision—if you stayed alert and open to the unusual that grew out of the usual. Fifteen years had given Joe Walesky a finely honed sense for the unusual. Nobody could stay a cop that long without developing a kind of sixth sense for trouble.

Everything here looked so normal and quiet that it positively spooked Joe. Nothing in the world could be this normal. There had to be something unusual here. Maybe its name was Ernie. That might explain his feeling of apprehension. He tried to relax a bit. Being uptight was a perfect way to tighten up the sphincter on that unusualness-lens in a cop's eye.

He pulled to a stop at the dock and got out. The freighter's steel hull loomed over him. "Ernie?" he called out.

Silence. Wind tattered in his ears. Gulls sailed through the air over the water several hundred feet away. Not a bird sat on this dock anywhere. Joe sniffed. What was that smell?

"Joe," said a voice at the rail of the ship.

Joe saw his brother. "Hey, Ernie. What's up with you?"

Ernie wore a baseball cap and sunglasses. He wore a khaki work suit like a gardener, and heavy gloves. "Come on up, Joe."

Joe had misgivings, but started up the metal gangway that led t the main deck, a climb of about thirty feet over a nasty drop into blackish water between ship and dock. He guided himself up along a chain strung over metal posts for that purpose.

Another figure appeared beside Ernie—another heavily clad man with sunglasses and baseball cap.

"Who's your friend?" Joe asked, holding the chain with his left hand, and instinctively keeping his other hand near his service handgun.

"Meet Lo," Ernie said.

"Hello," said Lo.

"Hello," said Joe.

As he neared the deck, Ernie reached out a gloved hand as if to help him. Joe reached for the hand and felt Ernie pulling him aboard. The hand felt a little funny, as though something came loose as Joe's weight tugged at it—several fingers, it felt like, but Joe dismissed the thought as absurd. At the same time, Lo stepped forth and extended both hands as if to help. Joe thought this was a bit strange as he swung onto the deck. "So, guys," Joe started to say. Both men stepped close, suddenly, so their faces were near Joe's. Black air streamed from their mouths.

Joe felt very distant, as if he were just going to sleep, and the two men grabbed him and pulled him back on board as he started to topple over backwards over that long drop into the cold water. As Joe fell asleep, he felt Lo carrying him like a mannequin toward the dark heart of the ship.

The things that happened deep in the bowels of the ship were strange and pleasant. Ernie came to say goodbye—just a brief exchange of looks, nothing said—and went away. Lo wrapped his arms around Joe and pressed him against the bottom of a rusty steel wall that smelled mushroomy at first but became fragrant somehow as Joe began liking the smell. Lo put his mouth against Joe's neck and bit him gently, spitting out a wad of dripping pulp. Lo's mouth had a bitter coagulant that Joe could smell, and the bleeding stopped. The coagulant came with an anaesthetic so there was no pain when the long black tube slid from Lo's mouth into Joe's jugular and traveled down into the pits of Joe's bowels looking for the stem cells it needed. Along the way, it sampled all the important organs to make sure it could match the blood type as the exchange took place.

Joe went through a blurry phase where it felt as though he were in both bodies for a time, and then only in the new one. Lo's body morphed into a new Joe. It was a perfect copy of Joe except the eyes were a little funny, but that could be helped by wearing sunglasses. Lo's body had begun to age already, and felt stiff like Styrofoam or cardboard at first, but with the new DNA from Joe, and all that fresh blood and brain fluid, the new body was as spry and powerful as Joe's old body.

The thing that had been Joe realized a lot of things now, like these bodies aged at various rates, and so it had only from 2 days to a week to live before it had to find a new host. It was now no longer human, but a spore. It must immediately begin cultivating the next human to inherit this mantle of glory, while its remains then became a bed of bracket mushrooms to sexually birth billions of spores and take over the world.

The thing that had had been Lo had now merged with the soggy remnants of the old Joe-body, including the skeleton and some throwaway body parts the mushroom people didn't need. As new-Joe (or was-Joe) slept a golden sleep in which it felt it was being welcomed into mushroom heaven, the old body deteriorated and became a colony of bracket mushrooms. These would reproduce the other way (sexually, with the fruiting body producing both male and female spores which then would fuse in the gills under the bracket heads and become new mushroom spores). Many fungi can reproduce sexually in this manner, but can also reproduce asexually through some form of cell division that still involves producing a spore to carry the genetic material. The latter was the function that the Peruvian jungle mimic species had devised to enhance their species' survival.

When was-Joe awoke, it felt great. It was free now. Free at last. The new body was already a little stiff, but it felt very strong. It felt right to be part of this community of living things, as opposed to being one lonely human spending years, if not decades, seeking to find a mate for a few hours of frenzied pleasure followed by dismal, declining years of being bad at everything, from burned barbecues to failed soapbox derbies to having your teenager call you a rat and walk out in tears slamming doors...not to mention divorce, alimony, more tears, more arguments, more slammed doors...surely the ways of the mushroom people were far better. Was-Joe felt righteous as it stomped up the rusty stairs in a series of dust clouds that it barely noticed. It slammed open the door, put on it sunglasses, and looked around at the world in a new way.

First, it called work. The dispatcher answered. It said: "This is Joe Walesky. I am going home sick."

"Sorry to hear, Joe. Just park the car and drop off the keys."

"Thank you." Next, it called home. Its wife answered. It told her: "Honey, I am going on a little trip. I'll be back soon."

"Joe? Are you feeling okay?"

"I have never felt better."

"You sound strange. Are you eating something?"

"I am just so very happy."

"Joe, is there another woman?"

"I won't be needing to address such bullshit anymore." It dropped the cell phone overboard.

Then it strode down the gangway. It didn't need to hold on to the chain. In a few days it might, as this new host body aged and needed replenishing. For now, it felt as if it had been pumped full of a new drug that made the world seem to be of shining silver, and made every fiber of its mushroom innards seem to tingle with electrical power.

It climbed into the police car and made a Y-turn on the wooden dock. It drove off down the gravel path at just the posted speed limit. No need to attract attention from these skin-bags. It got a nice salute going out the gate, which it returned with a smug little grin. It drove north to the Harbor Police headquarters by the Convention Center, and parked the car.

It spotted Cleve Bartlett, and waved.

Cleve waved back. "Hey, what's up, man?"

"I just came from the *Lima Voyager.*"

"Oh, really?" Cleve hurried over. "What's going on, man?"

Might as well get on with it, was-Joe thought. "I found the most amazing thing down in the hold.

"Oh really? What is it?"

"I'm not sure. Maybe you would like to come and take a look. Then we can write a report together."

"Oh man," Cleve said, "Linsey would be so thrilled to know we helped break the case. Yeah, I'll just—"

"No, don't go inside," was-Joe said.

"Why? I have to let my superv-"

"There isn't time," was-Joe said. "Don't worry about it. We'll cover that base later. Just get in, and I'll take you there."

Cleve looked at the building as if he knew he should do something in there— let someone know where he was going—but was-Joe was already in the patrol car and starting the engine. Cleve shrugged and got in at the passenger side.

"It's just a mile down the road," was-Joe said. "We'll be done and back before you know it." It backed out of the parking space and drove off down Pacific Highway between the Convention Center on the right and the Gaslamp Quarter and Petco Park on the left. Ahead lay Barrio Logan and the 32nd Street Navy Yard.

"So what is this thing you found?" Cleve said.

Was-Joe looked at Cleve and exhaled a cloud of black air.

Cleve sat back with a dreamy look, and felt contented.

Was-Joe felt an intense pleasure at its conquest—so soon, so well done—and the black tube came out of its mouth prematurely a few inches as if to look at the neck it was about to enter. It was all was-Joe could do to swallow the tube back down in order to get through the gate at 32nd Street without incident.

You will be so happy, it thought-emanated at the immobilized was-Cleve.

I already feel the joy, was-Cleve emanated back.

Chapter 46.

Linsey had a call from Louise Trost's executive secretary that Louise had called an important meeting for one p.m. that afternoon. "Nolan has set up a special isolation ward at UCSD Medical Center. They've got at least fifty people with Yellow Fungus Inhalation Syndrome, or YFIS, and they're opening satellite wards in the South Bay, East County, North County Inland, and North County Coastal because they're expecting hundreds more victims. This is a growing plague."

Linsey called Louise privately before then. "Louise, I have something important to ask. You know we've joked about this, but my husband is a topnotch writer and journalist. He's had two books published, one about baseball and the other about history, and I think it would be good if we had a historian on board to record all that's going on. I'm asking you to authorize me to bring Jack along and have him start documenting."

Louise could be heard sighing thoughtfully. "Let me think about it. You're right, we do need a historian on the project. Usually the Government provides someone. It's also a bit early to do this, but it's never too early to think about it. It's a slot I think is open, but I'm not thinking of hiring anyone fulltime."

"He's getting paid by the newspaper. That's legit. They'll be happy to have a scoop at the end of this, and we'll have an objective observer."

Louise laughed gently. "Honey, there are no objective observers. If I give the go-ahead, I want to do it legit. I'll put him on a part-time retainer, and you can have him work whatever hours he wants. I don't care. I'll pay him for fifteen hours a week, enough to make it official, but not enough to have him on the radar screen for now."

"Thanks." Jack would be so happy. And why not? Why let someone else scoop him?

"One other thing," Louise said. "When you come to the meeting, be in your field fatigue uniform, ready for a raid."

"Raid?"

"We're hitting Volcan Mountain."

So it was that Linsey and Jack appeared at the meeting that afternoon. Present were Louise, Linsey, Jack, Professor Nolan, and a dozen representatives from local law enforcement, the Mayor's office. Louise introduced a senior National Guard officer with Medical Corps insignia on his lapel as Colonel James Meyer, an assistant commander of a local hospital unit and medical doctor practicing at the Department of Veterans' Affairs hospital in the La Jolla section of the City of San Diego.

Louise sat at the head of the table, peeling an orange into a plastic grocery store bag as she spoke. She wore a pink sweater and seemed uncomfortable under the air conditioning pouring cold air in from overhead. "It's becoming clear that we have a disaster going on." She sucked carefully at an orange slice. "Doctor Nolan, can you update us on your research?"

"Sure, Louise." Nolan rose and introduced himself, then reported. "Our lab tests confirm that the deceased roofer, Mr. Milton, died from systemic shock and pneumonia following a direct inhalant exposure to the fungus that you see on the streets all over San Diego. Actually, the fungus has died down suddenly and significantly. Its population has suddenly collapsed, leading me to wonder if it has accomplished its purpose and we've moved on to the next phase. Yes, you all know the story of the mysterious crop dusting planes by now." He paused, looking at Linsey, while a stirr went through the room. "Lieutenant Simon has now located those planes for us." There was another stir. He continued: "Meanwhile, I have to sadly tell you that there have been at least ten more deaths similar to Mr. Milton's around the county. I believe these are not the intended result of the so-called crop dusting." Another stir swept the room. "I think we may be facing something larger and more sinister." He turned on the overhead projector while someone darkened the room. "Let me show you a few slides."

"Here is a slide of the yellow fungus, greatly enlarged. I could bore you with a whole lot of botanical, taxonomical terminology, but the bottom line is that it's a hitherto unknown subspecies. I have no evidence that it has been genetically engineered. Because of the wide variety and adaptability of fungi in general— there are about 60,000 species worldwide—my guess is that whoever did this found a suitable species, probably in one of the world's rainforests. The next slide will show you what I mean by 'did this.'"

Louise spoke up as a slide appeared, showing what looked like crosses on a white path amid rectangular structures. "This is an aerial photograph of the Anaconda Chemicals plant at Volcan Mountain. Lieutenant Linsey Simon of my staff has managed to locate the so-called crop duster planes that allegedly were crisscrossing Mission Valley, and clearly depositing the spores that led to the yellow fungus infestation. I'll say more on this a little later. Next slide."

A slide appeared, showing several large mushrooms clustered together on a grassy corner at a street intersection. Nolan took over, saying, "this is an ordinary cluster of poisonous gymnopilus1, or penetrating agaric, growing on the remains of a tree trunk the city cut down a year ago. They are a classic cap mushroom, with a whitish cap-shaped fruiting body on top and a tall, yellowish stem connecting it to its base. Under the cap are a series of fine dark-red what we call gills, which have nothing to do with breathing underwater, but are the membranes on which spores gather before they are released to drift away. The mushroom does not have eggs, like humans and other animals do, whether inside or outside the body. The mushroom reproduces by means of spores. What I want to call your attention to is the size of this cluster. Gymnopilus normally grows from about three to four inches high, but these exemplars are ten inches tall, or twice the normal maximum. Next slide."

The next slide showed a slightly different mushroom. There were a dozen or so of these light brownish, almost almond-colored umbrellas with curving stems, unlike the straight gymnopilus. On this one, the stem also became wider toward the bottom. "This is another example of hyperplasia, or excessive growth due to an increase in the number of cells. This is another poisonous mushroom, actually a relative of the first one you saw. This is the fiery agaric, which normally grows up to 8 inches, but these specimens average over a foot tall. That brings me to one of my main points for today. Next."

The next slide showed some cells dividing under a high microscopic enlargement. "These are cells of the penetrating agaric, caught in the middle of dividing. What I found was that the stems and caps of these mushrooms are saturated with a protein secreted by those yellow fungi, which has led me to suspect that the yellow mushroom introduces an Excitor enzyme that makes other fungi grow abnormally large, abnormally fast. In other words, someone wants to speed up the process of whatever they are engineering for us—and we don't know yet what that is. We only have one piece of evidence to date. Next."

The next slide showed one of the elongated bracket fungi. "This is a cluster of so-called bracket fungi that one often sees in humid rain forest environments, be it temperate forests like those on the Olympic Peninsula of Washington State, or jungle forests like in Central or South America. It is a type of fungus that feeds on rotting vegetation. This specimen, of which we have recovered a number of exemplars from the Lima Voyager and from a house in Coronado, seems to be an adaptation never before seen. The individual mushrooms, which form round shelf-like sconces, join at the edges to form a single mass. Their spongy tissue is inset with some algae, so this is technically a lichen—but there are bacteria and viruses involved. It's a complicated process I don't yet understand.

"Next—" The next slide showed a cross section of such a bracket fungus, with various inclusions of interest highlighted. "—is that this fungal body appears to have somehow gathered bits and pieces of human bones, hair, eyeballs, you name it. We have found stem cells as well as highly specific cells for skin, fingernails, mucosa. In effect, if you could unscramble the mess inside there, you could almost put a human being together. What's most interesting is that the human tissue has not decayed, but seems to be kept alive through the general nutrient and humidifacient properties of the host. One more thing: the DNA in the tissues seems to indicate that each of the bracket colonies contains the unique genetic material of a different person. What this all means, ladies and gentlemen, I don't know yet."

The lights went on and the slide show was over. Louise said: "I do know that we are missing several dozen people, including the crew and captain of the Lima Voyager, and I hope they are not inside these bracket things."

The Mayor's office spoke up. "Are you recommending one way or the other that we call in outside resources?"

"Absolutely," Louise said. "We cannot afford to sit on our hands and take chances. I'd rather be wrong than have a catastrophe we could have avoided."

Linsey saw Jack furiously scribbling notes. Louise was covering her behind, it was clear.

The National Guard colonel spoke up. "Dr. Nolan, can I safely assume that the State of California has sufficient resources to offer you at UCSD Medical Center?"

"For now, yes," Nolan said. "I can draw upon my department on the UCSD campus, which has an excellent Biology Department. You will remember, Colonel, that this city is a world leader in biotechnology."

The colonel nodded. "That gives me a small ounce of comfort, maybe." Weak laughter rippled around the table. "I assume you have no problem with my reporting upstream to, say, the Army Chemical Corps?" Those were the people who engineered counter-biological weapons, Linsey knew, and she assumed they had to cultivate biological bombs to develop counter-measures against them.

"So far," Louise said, "this is still not a classified matter. We're operating on an open principle, but trying not to cause panic among the civilian population." She pointed to Jack. "I have authorized a member of the civilian press to freely take notes and record comments, on the condition that he doesn't publish his stories yet. It's a fine line between Freedom of Speech and yelling Fire in a crowded theater. Mr. Simon is acting as our official historian for now, rather than as a newspaper reporter."

Someone asked: "Isn't it preferential and possibly biased to have one guy hog the news coverage?"

"Not at all if it's done right," Louise said. "It's common custom, or at least one approach, to have a single organization lead up the press pool. In that case, Mr. Simon is a senior writer for the city's metropolitan daily, *The San Diego Times*. When the story breaks, as we all know it will, Mr. Simon will release the initial story to all the media simultaneously. For now, as I said, he is acting as a Federal employee and as our official historian." She rose. "Thanks for coming. We all have work to do, and I appreciate your participation. I ask you all to keep a tight lip about this for a day or two. I'll convene this group again shortly."

As people left, Louise approached Linsey. "You ready to fly? You're going to be part of a raiding party at Anaconda Chemicals' Volcan Mountain complex."

Chapter 47.

Along with two dozen Navy SEALs and a San Diego City and County police SWAT team, Linsey and Jack sat in a large U.S. Navy helicopter. Not counting pilots and crew members, about 40 persons waited on board three U.S. Navy Knighthawk heavy lift choppers, most of them men. The choppers were undergoing final flight checks on a concrete runway at North Island Naval Air Station.

Jack whispered to Linsey: "This is the first time I've been in uniform since my navy days. Geez, what have I signed up for?"

"You asked for it, honey."

The ground crew waved their last signals, and the flight master pulled the door shut. The interior was air tight and heated. The crew members wore distinctive gray flight helmets and olive drab flight suits. The SEALS wore dark watch caps, Marine Corps-style fatigues with Kevlar flak jackets, and plain black combat helmets. They carried their usual variety of weapons, but each had some form of side arm and assault rifle. As a matter of routine, they handed around cylinders of dark, matte face paint. The SWAT people, which included a number of women, wore dark blue jumpsuits, Kevlar vests, web gear, and combat boots. Instead of face paint, they wore dark ski hats the left only eye and mouth holes open. They carried their police 9mm side arms and standard U.S. military M-16 assault rifles. Linsey was dressed like the SWAT people, while Jack wore his personal Glock. With them also was an official FBI camera crew of two women and one man toting lots of sophisticated, portable equipment. Navy and police personnel were purposely mixed together to develop some quick rapport on the half hour flight.

As if to complement their mission, the weather had turned raw. The heavy marine layer had suddenly rolled in, making the air gray and moist, visibility poor, and the airstream cool and damp. With a gut-wrenching twist and deafening noise, the chopper roared off the field at NAS North Island. As it rotated, Linsey saw the city skyline spin by. It looked like looming black buildings swathed in a fog of tiny dots of light.

It was late afternoon with two hours of daylight left. Louise had confided to Linsey that she didn't like the launch hour, but she didn't want to wait another day for fear the suspects at Volcan Mountain would remove the planes. More than anything else, what they were after was some residue from the cloud seeding mechanisms of those Cessnas. That clinches any doubt about the relationship between the yellow fungi, Anaconda Chemicals, and the death of people like the roofer, Hugh Milton.

Under the joint command of a Navy SEAL captain and a County Sheriff's Inspector, the flight rose up in unison. The choppers leaned nose-down toward the Pacific Ocean as they gained altitude. Approaching a cruising altitude of just over a mile, which put them above the marine layer and into bright sunshine that made the clouds below glitter like mother of pearl, the choppers headed due east in an arrowhead formation.

The team commander for their chopper was a young Navy lieutenant with a map in hand. He had a throat mike that fed into the main public address system, and with this he lectured his personnel on the mission ahead. "First thing I want to warn you about is that Volcan Mountain has a reputation for some nasty plane crashes over the years. We may run into some turbulence, because it's raining and thundering out there. That's a mountain climate that can be quite different from what you're used to on the coast. Classically, in the winter, people may be surfing and sailing in the bay, but an hour inland, where we are headed, they may be sledding and skiing. Up around Volcan there can be conflicting air masses pushing different ways. The mountain has very rugged terrain, with thick fogs, and just tends to suck planes in to their death. We'll be fine because we have experienced local pilots, and they're following all the proper safety practices. That said, let's talk about the mission."

Fifteen minutes into the flight, with I-8 a thin ribbon far below when the clouds lifted, Linsey was just beginning to soak up some of the information about how they were going to land in the middle of the runway, secure the planes, get test samples, seize this building and that, and wait for a battalion of combat Marines to arrive in trucks to take over the facility from the shock team.

An announcement came in an indistinct voice, at least from Linsey's viewpoint amid the huddled troops all around her. The team leader said, "New orders. We're turning back. Mission has been scrubbed." There was an audible sigh of disappointment from the gung-ho troops. "Sorry," the team leader said, "I don't know if it's the weather or what, but the circus is off." He turned slightly to listen to another bit of information. "Okay, rumor has it some Congressman has ordered us to stand down while an investigation goes on. Seems there has been a lawsuit filed against the task force to prevent them from employing folks like us on Anaconda Chemicals' property." He shrugged and grinned. No skin off his back.

Linsey was furious.

By the time the helicopters landed, and their teams dispersed, night had fallen. From across the harbor at NAS North Island, the city skyline looked magnificent. The green neon hexagons of the Emerald Plaza Hotel had become a signature of the skyline, amid a hazy wash of gold lights among brooding high rises. The marine layer had thinned late in the day, but now started rolling in again for a heavy morning fog.

Jack drove, and Linsey fumed in the passenger seat. "We were so close!"

"I don't understand it," Jack said as they cruised high up on the Coronado Bay Bridge. "That had to be raw politics. I can make some phone calls, Lin."

"No, better not. I'll talk with Louise first." She dialed, but ended up leaving a message on Louise's voice mail. She wondered how Louise was feeling about the news that her pet raid had been aborted. "The unknowns are probably moving the Cessnas to another state, if they haven't already."

"Not in this fog," Jack said. "And not at night."

That gave Linsey an idea. "Jack, are you game?"

"Huh?"

She explained her plan.

Chapter 48.

The night was cold and drizzly around Volcan Mountain. Fog rolled through the thick forests, and clouds reared up charcoal and black as if the whole mountain were smoldering, on fire. This was the weather that sucked planes out of the sky and threw them against the mountain with deadly force.

At the Anaconda Chemical plant on Atasca Ridge, perimeter lights burned with cold brightness. Fog rolled through the wire fence as if trying to deny their existence. Every hour, the white guard SUV labored along the perimeter ridges.

Down in the basin 500 feet below, several Cessnas still sat at the end of the runway. Corner lights illuminated the several rectangular buildings at the far end of the valley.

It was a silent scene. Nothing was flying tonight, not even toward the dawn hour. Several dark figures worked on the Cessnas, getting them ready to fly as soon as daylight came and burned off the drizzle and fog.

In that silence, suddenly, a loud noise echoed across the valley. The main gate above on the road burst open as its chain and lock were destroyed. The gate flew open in both directions as a heavy, dirty SUV barreled through—belonging to Ernie Walesky, but driven by Linsey Simon. Beside her sat Jack Simon, who held his hands over his eyes and mouthed a silent scream. The SUV barreled down the main street, into the valley below, toward the air strip. "Keep an eye out for that guard hummer, and have your camera ready," Linsey instructed.

Jack said: "Aye aye, Sir." As the SUV bounced along, fishtailing at times, he had trouble keeping the camera straight. He was trying to film the whole escapade, as she'd instructed. Half the battle would be the film evidence. The other half would be getting scrapings off the exhaust nozzles of the rain making foggers on at least one of the Cessnas. Ideally, they should have brought a pilot along to fly one of the planes out, but that couldn't happen on such short notice and under these conditions.

Suddenly inspired, Linsey stopped. "I've got an idea, Jack."

"Oh God not another one!"

While Linsey sat deliberating her next move, Jack kept filming. Ernie Walesky's SUV sat growling quietly and powerfully at the edge of the runway. The nearest Cessna was about 200 feet away, facing toward them. Linsey eyeballed the plane, while simultaneously looking around for that white guard vehicle with those two scary dudes. She and Jack had come armed, of course, with handguns, assault rifles, and shotguns, plus enough ammo for an extended siege, but the evidence collected under such circumstances would probably not be admissible in court.

"Look in the back, see if there's any rope—extra thick rope."

Jack clambered back and said: "There is a coil of something back here. Looks like inch thick braided nylon, blue and white, like for boating and stuff."

Linsey looked at it in the rear view mirror. " Ernie is or was a sailor, so that makes sense. I'm going to collect those scrapings from the plane." So saying, she drove down the runway toward the nearest Cessna.

"Honey, are you nuts?"

"I'm not going to hit him, Jack. Just relax." Driving past the plane, she eyeballed it and made sure the chocks were under the wheels front and back. Also, the propeller was horizontal. Good. She made a U-turn behind the plane and drove around it, so that she was in front of it facing in the same direction."

"What have I done?" Jack said. "I married an insane person."

"Sweetheart, this isn't our car, and those aren't our planes, so who cares? Duck your head—there may be some glass!" She backed into the Cessna at a high rate of speed. Jack ducked, holding his head in both hands. The SUV collided with the Cessna. Jack bellowed, and for a moment Linsey thought she might have made a mistake. Then she saw that her plan had worked. The car had gone under the plane's front end, forcing it on top of the car. "Quick, Jack, the ropes. Let's go!"

Eyes wide with terror, Jack helped her toss the nylon rope over the plane's wheels and around the SUV. They got the plane tied down, at least somewhat, when the guard vehicle's spotlight found them and started playing over the scene. Arriving up at the ridge, the guards driving the vehicle must have seen the gate sprung, and then noticed the commotion on the runway. They turned the SUV toward the air strip and raced down the road.

"Hand me the shotgun," Linsey said. As Jack fumbled with the heavy weapon, Linsey raced up the road. For a moment it was a duel of high beams.

Jack said: "You drive. I'll take care of them."

"That's the spirit!"

As the two vehicles neared each other, it looked like a near miss was about to turn into a deliberate ramming. "Those guys are crazy," Jack yelled. He leaned out the window and unleashed a series of shotgun blasts into the engine and front tires of the guard vehicle. The guards veered left, then right, then left again. Linsey tried to steer opposite their direction in the hope of flying past them. At the last moment, Linsey went left and they went right. As they sailed past, Jack unloaded several more shotgun blasts at the rear of their vehicle in hopes of flattening their tires.

As Linsey drove uphill and neared the gate, she looked back and saw that the guard vehicle had burst into flames. Must have hit the gas tank. Two figures bailed out as the vehicle exploded.

"My career is probably over," she said as she drove through the broken gate. "I enjoyed it while it lasted."

"Stop," Jack said. She did, and he potted the security cameras above the gate. Emptying another round of shotgun shells, he explosively demolished the camera and cut its mast in half. "If you go to jail, I might as well do the same. We can send each other notes."

"There's our car," she said. "I'll drive this thing. You get our car out of here, but pronto."

Minutes later, a strange sight could be seen heading south on a winding mountain road: a sports car racing full tilt, followed by a dusty SUV with an airplane on top.

Linsey kept looking in the rear view mirror. Beyond the broken fuselage, and the tail section hanging limply, rocking, over the back of Ernie Walesky's SUV, nothing was following her. The tie-down job wasn't too good, and the nylon rope appeared to be stretching, so that the airplane yawed back and forth. She spotted a parking lot for some large church, empty at this hour, and sailed into there. A row of street lights in the parking lot had caught her eye. She raced along, severing first one wing, and then, going the other way, severing the other wing. With the plane's landing gear firmly wrapped around Ernie's SUV, the plane wasn't going anywhere now.

Jack waited on the road. She followed him down the grade, past Julian, and down to Interstate 8. As luck would have it, the Highway Patrol didn't pull her over, and eventually she managed to drive into the parking structure of Louise Trost's high rise.

Timing was great, because Louise was just getting out of her car, and stood gaping as the SUV with the airplane wreck embedded in its roof pulled up along side her. It barely cleared the ceiling, by an inch. Jack pulled up in the sports car with a screech of tires. "Hello, Louise," Linsey said. "We did manage to grab one of those planes. Get Nolan over here to get samples from the rain dusting nozzles." As Louise gasped for breath and leaned back over her own car, Linsey said: "Are you okay?"

Chapter 49.

"Child," Louise said when she had recovered her aplomb. "Get out of that car and wipe all your fingerprints off."

"Oh yeah," Linsey said as she climbed out. "I get it. Nobody needs to know how this thing got here."

"I'd speculate the owner of that SUV drove the plane here."

"Right," Linsey said while wiping the steering wheel and shift knob with an oily rag from under the seat. "Ernie Walesky, one of the Lima Voyager crew members who has been missing."

Jack screeched down the ramp in his car and pulled up alongside. "You made it." He radiated respect and amazement.

"Get in," Louise told Linsey and pointed into Jack's car. "That's how you got here, got that? You came with Jack."

Linsey shrugged. "You want to take it from here?"

"I sure do. See the cars in here?"

Linsey saw a handful of car rear ends and rear windows.

"That's going to be a pissed off group of people when they find out this has become a HazMat Zone. Go on, get out of here, you two. Good job, Linsey."

"She gets the job done," Jack said in a faint, amazed voice. He looked at his wife with some fear. "Are you okay?"

"You mean, are we done doing insane things for now?"

"Next time, warn me and I'll stay out of the way."

As they drove out of the garage, she leaned back, squirming happily, and said: "You wanted to tag along, Jack. I have a feeling it's going to get far more interesting yet."

"Let's go home and catch some sleep," Jack suggested. "It's going to be a long day tomorrow." He amended: "Today." Groaning, he looked at the dash clock. *It was five a.m.*

At noon, when Linsey drove in to work, still tired, the scene on lower Broadway was not surprising. A city block was sealed off. Traffic police were rerouting traffic with temporary barricades. Blocky red Fire Department vehicles stood out among marked and unmarked vehicles from various agencies. Rather than fight it, Linsey drove up to Park Boulevard a mile away, parked her car, and took a red MTA trolley down C Street to the Transfer Station near the Santa Fe Depot. The trolley crawled slowly down the congested street—all of downtown was impacted. Nice job, Linsey, she told herself and almost grinned.

What was most surprising was the occasional two or three foot button mushroom growing out of dusty soil in spots where only grass managed to eke out a living.

Linsey found Louise standing outside the building along with about 1,000 other persons. "Good morning," Louise said drily. "Good timing. We're just about to get permission to go back inside. The parking garage is totally off limits and will be for days." Louise leaned close and whispered in Linsey's ear: "I'll keep your little secret for you so you won't have to pay for the rental cars, for the night shift people from the computer networking firm, whose cars are stuck in there."

"You should be glad you have your evidence," Linsey whispered back.

"I am, don't get me wrong." Slowly the crowd began to surge toward the newly opened glass portals into the main lobby. "Nolan has already confirmed that the cloud seeding mechanism on this plane, especially the nozzles, contains oodles and oodles of that same fungus that killed Hugh Milton. It's a smoking gun." She was silent while they rode up in a crowded elevator. When they entered the task force's offices, she flicked on lights and Linsey started up the coffee pot. Louise continued: "We found out that Congressman Metrick ordered the mission aborted yesterday, and it wasn't hard to find out through my own contacts that he's in Lee Collwood's pocket. Collwood's family, and Anaconda Chemicals, has been adding rocket fuel to Metrick's reelection campaigns for 20 years through the usual third party conduits. Don't forget, Linsey, this task force is joined at the hip to a bipartisan House committee designed to oversee Homeland Security. I can pick up the phone and call my boss in Washington D.C., or call any one of the Representatives on the committee. There is already a procedural inquiry in to Metrick's involvement, since he's not on the committee and sidestepped all the proper protocols in freezing our police action. That's a serious matter, even though he couched in a lawsuit."

"What did Nolan find, if anything, about the Yellow Yuck?"

They sat down at a small round table in the cafeteria with their coffees. Louise said: "He's more convinced than ever the yellow fungus was sprayed as an accelerator to make all the mushroom species in the area grow huge at a fantastic pace."

"Lots of these huge mushrooms around town," Linsey said.

Louise agreed. "People are starting to get used to it. Funny how humanity is. Can't stand each other, but will take for granted that a morel the size of their kid is standing next to them at the bus stop. What's your plan for the day?"

Linsey stirred her coffee thoughtfully. "I'm switching back from mushrooms to people."

Louise winked. "You've got the mushroom side covered, child. Anaconda can't recover their plane, though they've got 20 lawyers on it from here to LA and Phoenix. I've asked my friends in Congress to override Metrick's cheap little lawsuit and get the Anaconda plant at Volcan locked down so we can send investigators in pronto."

"Keep me posted on that, will you? Jack and I would like to go in and have a look as soon as possible." Linsey's phone warbled and she answered. "Yes?"

"Linsey, " said a muffled voice.

"Yes? Who is this?"

"Cleve."

"You sound like you couldn't get your shirt over your head this morning. Are you stuck?"

"I need to see you."

"Sure. Where are you?"

"Lima Voyager."

"I'll come right over."

"Come alone."

"Cleve, are you sure you are okay?"

"Come now."

The line went dead. Linsey frowned. Louise had left the room. Linsey left a voicemail for Jack, in case he wanted to tag along: "Honey, it's me. Lin. Cleve called. He wants me to meet him. Call me, okay? Love you." She stuck her head in Louise's office, but her boss was away—possibly in the can, but Linsey didn't want to keep Cleve waiting.

Chapter 50. Midmorning

Jack Simon sat on the patio at his and Linsey's house and tried to organize a plan of action on paper. Sitting in the shade of an outdoor café-style Cinzano umbrella Linsey had ordered from Italy, he sipped hot coffee and scribbled with an expensive ink pen on a quadrille pad. Jack's theory was that if you had an expensive pen and expensive paper, it should help your thinking. Unfortunately, it made him hesitant to put expensive ink marks on expensive paper. In the end, he resorted to his old favorites—a mechanical pencil and some cheap loose-leaf paper. His laptop sat nearby, just in case he decided to start writing. A news feed with AP and other images rolled through a constantly refreshed slide show on the screen, and he glanced up occasionally to keep up with events.

He'd hoped to go on the road with Linsey this morning, but she was in a series of meetings with Louise Trost at the task force office downtown.

Jack understood what he must do the instant he got hold of Linsey. He must get Linsey and Louise Trost to join him in a meeting with the newspaper's owners and his own boss, the executive editor. He had already asked the newspaper to take him off all other work so he could devote his full attention to a major story that would break soon. He had told Griff Wilkins, his boss, that he couldn't reveal the nature of the story yet but that it was related to last week's alleged crop dusting incident and the yellow mushrooms that had by now faded away. With the growing incidence of huge mushrooms all over town, any fool could readily make the connection. In fact, there were news people all over the world starting to note San Diego's infestation of giant mushrooms. Wilkins had given Jack 48 hours to either bring a report and fire the opening salvo so the The San Diego Times could break the story and scoop the world—or Wilkins would bring in a team of seasoned, independent professionals from around the country, hired direct by the U-T, to investigate and report. Already, Japanese and European journalists were arriving, and there were colonies of foreign journalists hanging around the hotels in Mission Valley, downtown, at the Convention Center, and in the beach communities.

Even from his patio, Jack could see a trio of intertwined cap mushrooms growing in the garden next door. They were almost eight feet tall and resembled the triplets of king palms or fan palms that San Diego gardeners were fond of growing.

Glancing across the table, Jack noticed his cell phone. It was off. He tried to turn it on, but the battery was low, so he went into the house and attached it to its recharger. Pouring himself another cup of coffee, he returned to the patio.

While he waited to hear from Linsey, he might as well get something going. He brought the portable house phone outside and dialed a number. Mrs. Nellie Walesky answered.

"Hi, Mrs. Walesky. Jack Simon here, Lieutenant Linsey Simon's husband?"

"Who?"

"The police officer who spoke with you the other day."

"Oh yes. And you're also a policeman?"

"Not exactly. I am a writer, working for the same task force that Linsey is on. In my spare time, I work for the Times."

"Yeah, and?"

"I'd like to come by and have a chat with you and the boy."

"You mean Jimmy."

"Yes. I understand he's been telling some stories about a terrible thing that happened to his mom and dad."

"Yeah, well, mister, I'm starting to believe him. I haven't heard a word from my sister and brother-in-law. At least my own worthless husband called once to say he's tied up, which means he's probably in a Mexican jail sweating off a hangover."

"Can I come by to visit you?"

"Yeah, sure. I have to go shopping later, but you can talk with the kids. Maribel will be there to help."

Jack took a shower and dressed in a moderately official outfit—summer khaki trousers, light leather knockabouts, a white shirt, narrow red tie, dark blue blazer. It was a preppy outfit that seemed more nonthreatening than some corporate uniform. Before leaving, he made sure the coffee pot was off, stove off, lights off, burglar alarm on, radio playing softly to give the illusion someone was home. Oh, cell phone—call from Linsey—he checked his voicemail. She wanted him to call her. He tried her number, got voicemail, left a brief note that he'd be interviewing Jimmy Mendez, and that he needed to speak with her asap (the upcoming meeting with Griff Wilkins). That done, he sprinted from the house, to his car, and drove to Linda Vista.

The late morning sun was intense in a cloudless blue sky, and Jack donned his sunglasses. He enjoyed the wind whipping through the sparse tendrils of his hair, but enough was enough—he put the top up on the gray Ford Mustang convertible.

The Waleskys' house, by contrast with the heat and light outside, was comfortably shady and gloomy, in a friendly rumpled way that smelled faintly of this morning's toast and stale coffee. The dominant smell at the moment came from the garage—detergent and fabric softeners, to go with a ton of laundry generated when one had two children running around and school was out.

Nellie Walesky was a heavy-set, gray-haired woman in a shapeless mumu the color of lime ice cream speckled with tiny strawberries and other fruits. She gasped a little when she walked, and waf miffing a few teef, so that she talked like dif. She sat Jack down in a brown couch in the living room and pressed a sweaty-cool ice tea in his paw. Then she went to the backdoor and bellowed: "Jimmy!

Maribel!" several times until Jack detected faint answering shouts in childish voices from afar.

Minutes later, the four of them sat together in the living room. Jack asked for permission to set up a small recorder on the table. He also had his PDA ready, with the stylus hovering over the text pad. He listened in horror as the boy began describing the same nightmare that Linsey had told him about.

Nellie rose. "I can't hear that story again." She trudged out into the kitchen with a distraught look on her lined features.

Maribel bit her lip and had wide eyes, but held Jimmy to comfort him, one arm over his shoulders. Jimmy told his story about the two impostors spooning in bed, and the black tube running from the dad thing's mouth into the mom thing's neck. "I have this nightmare almost every night. Annette, the social worker, says I have to get into therapy, but Aunt Nellie won't let them dope me up. I like to go out and play, ride my bike, play basketball, and I don't want to be on some stinkin' drugs."

Jack said: "Well, I'm no doctor, but I think it's good for you to ride your bike and play sports. Best thing in the world for a growing boy."

Maribel added: "Growing girls too. I play shortstop in girls' softball and I plan to be in the majors one day."

"Good for you," Jack said. Two normal kids, the thought. This black tube stuff can't just be a stray fantasy.

Jack thought about the guards in the hummer at the Volcan Mountain plant. What if they were some kind of invaders, from outer space or from some other dimension?

There was a knock on the door. Maribel opened, and in came a woman who resembled Aunt Nellie. Aunt Nellie came into the living room. "Kids, I'm going to Fashion Valley Shopping Mall. Aunt Joanie is going to babysit while I'm gone." Aunt Joanie was a heavy-set, graying woman with blue eyes and a red dress with rocking horses on it, in the same spirit as Aunt Nellie's lime dress with fruits on it. Scientists had discovered that pediatric nurses made children feel more at ease if they wore hospital scrubs with these sorts of colors and motifs—a set of knowledge already known by these grannies.

Nellie said: "Gotta get out of this house, and I have so much to do. Jimmy, I'll see about that soccer ball pump you need."

"Thanks, Aunt Nellie."

"Maribel, do you need extra leggins for softball?"

"I'm good, but I could use some thick crew socks."

"You got it, babe. Mr. Simon, nice to meet you." Nellie extended a hard, firm hand, and Jack shook it. With women like this, the world will be safe, he thought. She reminded him of his own grandma who had done much for him.

After Nellie left, Jack sat with Aunt Joanie and the kids and watched cartoons. It was very restful, almost like being home at his own grandma's house. He decided to stay put for a bit, while waiting to hear from Linsey. He made small talk with Aunt Joanie, while keeping eye on Jimmy to see if he said or did anything strange; but the boy just seemed utterly normal except for the grief that was tearing his life apart. Maribel served up ice tea for the four of them.

The phone warbled, and Jack opened. It was Linsey. "We've been playing phone tag. Where are you?"

"I'm watching Donald Duck with Jimmy Mendez and Maribel Walesky and Aunt Joanie from next door."

"You are nuts, Jack Simon."

"I'm an investigative reporter. This is important stuff."

"Okay," she said, laughing. "Cleve called and said he wants to meet me for some reason. He sounded a little strange. I thought he got his jammies stuck around his neck or something."

"Want me to come along?"

"Nah. You're way across town. I'm sure he's got something I need to sign, or he wants to have lunch, or whatever."

"Right."

He made more small talk with Aunt Joanie. Jimmy laughed, and Maribel patted him on the back, as he happily watched the road runner go beep beep and varooommmm while the stupid coyote had his head stuck in a board that went ratta-tatta-ratta-tattle. Maribel and Aunt Joanie laughed. Jack was thinking he might wander to the corner store and bring back a box of popsicles for everyone.

Just then, there was a noise outside. Maribel climbed over the couch and pulled up the curtain to look. "Daddy!"

Jack turned, leaned over, and lifted the curtain also. Standing on the curb outside was a man heavily muffled in a khaki outfit of some kind, with work gloves and a baseball cap, and black sunglasses that glinted in the sunlight. The man's expression was flat—unemotional, hard, enigmatic. Weird.

Maribel darted for the front door, but Aunt Joanie stopped her, caught her in an embrace with a pale, heavy arm. Her arm was sunburned red on top, and flaccid underneath. "No you don't. We don't know what condition your daddy is in, honey. Come on, you know the score. I'll go check him out first."

Maribel nodded reluctantly. She stood with her arms akimbo, tapping one foot, and Jack was sure that the spirit of Aunt Nellie was alive and well in that little girl. Ernie Walesky would get the riot act read to him either way. Jack and the kids stayed in the living room. Maribel turned down the cartoons. Jack noticed that Jimmy seemed pale, frozen, and agitated.

Scared.

Jack took one last glance outside. Ernie wasn't headed for the front door, but for the kitchen door at the side of the house. As the draped figure disappeared around the side of the house into the gravel driveway, Jack let the curtain drop back into place.

Aunt Joanie went into the kitchen, entering by a small hallway to the left. She let the dark oak bar-style swinging door rattle back and forth a while.

Jimmy and Maribel tip-toed into the dining room, from which Jack assumed they could spy on Joanie and Ernie. Jack sat in the comfort of the couch, which seemed to be trying to swallow him up. This household was so much like his own childhood home. It had taken him by surprise, reminding him of his own parent's frequent travel as journalists, and his own loneliness which Grandma Simon totally relieved by being a second mother to him. She was long gone now, many years, and Jack felt memories coming back, floods of pleasant memories—

A shrill, piercing scream rent the air. It was a scream like a dental drill, 1000 decibels high, capable of shattering glass and cutting like a razor blade. The scream continued on in one large lungful that seemed to have no bottom.

Jack was on his feet, running. The scream came from the dining room where the kids were. Jack burst through the door into the dining room and saw Maribel with her mouth open and a pair of eyes like billiard balls. Jimmy stood with his back to the opposite corner, as if he were trying to blend into the dark oak paneling. He was red as a lobster, and trembling. His mouth was open, his eyeballs bulged, and his lips moved in silent words—like someone talking in his sleep in the midst of a nightmare.

Jack pushed open the door leading from the dining room into the kitchen a few inches, and looked. Maribel's scream still echoed in Jack's tortured ears, but the dining room had fallen silent. The kitchen smelled like a newly opened grave as the fungus-loam smell filled it with the scent of drifting microspores.

There was Aunt Joanie, standing in a silent embrace with Ernie Walesky. She had her back to Jack and faced out the kitchen door. The kitchen door had slipped shut as Ernie must have stepped inside to embrace her. What the hell? She wasn't actually embracing him, but stood with her plump arms hanging limply at her sides. What tiny hands she has, Jack thought, little pale hands with doll fingers, for such a big woman.

Contrast that with those ridiculous heavy gray work gloves clasped in the red cotton amid the rocking horses wrinkled up above her haunchy butt. Ernie still had the sunglasses on, and that cap jammed down over his head, and the collar of his khaki work shirt standing straight up to cover his ears. Ernie's cheek rested against Joanie's ear, so that his mouth was open over the round opening in her neck. A shiny black tube thick as a curtain rod was still moving out of his mouth and into her jugular vein.

Then one of the gloved hands fell off, revealing a gray, desiccated stump with frizzled black cords hanging out. The baseball cap fell off, revealing the rot setting in at the mushroom man's bare scalp. He was missing an ear, and as the sunglasses slipped a bit, Jack could see the blackness of the pupils.

Maribel had gathered another zeppelin-size lungful and was screaming again like a jet flying through the living room. Jimmy stayed silent, trembling in his corner. His eyes were closed, and he appeared to be in another reality.

Jack backed away from the door and projectile vomited so that his breakfast and his coffee and Maribel's iced tea splashed on the wall and ran down looking like a watery milkshake. About six good heaves, and he was retching on empty. His throat and eyes burned, as he reached for a tissue box nearby and started cleaning his hands and face.

"Never mind that now," said Maribel. She had stopped screaming and had Jimmy by the sleeve with her left hand and Jack by the sleeve with her right hand. "We need to get out of here right now. Follow me."

Jack felt like a kid, running alongside Jimmy as they followed Maribel's fleet figure through the living room, out the front door, across the lawn, and to a neighbor's house. "Call the police nine one one," Maribel blurted as a neighboring gay couple, two men, stood in the doorway. "Please," Jack said, "do as she says. Call the police and tell them to meet me in the street. There is a murder in progress across the street."

The two gay men let Maribel in, and she towed Jimmy after her. "Lock yourselves in," Jack said.

"The police are on the way," said one of the men—Jack saw through the screen door that he held up a phone.

"Lock the door," Jack said, "don't let anyone in. And thanks."

"Right," the other man said and slammed the door shut.

Jack heard locks and bolts rattling. He heard Maribel's piercing voice: "Save my mom—don't let him get her."

"I will," Jack yelled over his shoulder as he ran into the street and whipped out his cell phone. Standing in the middle of the street, he called Linsey. He hoped he wasn't too late.

Chapter 51.

Linsey drove in her own Lexus to the San Diego Police substation at the bottom of a canyon near the Park Boulevard side of Balboa Park. She entered the park grounds—of one of the world's largest urban parks, with the large San Diego Zoo adjacent—from Park Boulevard onto Presidents' Way and turned right on the access road behind one of the large parking lots. The access road spiraled down amid enormous yellow eucalyptus trees. The trees, which sat on the hillsides above, had yard-thick trunks with peeling bark. Huge crowns of fine leaves hung down all around, making shade. Linsey drove down to find the parking lot deserted except for one or two police cars. The buildings were quiet at this time of day—probably locked up, or maybe with one or two administrative staff inside while the uniformed and detective agents were all out on patrol.

Linsey drove in a circle in the empty lot while fine leaf debris swirled up. Where was Cleve? He'd called earlier and asked her to meet him here. Her phone chirped, the readout said it was Jack, and she opened. "Hi, honey."

He sounded breathless. "Linsey, the kid was right."

"Huh?"

"The tubes in the neck, the mushroom smell..." He was gasping for air and trying to talk at the same time.

"Where are you, Jack?"

"In the middle of the street, outside Jimmy Mendez' aunt's house where I was before. Uncle Ernie showed up...or the mushroom person who was Uncle Ernie at one time."

"Jack, have you lost your mind?"

"Honey, no time for jokes. This is real. You gotta believe me because the proof is right there in that house. Cops on the way."

"I'll be right over."

"Wait. You said Cleve wanted you to meet him?"

"Yes. He's not here."

"Make sure he's okay. Stay there a while in case he shows up. I hope nothing has happened to him."

"If you say so."

"Check him out carefully first, to make sure he's not another Uncle Ernie. I don't know how they do it, but this guy has the neighbor lady in his embrace and he's got that tube going down her neck right there in the kitchen, just like Jimmy said."

"His memories must be jogging loose," Linsey said. "What on earth are we dealing with?"

"I haven't heard of any flying saucers or UFOs, so it must be of this earth."

"Hang in there, Jack, and I'll call you in 15 minutes."

"Right."

She made one last turn and parked the car behind the small complex of structures at the far end of the parking lot, housing the substation. She got out of the car and made sure her gun was ready and her cell phone was ready if she needed to call for help.

A few minutes later, a green luxury sedan came rolling down the access road. She hid behind the building and peeked. *Tourist lost? Cleve in a new car? What gives?* Behind the wheel was the beautiful social worker, Annette Lewis. *Huh?*

Annette pulled over and parked under a shady tree. She had a phone to her ear and appeared to be writing something. Linsey observed. When Annette put the phone away, Linsey searched her pockets and found the social worker's business card. She phoned and watched Annette pick up.

"Miss Lewis?"

"It's Mrs. Lewis. Who's calling?"

"Sorry. It's Linsey Simon. Lieutenant Simon? We met at Jimmy Mendez' Aunt Nellie's house?"

"Oh yes, how are you?"

"I'm fine. Just thought I'd touch base and see what' shaking."

"Not much is shaking, Lieutenant. I've been doing a little investigating of my own, trying to determine what part of Jimmy's hysteria is fantasy and what part might represent some form of real abuse."

"That's what Agent Cleve Bartlett and I were wondering too, after we left the other day. So where are you now?"

"I'm in Balboa Park, waiting for Officer Bartlett to show up."

"Oh?" Linsey felt suspicion growing. If she was married, and Cleve had asked Linsey to meet him here, what kind of odd triangle would this make?

"I called the Harbor Police this morning to see if I could interview both you and Cleve. They said you are working for some task force downtown and they'd get a message to you. They said Cleve told them he was going to leave the Harbor Police jurisdiction to drive here and take care of something personal. I thought I might catch him here and ask him a few questions. Oops."

"Oops?" As she echoed Annette's little exclamation, she understood: Cleve's Harbor Police patrol car was just then nosing down the winding access road. Leafy debris from the Brazilian peppers and eucalyptus trees rained down on the dusty hood of the black and white.

Cleve stopped in the middle of the parking lot as if looking—*for me*, Linsey thought. Something made her stay put, rather than step out to wave to him as she wanted very much to do.

Annette stepped out of her car and waved to Cleve instead.

Linsey watched as Cleve's head leaned out a bit. The two talked. He pulled over and parked parallel to her car. He got out and walked toward her, even as she walked under the shade of that big tree. Linsey squinted and wished she had binoculars, but she could see plainly what happened next.

Annette and Cleve stepped close to each other. She was just saying something with a pleasant smile. Cleve opened his mouth into an 'o' shape and breathed black air in her face. Her expression changed and she grew limp. Linsey's heart nearly stopped a beat or two. She realized with an icy shower of hurt feelings and fright that Cleve had meant for Linsey to show up so he could do this to her. Cleve quickly stepped in to catch Annette. As she grew limp in his arms, he did a half turn, almost a dance step, and bit her neck. He held her tightly to him, and a black tube slid from his mouth into her neck.

Linsey repelled backwards, repulsed and grief stricken. It was not the grossness or the horror of it. It was the fact that her friend was dead. She knew it. Someone must have gotten to him earlier, but from her perspective, seeing this was like seeing him actually get killed in front of her.

Leaving her car where it was, and keeping the building and trees between her and that horrid vision, she scrambled up the dark hillside until she emerged in full sunlight on the green lawn by Presidents' Way. There, she fumbled for her cell phone and pressed the pre-dial for Jack while running to find the nearest police officer.

Chapter 52.

Two squad cars arrive with lights and sirens from opposite directions. The sirens died down, but the lights kept twirling. Jack stood with his hands up, waving for them to slow down. He had Louise Trost on the phone, and she had just promised to call both Professor Shaun Nolan and the police chief. Four officers in dark blue uniforms got out of the squad cars, while slipping their nightsticks into their belt rings.

A sergeant of Asian origin said: "What's going on?"

Jack held up his press pass and wallet I.D. "Jack Simon. I work with Louise Trost on the anti-terrorism task force downtown. My wife is Linsey Simon, a lieutenant with the Harbor Patrol, who is also on the task force." He pointed to the house. "Inside there is a crime taking place, but I don't want you to rush in. You have to first understand what is going on. And it's a pretty fantastic story."

"You have one minute to make your case," the sergeant said. Already the other three officers were warily approaching the silent, dark house.

"There is some kind of take-over going on. I watched a man come home and embrace a neighbor lady. He slid a tube from his mouth into her neck and is doing something to her. I know you won't believe me, and I don't blame you. But you need to talk to your superiors before you go in there."

"I think you need help, sir, with all due respect."

"Please wait before you go in there." He waved his cell phone. "I can get your chief of police on the phone to you in a minute or two. You'll believe him."

"I believe you are very upset, sir, and we need to go into the house and see what caused you to become hysterical."

"I'm not hysterical. Sergeant, it's fine if you think I'm nuts, but if I say the four of you are taking your lives into your hands, give me the benefit of the doubt. Five minutes! Please!"

"Okay." The sergeant waved his men away into the neighboring yard. "Come with me, please. Stay by my side. I'm not arresting you." He walked over to his car while speaking into his collar mike. He spoke softly, but Jack understood: he was calling for backup, asking a SWAT team to go to standby.

A minute passed, while the sergeant held a little earpiece to his ear. He looked preoccupied, then puzzled. Someone was speaking to him, and he looked at Jack with dawning respect and understanding. "Yessir, I understand. Will do." The sergeant stepped up and patted Jack on the arm. "Sorry, Mr. Simon."

"I don't blame you a bit," Jack said.

"I have instructions from the Chief himself to isolate that house. We'll be evacuating neighbors and bringing in both a SWAT unit and the Hazardous Materials people from the Fire Department. I guess there is also some lady from the Federal Government on the way with a mycologist? Isn't that a mushroom specialist?"

Jack nodded. He didn't need to explain much. All he had to do was point to the basketball-sized yellowish mushrooms ballooning out of a neighbor's yard. "This is just a faint prolog to what you are going to find when you go into that house."

His phone rang. Linsey. "Yeah, hon?"

She was so out of breath she seemed to be sobbing for air. "Jack! They got Cleve and Annette Lewis, the social worker. I witnessed how it happens. Cleve blew black air in her face, full of spores probably, and instantly she seemed to go limp and be helpless. He's got his tube into her. I'm running to catch the nearest cops and get a net over the two of them."

Jack nodded. "Good go. Then we'll have two pairs of them and Nolan can do his mycology stuff on them."

"You know what?"

"No, Linsey, what bright idea did you just have?"

"I'm not going to get a whole lot of cops down there. I'm going to follow Cleve and see where he takes her. There must be a nest of them somewhere."

"Honey, please…"

"Jack, we have to know where this infestation is centered. It's going to do absolutely no good to cause a huge scene here."

"Honey—"

Chapter 53.

Jack was still pleading with her as she saw Cleve's patrol car slowly riding up out of the hidden parking lot below. She ducked down so he wouldn't see her. He was driving slowly enough, but faster than she could run. She would need to scramble back down the hill, get her car, and then find him. She watched to see which way he turned as he left Balboa Park. He turned right on Balboa Park, which would take him somewhere in the direction of the harbor.

Rather than scramble down the hill, she called Louise Trost. "Can you get me a chopper—STAT?"

"What's going on? I was just talking with your husband. You Simons are not Simple People."

"Louise, cut the crap. I need a chopper. I just saw Cleve put a tube in a social worker's neck and suck her life away."

"Ordinarily I would hang up about now, but after talking with your husband I'm convinced you can't both be nuts. After all, you come from different family trees. Where are you?"

"Balboa Park, the Park Boulevard entrance at Presidents' Way. There is a huge lawn here for a chopper to land on."

"Let me check. Hang on." She was silent a moment. "I'm on an emergency network, and I have priority."

"You talking to me?" Linsey asked.

"No, honey, I'm talking to the Highway Patrol. They have a chopper up over Highway 163 at Richmond Street, and it will be landing next to you in the next five minutes. That's the best I can do at the moment."

"Thanks, Louise. You are a doll."

"Just doing my job. Which way is Cleve headed? Give me the details and I'll have every cop in that part of town including the Navy and Marines on his case."

"Louise, hold off. I want to follow and see where Cleve goes. There must be a nest around here where those mushroom people hang out when they're not sucking on people's necks."

"Good idea, Linsey. Keep me informed."

As Linsey gave the number of Cleve's black and white, a chopper landed beside her. Linsey waved her gold badge. The chopper was an open four-seater with two men in jump suits and blue-gold helmets with shiny visors at the controls. They wore aviator sunglasses and had throat mikes.

She clambered on board, and the copilot checked she was securely buckled in. "What are we doing, Lieutenant?"

"You're following a black and white Harbor Police patrol car being driven by an officer who is to be considered out of control. He has a woman with him, African-American in a red business outfit, very fancy shmancy, probably unconscious. Both are to be considered armed and very dangerous. We need to locate them so we can quarantine them. We don't want to ourselves away, but we need to find out where Officer Bartlett is going."

As the chopper veered this way and that in strong, steady moves that left Linsey's lunch suspended in various places in mid-air, the co-pilot sat with his boots up on a steel bar and looked down with strong binoculars. He kept toggling from a medium field to a sharp focus, the same way Linsey used the little finder scope and larger viewing lenses of her telescope on the patio to locate a planet and then zoom in for a closer look.

"There he is," said the co-pilot. He pointed down among the tree crowns. She spotted the white roof and markings of Cleve's car and felt a lurch in her gut that made her want to cry. If only he could come back and have coffee and donuts with her—but those days were gone forever. A lot of things had suddenly changed for many people, she was sure.

"Just follow," she said.

The pilot nodded and hung back. He kept high enough so that the driver below would not notice the whine of his turbine engine or rattle of his powerful rotors.

"He is headed toward 32nd Street," the co-pilot said.

Lima Voyager, Linsey thought. The main nest. If not the main one, then the original one.

Chapter 54.

Montgomery Field sits atop Kearny Mesa. During Superbowl games it houses half a dozen to a dozen blimps that circle the stadium in Mission Valley. Year around, it is a moderate size airfield and a very busy one, bearing much of the local small plane traffic as well as prop-driven commuter flights to Los Angeles and other neighboring counties. Some amount of small cargo goes in and out.

Lee Collwood flew into Montgomery Field. He climbed from his converted Learjet and strode across the windy, sunny air strip toward a waiting van. The van had the legend Sunny Cleaners and a bunch of fake phone numbers and web page addresses on its sides. If anyone did call or email, they'd be put on hold or rerouted by answering services and webmasters until they gave up. It was a good cover for Blake's men. Their weapons were in a false floor in the van, under buckets and mops and other cleaning supplies.

Beside the van, Martin Delavalle stood waiting. Delavalle wore a sharp gray suit, light pink shirt, and dark reddish-blue tie, along with dark Oxfords and a plaid linen cap, sometimes called a newsboy cap, with a slouch top pinned to its visor and hanging over one ear like a beret. Natty dresser, Collwood thought.

As Collwood approached, the van's side door opened. Inside sat Thomas Blake's five surviving mercenaries. Blake himself got out of the driver's side to meet with Collwood and Delavalle.

"Well?" Collwood demanded. "Any action? News? Results?"

Blake shook his head. "We've gone to almost all the crew members' homes. The result is always the same. Nobody has seen the crew member. They know he's back from the sea, but he has called with some excuse to say he won't be showing up for a week or two. Some important mission, usually to get extra dough and make everyone happy."

Delavalle nodded. "Nobody's going to say no to that."

"Not good enough," Collwood said. "I need to locate everyone of those men. You see what this plague did to Lo. It infects men, turns them into walking spores for this mushroom pest, and they kill more people as they start to deteriorate."

"I want to go back to the Lima Voyager and start tracking from there," Blake said. As Collwood glowered at him, Blake said: "You ordered us to go house to house, looking for crew members. That's what we're doing. I tried to tell you you are micromanaging this operation."

"You get paid to do what and how I tell you," Collwood said.

Blake shrugged. "Hire a professional, then don't let him follow his nose? You're right—I get paid. I don't think we're doing this the right way."

"What's do you suggest?" Delavalle asked quietly.

"I would make this assumption," Blake said as he drew a diagram in the dirt at their feet with a long twig. "This circle is the city. Over here is the point of origin. Assuming they are still in the city, I would assume they have some kind of common meeting point. Some place of assembly when all else fails. If we could find that place, we might even be able to call them together—and then kill them all."

"Oh Lord," Delavalle said, turning suddenly away.

"What's the matter? Weak stomach?" Collwood said coldly.

"I didn't sign up for mass killing."

"These things aren't human any longer," Collwood said.

"Still—"

"Still what?"

Delavalle shook his head.

Collwood grinned. "Tell you what. We won't kill them. It's too late to cover up any longer, anyway. We find 'em, we notify the Government and become heroes."

Delavalle took a deep breath. "That sounds a lot better."

"For a minute there I thought we were losing you," Collwood said.

Delavalle said: "There are limits, even for me."

"Okay. Glad we know your limits now. Blake—"

"Yes, Mr. Collwood?"

"Do what you feel you need to do and keep me informed."

"Yessir, thanks."

As Blake drove off in the van, Collwood turned to Delavalle. "You know that I'm in a lot of trouble, don't you?"

Delavalle nodded as he stubbed pebbles with the toe of one Oxford shoe. "Yes. I understand the Congressional committee that Louise Trost answers to has overridden Metrick's stay order, and has officially seized the Volcan Mountain facility. How long can you dance away from them, Collwood?"

"They are investigating me," Collwood said, poker faced. "They aren't anywhere close to the truth yet. Neither are you."

"You're probably right."

Collwood watched the other man's flicker of expressions. Delavalle was about as loyal as a paycheck, if that. Right now, it was a good bet Delavalle was weighing whether he should quit and leave town, stick around and help Collwood in hope of cashing in as the ship sank, or else going to Louise Trost and becoming state's evidence. On the latter, there was little that he could bring, other than an unprovable allegation about the murder conversation they'd just had with Blake. Collwood bet that Delavalle would stick around a while.

"What do you want me to do?"

"Keep the operation going here in San Diego for me. I'll take care of my end. At year's end, we'll talk about whether you want to take the job permanently or some other option."

"You think you'll still be around by then?" Delavalle said with an impish, carrot-topped grin.

"You can lay money on it. Speaking of which—I'll have some for you shortly. Just to sweeten the pot a little."

Collwood winked and walked away, sensing Delavalle's stare at his back. Halfway to the jet, he glanced back and saw Delavalle slowly getting into his car—thoughtfully. Frowning. There was a man not to be trusted, Collwood thought as he leaped up the jet's stairs and waved for the pilots to take off.

Within the hour, Collwood's jet was in the pattern above Los Angeles—one of dozens of aircraft of all sizes and types circling to await their turn at landing instructions.

Syd Appelbaum met him on the private runway and whisked him away in a posh Lincoln Continental limousine. Syd was a small man in his upper 70s. He wore a business suit though he was retired, and leaned on a cane. His face retained a certain humor that came with age and the endlessly repetitive folly of human nature. He'd been in corporate as well as criminal law for many decades and had seen what he called the human cycle— predictably not pretty. "You're not dead yet," he told Collwood.

"I'm glad to hear that," Collwood said as he mixed himself a Campari and Soda on ice from the wet bar. "Drink?"

Appelbaum closed his eyes briefly, and shook his head. "I had lunch late at the Club."

Collwood sipped until he felt refreshed and braced. He sat back and nursed his drink. It was nice to smell the bitter liqueur with its sweet subtleties, and to hear ice crackling as the soda ate away at it. "So what's your scheme, Syd?"

"Oh, not a problem. I already have a call in to Metrick. He'll meet me for lunch tomorrow, and I'll spell out what he needs to do so we don't go ahead and publicize the story about his adventures with the latest Hollywood madam." He gave a dry, old-man chuckle through yellowed teeth. "We have at least 32 hours of him on camera with two dozen different women. There's more, but why wear ourselves out? It's tiring. He'll do what we want."

"And that is?"

"He will authorize a project. We'll backfill the details, because you know this will end up in a House subcommittee hearing even as it hits the press."

"Yes?"

"We'll say that Anaconda Chemicals had a secret Government project to do humanitarian pharmaceuticals research, and that something has gone horribly wrong but—and here's the important point—it's not your fault. We'll figure out a way to make some low-flying Air Force lackeys have to retire early. We might even pay them off so they aren't too unhappy. It will all work out, Lee." He patted his nephew's shoulder. "My boy, I saved your father's ass and his grandfather's ass more than once. We'll do it again, don't worry."

"If you can make a few San Diego cops unhappy at the same time," Collwood said darkly, "all the better."

Uncle Syd gave him that look he didn't like, nor understood, as if pitying him. "Don't push it farther than you have to, Lee."

Angrily, Collwood downed his drink, threw the cup aside, and he sat with his arms folded. He glowered at the back of the driver's seat. Uncle Syd calmly looked out the window. "I'm fixing your cash problem for you, sonny."

"Sorry."

"Keep your anger in check. You need to be cool. I'm going to move some money around through the travel office of the Chicago and New York facilities. In their cash pot, and then out to travelers' checks so that you'll have about a million bucks in walking-around money. You'll need it. Oh, and—"

"Yes?"

"Get rid of Delavalle. He made a phone call to Louise Trost's office to see what kind of information she needs. Just a probe, but it tells me he stinks."

"Yeah, I know that. I just need someone to run the San Diego operation. We're still a going concern, after all."

"You need someone else. Cut him loose before he learns anything more."

"If I fire him, with or without cause, he'll be over at Trost's office within the hour. He heard me talking with Thomas Blake about killing the mushroom men."

"Ouch. That wasn't wise, Lee."

"I know. I thought the more I get him sucked into what I'm doing, the more he incriminates himself."

Uncle Syd, usually calm, clapped himself on the knee. "That sets him up for a plea bargain, dummy."

"Okay, I'll send him to Peru."

Uncle Syd raised an eyebrow. "If he'll go—"

"Make it two million in travelers' checks. Money talks. Delavalle is more mercenary than Blake and his bunch."

"Ah yes. Morton brought him on board. Surprising. Wonder how and why Morton picked him up."

"Naïve. Morton didn't know anything."

"I hope you're right."

Collwood grinned. "He's a mushroom man now. I doubt he cares much about human affairs anymore. Probably doesn't remember me at all."

Chapter 55.

Linsey sat in the Highway Patrol helicopter and watched intently as Cleve drove the patrol car with Annette toward the 32nd Street Navy facility. She could clearly see the dark hulk of the Lima Voyager civilian cargo ship at her dock amid all the gray Navy vessels and cranes. She watched through borrowed binoculars as the patrol car rolled slowly along the tortuous gravel path amid wire fences. When the patrol car came to the dock, it stopped. Cleve got out and led a compliant Annette up the gangway. Dark figures came out to meet them. Cleve and Annette vanished into the ship. One of the figures—not Cleve—walked down the ramp, got into the cruiser, and took off.

Linsey got on her phone to Louise and explained what she had just seen. "I think we should follow this guy and see where he goes. He might lead us to another location of theirs. Before we pounce, maybe we can identify all of their main locations."

"Okay," Louise said doubtfully. "I'll give you another day, but I'm getting an awful lot of heat from the city, state, and Feds. We can't just stand by while this thing explodes out of hand. Nearly 100 people have died from the yellow fungus alone."

"Is that still a growing concern?"

"I think the numbers have shrunk. Shaun Nolan says he's more sure than ever the yellow fungus is some kind of agitator. There is a far more sinister purpose at work here, and the huge mushrooms are a direct result of that."

"So we need to focus beyond the crop dusting thing."

"Yes. We have sealed off the Volcan Mountain plant and we're waiting for an Army Chemical NBC team to go in." *Nuclear, Biological, and Chemical*, Linsey understood.

The car below headed toward the nearest on-ramp and then north on I-5. Near Morena Boulevard, it crossed through the maze of exchanges and ended up heading East on I-8.

"What's he doing now?" Louise asked.

"Heading east on I-8. Louise, with Cleve missing, and now his patrol car, this business is coming to a boil."

"Another one of your colleagues is missing—Joe Walesky."

"Ernie's brother! Let me guess. Ernie called Joe, did this black air thing to him, and Joe in turn did it to Cleve, who begat the new-Annette, and so forth. Ernie is at his house now, making a new Aunt Joanie, so Jack tells me."

"There had to be at least another one involved, because it appears to be a one-to-one thing. The mushroom person walking around is a spore, according to Shaun. The spore deteriorates in a few days and has to pass the genetic material along to another victim."

Chapter 56.

Jack was on the cell phone with his boss from outside the Walesky home. "Griff, it's out of hand. There are news crews all over the place. There are six reporters from various TV stations interviewing Aunt Nellie and the kids. I'm not telling you what to do, and I have to stay married to my wife, plus I'm under oath to Louise Trost and what not. If I were you, I'd set up a special team to cover this situation around the clock. I'll stay inside and keep my mouth shut, and I've been promised a major scoop if I do that."

"There's a book in it for you," Griff said wryly. "Sounds good, Jack. Do what you can. Do you have a camera?"

"Yep—a digital with spare chips, batteries, the works."

"Take all the pictures you can and put a story together that we can lead with as soon as they let you talk. I'll call Trost myself and ask how much longer she wants us to sit here and get run over by busloads of people from out of town."

As he hung up, a Fire Department Battalion Chief help up a yellow chemical suit kit. "Mr. Simon? The Mayor and the Fire Chief want you to go in with us if you'd like. We have our own camera crew, but you can be the public voice of record."

Jack brightened. As he put on the light plastic suit that totally enveloped his body and made him look like the other half dozen Fire and Police personnel wearing them—a cluster of yellow beach balls—his phone warbled. It was Louise. "I trust you are happy now?"

"I am glowing with joy. Is Linsey okay?"

"She's in a Highway Patrol chopper ringed by white hats."

"Perfect. We're getting ready to enter the house, Louise."

"Good luck."

Our first contact with the alien life form, Jack thought as he joined the line-up by the kitchen door. He glimpsed hundreds of spectators beyond the yellow police lines. Among them, he saw Nellie, Maribel, and Jimmy. They looked frightened, full of horrified anticipation, and grief.

A policeman in yellow chem suit, wielding a compact assault rifle, stood ready. Behind him stood a policewoman, in the same yellow, with a Glock automatic in both fists and aimed dead center at the doorway. Beside the kicker stood a third cop in yellow, holding a powerful flashlight up high and its battery in a suitcase type carrying case in his left hand.

"Everybody ready?" the team leader in the middle said—the battalion chief who had given Jack the suit. Jack was last in line, and missed his own Glock. Instead, he had a digital camera with flash in his hands, ready to take up to 140 high quality, 10 megapixel jpegs images.

"Go," the team leader said.

The kicker shoved the door open. A team of firemen wielding a steel battering ram nearby stood down. There was no resistance at the door. Like a snake, the six team members and Jack eased into the house. Everywhere they went, the powerful light darted back and forth. Jack knew the layout and called out: "Straight ahead into the dining room. That's my puke on the wall to your right." Nobody even snickered. They were probably all ready to puke.

The kitchen, including closets and cupboards, was clear. Everything sat in ghostly gloom and silence as if aboard a sunken ocean liner. They might as well be walking through the bowels of the Titanic. Going into the living room in one sinuous, sliding body, they explored on. "Nice job," the battalion chief said as they passed Jack's breakfast.

"I hope you didn't eat cheese with that," someone else said.

"Focus," the battalion chief said. "Enough jokes. We broke the ice. Now focus on the work or we could all die."

Jack told the battalion chief: "The living room is to the right."

"Small house," the other said. "Not a lot of hiding places."

They ransacked the living room. They turned chairs and couches, tables and chairs upside down.

"The garage," someone suggested.

"Outside," the battalion chief said. "We've swept the place. Nobody in here."

"How about the crawl space under the front of the house?"

"Okay," the battalion chief said. "Let's split up. Three on the garage, three on the crawl space."

As Jack watched, three of the people in yellow broke the lock on the garage and lifted the door. Three others pulled away a long piece of plywood covering the entrance to the crawl space. The garage was easy. Single-walled and big enough for one car, it was packed with typical household junk. The three explorers started passing out boxes, bird cages, skis, water equipment, a surf board, all the usual stuff, and no sign of Ernie and Joanie. Firemen trudged about on the roof with their normal fire gear on, but with oxygen masks. They used their picks to pry holes in the roof, looking for secret spaces. *Nothing.*

The man with the heavy-duty light lay spread-eagled on the gravel, and shone his light in while another man cautiously crawled to the entrance preceded by a Glock automatic held in both hands. "There's something down there in the corner."

"Can you see what it is?"

"Something long and dark."

"Sounds about right," Jack said—recalling the bracketed shapes Linsey had told him about from inside Lima Voyager.

"Get a hook in there and see if you can pull on it," the battalion chief said. "Have a gun ready, and we'll have both your feet in hand so we can yank you out."

That is a brave man, Jack thought. He tried to make himself small as he got in close to take pictures.

Fifteen minutes and a lot of sweat and tension later, out came an abandoned, rotting Boy Scout tent. Everyone stood around and scratched their heads.

"We had to have missed something," the battalion chief said.

Jack said: "From what I'm told, this thing always likes to nest against a baseboard horizontally close to the floor."

The battalion chief exchanged looks with the on-site police inspector. The latter shrugged. "Go in with your hooks and axes and take the baseboards apart."

Fifteen minutes and a lot of hammering and racket later, including the scream of tortured nails coming out of wood where they'd been compressed by half a century of drying, and there still was nothing. A thick dust drifted in the air.

The police and fire bosses looked at Jack, who, by default, had the most knowledge of the situation, and it wasn't much.

Jack raised a finger. "Wait!"

Everyone looked at him. He sniffed. "I smell weird soil."

"I smell it too," the cop who'd been the kicker said.

"That's a sign that you got close." Jack strode to the door. He pointed to the kicker and another man. "You two, grab crow bars and follow me." Together, they went back into the deathly silent, shadowy house which now was a total wreck. Drywall up to a foot high was gone, and daylight shone in with sharp spikes through the bottoms of the broken walls. Dust drifted thickly. Dust that had lain in these walls for generations, sealed up on some summer construction day back when life was black and white, Eisenhower was president, and the first Disney lunch boxes were carried to school.

Jack stepped forward one step at a time. His feet crunched on rubble. The others crunched along behind him. Hardly anyone dared breathe. The smell of mushrooms got stronger toward the bathroom. Jack nudged the door open with his foot, while keeping the camera ready to start shooting. The smell became overpowering.

Bathtub, sink, waste basked, shower curtain...

Bathtub was empty. Nobody hiding behind shower curtain.

Then Jack saw liquid oozing on the ground. He knelt down and touched it with his gloved finger. It looked like greasy water. Not rusty, like from old pipes. Nothing fecal or pissy. This looked more like it had floating mites of white in it like...he rubbed some between his fingers...greasy...like decomposing human fat tissue, but without the heavy cadaverine odor.

Jack pointed to the 40-gallong water heater that was built into the wall, with its other side in the garage. The ooze came directly out of the wall, leaking through the caulking around the bathtub, and down onto the floor around the top of the tub.

At Jack's signal, the two men with him used their steel hooks and bars to pull the wall apart. The smell of loam and mushrooms was unmistakable, along with a noticeable corpse smell.

"Oh God," one man said, and the other turned away. He could be heard retching into this suit and ran outside.

Jack and the remaining man stood looking at the inside of the crawlspace. Lying along a hidden space beside the water heater were two bodies, if one could call them that. One was the late Aunt Joanie, who had lost about 100 pounds of water and fat, which had oozed out into the bathroom and decayed in the afternoon heat. She looked withered like a dying grape, covered by white fungus like a fine mist, but Jack knew that a nonhuman resembling a far younger and more attractive Joanie would rise out of his union. Embracing her, and embraced by her, was the late Uncle Ernie. He'd been late getting his victim, and was already decaying when he'd taken Joanie. One could still see the anguish on his crumbling face as it rotted away like the brown and dry husk of an apple left on a barn windowsill. He still had one gloved hand lying over his mid section. Dead, tangled black hose still dangled from his mouth and entered her neck, but now her mouth was open and a fresh black hose extended from her mouth directly into his brain via his left ear. She was becoming the new walking asexual spore. She was sucking his identity, his memories, his marrow and brains out of his body. They were exchanging genetic material and at times it almost seemed one could see minute visible changes—a ripple under the arm skin, a bubbling of the belly skin, a shudder in the cheek skin.

Most remarkable of all, however, was the fact that the former Uncle Ernie had already started coming apart into two dozen or more semi-circular bracket mushrooms whose faint gray caps were speckled with faintly darker round spots like a form of camouflage. In its mordant way, it was very beautiful.

The cop choked out his words one disgusted, tortured syllable at a time: "What-the-hell-are-these-things?"

Jack said quietly: "A life form that wants to replace ours and be master of the earth."

A central dilemma suddenly occurred to him—something nobody else realized. He went outside to call Louise Trost. It might be too late to save mankind and the earth.

Chapter 57.

"Where is he going?" Linsey muttered as she sat in the Highway Patrol helicopter.

Below them, the Harbor Police car driven by an unknown person—or alien, or ex-person, whatever one properly called the mushroom people—was driving eastward at a sedate pace of 55 m.p.h. As it left the El Cajon city limits (past San Diego, past La Mesa) it speeded up slightly to the legal limit of 65 m.p.h.

"He's staying out of trouble," the pilot said. "I have 30 minutes of flying time left and will have to set down in the next 15 minutes. There is a Highway Patrol helipad out here at—"

"Look!" the co-pilot cried out. He handed Linsey the binocs.

"Holy Tomato," the pilot exclaimed.

Linsey looked down and noticed a glowing light in the windshield of the speeding patrol car. At first she thought it was a reflection of the sunlight, but the car was heading east away from the evening sun descending on the ocean miles behind it. As she looked, she noticed another dot of light glowing with incandescent intensity in the front seat.

"What's he doing?" the pilot asked.

Linsey said: "It looks like he is lighting road flares and laying them on the dashboard."

"I see smoke trailing out of the windows," the co-pilot said.

"Oh man," the pilot said gravely. "Put out an alert."

"Right." The co-pilot radioed CHP units to pursue, to block, to clear the path, to do whatever they must to save lives.

"The whole trip out here was a diversion," the pilot said. "He's committing suicide down there."

"It goes to show that they have no regard for their own lives. It's throwing itself away casually just to lead us from the ship. That probably means they knew we were up there."

"But do they care anymore," the pilot said while the other man chattered with his base station radio operator. "Or are the so far along that it doesn't matter anymore?"

"I don't know," Linsey said. Below, the black and white unit started to trail a heavy tail of thick black smoke stretching a quarter mile behind. As she watched, pale flames began to lick up around the roof in the rear. The flames got more intense, darker, orange, finally red. Then the trunk lid blew off as the gas tank exploded. Like a missile trailing black smoke, the patrol car burst totally into

Chapter 58.

The Sunny Cleaners van sat parked on the heights in Barrio Logan under the ramps leading up to the Coronado Bay Bridge. The door was open and the supposed cleaning crew all sat in the grass in a small park, eating sandwiches and drinking soda. They looked like an innocent crew of youthful men as they laughed among each other, played a little soccer, or cooed at a small dog led on a leash by a young girl.

Thomas Blake eyeballed the ship in the 32nd Street yards with binoculars. What he saw interested him greatly. He counted at least twelve figures moving around on her deck. The dock, the ship, and the decks were noticeably coated with several shades of a reddish fungus. Sort of brick or Mars colored, or burnt sienna. Maybe the crew had come back. Was it possible? But what for? Were they now like the missing Chen Lo—mushroom people? One way to find out—pay a visit.

He gave the men ten more minutes to finish their meal. Then he ordered them into the van. He drove slowly down to 32nd Street and passed through the guard gate. He had a pass specially signed by Mr. Collwood, and his men all showed their I.D. cards (fakes) and signed in. Nobody suspected that his cleaning crew were highly trained killers, nor that the floor of the van contained assault rifles and ammo. Each man had his favorite web belt and gear stashed in there, always including at least one or two good knives, cable cutters, all the essentials.

"Busy place today," said a female Navy guard, a blonde with pimples. She looked trim and athletic in her Shore Patrol uniform with black boots and white puttees.

"What do you mean?" Blake asked.

"Oh, they had a large truck in there this morning. Had trouble backing it in and getting out."

"We're just the cleaning crew," Blake said.

"Ship looks like it needs it."

"What did they truck away?"

"Beats me. We don't inspect civilian cargo. We should, I suppose, but we have our orders."

Blake nodded. Inwardly he snorted: Collwood probably has his pet Congressman fix things like that. Not that he knew of any such pet, but didn't all the really rich have some sort of mouthpiece in Washington on payola? Blake's interpretation of his life's experiences was such that his opinion of Third World corruption was converging with his newly forming observation of the more sophisticated but equally morbid and probably more dangerous corruption in the First World. He wondered what Collwood would have been anxious to sneak out the door—if it was Collwood behind it, not someone using Collwood for cover.

He drove slowly and observantly along the gravel drive among the Navy properties. Nothing looked out of place. He was sure there was surveillance, but they'd be in and out before anyone could get to them. He came to the dock and stopped. The men quickly opened the floor. They donned their combat gear and picked up their ammo and weapons. Each man had an O.D. poncho to cover what he was carrying.

There was a coating of that brickish or Marslike dust, probably pollen or spores or whatever, and a mossy fungus underneath clinging to stone, wood, or iron with equal tenacity. One could almost see the red dust moving slowly through the air.

First thing he did was cut the phone lines, in case someone wanted to use a land line to call out for help. Not much point in these cell phone days, but no sense skipping a measure.

He sent one man up the gangway about halfway, unarmed and without a poncho, to see what kind of attention he could attract and then say "I'm just the buffer, man. Is this the right ship?" or some stupid line like that, spoken with an accent.

No sign of life. The man returned and picked up his gear, then ran up the gangway and sprang on deck. Looking about, he signaled all clear. Blake sent the men up one by one, and each man jumped on board and ran for cover. One by one, they could not all be taken out at once. If there was an ambush, one man might go down but the others were well trained and fast. This had to go quickly now.

Brick-like red dust swirled with graceful, infinite slowness in the air around them. Nobody was coughing or sneezing yet, so Blake filed it away for future reference. He and one other man ran up into the bridge area and scouted around. Nobody in sight. Just in case anyone were in a closet or toilet, they rolled tear gas in and closed the doors. That would make them come popping out, but nobody did.

"I thought you saw a dozen men up here," his companion whispered.

"I did. They must be somewhere on board. Look, it's worth the try. If those dozen are the missing sailors, we've accounted for half of them and our job is nearly done."

"I'm with you."

Together, they went around the main deck from door to door, cabin to cabin, checking it out, popping in tear gas where they preferred not to enter. This way, they made a circuit all the way around, under the watchful eyes and gun muzzles of their four fellow mercenaries.

"It's time to go below," Tom Blake told his men. "Eyes on the backs of your heads."

"Got it," several men murmured. "Let's get it done."

Down the steps they went into the darkness. Each man had a police-style steel flashlight with six batteries that could be used as a club if all else failed. Down they went into the increasingly earthy smelling darkness. Six darting flashlight beams made for a peculiar disco-like ambience—all they needed was loud music, Blake thought hyperactively. He liked to use blue pool hall chalk to keep his fingertips dry, and he rubbed and rolled a cube of the stuff in one hand while keeping the other on his assault rifle.

They came to the main area of the A Deck below. The air was stifling down here. "Somebody open a hatch or two," one man protested.

"Don't touch anything," Blake whispered. "Stay focused. We can be in and out in twenty minutes if we don't get sidetracked."

"This is spooky as Hallow E'en Night," someone whispered.

Garlands of cobwebs hung from the ceilings, along with torn electrical cords, an open overhead panel, and other items. The walls were wet and streaked with rust. The overwhelming atmosphere was one of rust color, like the brick dust outside, and humid. "Air conditioning for mushrooms," someone whispered.

Blake could almost believe it. "Focus!" he ordered. "Sweep!"

They went from cabin to cabin, kicking steel hatches open and zigzagging their ready-to-shoot poses left and right. Shafts of their own light darted and stabbed all around them in that mad psycho dance floor whirl. *Silent disco. Nothing.*

They went down another deck, repeating the same process. The space got narrower. Along the keel in the center was a round chamber for a long worm gear running from the oil burning engines up front to the propeller at stern center below the water line. An old ship, Blake thought, and well in need of retirement. What kind of master had run this ship? This was heaven for a crew of pigs. Blake was no sailor, but even he would have had this crew scrubbing, scraping, peeling, and painting.

Finally, on the lowest deck, the stench of mushrooms grew until the underlying rot was nauseating. "If those are mushrooms," someone said, "they are rotting."

"Over here!" a man shrieked. "Come look at this!"

They warily surged forward, and came to a scene Blake thought resembled something from hell. In a large forward cargo hold about twenty feet square and ten feet high, lay the bodies of at least a dozen men. *Not men, but mushroom men. Dead ones.*

Lights darted over the contorted tangle and heap of bodies, the gaping eyes and mouths, the stiffly upraised hands, the sprawled legs. Oddly, the usual

Norway rats were nowhere to be seen. This must not be their kind of feast, Blake thought grimly. He could not see a single insect, not even the hardy cockroach. Something was very bad here.

"Didn't the boss tell us to look for all these damn bracket things along the lower bulkheads?" a man asked.

Another said: "I thought the ship was full of them."

"Now we know what Collwood's trucking crew removed from here this morning," Blake said.

"I smell something fishy," a man said.

"Let's get out of here. They're all dead."

With a last look over the dim, gray field of dead mushroom men, Blake turned and headed topside. "Let's evacuate.".

When they came to the last deck, they found that the hatch had been closed and sealed over them. Blake felt an ominous sort of dread and fear and anger all mixed together. Someone had lured them in here and betrayed them. *Who? Collwood? Why?* And he'd severed the land lines, so they couldn't call out.

"Radio's topside where we can't get to it," a man whispered.

"We're screwed."

Blake whipped out his cell phone. He shook it. "Dead. Someone has killed the local cell. We're going to die in this rusting bucket with those dead sponges down below."

"Keep cool. We'll pry open a hatch and climb out."

An hour later, after trying every hatch they could find, every possible exit, they found that they were all sealed shut and beyond opening. Rusted? Or purposely sealed. Blake was summoned to the main hatch leading up top by a man who held his finger over his lips. "What is it?"

The man whispered, pointing upward. "Can't you hear it?"

Blake signaled for total silence and then listened intently.

He heard a steady hiss. Shrugging, he looked questioningly at the man who had summoned him. The man said: "Someone is welding the hatch shut. They probably welded all the porthole covers and other hatches shut. We're trapped in here."

"Listen!"

The hiss stopped with a popping noise. Steps could be heard. Then silence. Then the starting of two or three car engines. "That's someone driving our van away."

"It could be years before anyone comes and looks in here."

What bothered Blake most was not dying, which was bad enough, or starving, or even drinking the filthy water in here. It was that the flashlights would be dead in a few hours. There would be total, oppressive, silent darkness. *A floating tomb.*

Chapter 59.

"What on earth is that?" The President of the United States made a face as he pointed to the projection screen on he wall of the Situation Room at the White House.

POTUS was watching an unfolding disaster in San Diego along with two dozen government officials including the Surgeon General and other health experts. On the screen, official Navy and Marine Corps footage, as well as up to the minute CNN and MSNBC reporting, featured a kind of fuzzy cloud covering the 32nd Street Naval facility. "We believe that this Fuzzy Cloud, as it's being called, is made of fungal spores, Mr. President." So said the Commander of Naval forces in San Diego from his emergency office at NAS North Island.

"Is it spreading?" POTUS demanded.

"It's possible. Wind could carry it inland," said the Air Force meteorology colonel in the room.

"How fast?"

The top Army mycologist, a brigadier general, said: "Not much is known yet about the characteristics, the life cycle, the DNA map, of this organism. We believe it's fungal in nature, and spreads spores on the wind. That said, it could take generations for it to actually get beyond the city."

"Generations?" POTUS asked. "You mean years?"

"Nossir. I'm talking mushroom generations. They can pop up overnight. I'm talking days. In other words, picture this, Mr. President. From each origin, a ring spreads out, or an oval, whatever the wind pattern happens to be. That's how far the spores radiate in all directions. Let's say it's 100 feet per gust of wind. Maybe 1000 feet per day. Some number of the spores land in a damp, dark spot and flourish. If conditions are right, a new mushroom springs up overnight. Remember, we've heard from Dr. Nolan that person or persons unknown were crop dusting with an Accelerator fungus that gets the other fungi all worked up so they produce bigger, faster, sooner. Each new mushroom dumps two million or more spores per minute and becomes the origin for new circles. Now you have dozens of new origins. Each of those spreads its spores in a circle around. Well, you can see, Sir, that within a few weeks the circles are going to cover many square miles. And that's just the simple picture without a lot of scientific mumbo jumbo."

"What do you recommend, General?" POTUS asked.

"Honestly? I'd evacuate San Diego. Go in and bug bomb the area until nothing can possibly survive, especially not the fungi."

"With what?"

"A cocktail of detergents, fungal infestations, rots that kill other fungi and then self-destruct—whatever we can throw at it."

An admiral reminded him: "Don't forget we have several atomic submarines tied up at Point Loma, just across the harbor. We have aircraft carriers sitting at North Island."

"Sail them out, get them out now," POTUS said.

"Sensible idea, Sir," said several senior admirals and generals. Within minutes, couriers ran from the room to send official orders signed by the Chief of Naval Operations.

"What else?" POTUS said.

"Tens of thousands of hotel workers, local residents, people working downtown—it will ruin their economy."

"We'll deal with tourism later," POTUS said. "Get everyone out in an orderly fashion while there is still time. Listen to this." He flicked a button on the intercom before him.

A woman's voice spoke. "Am I on, Mr. President?"

POTUS said: "This is Louise Trost, regional chief of the anti-terrorism task force of Congress in San Diego. Tell them about the casualties, Louise."

"Mr. President, over 100 persons have now died from the initial dusting of Yellow Fungus, as we call it. I'd say another 1000 are sick and will probably recover. However, the city is becoming increasingly infested with huge, overgrown mushrooms that are filling the air with spores that can only be toxic in many cases when breathed or ingested. My specialist here, Dr. Shaun Nolan, has estimated that over 50,000 persons have already been exposed, and an unknown number of those are in danger of dying. The emergency rooms are already filled to capacity with respiratory problems, secondary infections, blood disease, and other problems. If we don't evacuate, it will mean not only a medical catastrophe, but a public relations nightmare. You can carry the implications from there."

"Thank you, Louise." POTUS raised his eyebrows and looked around. "Comments?"

"Evacuate," someone said. Soon a chorus of voices rose, saying the word over and over. It was a voice roll call for not only medical realism but also political survival.

Chapter 60.

The air down around the Gaslamp District, around Petco Park baseball stadium, around the Convention Center and the great harborside hotels, was filled with clouds of drifting spores.

From Broadway downtown to the edges of National City, a frightened but orderly evacuation was taking place. Military and police occupied every street corner. The National Guard in their familiar MP uniforms were out in the thousands to make sure there was no panic, no looting, no fighting. School buses were marshaled to carry out those unable to walk due to age, extreme weight, illness, or similar problems. There would be a primary collection center in the former Jack Murphy Stadium at the far end of Mission Valley. Plans were to establish yet another evacuation center in El Cajon, and to have these center leapfrog each other until the need to evacuate was past.

Mushrooms of all shapes grew to fantastic sizes, some by now as tall as a grown man. There were a thousand different shapes, too. Some looked like huge button mushrooms on thick short stems. Others had thin straight stems with wavy caps. Other caps were rounded, or resembled Asian peasant caps. Some even looked like umbrellas that some imaginary wind had turned inside out—those, in particular, showing their brown gills greased with sticky spores. Clusters of fine green mushrooms grew together on stems curving away from each other. Many mushrooms had no visible stems, but attached like scallops or sconces or wavy clam shells around gutters and garden walls.

Through it all streamed a steady flow of men, women, and children bringing what belongings they could carry. Many were evacuees from luxury harborside condos. Some were restaurant workers leaving at the end of their shift, or hotel maids, clerks, messengers, and parking valets. A few were staggering or coughing. A few more came by on makeshift stretchers carried by unarmed Navy men half in, half out of uniform.

Chapter 61.

Martin Delavalle had a woman with him when the knock came on the door at three in the morning. Still slightly drunk from the night before, Delavalle rolled out of bed. He patted the woman's behind and staggered over to the door. The knocking continued the whole time.

"Yeah, yeah, hang on." He peered out through the peep hole and saw a gold police shield against a gray background.

The knocking intensified, and a handful of fat fingers roughly thrust some kind of paper up to the peep hole. "Police! Open up! We have a warrant."

The woman sat up in bed. "What is it, honey?" She was a common prostitute he'd picked up on El Cajon Boulevard that evening after drinking at a pub near 70th Street. "Oh God," she said, getting into her clothes. "Let me out of here."

The door was rocking on its hinges by now.

"Hang on, you Gestapo bastards!" Delavalle bellowed. "I'm getting my clothes on."

"Mister, I don't know nothing," the young Hispanic girl said. "Tell them I ain't done nothing."

"Quiet, Maria." He didn't know her name, but Maria was good enough for both of them.

He opened the door and saw the huge red haired guy, probably sixty, and mostly gray, but still very much a red haired guy, standing outside. The giant wore cowboy boots, tight black jeans, a gray jacket, white blouse with turquoise bolo, and a cowboy hat. "Mr. Martin Delavalle."

"That's me."

"I am Detective Captain Enderdoss, and I am highly upset that I had to get out of bed to collect your tired ass." He waved a sheet of paper. "This is a warrant for your arrest. You are charged with a whole sheet of very bad deeds, including trafficking in illegal drugs, crossing state lines to conspire, conspiring in the first place, thinking about conspiring, conspiring to conspire, and a whole lot of other shit that's all written down here." He handed Delavalle the paper.

Delavalle glanced at it. "This is all a bunch of baloney."

Several uniformed city cops stepped in and turned Delavalle around to search him for weapons. They handcuffed him and laid him belly down on the carpet.

The girl grabbed her things and tried to make an escape, stepping on Delavalle with her high heels. Enderdoss raised a thumb over his shoulder and growled: "Book the bitch. I've seen her around. She's got a sheet with us. Prostitution."

Delavalle lay face down on the carpet of his leased luxury condo. "This is all bogus, officer, and I plan to sue."

"You can call your liar from downtown," Enderdoss growled. "Take him away and book him, guys. I'm going back home to bed."

At four a.m., a rumpled county defender showed up at Delavalle's cell. "How are you doing?" the 40ish man with more beard shadow than an English country hedge asked.

"Not too good. I know what they're after. They want to bust Collwood."

"Who?"

"Sit down—I'll explain. I'm expecting a phone call."

"Oh, really?"

"Yes. From a Louise Trost—who now owns my nuts, and she's going to set me up as state's witness. Tell her I said yes."

At nine a.m., having catnapped and feeling more tense than awake, Martin Delavalle and his lawyer sat in a room resembling a concrete bunker with steel doors. In walked Louise Trost with two FBI agents. "Hello, Mr. Delavalle."

"Yes."

"Pardon me, child?"

"I'll plea bargain or whatever."

"Honey, I'm planning decades in prison for you. Don't you give me any lip now, or I'll add decades to that."

"Louise," Delavalle said, "you're overplaying it."

"We'll see about that."

"Take me, I'm yours. What do you want?"

Louise folded her hands on the desk and looked him intently. "Child, you can either play ball or play with your balls. Either way, I'm going to cook your goose—well done, rare, medium rare, or broiled black as a charcoal briquette—no matter to me."

"What do you want?" he asked, knees shaking.

"I want Collwood on a platter with an apple in his mouth."

"I'll do everything I can, including giving you the apple."

She set a little recorder on the desk and pressed a button. Delavalle winced and felt chagrin as she played for him a conversation in which he seemed to agree to round up a group of men and kill them all at Collwood's request.

"It's nothing like it sounds," he said. "That's an illegal wiretap and you know it."

Louise grinned malevolently. "Child, you are no poker player. You are dealing with years of your life here, so start singing for your supper. I want the goods on Collwood, and I mean for real. Don't you dare mess with me. Don't even think about it. Now sing, my little canary."

Chapter 62.

For tens of thousands of desperate people on the move with children and what belongings they could carry, the thing they seemed to have in common was blue or white surgical masks. Jack Simon was on the cell phone with Linsey. "Where are you?"

"I'm stuck in the East County. The roads are jammed and I'm trying to hitch a ride in on a police chopper, but they're all busy."

"At least you're safe. I'm here in Linda Vista with the Waleskys. Ernie showed up and mushroomed the lady next door. Ernie himself is a fungus."

"What about Nellie and the kids?"

"I'm going to try and evacuate them to NAS North Island as persons of interest in a police case. I have Louise's permission. In fact she wants Jimmy where Federal investigators can go over his story with a fine toothed comb."

"Keep in touch. Love you."

"Love you. Hope we can be back together soon."

The streets were in chaos, since the entire area of San Diego west of Highway 163 was being evacuated, and Louise had hinted further evacuations might take the perimeter all the way out to I-805. Something like a quarter to half a million people were on the move. It was late spring, but evenings were chilly for San Diego, sometimes with fog and drizzle along the coast, and mornings were generally heavily overcast with May Gray and June Gloom, as the marine layer effect was known.

Thousands of people were on the move, carrying clothing, radios, toys, furniture, children, even old people. Amid all that chaos, police and National Guard and ad hoc volunteers moved gently keeping order. So far, everyone was well fed and had plenty of fresh water—regional grocery chains and retailers were rushing all manner of supplies to the area. Doctors and nurses from all over Southern California were setting up clinics at major intersections, where refugees might be passing.

Even so, Jack had difficulty organizing an air lift for Jimmy Mendez. He had to keep it quiet, or more persons might demand to be flown out—even though the destination was across the water a few miles rather than east where the exodus was heading. Jimmy demanded that Aunt Nellie and Maribel go along, but the one chopper Louise managed to send through could only hold either one adult or, pressing it, two children. Jack volunteered to drive Nellie down to a checkpoint near Pacific Highway at Washington Street by the old Marine Corps Recruit Depot, where they would be ferried across by a Navy chopper that was shuttling back and forth with important persons, medicines, and the like. Thus, around noon, Jack stood with Nellie and the children atop an old two-story brick building with a hot, tarry roof. Down below, a river of humanity flowed past in the streets and sidewalks. In his heart, Jack wasn't sure he'd even be able to get his car out of here. On cue, a chopper borrowed from the U.S. Marshals Service swooped down on the roof top. A whirlpool of hot air and grit blew up. Jack's neck and face stung. On board was only the pilot. As Nellie and Jack secured the children in their seat belts and shoulder harnesses, they heard an outcry from below. A mob was beating doors in to reach the chopper. *Totally irrational,* Jack thought, *dangerous, scared, mob mentality.* The chopper lifted, turned, speeded westward.

Simultaneously, with several lunging roars, a group of men in gang-like clothing (khaki shorts, white tank tops) broke the door down and surged onto the rooftop. A few fell down and lay bruised and dazed on the hot tarry gravel. Others shouted and cursed and waved fists after the chopper. Then they turned toward Jack and Nellie in their rage, thinking they were somehow complicit in whatever hallucination the mob was having. Seeing only a heavy, middle-aged grandma type and a hatless, disheveled balding man who had not shaved in days, they relented and resumed their trek downstairs and eastward.

"Urban living," Nellie said. "With Ernie gone, I'm moving to a town of not more than 200 people somewhere in Kansas."

"At least the kids are safe." Jack took her by the arm and led her down dark, narrow stairway.

"Thank God," Nellie said, wiping a tear away. "I want my Maribel back as soon as possible."

A pharmacy on the first floor had been partially looted and now three policemen stood guard with M-16s held before their chests. Jack guided her across the street. It was like swimming upstream in a raging river. They found an alley running crosswise to that current, and followed a narrow path through a small wood to the next street down. They were in a landlocked neighborhood, climbing down through back yards and paths to get to Friars Road, which would be a madhouse also. Jack tried calling Louise again to see if there were another chopper out, but he did not expect that he and Nellie would merit such help, and in any case Louise didn't return his calls for now.

Nellie was having trouble breathing, and they had to rest more and more often. "Are you on any medications?" he asked.

She shook her head. "I should be for my blood pressure, but can't afford it." She fanned herself with a pudgy hand. "I need to live for Maribel. I have to go slow, Mr. Simon. Maybe you should leave me here. You have important things to do."

He sat down beside her. "So do you, Nellie. You know what? I don't care about the story that much anymore. I wish none of this had happened. Linsey and I have been putting off having kids for years because of our careers. Our damned ambitions. You have something far more important to do—get to your daughter. I'm going to help you do that."

Nellie looked shocked and ready to cry. "You are very kind," she gasped.

"It's the right thing to do," he said. "When you're ready, we'll go another block. Maybe we'll find a store and buy some water."

Chapter 63.

Linsey managed, with luck, to hitch a ride on a California Forest Service DC-4 heading west to refuel at Montgomery Field before flying north. That at least got her to Kearny Mesa, and from there she could walk through Serra Mesa and downhill to the stadium in Mission Valley. The streets were clogged with refugees streaming through Linda Vista. She called Jack, and learned he was heading down into Mission Valley. "We must be two or three miles from each other," he said forlornly.

She told him: "You should head toward the newspaper offices. That's only about mile or so from where you are."

"A good reporter doesn't head in when a story is going hot."

"You have Nellie with you. She can't walk much further."

"I know. It worries me. She might need oxygen soon."

"Stay where you are, Jack. Try to flag down a police car or some other emergency vehicle. Get her to someplace where she can be looked after in case of a heart attack."

" Good idea. Maybe you can take over my story for me."

"I might as well," she said, more in frustration than humor. "I've felt useless as a bump on a log since yesterday. Got decoyed away by a mushroom person who committed suicide out near Alpine. Then my CHP helicopter had to set down, running out of fuel, and I was stuck in the East County overnight."

"It's been a madhouse here. Stay away from the mob that's heading east. Some of them are starting to turn violent."

"Thanks for the warning."

"I had a major insight, Linsey."

"What's that?"

"I think the other shoe has yet to drop."

"What other shoe?"

"I have a feeling that what we've seen so far is nothing yet. You know all those big bracket fungi? I saw one today—it is the scariest thing I have ever seen in my life."

"Why, sweetie?" She felt a sudden deep concern.

"You had to see it. Ernie Walesky, embedded in a wall with Aunt Joanie sucking his DNA and fluids out. She was getting cuter and he was getting uglier. He was like a ghost image of himself, divided up among a couple of dozen grayish plates with darker gray spots on them. And you could read the anguish in his face as the last of his humanity drained away."

"Ick. I'm sorry you had to see that."

"Me too. I have a feeling we will all be seeing more of that." She could hear him sucking in a sobbing breath. "The scary part is that I think something more is going to happen. It's not just that those bracket things are going to sit there and shoot out billions of spores to populate our world with more of themselves."

"Oh?"

The connection went dead. She shook her cell phone. *Dead.*

She stuck the cell phone in her pocket and stood in the middle of Montgomery Field. She could see streams of people moving down Aero Drive at the southern end of the airfield. Louise wasn't answering her calls at the moment. Her boss at the Harbor Police HQ was out in the field and only answering a special emergency phone frequency that she couldn't access. She relayed a message to Louise and Harbor Police that she was at Montgomery Field and would try to make her way back west. She wanted another look at the Lima Voyager. What had yesterday's dead mushroom driver been so anxious to hide?

As she walked down the street, she glanced at a newspaper dispenser and stopped cold. Just above the fold on one side was a two-column local news story about a horrific car crash in El Cajon. She dropped in a couple of quarters, retrieved a paper, and stood fumbling through the pages to the East County jump. There it was: James Robertson Jr., driving such and such, struck by an apparent suicide driver...she skimmed through the details. Jack had mentioned that a James Robertson had failed to appear for an interview with two South Americans, and now he was the only one of the three left alive. Treated and discharged from Grossmont Hospital. Case being investigated for possible terrorist angle among other things....Linsey tossed the paper aside and took off running.

Chapter 64.

Louise Trost was tied up in a major conference at City Hall. This was now a regular show called the Daily Circus. It started with a closed meeting for one to two hours, and then became more of an informative meeting for the public. Only in the second half were news media allowed in. At the moment it was still Part I.

Professor Shaun Nolan, the mycology expert from UCSD Medical Center, was at her side. Present in the small amphitheater were the Mayor and several City Council members; fire and police authorities; National Guard and other Federal representatives; the state's Lieutenant Governor and his assistants, who had all flown down from Sacramento overnight; and a mix of journalists (sworn to silence for the moment, but documenting the proceedings for history) and expert witnesses.

A dominant figure was the four-star general commanding the California National Guard. General Reginald Quentin Stark seemed to be on the verge of declaring martial law and taking charge of the entire theater of operations. The Governor had already empowered him to do so if he and the Lieutenant Governor felt the situation warranted it, but the top Federal military officer in San Diego, a very senior Navy four-star, Navy Admiral Edgardo Malayan, was not ready to put his atomic submarines and aircraft carriers and other heavy weight vessels under Malayan's command. When Stark huffily suggested Malayan move the ships out to sea, the admiral retorted "on whose budget, with what safety procedures, and with what resources given that every available sailor and Marine is out on shore duty protecting stores, helping refugees, and so forth."

Louise knew she was outgunned and kept her head low. Had there been a Congressman present, her position in this elbowing match for power might have been stronger—unless it was Collwood's boy, Metrick. Rumor had it Metrick was about to be subpoenaed if not actually indicted on various corruption charges resulting from four separate investigations here and in Washington, D.C. In that atmosphere, she merely offered the council of her associate, Dr. Nolan, in conjunction with the testimony of several Army biological warfare experts present.

Nolan told them: "The city is effectively under a full frontal biological warfare attack. I am not suggesting one way or another that there may be a human enemy. My suspicion is that perhaps one or more humans tipped a delicate balance somewhere, and unleashed forces that have been kept at bay for eons. The good news in that is that, if there is a counter-force, we know we should locate that counter-force and use it to combat this horror that has seized our city."

General Stark said: "That's the first encouraging word I have heard so far. And the most intelligent. Professor Nolan, thank you for offering a candle in this terrible darkness. Have you any idea where this counter-force lies?"

Nolan said: "I have associates—a growing number of mycologists from UCSD and from all over the country and in fact around the world—testing every hypothesis they can think of. By now it's clear that, for reasons yet to be fathomed but probably having to do with greed, the owner of Anaconda Chemicals tried to smuggle in a shipment of some deadly fungus. We know the Lima Voyager traveled from here to Asia, then to several Latin American countries before returning to San Diego. On the return trip, disaster struck as this malignancy took over the ship."

"What is this malignancy, Professor?" the Mayor asked.

"Your Honor, I believe some very complicated symbiosis is at work. You should know that there are at least 60,000 fungus species of all types in the world. They are very variegated, ranging across a broad spectrum of adaptations to every climate zone conceivable. It is highly likely that this species has had human contact in the past. Somehow, in ways I do not understand yet, it has formed a kind of bypass in its reproductive procedure. That is to say, fungi have evolved with capabilities to reproduce either sexually (with a male and female gene set converging to form a new stem cell, if you will) or asexually, with a spore that carries the entire gene set, the entire DNA map, from source to target. If my surmise is correct, what we are dealing with is a mimic. Somehow, a transitional form of it attaches itself to a human, and robs that human of not only life, but also of its DNA. In effect, the gene pool of this species is constantly enriching itself. It may have started as a typical saprophytic species, feeding on the decaying residue from living matter that has died, like a fallen tree or a rotting fruit; or it may have started as a parasitic species that feeds on a living host, like a fruit that hasn't fallen yet—that's the rotten spot in your apple, for example, or the athlete's foot between your toes. In a third case, it may have started as a symbiote, a fungus that enjoys a mutually helpful relationship—lichens, for example, which are composed of two life forms—a fungus, with algae embedded."

He strode back and forth, hands in pockets, as if lecturing in a university classroom. "Whatever its origins, at some point it interacted with humans and was already predisposed to predating upon our flesh and our DNA. My guess is that the victim becomes a spore, a carrier."

"Why are they picking on us?" a woman asked, followed by a rumble of tired, scared laughter."

"The fact that many mushrooms are deadly poisonous to some species and yet can be eaten with great zest by other species suggests some evolutionary defense mechanisms over time. If you are a mushroom and want to have your spores carried around by some animal, you'll want to taste good to that animal. If there is another animal that likes you so much it will eat you into extinction, you'll want to be poisonous and smelly and distasteful to that animal. That's a silly way of saying it, of course, because I'm not sure plants and fungi actually think about things" —he paused, hoping for laughter that didn't come, which reminded him how creepy this whole situation was, and made his spine crawl—"more likely, only those mushrooms survive that happen to have just the right characteristics for that environment. But that's a discussion for another day, if you ever want to take one of my courses at UCSD."

"How can mushrooms walk around?" someone asked.

"Good question. I wouldn't have believed any of this myself unless I had seen it. Sometimes I still think this is all a bad dream. Basically, most fungi are a bunch of cells strung together with very fine threads called hyphae. Individually, hyphae are practically invisible. Together, they make up a foofy, dry looking mass called a mycelium, which is the thing you see, that you call a mushroom or a fungus. Moreover, hyphae are known to gather into tough strands. That's what makes a stem able to support the weight of the cap, for example. In some symbiotic species that live underground together with tree roots, the hyphae develop into long, tough, rubbery black tubes that intertwine with tree roots in a mycorrhyzal relationship. I might also point out that many plants have xylem tissue, which conducts water, nutrients, and useful compounds through the plant's body. Taken all in all, without boring you with endless technical terms, I would merely point out that nature is endlessly inventive. All the basic ingredients for functionality are already present in most species. Remember also that almost the entire palette of life on earth, from the polar regions to the deserts, from the bottom of the sea to the deepest jungles and to the birds flying everywhere, rests on the DNA map and its million ways of propagating itself. Thus, is it really that far-fetched to think that a DNA-driven fungus might be compelled to have a symbiotic or parasitic relationship with a DNA-driven human being? In a parasitic relationship, the host eventually perishes, as in this case, I fear."

Admiral Edgardo Malayan said: "Doctor Nolan, how close are your people to giving us a weapon to fight this plague?"

Nolan shook his head. "All I can tell you is that we are proceeding on the assumption that the organism attacking mankind is what we call the Offensor, and that somewhere on this earth it has been held in check somehow by a rival we are calling the Defensor. If we can find and employ the Defensor in time, there may be hope."

"Or else?" Stark said.

"Or else," Nolan replied, "soon the entire earth will resemble the harbor front of San Diego—a fungal paradise in which no human can survive."

Chapter 65.

Jimmy Mendez was grateful for Maribel's presence on the chopper whizzing over San Diego. Often, they had fought like cats and dogs. Now they held hands and clung together.

"Pretty cool," he admitted as he looked down over the trees around the San Diego River as it wended its way through Mission Valley toward its delta and the Pacific Ocean.

"I wish my mom could see this," Maribel said.

"You kids hang on tight and stay put," the pilot said kindly. Jimmy admired the man's uniform and gun. He wore a brown bubble helmet like an astronaut, and a brown jumpsuit with these really cool lace-up boots. "I'm gonna get mom and dad to get me some of those and a toy gun," Jimmy said.

Maribel said sadly: "I don't think we're ever going to see them again, Jimmy." She squeezed his hand.

"Stop reminding me!" he yelled, but held her hand tightly.

It was supposed to be a flight of no more than 15 minutes from Linda Vista, crosswise over Mission Valley, over downtown San Diego, across the harbor and bay a mile, to set down safely on the runways at the Naval Air Station.

As the helicopter roared over the rooftops downtown, it started making bucking motions.

"What's going on?" Jimmy and Maribel yelled in fear.

The pilot's expression behind his dark visor was unreadable, but he was gripping the stick with both hands and making body motions to one side as he tried to bicycle his floor pedals.

What happened next was all in slow motion, or so it seemed.

Maribel started letting go with that piercing scream of hers.

Out of the corner of his eyes—while he held his ears and tried to kick Maribel to make her stop screaming and hurting his ears, which was hard because they were strapped together in the seat—Jimmy saw the tail come swinging around on his right. As he watched, one of the rotor blades broke off. It glinted in the sunlight as it flew twirling away.

"Got to set down," the pilot said. They were the last words he would ever utter. The chopper lost altitude fast. Below were the empty streets—littered with abandoned vehicles and debris. Below to their rear were the highrise office buildings and condo towers. Ahead and below was the long, multi-story glass tube that contained the main passages of the Convention Center—at least two blocks long, a quarter mile of curving, slightly tinted glass. The sail-like roofs of the Convention Center loomed ahead. To the right were the towers of two huge high rise hotel towers joined to the Convention Center by passageways, garages, and storage areas.

For a moment it looked as if they were going to crash at over 100 miles per hour into those white roof-sails. Maribel was still screaming. She could hold a blimp worth of air in her lungs, Jimmy thought. He held his ears and sat paralyzed watching the great roof structure fly at them. Then the chopper dropped straight down as the pilot made some desperate moves to avoid hitting the roof. The tail spun all the way around in a dizzying circle. The chopper crashed through the glass roof and one second later smashed into the upper story walkway. As the chopper went through the roof, the right side was sheared off—so close that Jimmy felt the wind on his fingers like a hammer.

Maribel's scream ended suddenly.

The chopper's fall was broken and it landed on its side and did a little dance in a half circle while the top rotors beat themselves into pieces on the carpeted floor and concrete showed through.

Jimmy went black as the cockpit shattered around him

Chapter 66.

Jack flagged down a passing sheriff's deputy, who saw that Nellie was in trouble. The deputy had oxygen in the trunk of his car.

"She is having a heart attack, I think." The deputy called for a Life flight chopper, which arrived 15 minutes later. In this manner, Jack got a ride into Hillcrest, where the old UCSD Medical Center highrise dominated the skyline. Along the way, the female flight nurse told him: "She's stabilized and we'll get her on I.V. and get her into the E.R. We'll take it from there."

Jack phoned Linsey to tell her of his whereabouts. He was standing in the lobby of the hospital, where hundreds of people were camped out and the TV was on.

"Breaking story amid all these many breaking stories. We have just learned that emergency personnel have given up trying to recover the U.S. Marshal's helicopter that crashed into the Convention Center about two hours ago. It was presumed that the pilot and both children are dead. Now a Marine Corps helicopter dispatched to investigate reports seeing a child waving through the broken canopy. Our news chopper is on the scene and here is what Leanne Radzick is seeing:"

The woman's voice cut in. "Thanks, Bob. As you can see below, in the uninhabitable area filled with clouds of drifting, poisonous spores, it looks like at least one of the children survived and is waving for help." As Jack stared transfixed, he recognized the tiny figure of Jimmy Mendez. That was some kid. "Several Navy SEALs have volunteered to fly in and rappel down, but there is absolutely not one heavy lift chopper available at the moment. Commanders here are making tough decisions. There are rescues in progress up and down the coast as well as inland, and this child is somewhere on the to-do list."

Bob said: "Can you get close?"

"We can get kind of close, and I would love to drop some supplies—if I had wings I would fly down there—but there is the fear of the glass roof collapsing and making the situation infinitely worse if not fatal."

"Is there radio contact with the downed chopper?"

"Negative. I'm looking through binoculars, and it looks like the helicopter went down quite hard."

"Can you still see the little boy?"

"No. I'm afraid he seems to have vanished."

Jack stared at the screen. He saw a wrecked aircraft lying in a heap at the bottom of a very large glass and steel structure.

The newswoman wrapped up: "Bob, it will be getting dark soon, in this long and terrible day that seems to have no end. We will be forced to return to base, and frankly I think there is now a fuel shortage that will prevent us from flying again tomorrow. This crisis seems to deepen by the hour."

Chapter 67.

As night fell, the invasion of the mushroom people entered into the ultimate phase. Professor Shaun Nolan was one his way home for a change of clothes and a shower. He felt exhausted and wished for a good night's sleep. He was stuck in traffic at the foot of Washington Street and India Streets, when he saw a sight that made him recoil in abject horror.

Of course. It had to be. He stepped from his car, oblivious to danger, as the monstrous being walked past him. He saw a being unlike anything ever seen on earth—about six feet tall, with two legs and two arms as the human segment of its DNA map would dictate. Looking at it from the front as it approached was hideous enough. Its skin was brown and scaly, with green and yellow fuzz indicating some kind of secondary fungal infestation, like the world's worst case of eczema on a human—or better yet, total psoriasis to the extent that it looked like barnacles.

This nightmare thing had to be the senior partner of the formerly human crew members walking about. It was naked, had no visible sexual organs. Its face was a sort of tin-can mask with a slit for a mouth, from which a flat mycorrhyzal organ like a snake's tongue, but with multiple fringes rather than a split into two points, flicked around sampling the air for smells. It had two black button eyes with white sclera that darted left and right as it looked for—*what? Enemies? Prey?* What was that on its back? Looked like foot-long brown wings or fins or something, trailing in the shape of the entire body. Legs, arms, torso, even head, had this brown structure trailing like rotting goldfish fins. Those must be gills, the sporing organ, like the grotesquely magnified underside of a button mushroom. Straggling human refugees, seeing its rear side, started screaming.

When the being walked past, Shaun Nolan felt a visceral fear, loathing, and disgust he had never imagined possible as he got a better look. Its entire back was composed of one entire mass of gills that yawned slowly open and shut, as if breathing, and a clouds of microscopic spores emanated from among the gill slits. Hundreds of fine gill edges were visible amid the brown structures like pea pods that opened and closed like kelp waving underwater. The being was heading north along Pacific Highway. Out of town. To spread this horror as far as possible. More of its kind would roost in hidden places in the form of bracket fungi with human DNA, until they had grown into something like this creature, and then those would walk another ten or a hundred miles or whatever. It would not take long before these creatures populated the entire earth.

The perfect mimics of humans were the first stage in this reproductive cycle. Call them Offensors Lite. These other monstrosities were the real Offensor, the B-52 bomber of the fungal domain of life.

Coughing—the spores must be bad for human respiratory organs, possibly fatal, but that would remain to be seen—Shaun got back into this car. He now understood the full life cycle of the mushroom people. The final wave of their attack had begun. All else until now had merely been prelude.

As he drove around the harbor district in helpless fascination, hypnotized by morbid curiosity, he saw more and more of them. They lumbered away from their hiding places in small warehouses in the harbor district. According to Navy reports, gate guards had seen at least one truck pull in at the *Lima Voyager* and offload unknown objects—probably the bracket fungi.

Nolan got out of his car, half crazy, and walked the streets. He saw one after another of the creatures. He saw one take a screaming woman, blow black air in her face, and put its tube in her neck as Linsey and Jack Simon and more lately others had described. The little kid, Jimmy Mendez, had been right. His father had become the victim of the Offensor, and had next taken Jimmy's mother's life. Each time this happened, a bracket colony was left behind and that became a true Offensor.

Nolan saw one Offensor climbing out of a bedroom window in a cheap hotel. He saw another smashing a store window to enter because it saw a light in back and assumed it would find a human inside to eat.

When he had seen enough, Nolan wanted to return to his car. Instead, he suddenly screamed in blind panic, and ran across a street like a horse fleeing a fire by running into the burning barn. Better to die than see another of these things, or worse yet, be touched by it, have that tube in one's neck. As he ran across the street, he heard a screech of brakes and felt an impact against his side that sent him flying—into darkness.

Chapter 68.

Jack Simon felt useless. And he was determined not to be useless for long. Linsey's cell phone appeared to be dead, so he couldn't reach her for advice. Louise's personal assistant finally answered and said Louise would get back to him—she did daily briefings with the brass.

Idly, Jack called a friend in La Jolla. This woman, Nancy Sullivan, was a suburban stringer for the paper in the North County. "Nancy, it's Jack Simon."

"Hey, Jack. Long time no see. Hey, how are you taking all this mushroom stuff?"

"I'm right in the middle of it, Nancy. Wonder if you can do me a big favor. It might mean saving two kids' lives?"

"Wow. If I can help, yeah, sure, being a good citizen, what do you need." He told her, and she agreed to try.

An hour later, two ultralight planes came sailing down the coast at about 1,000 feet. Just dots in the sky, Jack watched them through binoculars as they banked left and turned inland. They approached his location atop the venerable Mr. A's Restaurant building (Bertrand's at Mr. A's) just north of the downtown area. At one time just about the tallest building in San Diego, it still was a local fixture every Christmas season when its upper edges were strung with thousands of green and red lights to give the illusion of a wreath wrapped around the building.

The ultralights buzzed closer, until Jack didn't need the binocs any longer to make out the two pilots—each wearing an orange jumpsuit and white helmet. Like big bumblebees, the two craft one by one sailed up to the roof, slowed, and dropped to a landing. It didn't take much for one to roll to a stop, and Jack ran alongside to help pull each one to a stop.

Nancy Sullivan climbed out and introduced her dad, John, a trim tall man of 60 or so with the weathered face and devil-may-care blue eyes of a longtime daredevil. Nancy handed Jack the orange flight suit and helmet he had requested. "I hope you find the kids in good health," John said.

"Thank you," Jack said. "If I live to tell the tale, I'll mention you guys in my story." He stepped into the flight suit.

Nancy said: "Everyone in town has a story."

Jack pulled the helmet on. "Give me a quick refresher." He'd flown with them off the Glider Port cliffs above La Jolla a number of times but it was a few years back and he was rusty.

"I'll check you out as best I can," John said. John eyeballed the rooftop. "Looks a bit tight, but I think we can get airborne. Nancy, I'm going to fly ours down to the street and pick you up. We'll take off down the steep slope at B Street."

"Sounds like a deal, dad." She turned to Jack. "Let me show you the controls. This is a new model you may not have seen before. Once you are airborne, it's pretty simple. The tricky part for you is going to be landing."

"I understand that."

"They said on the radio that you can't walk on Pacific Highway or any of the surface streets in the harbor area because the air if full of spores. I couldn't find a breathing kit for you."

"No problem." This is so crazy to begin with that I'll just wing it anyway, oxygen mask or no.

With a deafening racket, the motorcycle size engine in John's two-seater nylon and aluminum craft spun the twin props and the tail rotor into blurs. Rolling briefly, the craft just barely cleared the stone railing dropped out of sight. "Oh my god, dad!" Nancy screamed and ran to the edge. Jack followed, and saw that John had successfully recovered and was even then half a block away and rising above the street. Nancy seemed weak with relief. "Are you sure you want to do this?" Jack nodded. She gave him a walk-through, and then, with a peck on the cheek, sprinted down the stairs with her cell phone glued to her ear.

Jack was on his own. He took the plane as far to one end of the roof as he could. Then, tracing John's path, and revving to max power, he felt himself being hurled into the air. This smaller one-seater was easier to maneuver than John's, he figured as he stabilized and turned toward the harbor.

He saw the distant speck of John's craft setting down among the tall buildings around the extremely steep B Street hill. Heading in that direction, he quickly started to gain on the downtown area with its skyscrapers all standing close together.

He spotted John at the top of B Street in the middle of the intersection at Tenth Avenue. They waved to each other. It would take Nancy a while to get there on foot. He wished them a safe journey and continued his steady buzzing journey southward over the rooftops of Banker's Hill and Little Italy. The airport was shut down, but some of its lights were still on—haphazardly left on, perhaps, as staff and passengers fled. There had not been a civilian carrier landing here in several days.

The green neon lights forming hexagonal hoops atop the Emerald Plaza were still on. Their familiar shapes were a signature element of San Diego's night skyline. On his right, the first of the highrise condo towers started appearing. He was flying among the buildings at the 20th floor level. The magnificent 1930s County Building passed on his right.

He saw abandoned vehicles and a great mass of debris—everything from mattresses and bed sheets to windblown books and magazines—on the streets below. He could see the roiling arms of spore clouds, and instinctively took himself a few hundred feet higher. He saw an overturned pleasure-riding carriage, and its dead horse starting to bloat in the hazy sunlight. It was clear up here, but patches of fog remained below, mixing with spores.

Jack followed the line of India Street until he came to the MTS Trolley Exchange Building near the Santa Fe Railroad Station. There he angled west a bit to avoid getting near any more high rise buildings and their unpredictable drafts.

Still, as he flew over the fantasy ramparts of the huge old power station, now a big cube full of condos, he felt warm and cool winds shake him from side to side. Quickly, with his stomach lurching, he banked right and flew out toward the Star of India, the world's last iron-hulled sailing ship that had in the 1800s sailed back and forth with cargo and passengers between the Isle of Man and Australia.

According to his fuel gauge, which he hoped was right, he still had a quarter tank. He leveled off at 400 feet and sailed over the waters past the aircraft carriers tied up at NAS North Island. He flew past the old tourist attraction of Seaport Village on his left, and saw the great hotel towers and the Convention Center beyond that. Flying over a forest of masts—in happier times, the well to do could anchor their yachts and sailboats behind the hotel and go in for a steak, a swim, or a night's sleep.

Hugging the top of the glass tube—must be a quarter mile long, he thought—he sought a place to land. There wasn't one. The top of the tube was round and if he tried to land there, he might well slide off and fall several stories to his death.

He spotted the hole where the chopper had punched through several large, curving panes. He saw the wreckage inside, but no sign of life. Worse yet, he saw several large white shapes—mushrooms the size of automobiles—on the carpeted floor around the wreckage. There was no way he dared stall and then drop at least fifty feet to the concrete floor beside the chopper.

At the end of the building was a large open air plaza several hundred feet square. It was covered by a roof resembling a complex of gigantic sails undulating in a liberal reinterpretation of the Star of India's sails a mile or so north. As he came around the turn, having run out of building, he understood the opportunity: he angled around and approached the building dead-on. There seemed to be just enough clearance as he sailed over the hand railing and under the sail-roof. Ahead beckoned about 4,000 square feet of mostly clear space—empty, shining concrete that functioned as an open-air dance floor capable of holding 1,000 persons or more. Only now it was covered with various types of mushrooms. He landed and came to a rolling stop beside a towering white mushroom with an umbrella-like cap six feet across. A mist of fine black and green spores drifted down from the fleshy gills and frills underneath.

Jack ran for the entrance on the second floor. Luckily a small service door was open. As he had hoped, the infestation on the second floor inside wasn't as bad yet as it was out on the streets. He ran down the carpeted hall inside a surreal tube of glass and metal that looked like the inside of a giant space city. Rings of dark violet neon enhanced the effect of running through a series of giant circles or hoops. Now he saw the wrecked helicopter lying on its side a few hundred feet ahead. He had to dodge between big, puffy shapes and tall slender shapes and things that seemed to be hovering above just waiting to swoop down. Even here, outlined against the brightness coming through the glass, he could see a light rain of spores falling. In one corner, a huge round thing, which looked dark green, opened a hole in its top and emitted a gasp of black spore air. "Jimmy! Maribel!" *No answer.* He smelled the dead pilot before he saw him. The man's twisted and smashed body lay tangled in steel and broken glass. There was nothing anyone could do for him. No sign of the children—at least not in the wreck, which was probably good.

Jack ran on. "Jimmy! Maribel!"

Silence.

Chapter 69.

At the Daily Circus, Louise Trost was relieved to see that someone in Congress had adopted the suggestion Louise had quietly made up the chain to resolve the turf battle. Finally, orders had come down from both Washington and Sacramento. Along with the declaration of martial law by the Governor, and the declaration of a disaster area by the President, had come a Pentagon order that all waterways and land within 100 feet of shore were to be under Admiral Malayan's command, while the rest of the City of San Diego fell under General Stark's command. The Mayor of San Diego, working with the Lieutenant Governor who remained in the city, and the Governor, was to manage the civil courts and administrative services as a check and balance on arbitrary power.

As part of the deal, Louise's office was to remain in an advisory and liaison capacity in its primary function as an anti-terrorism apparatus. Louise had successfully put forth the case that this was a most opportune time for terrorists to strike—if in fact they were not behind this catastrophe in the first place.

As Louise quietly sat in, the rest of the meeting was taken up with horrified tales of the new, 'hard' mushroom people, as a reporter for the Los Angeles Times had dubbed them. The other ones, who looked human, were the 'soft' mushroom people. Some of the reporters had begun referring to the invaders as 'morels,' after a type of edible delicacy that was as ugly as it was tasty—like a sponge half-eaten away, whose acne-like cavities were the spore generators rather than gills. Some silly, giggling young female singer had referred to the invaders as 'truffles,' but the deaths and the suffering and the fear quickly banished such ghoulish humor from the media. There was, after all, some modicum of shame among the newserati; and it was beginning to seem that their bad behavior in recent years had been due in large part to boredom. Now that there was a real enemy threatening to demolish mankind, the news organs no longer needed to boost ratings by staging fake debates among vapid and venomous talking bedsores. *So much for that*, Louise thought.

Louise left the Daily Circus, which was being held on neutral territory on the UCSD campus. Her new emergency office, since downtown was off-limits, was in a room deep in the UCSD Main Library. She locked her office door, made coffee, and started returning long-overdue phone calls. First, she called Shaun Nolan, who had just been released from the hospital. "How are you, Shaun?"

"Stiff, but basically okay and eager to get back to work."

"What happened?"

"I saw the new kind of invaders, the 'hard' type, and panicked. Ran into the street screaming and got hit by a car. At least, that's what I'm told I did. Luckily, I got hit by a police car, and they weren't speeding."

"Will you be at work today? I missed you at the Daily Circus, but I heard you'd had an accident."

"I'm sore around my left hip, but doing fine otherwise. If you saw one of these creatures…"

"I've seen pictures. That's enough for me. Get better quickly—I need your expertise."

"I'll be there tomorrow to offer some more testimony."

"Good."

She called Jack. "How are you, Mr. Simon? Behaving?"

"I'm in the Convention Center looking for Jimmy Mendez and Maribel Walesky."

"You pick a bad time to make jokes."

"I'm serious, Louise. And you sound like a stuffed sea lion."

"Pardon me?"

"You're getting stuffy. Come down to earth."

"Jack, are you effing nuts? Been inhaling that spore stuff?"

"Probably. There are spores all over here."

"Enlighten me. We'll discuss the sea lion thing when you are within reach of my claws."

"I'd love to be in range of your rescuing hands, lady. It's pretty scary here."

"How did you get there?"

"Borrowed an ultralight plane from a friend."

"Jack."

"I'll be okay. I promise."

"Take care of yourself. Call me if there is anything I can do. By the way, if you had to sit through the bullshit I do each morning with those stuffed shirt flag officers, you'd start sounding like a sea lion too. A very stuffy one."

"Remember to let the air out, Louise."

She laughed. "You too, hot shot. Hope you find those children." She got a little misty and added: "In case the mushrooms get you, let me be the first and maybe last person to tell you that you're a hero."

She returned calls from Linsey. "Hi, honey, how are you?"

"Stuck in Mission Valley. I've been trying since yesterday to get from Montgomery Field to 32nd Street."

"That whole area is shut down. If you breathe the spores there they'll kill you. Are you walking?"

"Yes, it's all I can think to do. My department doesn't answer—I guess there is nobody working the harbor these days, so we don't need to exist."

"I have some really scare news for you. You ready?"

"Oh God, now what?"

"Jack borrowed an ultralight plane and flew to the Convention Center to look for those two kids."

"Oh my God. What next?"

"Just thought you should know." She waited in silence, expecting Linsey to start crying.

"Louise, I have a theory."

"Good. So does everyone."

"I'm serious. I need to call Dr. Nolan. I'll call you back."

"Pray for Jack, honey."

"I've prayed years for Jack." Linsey's voice thickened "He'll take care of himself. He'll figure something out."

Chapter 70.

While jogging down into Mission Valley, Linsey called Jack. She wanted to talk about Robertson, but Louise's story had her floored. "Honey, tell me Louise Trost was kidding."

"Wish I could." He sounded as if he were breathing hard.

"Are you really in the Convention Center?" She was suddenly blown away with worry.

"Yes. It's spooky as hell. No sign of the kids. The chopper is wasted, the radio is out, and you can smell the pilot from 100 feet away; nothing anyone can do for him."

"Can I help?"

"Stay out of here. Whatever you do, don't try to rescue me. This place is like a house of horrors, with all these giant mushrooms still growing, spewing out spores, inflating, deflating, I don't know what else. I see one out there on the street, a tall one with a long stem and a wide, flat cap, that seems to keep bending over and straightening out."

"Where are you now?"

"Circling the San Diego Marriott and Marina. I'll have to go out on the upper deck of the Convention Center and then run like hell to the next section. As long as I stay up high, I'll be okay."

"How will you get out, whether you find the kids or not?"

"If they're—gone—I can fly out by myself. If I find them alive, we'll climb as high as we can. The Manchester Grand Hyatt has one tower at least 40 stories tall, the other about 33 stories tall. It might take the mushrooms a while to get that high." He added: "You sound out of breath yourself."

She said: "I'm on my way to your office. I need to find the phone number for your guy who never showed up—Robertson."

"Oh yeah. What about him?"

"He was in a car wreck. His two Indian friends are dead. Looks to me like someone rammed them on purpose."

She could hear Jack whistle. He said: "Sounds like he was for real. No wonder he didn't show up. He was in an ambulance while Dylan and I were chatting over finger food."

"Where is the phone number? On your desk at the office?"

"Why don't you just call them?"

"Lines are clogged. Nobody answers. I'm on foot and going as fast as I can through streets that are either dead-empty or jammed with foot traffic." As she spoke, his cell phone went out and she yelled in frustration, thrust the phone in a pants leg utility pocket, and picked up the pace. She could see Mission Valley spread before her. She still had a few difficult miles to go.

The roads were terrible—filled with slowly walking tourists and people from downtown and the beach communities. Suddenly, thinking of poor Cleve, she felt overwhelmed. She felt as if she couldn't walk another step. Her feet felt heavier and heavier, and she plopped down on a little grassy berm. Her eyes were full of tears, and she dimly could see hordes of beaten, sullen people shuffling past with their belongings, but they barely had eyes for her, only for the road ahead. She rested her elbows on her knees with her hands dangling between her legs. Putting her forehead on her forearms, she started bawling loudly. Tears flew from her eyes, bounding off her arms and her combat boots and into the dirt. Poor Cleve. How she missed him. So many people lost...and now Jack in that hell hole in the harbor!

Chapter 71.

Linsey's phone warbled—Louise.

"Yes?" She'd been sitting, sniffling, and now she wiped dirt and tears from each eye orb.

"Linsey, are you okay?"

"Just going nuts a little bit about Jack and Cleve and all the others..."

"I know. I feel it too. I'm hoping for an end to this situation. As soon as I can free up a resource, I'll try to put people in there to extract Jack and the kids if—" She stopped but Linsey knew: *if they are still alive.*

"I'm heading east along Friars Road" This major artery was a parking lot of abandoned vehicles. Some of them were on fire. Abandoned clothing, shoes, toys, laundry baskets, all manner of debris littered the road. Some people had dumped bags of frozen food that were now melting and starting to rot in the sunlight. "I am trying to get to Jack's office." She explained about Robertson's accident.

"I'll see what I can do on my end," Louise said. "Tell you what. You're near the Hazard Center. See if one of the coffee shops there is open. Take a rest and wait for my call back. I might be able to coordinate something."

"Oh, you're a wonder."

"That's my job."

"Being a wonder?"

"No, coordinating things. If it turns out to be a wonder, all the more credit for me."

Despite the grim situation, Linsey had to laugh.

Linsey walked several long blocks from the Fashion Valley Shopping Center, over the 163 overpass, across the San Diego River, and over to Friars Road. The Hazard Center was one of two complexes with hotels, shops, restaurants, and a movie theater between the Mission Valley and Fashion Valley Malls. That was in normal times. As she walked through the littered arcades, some with smashed windows and looted stores, she noted that some of the lights were still burning. That meant they had power, for the time being. She smelled hot coffee. Clambering through a wrecked store window, she entered a coffee shop near the bookstore. The employees were long gone, and the place had been gone over, but there were a few pastries left in a corner of the cooler display. She stepped over broken crockery and spilled liquids until she found the pieces of a toppled coffee maker. Soon she had a fifty-cup brew going and sat munching on pastries while a gorgeous smell filled the air.

As she waited, she spoke several times with Louise. "Good news, Linsey, I have a County chopper available. Coming in from El Cajon with an empty seat. They are putting Mr. Robertson on board as we speak and he'll be with you in ten minutes, God willing."

As promised, a chopper set down on the high roof of the Red Lion Hotel, then took off with a loud roar in the direction of downtown. Linsey stood waiting outside the coffee shop as a figure appeared in the distant hotel doorway and made his way toward her. He walked stiffly and with a slight limp. His face had a bruise on one side, and his left arm was in a sprain brace.

James Robertson Jr. was a heavy-set man of about 50. He stuck out his free hand. "Lieutenant Simon?" He was nearly gray, with a jowly, florid face and sympathetic, watery eyes. He wore hiking boots, jeans, a white T-shirt under a greenish plaid shirt, and a Padres baseball cap. Plain and worn, but clean. He came with his fists jammed in his pockets. No documents.

"We're us," she said for both of them. "Call me Linsey."

"Call me Jim."

"Looks like you took a beating."

"Tell me about it," he said with a groan. "I'm supposed to be home in bed, doped up and resting, but this is too important. I do need to sit down before I fall down."

She pointed at a wrecked coffee shop. "Come on. I'll buy."

He sniffed appreciatively. "Smells like fresh coffee."

She offered her arm, and he leaned heavily on her. They clambered over the shattered glass and debris. She showed him to a plastic table and two plastic chairs she'd set up, and served coffee and pastry. She had assembled napkins, sugar, powdered cream, and wooden stirrers previously.

"Down to business," he said licking his stirrer.

"What is it that you want so urgently to tell us?"

"My father handed over a bunch of papers to Collwood. My father died last year."

"I'm sorry to hear that."

"Have you figured out the basic story about the fungus.?"

She shrugged and recited what she knew. "Collwood brought it in on that freighter, but it looks like the freight was stolen."

"It wasn't stolen, Linsey, it came to life. He was just looking for some fancy pharmaceuticals to revive his company, and he was grasping at straws. Very evil, very desperate, but ultimately a shallow, foolish man. My father sold him the keys to hell, and what he bought got away from him."

"How do you mean, Jim?"

"My father was in China after the war and got his hands on some important papers abandoned when the Japanese surrendered in 1945. The Japanese had learned of a secret Inca mushroom storage place in the jungles. Maybe the Inca wanted to use it to get their empire back from the Spaniards. Who knows? The Inca are gone, and so are the Spaniards. This fungal stuff has been in the jungle probably for ages. You see, here's the key. It's two opposing families of funguses, from what my dad and Paco and Marie were able to explain to me."

"Offensor and Defensor," Linsey ventured. "We're working on that hypothesis. Our mycologist, Dr. Nolan, dreamed it up."

"It's real. For ages, the Defensor fungus has surrounded the Offensor which exists only on one island hidden in the mountains. They are mutually dependent, somehow, and yet mutually extinguishing. They balance each other out. And Collwood sent mercenaries down there and upset the balance. The natives sent Paco up here to see what could be done."

"Your dead friend."

"Yes. He was not only a shaman, but his daughter spent years in the U.S. and knew the ways. He was the best of their people for the job."

"I thought they were a secret bunch deep in the jungle."

"They are, but the outside world beckons. They keep their secret among them, this small tribe, even as they bring jungle goods to market in distant mountain towns. Marie was the first to reach the United States."

"Must be one of the best kept secrets on earth or our Government would know about it."

"Yes. They defeated the Japanese. Killed their two pilots with arrows. Japan never did get this stuff or they might have won World War II and killed half the world to boot. But the natives were used to keeping secrets. The Incas' last hiding place, the mountain city of Macchu Pichu, is about an hour's air flight from the fungal island. The native tribe were put there by the Inca centuries ago to be guardians of the mushrooms. And the mushrooms were sacred to the gods, like in many early societies including Ancient Egypt. Until Collwood's guerillas blasted through, the natives had never lost a spore to enemy foreigners. Now the genie is out of the bottle."

"Can it be put back in, Jim?"

"Maybe. That's what Paco was here to engineer. He was biding his time. Waiting for Collwood to do his thing, waiting for the danger to become evident. Then his plan was to use his own counter-measures. Because, face it, the natives guarding the Defensor spores are the only human, thinking people involved down there. There is no reason, no mercy, no rationality on the Offensor side. It's a pure parasite, opportunistic, ready to jump at every chance to seize a living being and turn it to its advantage. Here." He fumbled in a shirt pocket. "We made copies of much of it before my dad sold it all to Collwood. Look here." He showed her several old, fading color photos —different views of what looked like a cave or a cleft in a tall mountain face. A waterfall dropped from high up. There was a lake at the bottom with steam on it. There was an island in the middle of the lake. The island was heavily overgrown and green, but there appeared to be buildings hidden in the brush. And giant mushrooms—her fingertip tapped that image repeatedly.

"An island in a crater lake. Many different fungal species growing around an old abandoned Native American city. A city overwhelmed by fungi. An evolving horror."

Linsey kept tapping the picture of that island. "This is where Collwood got the fungi?"

"Yes."

Linsey sipped her coffee thoughtfully. "Hmmm. So it seems that we know where Collwood got this stuff from. We could send people down there to find this spot—"

"It's all in Karasawa's journal. The exact location."

"If we sent people down there, they could bring back whatever keeps the Offensor in check."

"Right," James said. "The Defensor that Dr. Nolan has talked about. It's worth a try, Linsey."

"You've done very well, James."

"I'm sorry I didn't come forward sooner. My dad wanted me to wait until he was dead. I had no idea of the implications."

"None of us did. Probably not even Collwood." An idea dawned on her. "Say, where did this Paco guy stay?"

"Not sure. He was one of these scary dudes that can fit in with the scenery wherever he went. I watched him will himself to die. He saw his only child dead before him, and he died holding her face in his hands. It was love unto death."

"Sad. But you know, Jim, I have an idea."

He stared at her. "Has your husband ever mentioned that you look scary when you are on that wavelength?"

She nodded. "This is the time to get scary, my friend, when it counts." She whipped out her cell phone to call Louise. "We need to get you home, James, and I need to find Paco's hangout."

Chapter 72.

Lee Collwood hung up the phone as he sat in his office at Anaconda's parent plant near Brawley. He looked out his office window and saw the helicopters coming from San Diego. He'd just finished speaking with a sobbing Metrick. His man in Congress was done and would be singing like a canary. Lee knew he was finished.

He went to the pool area, unlocked the liquor cabinet, and took out a bottle of the finest scotch. He wandered into the living room and got his gun out of the cabinet. Then he climbed into his golf cart, rode out through the huge garage, and drove out through the still rising gate. All the while, he kept tipping that quart bottle up over his lips, until the burning liquid ran down his chin on both sides. Soon, the sky seemed to be turning as his vision blurred.

About a mile out on the desert, that ancient seabed, the golf cart ran out of juice. Lee Collwood finished the last of his quart bottle, hoping it would stop his heart. But the Collwoods were made of sterner stuff. Armed with Collwood genes and a Glock automatic, Lee walked till he could walk no more, and crawled.

He crawled on the burning-hot glassy gravel and felt the sun beating down on him. A scorpion darted past and refused the opportunity to administer a killing sting. Somewhere, a rattle indicated that a big desert snake was after more appealing game. *Not even the desert's most insidious killers want anything to do with me*, Lee thought. *Screw them all.* He laughed at the irony of it—that snakes and scorpions would not claim one of their own, and perhaps the devil himself would refuse Lee entry into hell. Laughing wildly, he lay on a ridge overlooking a shallow valley and put the gun to his head. The Collwood body engine was pumping with vigor and strength, and no heart attack was imminent. Nor did he have the courage to shoot himself in the temple as he'd planned. So he discharged the gun into the air.

"I know you're out there," he called. He fired again. The shot echoed back and forth in the dry canyon and the gulch. He fired again and again until the gun was empty, and then he threw it from himself. "Come find me," he called out. "I want to pass into the next circus." With those words, he passed out face down in the hot glass shards that passed for desert sand, here on the lower spurs of the hell not all that far away—Death Valley.

Chapter 73.

"Jimmy! Maribel!"

Jack ran from abandoned conference room to abandoned conference room shouting their names, but he got no answer. The vast, tubular glass hallway with its futuristic glowing neon rings was silent. Reality and fantasy had meshed as giant mushrooms grew all around. There were round ones, tall ones, even cubic ones big enough to swallow Jack if he got close.

Then, behind a stairwell, Jack glimpsed a brief hint of motion. He ran toward the stairs, only to see Jimmy's fleet figure running away. Quick, like a shadow, the child ran. There was something odd about him. His face looked dark, as if dusted with war paint. "Jimmy, I won't hurt you! Where is your cousin?"

The boy stopped. He turned around and stood very rigidly and seriously. "Are you really Mr. Simon?"

"Yes! The mushrooms haven't gotten me. What about you?" As he walked toward Jimmy, another figure stepped out from a huge flower pot across the hall. *Maribel.* His heart skipped a beat. *Same rigid posture and dark face. Staring eyes.* He stopped, wondering if they'd blow black air in his face and stick tubes down his neck.

To his surprise, both children started laughing and dancing up and down. "Yay, we're going to be saved!" They ran and hugged him before he could cautiously back away.

"Let me get this straight," he said, "You aren't mushrooms, and I'm not one. Is that right?"

He squatted down, and they hugged him. They felt warm and normal. "How did you survive that crash?"

Maribel said: "Who knows? We were buckled in together, and the left side crashed, hard, killing our pilot. Poor man. He was oozing…" She closed her eyes, trying to shut out the horror.

Jack hugged them close. "We're not out of the woods yet. I came in a tiny one-man airplane that may not even carry one of you on my lap. If I try to take you out one at a time, and if we crash, we'd really be in mushroom soup down there on the street with those hideous things walking around."

Jimmy grabbed Jack's collar in a death grip. "We saw a couple of them walking by earlier today, down on the street. They are soooo gross. This guy looked like his back was crawling with huge snails or something."

Jack said: "Look, let's stick together. Flying you out one by one is a bad idea. Whichever of you I come back for would have died of fright by then. What we want to do is get over into the Hyatt and up to the 40th floor. That's as high as it goes. We should be safe until they can rescue us, maybe right off the roof."

Taking the two children by the hand, he walked in the middle as they headed north through the whispering glass corridor. They stopped several times, thinking they heard something moving up ahead, but it was probably just a gust of wind hitting a door someplace, and sending gusts shivering through the building. It was eerie to be alone in this vast structure capable of comfortably handling many thousands of people, probably tens of thousands.

Across the street they did see a shadowy brown figure moving beyond the mushroom-overgrown hulk of three abandoned red trolley cars. The figure moved quickly, as if it were hunting something.

Wind kicked up outside, coming from the south, and the sky started to glow red as if evening were coming early.

They made a run for it from the north end of the Convention Center, across the mushroom-encrusted concrete plaza, past the Marriott with its twin towers, in order to reach the Hyatt.

What a fantasy scene! In the middle of the debris-littered street stood several mushrooms 40, 50 feet tall. They had developed cellulose cell walls, like trees. Their stems had become tree trunks, and black spores rained down. The trolley tracks were completely blocked by a stalked puffball whose fruiting body was as big as one of those giant concrete mixers mounted on the back of a truck. As they looked, its top had an open black hole from which a constant series of puffs emitted clouds of spores. Deadly looking bright green mushrooms stood everywhere with something dagger-like about their streamlined caps. There were round white ones with red spots, and boxy red ones with white spots. There were mushrooms big as cars with long trailing fronds. There were grotesque things resembling dead men's fingers and shrunken heads and medusa's hair, and all manner of nightmarish apparitions.

The man and two children were insignificant little life forms running across an empty concrete plaza, in front of a great abandoned hotel, and then up the ramp to the main entrance of the Hyatt. As they cautiously entered through the glass doors, Jack looked back. He saw a brown snail back running toward them from behind the trolley.

"We've been spotted!" Jack cried. Together, they ran into the lobby. He glanced back and the thing was still running diagonally across the street toward them with its trailing gill slit covers or fins or whatever they were flapping in the wind. It ran powerfully on thick legs, and its powerful arms terminated in clenched fists much bigger than Jack's.

Maribel looked as if she were ready to start screaming again. Jimmy punched elevator buttons. For a moment they stood in a time warp in the magnificent lobby. And magnificent it was, emblematic of a new age that seemed to have started in wonderment and was going dramatically sour as had most previous dramatic ages in history. The lobby had been designed to dwarf the onlooker with spectacle and lighting. Huge chandeliers like those on the Titanic hung down; one could almost imagine the deep, cold sea water swirling through its ornate rows of pearls. The lobby was a cathedral in dark wood—oak, mahogany, ceramic, fake, plastic, who cared. Its square pillars were the size of elevator shafts and tastefully paneled. Clerks manning the desk had been dwarfed by huge murals and by lights big as elevator cages and resembling hourglass fantasies. Everything had been made bigger than life, as if to sweep the functional harshness and minimalism of the century of Hitler and Stalin and related ogres into the dustbin of history.

Now the lobby was an underwater landscape of fungi. Thin, tall ones on wavy red stalks reached almost to the ceiling. Globular blue and green ones seemed to float in midair on spider web-like attachments. A thing that looked like a lamp stood in a corner. In fact, half the mushrooms they saw here glowed in the dark. Bioluminescence had found its need, its evolutionary calling, a switch had been dripped in the DNA accelerated by the Yellow Spray, and here was a lobby more fantastic than ever.

Maribel screamed her high, thin scream that seemed capable of cutting through glass—the door flung open and the grisly looking gill monster came charging toward them. Its black tongue already stuck out as if anticipating the taste of them. The floor shook with its pounding feet.

The elevator rumbled open. Jack snatched the kids into it. Jimmy and Maribel hammered away at all the buttons, and the door shut just as the gill man's weight slammed against it. The kids were thrown down at the impact and Jack had to brace himself as the cage rocked, but the elevator was on its way up. "You pressed all the buttons!" Jack exclaimed. "It's going to stop at every floor!"

Maribel screamed again, this time a series of piercing alarms, one for every exhaled breath. Jack put his hand over her mouth and said: "You're going to hyperventilate and pass out."

Jimmy tore open a metal box and pointed to the controls there. The door rumbled open and went *ding!*

Maribel slammed her palm on the button for the 40th floor.

They heard the pounding of the gill man's feet coming up the stairs just on the other side of the wall. The door burst open, and the gill man came flying across the floor.

The elevator door slowly started to shut. The gill man, who had skidded across the fungus-coated floor and had started to run the wrong way down the hall, turned with an audible snarl and came charging directly at them. Again it slammed against the door just as the cage started rising.

The elevator rose slowly and steadily. "I disabled the local access," Jimmy said, "and put it on emergency override. It's going to shoot right to the top."

"Great," Jack said, "but it's not shooting. It's whispering slowly along the way my grandma used to drive."

"I don't hear it outside anymore," Jimmy said.

Gravely, Maribel said: "I hear it in the stairwell next to us. It's running ahead of us."

Jack looked up at the slowly moving floor-number lights. If only he had his Glock, or at least a baseball bat. They heard a thud far above. The cage began to shake.

"It's getting into the shaft above us," Jimmy whispered.

Maribel reached into the emergency box and yanked out the wires to the override mechanism. Jimmy shouted: "Lobster skull! What have you done?"

"No, she's on to something," Jack said. "It's all timing now, or we are dead ducks."

Maribel pressed the button for the 35th Floor, and the elevator stopped. Just then, a heavy weight smashed down on top of the car. The door opened, and Jack pushed the children out. Pressing L for Lobby, he stepped out. The ceiling of the car exploded in sheets of torn plastic and wood splinters as the gill man threw himself with superhuman strength through the service door without bothering to open it. He hung for a second in the opening, and needed to ease the sensitive gills and fins on his back through. In that moment, the door just rumbled shut and the elevator started down. Jack heard a series of explosive bangs as the thing hit the walls with its fists in a rage. It was smart, still having some human DNA as well as inherited memories and instincts stolen directly out of the brains of so many in the chain of past victims—stolen the very electro-bio-chemical shapes of electrons that formed images and memories and snatched them electro-bio-magnetically into its chain of predecessor fungi. It was smart and might or might not remember how to stop an elevator. Jack took the children's hands, and together they ran up the concrete stairwell. Even here, it smelled of earth and there was a light powdering of fungal growth, like white moss in places red and green like peach fuzz.

There was a bar on the 40th floor, from where one could look down on the Gaslamp District and Petco Park and the harbor as if looking into a box of toys. Even aircraft carriers looked like matchbox toys from here. As they ran past the elevators on the 40th floor, Jack saw the numbers moving upward: 10, 11, 12…slowly, but surely.

"Hide in the ladies' room," he ordered, "lock yourselves in."

He ran to the bar, grabbed three or four bottles of rum and vodka and some matches and paper napkins. He ran back to the elevator doors and put his burden down. He heard the smashing sounds in the shaft below as the enraged gill man roared for his victims.

28, 29, 30... read the flashing floor number lights.

Jack grabbed a fine table. He smashed it on the ground and against the walls in a rage of his own. When he had one leg left, he used that to pry the elevator doors apart a few inches.

34, 35, 36...

Rip the cap off, stuff paper in, light, and drop the first bomb.

He glimpsed the dark brown shape of the gilled and finned creature sitting on top of the elevator already reaching out with one crusty, shining hand. It spotted the first bottle dropping and roared in fear as it dove down into the elevator. *Perfect.* The elevator burst into flame. The gill man roared and smashed the walls with its fists.

Jack dropped the next two flaming Molotov cocktails one by one so that they fell into the elevator. The screaming stopped but the pounding continued. A wall of heat, and a smell like burning—something disgusting, like barrels of flaming spit or toe jam—rose up and almost knocked Jack unconscious. He had one more bomb to go, and he dropped that in to the car as it rose above the 39th floor. As he reeled back from the heat and smell, he caught a glimpse of the trapped thing writhing while it burned—and still it looked up with eyes filled with hate as they slowly dimmed.

The elevator mechanism went into failsafe mode, and the mechanical automata took over. The elevator stopped rising and rapidly descended toward the bowels of the hotel underneath the lobby trailing a shaftful of fire and dead-gillman smoke.

Jack lurched away from the elevators and gathered heavy tables to push into the entrance and block the elevator shafts. Working manically, he chained the stairwell doors together so they couldn't be opened from outside. Pouring himself a glass of fine scotch and a tall glass of ice water, he rummaged until he found some pretzels and then sat at the window overlooking the phantasmagoria far below. It all looked so normal.

The kids poked their heads out of the bathroom. "Is it gone?"

He nodded. "It's dead. Burned up. Gone to hell. You can come over now and sit with me. Maybe we'll rest a bit and then I'll take a look on the roof.

Chapter 74.

Linsey sat in the shattered coffee shop with Jim Robertson when her cell phone chirped. It was her husband. "Hi, Jack. Are you okay?"

"I have the kids and we are safe for now. I just killed one of those gill men."

"Geez, be careful. I so wish I could help you. I'm stuck here in Mission Valley. Has Louise contacted you?"

"She did earlier. She said she'd fix something up."

"Don't run your battery down."

"We're barricaded in the bar on the 40th floor of the Manchester Hyatt Grand San Diego Hotel."

"I'll call Louise and see if she's able to send someone yet."

Linsey called Louise's office, but got only the executive assistant, who promised a call back as soon as Louise was free from yet another meeting.

Linsey called Shaun Nolan. "Are you feeling better?"

"Yes. Sorry for the uproar."

"Dr. Nolan, I understand you have gone on TV and radio to warn against a horrifying new version of the mushroom people."

"It's the real version, Lieutenant Simon. What I saw with my own eyes down in the harbor district resembles a cross between a man-sized cockroach and a bedsore walking around."

"My husband and some children are trapped there. I think I may know how to fight these monstrosities."

"I bet you do. Can we meet?"

"You'll need to extract me and a wounded man."

"I can do that. Just tell me you can save the world."

"Huh?" She laughed nervously.

"Louise has put a tool at my disposal to help with the research. I just need to justify the use—you know, the old paper trail and all."

"I'll show you how to kick ass, take names, and save Earth."

" I'll make a note of that for Bookkeeping. Where are you?"

"The Hazard Center in Mission Valley."

"Stay put. I'll come and get you."

"How?"
"You'll see."

Chapter 75.

Linsey sat in the wrecked shop with Jim Robertson, both sipping coffee gone cold, when her cell phone warbled.

Nolan said: "You can come outside now. We're ready to go."

She and Jim heard the roar of a big engine as she helped Jim climb out over the debris. The engines weren't so much deafening as numbing. Wind whipped around her head. She squinted and grimaced, looking up. First she saw the mooring ropes hanging down at an angle. Then she saw the huge yellow letters on blue background: Goodyear. Then she saw the cabin underneath the blimp's enormous bulk and the man waving from the enclosed gondola. Three men, actually—a pilot, co-pilot, and Shaun Nolan. The blimp came down as low as the pilot dared on the street behind and below the bookstore—she gladly ran down a flight of stairs and ran to get on board. Immediately, the copilot slid the door shut and the pilot took her up with a roar, just as a half dozen men appeared from nowhere—bearded, dirty, drugged, seeking a ride or some loot or just plain raising hell.

"I wanted to surprise you," Nolan said.

"How did you get this airship?" she squealed. She looked around at the compact but spacious interior with its passenger seats and a table for desk work.

"Louise got Goodyear to donate a resource to help me in my efforts to figure out the secret behind this mycoplague."

"We need to set Mr. Robertson down someplace where he can get home safely. We owe him a lot." They clambered inside and buckled up in comfortable, bus-like seats. When the doors closed, the noise was minimal.

"No problem," Nolan said. "How about the roof of UCSD Medical Center for now?"

"No," she said. "We need to get into El Cajon. Our solution is waiting there for us."

"Are you sure?" Nolan said, biting his lip. "I have major commitments elsewhere."

She explained quickly, and, at Nolan's nod, the pilot headed toward the East County.

Jim said excitedly: "Hey, I just remembered something. Paco's daughter, Maria, had a driver's license and I think he stayed with her."

"Bingo," Linsey said. "Let's get Louise on the horn, and have her check the DMV."

Within a half hour the blimp hovered above a house in eastern El Cajon. Already, city police units had converged on the house. The blimp nosed down close enough to let Jim off on the flat roof of a neighboring bakery, where the owners—loud, friendly men with white hats and big mustaches and dark hair—helped him down the stairs and out of sight.

Nolan and Linsey met an El Cajon police detective named Cordoba—heavyset, graying, wearing a suit, lots of acne scars under a short black mustache—who escorted them into the house. Fire Department units stood around, along with little cars from all sorts of strange agencies. "At first I thought it was a drug place, maybe a meth lab, but the signs are all wrong." People in hazmat suits came along, bringing suits for Nolan and Linsey to wear. She wasn't surprised to find hers claustrophobic and sweaty, from the plastic booties up to the bubble helmet. Cordoba also donned one.

They entered empty, cold rooms where people (Paco, Marie) had once lived and were never coming back. There was a haunted loneliness about the dark rooms and hallways. People looking like spacemen shuffled about looking at things or carrying objects. The house was plain, but spacious. "In the garage," Cordoba said, showing them ahead with a wave of the hand. Linsey stepped into a cool, dry garage whose walls and floors were stacked with carefully sealed, clean 2-liter plastic soda bottles. "That's no cola drink in there," Cordoba said. "Don't touch anything!"

"That's it," Linsey said. She felt Nolan's excited grip on her arm as they watched spores filling the bottles like fine powder.

"The Defensor," Nolan said. "Your premise was right. Paco wasn't just here to look and wait. He was actively culturing the small sample he brought with him. It will take a few days to get a huge amount going. There is enough here to start cultivating—why, I bet we can be spraying counter-fungus within hours. I know how to grow this stuff!"

Chapter 76.

By his second day in the Manchester Hyatt Hotel , Jack found a special access ladder leading to a hatch that opened onto the roof. Cautiously, he opened the hatch and looked about. No sign of any gill men. There were a few small mushrooms around, but none of the grotesque giants down on the street.

It was midafternoon and the sun was starting to move past its midpoint in the Western sky. Wind whipped around Jack's thinning hair. Reddish-golden sunlight felt good on his skin.

He pulled the hatch shut, locked it from inside, and clambered back down the ladder. The kids were where he'd left them—wrapped in oversized waiters' coats and sipping hot chocolate while looking down at the city from high above.

"How did you kids get that red stuff all over you?" he asked.

"It was blowing all over in the wind," Jimmy said.

"Didn't you notice?" Maribel said. She laughed and took a paper napkin, dipped it in water, and rubbed Jack's face. She showed him the napkin, which was soaked and covered with a kind of brick-red fungal rot.

"Argh," he said, wiping his face.

"No, leave it on," Jimmy said, "we found that it kept the spores off our skin. It's some kind of magic dust."

Jack stared at them. Of course!

He phoned Linsey. "Honey, the antidote to this fungus plague is another fungus. It's this red stuff that's spreading in the wind already coming from the Lima Voyager."

She was excited. "I'm a step ahead of you as usual, honey. We have a lifetime supply of the stuff, and we've already started spraying. In the big picture, we'll use the marine layer and the daily fogs. We'll get those cloud seeding planes of Collwood's from Volcan Mountain, and we'll crop dust the entire city with this red stuff. I'm pretty sure this is very powerful stuff and will stop all this chaos in its tracks. The Offensor and Defensor will neutralize each other, and we can proceed to scrub the city clean so that life can get back to normal."

Chapter 77.

Louise Trost sat wrapped in a shawl as Martin Delavalle, Lee Collwood's San Diego CEO and, frankly she thought, Collwood's patsy, finished giving his testimony to detectives.

"Thank you, Mr. Delavalle," she said. "We already have a subpoena in work for Mr. Metrick to testify against Collwood, and Metrick may get off with just resigning from Congress while we nail Anaconda Chemical."

"And I?"

"We'll make sure it goes easy on you. You have a long record of dishonesty, Mr. Delavalle. We don't have the time, the patience, or the resources to put you away here at the moment. People like you are your own worst enemies. I'm sure you'll move on and get yourself indicted elsewhere. It was good of you to explain the business with the red stuff, though."

"I deserve a break," he said. "If you can rescue them, I may have saved half a dozen men from dying in that ship."

"I commend you for that, and it pains me, but I have no resources to find and help them. Like yourself, they may be victims of their own greed and foolishness. And now I wish you good day." As he rose, she waved him off saying, "Don't let the door hit you in the ass on the way out."

Chapter 78.

Three choppers full of SEALs and Navy technicians, all in yellow protective suits, roared toward the Lima Voyager. One by one, each touched down on he ship's small helipad and disgorged passengers and equipment before flying back to NAS North Island.

A large Sea Knight flew from USMC Air Station Miramar to evacuate people. SEALs stood guard, while Navy techs spotted the hatch over the main stairwell that had been welded shut. Dragging a bottle of gas and their blow torch and other equipment and started blazing away at the hatch. The welder wore a face mask and peered through a smoky glass window at his incandescently bright light. Minutes later, they used crowbars to finish prying the hatch open. SEALs shone powerful lights down the gangway. "Hello? Anyone home?" they called out. "Drop your weapons. Come out with your hands on your heads."

The men who climbed up had long since tossed aside their weapons. They were red-streaked ghosts, glad to be alive, overjoyed at their rescue from the jaws of a slow and agonizing death. They had stripped down to their shorts because of the heat below, and their bodies were smeared brick-red with rust or brick dust—the SEALs had no idea. Two unconscious men had to be carried. All desperately guzzled water offered to them.

With excellent timing, the Sea Knight roared in and made the air dance with red dust. As the SEALs stood watch with their weapons ready, the Navy techs abandoned their welding equipment and climbed on board the hovering helicopter. At the same time, evacuation specialists in white medical garb rushed out to help the weakened mercenaries onto stretchers and get them on board. There was an element of haste for fear that the gill men might attack, for they seemed to be multiplying and becoming bolder.

As soon as the mercenaries were secured, the SEALs were the last to board, and the Sea Knight roared off in the direction of NAS North Island.

It was getting late in the afternoon, and the water had a sleepy golden sheen below.

Chapter 79.

As he lay on the cooling desert sand as night fell, Lee Collwood finally admitted to himself it was the end of the road. This could all have been over already.

He had sat at his desk in the loneliness of his office at the main plant outside Brawley, held his Glock to his head, and thought about pulling the trigger. He thought about calling this one or that one of his ex-wives, but they hated him and would laugh at his suffering now. He didn't have the courage to do the deed, and put the gun down. He forgot about it as he rose.

He'd thought of the captain of the Lima Voyager, Tidjeman. Poor stiff, he thought. It was rare that Lee Collwood felt sorry for anyone but himself. It wasn't my fault, he thought. The whole episode had come to a bad turn because nobody had known the fungus was so powerful, and that it would seize the day. It wasn't his fault, like everything wasn't his fault, but this time he was too tired to fight anymore. Subpoenas and indictments were on the way, and he didn't feel like fighting them because he knew cash was running out and he didn't have the brains to figure out any way to save the company.

So he'd filled his canteen with water, stuffed a bag full of crackers and peanut butter, and set out into the desert outside the Brawley plant.

Somewhere out there, he knew, rested the bracket colony created when Thomas Blake's mercenary Lo encountered the mushroom person that Tidjeman had become…the same Tidjeman whom Collwood had battled in the hallway of his home in University City with the spooky severed head looking on from across the room.

Lee Collwood walked out into the desert into the area where he knew Lo had lost his life to Tidjeman's ghost. Somewhere out here in a safe and secure place chosen by was-Lo, a bracket colony lay nestled and waiting for its birth as a gill man.

Lee had drunk himself to a near stupor, but now that was starting to wear off. He turned over so that he could see the sun turn red in the sky and decline toward the horizon. It was cooler in the desert around this hour, and things that had boiled in the sun now cooled off and emitted sweet smells.

When he heard the snap of a twig behind him, he turned and laughed. "Just when it was getting good," he muttered in a faint voice, meaning how sweet and beautiful a place like this desert could smell in the cool of evening.

The being coming at him with outstretched hands was covered with snail-like gills. Collwood assumed that, behind that stony mask, some faint memory of Tidjeman survived, and that the ghost of Tidjeman felt considerable rage toward

Collwood for sending him into such a dangerous situation without warning. As he had done much of his life, Lee laughed. When the creature took him by the head and snapped his neck, Lee's last thought in sinking toward peaceful oblivion was "Thanks."

Chapter 80.

Linsey called Jack from the blimp, which was heading west toward the Harbor area. "Honey, I'm en route. That blimp you see will be us. Get the kids up on the roof so we can snatch and grab you."

"Okay," he said. " Jimmy and Maribel figured out the Defensor thing all on their own."

"They'll be mycologists before long," Nolan said proudly.

"Can't wait to see you," Jack said. The radio crackled.

"I can't wait. Love you to smithereens. Soon!"

Nolan studied the pictures Jim Robertson had given Linsey. He did the same tapping thing that Linsey had done. "That red stuff along the edge of the crater. That's the Defensor fungus."

"Look closely and you'll see some Native Americans too. Their faces and hands look red, and they are carrying weapons."

"Defenders," Nolan muttered thoughtfully while studying the image. "Defensor, defenders. Hmmm. We'll get this neutralized and totally confined to down there, and maybe figure out a way to wipe it out but keep small samples for research and pharmaceuticals."

"Here we are, approaching target," the pilot interrupted.

Linsey pressed her palms and face to the glass and looked for Jack. She saw him on the rooftop of the Hyatt, holding the Jimmy and Maribel by the hand. He looked exactly right that way, she thought, and waved to him. She smiled, thinking it was time to get her own gills in gear with Jack's help.

On the earth below, thousands of police and military personnel prepared to hunt gill men to the last specimen. There would be exemplars of their race kept pickled in large jars for scholars to gaze at. The Indians of the Peruvian rain forest would continue their age-old service of the mushroom gods and keep the world in balance by protecting the crazy place where men went and died and then came back as walking spores. The soil in the ages-ago abandoned city contained many visitors, including the two 1944 Japanese pilots who had sunk dying into the fungus-rich soil, only to be reborn as mushroom men—whom the Indians had stopped in a hail of arrows before they could go forth and wreak the damage Collwood's operatives had. Collwood's men had killed several of the Indians, who only had bows and arrows. In the future, the Indians would be better prepared. Louise Trost's task force would send them the latest in laser-guided shoulder-fired missiles to stop any terrorist who tried to seize the fungi for evil purposes.

The blimp puttered in for a touchdown, turning masterfully so that her golden side caught the late sunlight full-on and radiated a sense that all would be well again. As she nosed down over the hotel's roof, Jack ran forth with a child at each hand. Crew members helped Jack and the two squealing, happy children on board. Linsey and Jack fell into a tight hug and kissed, while the engines roared all around them, and the blimp ascended from the hotel. The airship rose up and turned majestically to inland to deposit passengers, and then to bring Dr. Nolan to his lab up the coast at the University of California, San Diego. He rubbed his hands together and told the children with glowing eyes: "We have a lot of work to do!"

The water below ran like liquid gold. The wind was fresh and crisp, offering yet another chance at killing the Offensor spores and bringing some normalcy back to the world. With Cleve and so many other good people gone, it wouldn't be the same world again, but this planet that had endured billions of years. The show would go on—with or without people.

A colorful sunset was shaping up on the western Pacific horizon. A row of clouds portended a sea storm that would cleanse the air. Playing with the controls on the pilot's lap, Jimmy Mendez crowed: "It was a close call—!"

To which Maribel, sitting in the co-pilot's seat, finished the heroic outcry: "—But Earth is saved once again!"

Jack held Linsey tightly and silently, rocking her gently from side to side as they stood by a rear window. Jack whispered to her: "I didn't think I'd ever see you again. I think I'm the happiest guy on earth right now."

Linsey closed her eyes and gripped Jack tightly. She laid her cheek on his shoulder and whispered back: "I'll let you write that big story—soon—but first, just one more little bit of very personal and important business, as soon as we're home alone."

More Info: Worlds of John Argo

John Argo is a writer of Science Fiction, Dark Fantasy, and Science-Horror Fiction (SH, or Dark SF). We also call his work Subversive Fiction (SF). He lives with his wife and family in Southern California.

His two primary lines are science fiction:

Empire of Time: a sprawling future history covering eons and light years. Titles include *Time Train*, *Mars the Divine*, *Escape from Prison Planet or Die*, and more.

DarkSF (or Science Horror): stand-alone novels unified by their dark, thrilling atmospherics, cinematic visuals, and often poetic language. Titles include *Doom Spore*, *This Shoal of Space*, *Monopol City*, *Day Flies*, and more.

Neon Blue, a suspense novel, was the first proprietary novel to be published online in HTML format to be read online (not on portable media). More at the Clocktower Books Museum.

Whenever you read a John Argo story or novel, no matter how dark or thrilling, you will usually also find a love story. In his tales, we travel to the far sectors of the human existence, while the characters' search for meaning glows like a lantern in darkness. Trust John Argo as a frequent traveler and tour guide along highways through imaginative space and time.

John Argo's web presence is at Clocktower Books (online since 1996). John Argo is the SF/F/H pseudonym of Jean-Thomas Cullen, who also publishes thrillers and nonfiction as John T. Cullen.

www.johntcullen.com

Please visit Metrowebplex.com, the hub of this author's publishing (over thirty books to date, and many more on the way).

More Info: Clocktower Books

= online since 1996 =

Clocktower Books was, to our knowledge, the world's first publisher ever to publish real digital, proprietary (not public domain), novel-length fiction (books, novels) online in digital format for download. Note carefully: proprietary, not public domain (which Project Gutenberg and others were already doing); for reading online in HTML, not on portable media (which a few others were already doing). Most telling: Clocktower Fiction, our first presence on the Web—that domain was created in December 1996 as an umbrella publisher for our already existing websites (neonbluefiction.com for suspense; and thehauntedvillage.com for SF/F/H, which is now hauntedvillagesffh.com).

We launched this program in 1996, using an innovative process of publishing weekly serial chapters. Readers who needed to know the outcome, and couldn't stand the suspense, could email for a complete digital text file anywhere in the world. We received raves and kudos from around the globe. We used this serial chapter method to publish three John Argo books over 1996-1996: *This Shoal of Space* and *Pioneers* (both SF); and *Neon Blue*, a suspense novel. All three novels were bestsellers in the earliest e-book forums, including the original Barnes & Noble website in 2000, and other venues including Rocket eBooks. See the publisher website for more info:

www.clocktowerbooks.com

Learn about the history of Clocktower Books at the Clocktower Books Museum website (museum.clocktowerbooks.com).

Publisher's Dedication

(Circa 2007:) **To** *Deep Outside SFFH,* the world's oldest professional web-only magazine of science fiction, fantasy, and horror (speculative & dark fiction), launched April 15, 1998. An archive site is still maintained (*www.deepoutside.com*). Small but mighty, the magazine was and is an innovator stressing quality over quantity, equally valuing literary and commercial components of short fiction, promoting the particular strengths of digital media without losing what has been great about print media. The magazine continued uninterruptedly publishing online as *Far Sector SFFH* (*www.farsector.com/*) until January 2007 under the sole proprietorship of John T. Cullen, with help from a team of dedicated authors and editors. Far Sector SFFH has an entry at the online SF Encyclopedia, while Deep Outside SFFH will be featured in Mike Ashley's fourth in a quartet of scholarly books on the history of SF magazines (Liverpool University Press).

Strengths include new modes of distribution that break from the past and work with innovators like Fictionwise (*fictionwise.com*). *Deep Outside SFFH* (originally *Outside: Speculative & Dark Fiction*) became the first such web-only magazine to be listed in Writer's Market (1999 Edition) alongside the pulps. Founders were John T. Cullen and Brian Callahan. Significant contributors have been A. L. Sirois, John Kenneth Muir, Dennis Latham, and Shaun Farrell, plus of course all the authors we published over a decade. We published many unknown newcomers, as well as established talent. Some of these authors already had won prestigious awards (Pat York, Nebula), while others went on from obscurity to win important awards and nominations (Tim Pratt, Ted Kosmatka, and many others).

Most important, of course, is content. While digital innovations are exciting, there is no substitute for good old-fashioned storytelling from fine authors like Dennis Latham, Pat York, Melanie Tem, Joe Murphy, A. L. Sirois, Joel Best, and many others the magazine has sent to your viewing surface.

Message sent back in time to the Futurians of the 1930s: *"We have landed in the future, which we find to be exhilarating. Maybe 'breathtaking' and 'terrifying' would be better adjectives. Humans are still behaving stupidly, and wantonly killing each other, so we add 'disappointing.' Will send full report soon. Aim your crystal radio sets to the following coordinates..."*

John Argo and Clocktower Books Present

Stunning and poetic far-future history by John Argo in the tradition of Cordwainer Smith's Classic Norstrilia and other tales of the Instrumentality.

Jean-Thomas Cullen Presents

A sentimental, clean romantic story set in contemporary Connecticut. A young war widow has become a Sleeping Beauty, stung by the loss of her soldier husband, and works as a librarian in the tiny town of Emery. One hot summer day, just looking for a cool spot while his car is fixed, Prince Charming stops by in the form of a young millionaire who has suffered a painful divorce and isn't really looking for love. Neither is she. But old Cupid shoots them both with his arrows, and the ground moves beneath their feet…

Valley of Seven Castles: A Progressive Thriller

Set in tomorrow's Europe, in a world gone global and run as one big feudal state by a thousand zillionaire families, here is the world's first progressive thriller. A U.S. Army deserter running from a crime he didn't commit, and a young California woman who sold herself into a modern form of five-year slavery to pay her mother's final hospital bills, are on the run. With them they carry the plans for a new warplane fuselage that must not fall into the wrong hands. Chasing them from Paris to Luxembourg is the Chinese billionaire who murdered a young Luxembourg engineer in London and wants his toy back. In the spirit of John Buchan's 1915 *The Thirty-Nine Steps* as well as Alfred Hitchcock's 1935 movie version *The 39 Steps*, plus a big surprise (see Thrillerology in the novel). Add to that the pace of the 2002 thriller movie The Bourne Identity starring Matt Damon and Franka Potente, based on a 1970 thriller novel by Robert Ludlum, and you have a first-class read.

(cover image next page)

Valley of Seven Castles
A Luxembourg Thriller by John T. Cullen

PROGRESSIVE THRILLERS SERIES

Also By John Argo: YANAPOP

Here's a thriller unlike anything you've ever read. Think of the dark comedy movie After Hours (Martin Scorsese, all-star cast) which is considered one of the funniest (and craziest) films ever made. We agree. Think of Linda Fiorentino in The Last Seduction, Jack Lemmon in The Out-of-Towners, and how about Thomas Pynchon's classic novel The Crying of Lot 49. YANAPOP (stands for Young Adult, New Adult, Participating Older Persons) is the name of a giant (fictional) entertainment corporation in Los Angeles. It's the love story of Martin Brown and Chloë Setreal, and how Martin became Odysseus in his insane and dangerous journey to reach his Penelope.

Nonfiction by John T. Cullen: Dead Move

John T. Cullen, a San Diego author and scholar (BA, BBA, MS) applies his journalistic and historical expertise to solve a long-standing true crime. During Thanksgiving Week 1892, a stylish young woman (about 24) officially called The Beautiful Stranger by the Hotel del Coronado near San Diego, checked in under a false name and died a violent, mysterious death a few days later. Her case became a national sensation full of notoriety overnight because of allegations of affairs with men in high places. It was a Victorian scandal of epic proportions, resulting in the famous ghost legend at the hotel. John T. Cullen, basing his research entirely on true history (no ghosts were harmed), provides the first ever plausible explanation of what really happened—including a coverup of global proportions. See also Lethal Journey, the noir gaslight mystery thriller he wrote to dramatize Dead Move, on which Lethal Journey is closely based.

(cover image next page)

The nonfiction analysis (*Dead Move: Kate Morgan and the Haunting Mystery of Coronado*) is contained in the dual edition (two books in one) *Coronado Mystery*. The dual edition also contains the full text of the novel *Lethal Journey* (see next page).

Thriller by John T. Cullen: Lethal Journey

Closely based on his nonfictional scholarly analysis of the 1892 true crime (*Dead Move*) here is a dramatization treated as a gaslight era noir suspense thriller.

Ray Bradbury Loved This One:

Ray Bradbury wrote a personal fan mail note to John T. Cullen in January 2008, praising this little gem, a novel that is a tribute both to Charles Dickens' classic A Christmas Carol, and to Ray Bradbury's dark but playful fantasies.

Lots More Where These Came From...

Please visit the website of Clocktower Books for a full listing of our exciting fiction and nonfiction books, articles, and short works by a variety of talented authors.

www.clocktowerbooks.com